Suddenly she turned, wrapping her arms about his neck, and pressing her body into his. "Kiss me, Joe. Kiss me like you used to. I always loved it when you kissed me senseless."

Gently he tried to disengage her arms. "Annie. Sweet, sweet Annie. You're killing me. We've got to stop before things get out of hand." He had fifteen years worth of love and lust to share with this woman. But now was not the time. Not when she was so vulnerable. When they finally came together he wanted her to be one hundred percent willing and two hundred percent aware of with whom she was making love.

"Kiss me. Just one kiss and then I'll behave."

He felt himself being pulled under. "Promise? You'll stop after one?"

She nodded. "Promise." ·

Taking her head between his hands, he lowered his mouth to hers, and at the first touch, Joe knew he'd come home. . . .

By Millie Criswell
Published by Ivy Books

THE TROUBLE WITH MARY
WHAT TO DO ABOUT ANNIE?
THE TRIALS OF ANGELA*

*Forthcoming

WHAT TO DO ABOUT ANNIE?

Millie Criswell

IVY BOOKS • NEW YORK

This book contains an excerpt from the forthcoming paperback edition of *The Trials of Angela* by Millie Criswell. This excerpt has been set for this edition only and may not reflect the final content of the forthcoming edition.

An Ivy Book
Published by The Ballantine Publishing Group
Copyright © 2001 by Millie Criswell
Excerpt from *The Trials of Angela* by Millie Criswell © 2001 by Millie Criswell.

www.randomhouse.com/BB/

Library of Congress Catalog Card Number: 2001116593

ISBN 0-8041-1951-1

Manufactured in the United States of America

First Edition: August 2001

10   9   8   7   6   5   4   3   2   1

For all the wonderful conversation,
fabulous food, and fun times,
this book is dedicated to my very dear friends,
Chris and Bob Heggan.

ONE

*"An old maid who marries
becomes a young wife."*

Being a bridesmaid sucked!

Even if you were the maid of honor.

And weddings were totally overrated.

Annie Goldman knew this because she was presently in one—her best friend Mary's, to Dan Gallagher.

It wasn't bad enough she was dressed like a rose-tinted marshmallow, surrounded by other rose-tinted marshmallows. No, she had to endure wearing the hideous tulle headpiece—a headpiece even Queen Elizabeth would have objected to. And everyone knew Liz, who probably carried Prince Philip's family jewels in those frumpy purses she toted, had no taste.

Sophia Russo, Mary's mom and dictator extraordinaire, had insisted that her daughter could not be married without bridesmaids in tulle headpieces. Most likely tulle was some type of fertility material—Annie sure as heck hoped not!—because Sophia was planning on lots of grandkids.

Annie had never been a maid of honor before, and she had no intention of ever being one again. The reasons were numerous: The clothing was hideous; you had to hold the bridal bouquet; make sure you didn't fall on your face while marching up and down the aisle; and you were forced to wear a serene smile, which gave you the appearance of suffering from a serious case of gas.

Though on the latter she was covered, because her father, Sid, seated five pews back—and trying not to look too Jewish among all the Italian Catholics, despite the fact he wore a kippah—carried chewable Maalox with him wherever he went. Of course, if her father should happen to forget his antacids, one just had to search through Gina's purse to find a drug supply second only to old man Moressi's pharmaceuticals.

Her mother wasn't a drug addict, just a hypochondriac who believed in being prepared.

Gina Goldman was the Boy Scout of hypochondriacs. She had more ailments than Baskin-Robbins had flavors. What would be a headache to most people was a malignant brain tumor to her mother. Thirst translated into diabetes, a stomachache to ulcers, and on a particularly bad day a mild rash was usually construed as flesh-eating bacteria.

Dr. Mankin had given Gina a clean bill of health after her physical last week—her weekly physical—but she refused to believe she wasn't dying, which drove Annie's father crazy.

"The woman's a nut! She's healthy as a horse and still she kvetches! She should go in good health." Which, in reality, meant quite the opposite.

Annie had been surprised—stunned, really!—when her mother had shown up at the church today, because this morning she'd been dying of food poisoning.

"God forbid, but if I should die today, Annie, you'll take the Limoges china. I don't want the Goldman girls to get it."

Gina despised her sisters-in-law, who had never really accepted a *gentile* into their midst, but she was fond of

Mary, liked and respected Mary's brother, Joe, and so had made a special effort to overcome her latest fatal affliction.

Father Joseph Russo was performing the mass and the ceremony today. And he looked damn good in his vestments! The ladies of the parish called him Father What-a-Hunk behind his back, and it was more than fitting.

The priest was well over six feet tall, dark-haired, brown-eyed, and had dimples in his cheeks that put Shirley Temple to shame. He'd been compared to everyone from Mel Gibson to Rupert Evertt, though Rupert was purportedly gay—a major waste to womankind!—and Annie knew first hand that Joe was not.

Joe would be mortified if he knew what was being said about him. Unlike Annie, he didn't draw attention to himself, so she thought it might be prudent and very amusing to enlighten him. It was the least she could do.

There was no doubt that his holiness was a hotty. Under those vestments lurked the body of a man who worked out on a regular basis. Sinewy forearms, bulging biceps, muscular chest, and . . .

Well, it wouldn't be prudent to venture below the waist while in church. She didn't want to be struck down, smited a mighty blow, turned into a pillar of salt— No, wait! That was Lot's nosy wife.

The man should have been called Father What-a-Waste, in Annie's opinion, because celibacy and Father Joseph Russo just didn't go hand in hand.

"I, Mary Russo, take you, Daniel Gallagher, to be my husband, to have and to hold from this day forward, for better or for worse . . ."

As his younger sister recited in a whisper-soft, dreamy

voice the vows that would bind her to Daniel Gallagher forever, Joe's gaze slipped from the lovely bride before him to the woman standing solemnly next to her.

Or as solemn as a maid of honor could look sporting hair the same rose color as her form-fitting satin gown.

The beautiful woman was anything but maidenly. And she certainly wasn't demure. She was outspoken, outlandish, and quite unorthodox, a free spirit who was totally unconventional.

Annie Goldman had captivated him from the first moment he laid eyes on her: she was six and as scrawny as a gangly filly; he was eight, just as scrawny, and had no use for girls.

Not then, anyway.

For an instant their eyes locked. Hers widened in appreciation, then narrowed slightly before she hurriedly looked down at the pink baby roses in her hands, while his filled with regret.

If only things had turned out differently.

His soon-to-be brother-in-law cleared his throat loudly, drawing Joe's attention back to the bridal couple and the matter at hand. They looked confused and a little bit dismayed. Not that he could blame them.

Smiling apologetically, he continued on with the ceremony. His sister's wedding would be his last official duty as parish priest of St. Francis of Assisi's Catholic Church, though nobody knew it as yet.

Joe was hanging up his rosary beads after today and quitting the church.

It hadn't been an easy decision, but it had been one a long time in coming. He'd grown disillusioned with the church—or more, his lack of contribution to it. He'd become a priest for all the wrong reasons, he knew that now. And though he wasn't one hundred percent certain quitting was the right thing to do, he intended to go through with it.

He had feelings that needed to be sorted out and dealt with. Feelings no man of God should possess within the confines of a church—or outside of it, for that matter. And questions that needed answers, like: *What to do about Annie?*

"You made an absolutely gorgeous bride, *cara,*" Annie told Mary later at the reception. The music of the Paisans, the band that comprised five Russo male relatives of various ages, from fifty to eighty, blared loudly from the overhead speakers.

They weren't the Beastie Boys, but they weren't exactly Guy Lombardo, either.

"Uncle Tony's version of *That's Amore* is going to make Dean Martin turn over in his grave," Mary said, looking uncertain and apologetic at the same time. "But they came cheap. My father's brother practically begged for the gig. Or so I was told." Her expression remained skeptical.

"Meaning they were free, right?" Annie knew Mary's mother was big on bargains and saving a buck. Sophia had finagled a deal with the VFW, so the reception could be held at their large banquet hall. Never mind that a Sherman tank sat in front of the building.

"So what if there's a tank? " Sophia had told her daughter when Mary expressed concern. *"The trouble with you, Mary, is that you're not patriotic. Those old geezers risked their lives to save us from the Nazis, so you could get married in this hall."*

Sophia had a thing about Nazis. Especially now that she couldn't voice her sentiments about the Irish. At least not aloud. Mary's new husband was of Irish descent, and Sophia had been forced to rein in her tongue. A blessing for everyone concerned, Annie decided.

"We have to feed them, that's about it," Mary said. "Thank goodness Marco agreed to cater the event. At least I know the food will be good."

Marco Valenti was head chef at Mary's restaurant, Mama Sophia's. He was temperamental as hell, had the disposition of Attila the Hun, but was an excellent cook. If you had a thing for the Pillsbury Dough Boy, Marco was your man.

The irritating little chef was presently teaching Annie how to cook, and she was driving him nuts in the process, which seemed a fair exchange. Paybacks were tough. And Marco had annoyed the heck out of her on more than one occasion with his bossy ways and air of superiority.

Mary shook her head and winced when Uncle Tony hit a high note only a dog could appreciate. "The way they sound, I guess it's good we didn't have to pay them."

"Such a deal!" Annie mimicked her father perfectly. "What more do you want? Gabriel coming down from heaven and blowing horns? Free is good."

"Mary!" Sophia Russo shouted from the other side of the room, waving frantically at her daughter, an impatient look on her face. "Come on. The photographer is waiting."

Dan was trapped between Sophia and Mary's aunt Josephine, who was sniffing his coat sleeve and looking altogether too blissful. (Admittedly, Aunt Josie had a few problems.) He, on the other hand, wore the pathetic look of an abused, neglected puppy.

"You'd better go, kiddo. Dan's in need of rescue, and I don't want your mom accusing me of ruining your wedding by monopolizing all of your time."

"Will we get a chance to talk again before I leave for the honeymoon?" Mary asked.

Annie shook her head, feeling sad at the thought that life as they knew it would be forever changed. "Not unless Dan wants to engage in a little ménage à trois tonight." She smiled wickedly. "On second thought—"

"Annie Goldman, shame on you! This is my wedding day!" The bride did her best to look indignant, but she was laughing and couldn't quite carry it off.

"*Oy vey!* I was only kidding. Now, go. Be happy." Hugging her around the waist, Annie kissed Mary's cheek, surprised by the tears suddenly flooding her eyes. She wasn't a woman normally prone to tears. Annie had made a career out of hiding her vulnerability and the sorrow buried deep inside.

"Have a wonderful time in Venice, and a wonderful life with Dan. And call me when you get back. I want to hear all the pornographic details."

From the other side of the room, where he stood next to the garish four-foot-tall silver champagne fountain that was spewing forth bubbly like an out-of-control geyser— that his mother had insisted they needed so his father wouldn't come off looking cheap in front of the relatives, a major factor in any Italian social gathering—Joe observed Annie.

She was guiding Dan's son, Matthew, onto the dance floor. The eight-year-old boy had been looking somewhat lost and left out during the festivities, and it was so like Annie to come to the child's rescue.

Bending over, she bussed him on the cheek, and the kid's face reddened before he wiped her kiss away with the back of his hand, making Joe grin. He could distinctly remember doing the very same thing when his mother's sisters came to call. Aunt Josephine and Aunt Angie were big on kissing, pinching cheeks, and patting bottoms. The two women majored in mortification.

For all her tough exterior, Annie Goldman was a tenderhearted soul, a real soft touch. Though she'd be horrified to learn anyone thought so. She was also a woman who professed indifference, who liked playing it cool and detached.

But Joe knew otherwise. From the moment he'd taken Annie to her homecoming as a favor to Mrs. Goldman, who didn't approve of the boys her daughter associated with, he realized she was someone special.

But that hadn't always been the case.

Joe had been in his sophomore year of college and not at all thrilled by the idea of dating his little sister's best friend, who was still in high school. He'd never really paid much attention to Annie Goldman while she was growing up, though she'd been at the house almost every day, hanging out with Mary and making his mother crazed.

She'd always been a little wild and unconventional, her clothing over the top. After all, how many teenagers dressed up as Rita Hayworth's Gilda to go to homecoming?

Annie Goldman just wasn't his type at all.

Or so he'd thought.

But Joe learned soon enough that there was substance beneath Annie's flash and flamboyance. She was smart, funny, and could talk intelligently on any number of topics. And she was much more mature than the other girls her age.

He'd been drawn to her wit, infectious laugh, and very ample charms.

Annie had a body made for sin. And Joe, at twenty, had been ready and willing to break a few commandments.

There was a bit of the forbidden about Annie. Like Adam to Eve, he'd been lured by her blatant sexuality. He still wanted her, despite everything that had happened between them.

Loving Annie had been incredible, losing her unbearable. And he had only himself to blame.

Annie laughed at something the child was saying, and the husky, sensual sound drew Joe's attention back to the present, skittering down his spine like a feather on bare skin.

Filling a glass with champagne, he took a sip, then gulped a great deal more when the woman began moving across the crowded floor, in his direction. Undulating, was more like it. Annie moved like a tidal wave, and he felt like a man going under for the very last time.

"Well, well, if it isn't Father What-a-Hunk," Annie said, arching a brow at the champagne glass in his hand. "Are you trying to drown your sorrows? That's so unpriestlike. I'm actually quite shocked that you're imbibing like the rest of us mere mortals, your holiness." She failed to keep the animosity out of her voice, not that she tried very hard.

"Father what?" Joe asked, and she shook her head and moved to fill a glass for herself.

Though he was tempted to tell Annie of his decision to quit the church, he wouldn't. Sophia was likely to go ballistic when she heard the news that her precious son, the priest, was turning in his clerical collar, and he wouldn't let anything ruin his sister's special day.

Mary's decision to marry Dan Gallagher, the sportswriter-turned-restaurant-critic—the very man who had trashed her restaurant—had been an agonizing one.

Thanks to his mother's overwhelming, controlling personality, all three of the Russo children had had issues to deal with while growing up. Mary's was a fear of commitment and failure, and it had taken a great deal of persuading and patience on Dan's part to bring the stubborn woman around to his way of thinking.

Of course, now that she was married and had taken over the role of mother to Dan's son, Mary said she couldn't think of a time when she'd ever objected to becoming the journalist's wife.

And wasn't it just like a woman to forget the important things in a relationship?

Flashing a smile in Annie's direction to cover his discomfort, Joe said finally, "I drink communion wine all the time, so I guess you can't call me a teetotaler."

She shrugged. "Whatever. You did a nice job on the ceremony today. I was impressed with all the Latin you spewed forth, not that I understood a word of it."

Her compliment took him by surprise. Annie had very little good to say about him these days. "It comes with the territory."

Joe's gaze drifted to the dance floor, where his parents were dancing, as was his sister Connie and her proctologist husband, Eddie Falcone, who took a great deal of ribbing from the Russo clan because of his medical specialty. Mary ungraciously referred to the poor guy as "the butt doctor."

He didn't miss the wistful smile crossing Annie's lips as she watched the laughing couples crowding the dance floor. She loved to dance, to participate in anything having to do with music. "Would you like to join them?" he asked. "I'm a bit rusty, but I think I can manage without doing you serious injury." He held his breath, wondering if she would take the olive branch he proffered.

Blue eyes widened at the invitation, then her cheeks warmed as she sipped more of the bubbly liquid while contemplating her answer. Finally, she said, "Why not. Even though the band sucks big-time, I'd hate for all that music to go to waste." It was only a dance, after all.

"It won't ruin your reputation to be seen dancing with a priest?" he asked, leading her onto the dance floor, a teasing smile hovering about his lips.

"I don't give a f—a fig about my reputation. Or haven't I made that clear over the years, Father Joseph? And since you're dressed in a nice suit, instead of your holier-than-thou garments, I guess I'll take my chances."

They began moving about the floor to the romantic strains of a Frank Sinatra standard, and it didn't take Annie long to become *bewitched, bothered, and bewildered* by Joe's nearness. Though she hated to admit it, even to herself, it felt wonderful to be held in his arms again. It had been a long time.

Fifteen years was a very long time.

Cursing inwardly at where her thoughts had taken her, Annie decided that when the song ended she would make her excuses and drift off to the other side of the room, away from the man's charms. The sexual attraction that had always existed between them was still as potent as ever, and she had no intention of repeating past mistakes.

"I was watching you when the bridal bouquet was tossed," Joe said. "It was nice of you to pretend to miss it so our cousin Rosemary could catch it." Tipping the scales at over two hundred and fifty pounds, poor Rosie needed all the help she could get. The overweight, unmarried woman hadn't met a cannoli she didn't like.

"I'm not looking to get hitched, so it wasn't that great a sacrifice."

"You're a lot nicer than you give yourself credit for, Annie. I watched you with Dan's boy earlier. You're a natural as a . . ." he hesitated a moment, then whispered, "mother."

White-hot pain stabbed into her breast, and she sucked in air, trying to maintain her indifference. "Speaking of mothers, yours has been giving me the evil eye, so I'd better go. I can't afford to have any curses put on my head."

Before she could make good her escape, the Paisans began playing a tarantella, and Joe latched on to her hand, dragging her into the circle of energetic Italians. They were clapping their hands above their heads and singing loud enough to raise the dead as they cavorted to the lively folk dance.

"Let me worry about my mother," he told her when she started to protest again.

Someone thrust a tambourine at Annie, and she was soon banging it and singing as loudly as the rest of them, forgetting all about where she was, and whom she was with, as the magic of the music took hold.

"I am totally out of breath," Annie admitted after the dance ended, clasping an open palm to her chest. "I can't dance another step right now. But it was so much fun."

Joe's grin widened as she sucked in huge gulps of air. "And here I thought you were in shape from all those aerobic exercises you're always doing." Her tight, compact body gave testimony to that.

Concentrate on something else, he told himself, lifting his gaze to her mouth, to the fullness of her lush rose-petal lips, which proved to be an even bigger mistake. Annie had a mouth that fueled erotic dreams even a priest wasn't immune to.

Pausing mid-breath, Annie shot him a look that would have withered lesser men. "I am in shape. And I haven't heard any complaints from the other men here tonight."

"And you'll get none from me," Joe said quickly, hoping to avoid an argument. "Come on, let's go sing some karaoke. I've always wanted to try it." There were a great many things he'd missed out on these past years, and he intended to rectify that, starting tonight.

Tonight was for new beginnings. He'd worry about the consequences tomorrow.

She looked at him as if he had suddenly become possessed. "What? Have you lost your mind? A priest singing karaoke? Your mother will faint dead away."

Smiling in conspiratorial fashion, he winked. "That's too good to pass up, don't you think?" With a sigh of misgiving, she relented, allowing herself to be led up to the bandstand.

"I'm not singing, just as long as you know that."

"I never took you for a chicken, Annie Goldman."

"And I never took you for a jackass, Joseph Russo."

Swallowing his smile, he settled her down onto a chair, told her to wait, and moved to talk to the guy in charge of the equipment.

A few moments later, Annie watched nervously as Joe grabbed the microphone and the screen before him lit. She had a bad feeling about this whole stupid idea. Then the music started playing, Joe began to sing, and she almost fell out of her chair.

"You fill up my senses . . ."

"Annie's Song." She sucked in her breath at the familiar strains of the John Denver classic. It was her song. The song Joe used to sing to her when they were dating—the song he had sung the first time they'd made love. A large lump lodged in her throat at the memories it conjured up.

Damn you, Joe! Damn you!

Cursing herself for her moment of weakness, she quickly regained control of her emotions.

"Come let me love you. Come love me again."

In a pig's eye! she thought, knowing *that* was never going to happen. Not again.

How could Joe do this to her? Didn't he realize what that song meant to her? He was obviously more callous and unfeeling than she'd given him credit for.

Noting that several curious onlookers had gathered in front of the stage and were now staring at her with stupid smiles on their faces, as if she were the "luckiest girl in the whole USA," to borrow a line from one of those hillbilly songs she detested, she felt trapped and angry.

Squirming restlessly in her seat, Annie wanted nothing more than to bolt. Except, that is, to kill Joseph Russo. That she wanted in the worst way.

Forcing a smile that was really more of a smirk, she kept her rage carefully hidden when he came to kneel down before her, and silently enumerated all the hideous things she was going to do to Joe when she got the chance.

Out of the corner of her eye, Annie caught Sophia Russo's hateful glare. She was obviously furious at her son's public display toward a woman she detested.

The woman's anger almost made Annie's pain bearable. Almost.

But not quite.

TWO

"Don't spit into the well—
you might drink from it later."

Annie had what psychiatrists often referred to as a split personality. It wasn't the stark-raving mad kind caused by an insane mother who tied her child to a piano bench with a dish towel and made her hold her pee until she burst. (Poor Sybil!) And it wasn't the kind that sent Joanne Woodward splintering into triplets in *The Three Faces of Eve*.

No, Annie's split was more or less religion-induced, caused by a Jewish father who would take hold of one arm, a Catholic mother who would grab the other, then pull, tugging her from one side to the other.

"She'll be raised a Jew!" Sid Goldman would shout during their tug-of-war. *"It was good enough for me. It'll be good enough for Annie."*

To which her mother always replied, *"Over my dead Jesus!"* before making the sign of the cross, as if her husband were a member of the bloodsucking, overbite set, and she had the means to ward him off.

"I'm Catholic. You knew that when you married me. Our daughter will be raised in the only true apostolic faith."

It was at this point that Sid would shake his head, throw his hands up in the air, and shout, "Oy! *I should have listened to my mother and never married a* shiksa. *Marrying out was a big mistake, a catastrophe. The* rabbi *warned me. But did I listen?"*

"Now I'm a mistake? A catastrophe? After thirty-eight years you say these things to me?"

You could also insert five, ten, fifteen, twenty years, and so on, because Gina and Sid had been having this same conversation since the day they exchanged their marriage vows before the Justice of the Peace.

"You, Sid Goldman, are a schmuck *and a* mamzer.*"*

Even though her mother was Italian, when it came to cursing her husband, Gina didn't let ethnic prejudice get in her way. A prick and a bastard were the same in any language.

Staring at the massive double doors of St. Francis of Assisi's Catholic Church, Annie shook her head. The fact that she'd been thinking about her childhood, and how she'd been batted back and forth like a Ping-Pong ball between Judaism and Catholicism, came as no surprise. The surprise was that she had survived her childhood with most of her sanity intact.

And it wasn't any wonder that going to a church or synagogue freaked her out. It was actually a minor miracle that she didn't break out in hives at the thought of meeting up with the Father, Son, and Holy Ghost.

For all her parents' tugs-of-war, their touts about Jews being better than Catholics, and vice versa, in the end Annie had chosen not to embrace either religion fully. It would have been admitting that she loved one of her parents more than the other. She didn't. She loved them equally, or as much as any child could love parents that drove her crazy.

Of course, there was another reason she shied away from the church and organized religion. And that reason was at this very moment waiting on the other side of those forbidding oak doors.

Annie hadn't stepped foot in a church or seen Joe Russo since Mary's wedding. But when Mary had called earlier this afternoon, asking Annie to pick up her brother, she hadn't been able to refuse, though seeing him again was at the bottom of her favorite-things-to-do list.

It was true: She and Joe had had a great time together at the reception. They danced, flirted, and acted like fools. Maybe it had been the champagne, or the fact that weddings always made people nostalgic for happier times.

Or maybe it was just temporary insanity. That seemed the more likely possibility.

But whatever it was, they'd had fun, up until the moment he'd made the mistake of dragging her up onstage and singing to her, of forcing her to remember things best left forgotten.

And it was also true that she had been attracted to Joe for as long as she could remember. As a child, she had idolized Mary's older brother. As a young woman, she had dated and fallen in love with him. And believing Joe felt the same about her, she had surrendered herself to him, totally and completely, like a lovestruck, stupid, naive fool.

And then she had gotten pregnant.

Terror didn't even come close to describing her feelings at the idea of becoming a mother at eighteen. She'd been such a kid herself, spoiled and pampered by her parents. But Joe had been wonderful, had reassured her that everything would work out fine. They made plans to marry and rent an apartment near his college, so he could continue with his studies.

And then she'd lost the baby, and her whole world had collapsed.

Joe's promise of undying love had all been a sham. His vow to care for her, support and love her, lasted only as long as her pregnancy. After the miscarriage, he had withdrawn into himself, and then had finally left her, to join the priesthood.

It had been the final insult.

She was still humiliated, and angry at him for dumping her, for breaking her heart and turning it into chopped liver.

After all, how does a woman explain to the world, to her friends, that she's been set aside for the church? That a man found celibacy preferable to her? That she sent men running to find sanctuary from her potent appeal?

She couldn't.

She just lived with the heartlessness of his actions and seethed inwardly.

She could compete with another woman, but how could she compete with God?

Deciding that there was no good reason to let an opportunity to harass Joe go to waste, Annie pulled open the heavy door of the dimly lit church and entered, making her way toward the confessional, where Mary had instructed her brother would be waiting.

There were few things in life better than sex. Except, perhaps, for getting even. You didn't have to be a Jew or a Catholic to realize that. In fact, Italians were masters at the whole vendetta thing. And since she was half Italian, and since sex was definitely out of the question . . .

Slipping sight unseen into the confessional, she heard a rustling on the other side and smiled inwardly, knowing the words she was about to speak weren't totally untrue.

"Forgive me, Father, for I have sinned."

Searching the confessional for his favorite ballpoint pen while he waited for his sister, Joe froze at the sound of Annie's voice, then formed the uncharitable thought *No kidding!* before sliding the partition back.

"What are you doing here, Annie?" She had avoided him like the plague since Mary's wedding reception, refusing his phone calls, and ignoring him completely the few times he'd seen her at the restaurant. And that had hurt—as, he supposed, it was meant to.

"Aren't you going to absolve me of my sins before I tell you why I'm here, Father?" she asked in a deceptively innocent voice.

He could barely make out her features through the confessional screen. But he didn't have to see Annie to know she wore a teasing smile—a smile that held more promise than she was willing to give.

They'd gotten along well at the reception, and he'd briefly entertained the hope that maybe things would work out between them. But he knew that was only wishful thinking on his part. Nothing had changed, not really. They were still two very different people, with very divergent philosophies on life.

"Madonna meets Dr. Spock," was how Annie had always described their relationship. He guessed there was some truth to that. He had always been far more serious and grounded than she. Unbridled passion versus restrained practicality about summed it up.

And it was clear that she'd never forgiven him for leaving her all those years ago. He'd barely forgiven himself.

"That would take much longer than I have," he finally replied. "And as I'm sure you've already heard, I'm out of the absolution business. I'm no longer a priest."

"So what are you doing here, then?"

"I just came by to clean out my office, pick up the rest of my personal stuff, and take one last look around." The thought of leaving saddened him. He would miss St. Francis—the choir, the kids, hearing the confessions of his parishioners, their problems, and offering what counsel he could. But he knew it was time to move on, to make a new life.

And resurrect part of the old one, if he could.

His life would never be complete without Annie in it. It had taken him fifteen years, and a lifetime of prayers, to make him realize that. He couldn't serve two masters, and his heart had finally won out.

"What a pity you're no longer a priest. I've never gotten it on with a priest before. It would have been—"

"Shut up!" Joe's voice hardened in anger.

Even though no one was around to hear Annie's brazen remark, it still angered Joe that she would say such a thing in a church. It wasn't that he was a prude, far from it, but Annie was . . . well, she was just too outspoken for her own good, always had been, and she knew exactly which buttons to push to get a reaction.

"Why are you here? I thought Mary was coming by to pick me up." His sister, just back from her honeymoon, had promised to be at the church by two o'clock to help cart his belongings over to his new apartment—the same apartment she had vacated after her marriage to Dan Gallagher.

They'd agreed to meet at the confessional, for old times' sake. Mary had never believed in the theory that confession was good for the soul, while he had strictly adhered to the teachings of the church, and had pushed and prodded his sister to unburden herself. Her resistance to his insistence had been a running joke between them.

Confession was a moot point, at any rate, since he was no longer a priest. Although his mother had made him promise that he would administer last rites if she "dropped dead," which, she assured him, would be soon. Apparently his decision to quit the church was sending her to an early grave with the same velocity as a bullet train.

But then, Sophia Russo had a flair for the dramatic.

His mother foolishly believed that she derived her standing in the close-knit Italian community from his being a member of the church hierarchy, and that she would now have to hide her head in shame because of his decision.

From the day he'd been ordained, she'd referred to him as Father Joseph, never Joe. She'd set him up on a pedestal, envisioned him as pure and unsullied, even talked about him becoming Pope one day—a topic that usually sent his sisters into gales of laughter every time it was mentioned.

Therefore, it had been a particularly bitter disappointment when Sophia learned that Father Joseph was now just plain old Joe. Father Joe, the priest, had become Joe, the unemployed—a problem he would soon have to rectify.

His meager savings had dwindled, and he had to find a way to support himself. The church had always provided for his needs, but now he would have to take charge of those matters himself.

Finding a job was the first order of business. Not that he was qualified to do much, in a job market where computers ruled and experience counted.

What did ex-priests do, besides write novels or become television evangelists?

Being totally on his own was a heady feeling, but it also made him nervous. He hadn't met the lofty goals he'd set for himself as a priest. What made him think he could succeed in the secular world?

And what was he going to do with the rest of his life? That was the big question, and one he didn't have an answer for.

Exiting the confessional, Annie came around to where the former priest was standing. It was strange to see Joe dressed in jeans and a T-shirt, looking so normal, so unpriestlike. So handsome. It was even stranger to hear his voice raised in anger, but she supposed she deserved his wrath. She'd meant her comment to be funny, but Joe had apparently lost his sense of humor.

"Mary's still at Matt's parent-teacher conference. She called and asked me to pick you up, so here I am."

Reaching into the pocket of her white cotton shorts, she extracted a key and handed it to him. "This is to Mary's old apartment. Mrs. Foragi said you could have the locks changed if you want."

"I don't see any reason to."

Joe pocketed the key, and Annie's eyes followed the movement. Their eyes met. His smile grew knowing. Her lips thinned.

"I can give you a good reason: I've got the spare."

"Great! Maybe you can come in and clean up the place from time to time." Her look of outrage amused him, as did the color of her hair. It was sapphire blue and matched her eyes.

Annie changed hair color as often as most people changed underwear. Mary insisted that the unorthodox woman was making a statement, but Joe had never been able to figure out exactly what she was saying. He wasn't altogether sure he wanted to know.

"When hell freezes over, Fath—"

"*Uh, uh, uh.* Remember, it's just Joe now."

His grin produced two deep dimples, and Annie sucked in her breath, remembering, and wondering why she allowed Joe Russo to get to her. He'd been under her skin since high school. They shared a history.

They had no future.

"Come on, *just* Joe. I'm double-parked, and I don't want another ticket." She already had a glove compartment full of them. Her father warned that if she didn't pay them soon, the police would arrive on her doorstep unannounced and haul her off to jail in handcuffs.

Joe folded his long frame into the front seat of Annie's silver Mazda Miata and whistled appreciatively. "Is this new?"

She shrugged, trying hard not to look overly proud, but failing. Buying the car had been a goal she'd set for herself. She hadn't realized many of the aspirations she'd set forth in life: building a career in social work, finding Mr. Wonderful and getting married, living happily ever after. So she'd been determined to achieve this one small objective.

"Used. But it's only a year old, and I got a good deal on it." The car had been her first major purchase since taking the job as manager/hostess at Mama Sophia's.

He glanced up, noting the black ragtop. "It's sporty."

"Yeah, well, I'm a sporty kind of gal." Actually, except for the forty-five minute daily aerobic workout she did unfailingly, Annie wasn't into athletics or sporting events, not like Mary.

The Gallaghers attended all of the Orioles baseball games, and had already obtained tickets to the upcoming fall season of the Baltimore Ravens football team. Of course,

Dan's position as *The Baltimore Sun*'s Sports editor pretty much made that a necessity.

"Maybe you can introduce me to your car salesman," Joe suggested. He smoothed his hand over the leather dash, like a lover's hand caressing bare flesh, and Annie's mouth suddenly turned into the Sahara desert. She tried to swallow, but couldn't work up enough spit.

Damn her for remembering how it used to be between them.

"I need wheels now that I'm not driving the church van any longer."

"I doubt Sonny Brando"—no relation to Marlon, despite the car salesman's repeated assertions to the contrary— "will cut you the same deal he cut me." Her smile grew wicked. "Unless, of course, he's suddenly become interested in men. Though I'd be surprised to learn that after—"

"Save it, Annie. I'm not interested in hearing about your conquests." His eyes hardened, resembling bits of coal.

Maybe it was the fact that he'd sang that damn song, or maybe it was because she felt justified in getting even for everything that had happened between them, but whatever the reason, Annie wanted to annoy Joe, and was inordinately pleased that she'd succeeded.

Let him think the worst about her and Sonny, Annie thought. Not that anything had happened between them. She had better taste in men than the owner of Sonny's Auto Circus. Not that the man hadn't tried. Sonny always tried. But she wasn't interested in her former high school classmate. He was too slick. Literally! His hair held more grease than the crankshaft of her Miata. She was sure if he ever jumped into a swimming pool, he'd create an oil slick bigger than the *Exxon Valdez*.

"Your loss," Annie said finally. "After all, I have so many interesting stories I could tell."

"I bet you're a regular Scheherazade, but I don't have one thousand and one nights' worth of interest." Bad enough he'd had to sit back all these years and watch her go through a procession of men. Joe couldn't bear thinking of them as lovers, though he knew they probably were. Annie had never made it secret that she liked sex.

Suddenly a car pulled out in front of Annie, stealing her attention. She stomped on the brake to avoid hitting it, then blasted the horn, leaning into it for all she was worth. "Watch it, moron!" she shouted out the window, and the guy in the red Mustang flipped her off before speeding away. "*Eizel!* Idiot!"

"Nice," Joe remarked. "I don't suppose you've heard road rage can get you killed? And cursing, whether it's in Yiddish or English, isn't considered ladylike." Damn, but he sounded self-righteous and preachy! That, he supposed, was going to take a while to fix.

She rolled her eyes. "Whatever. So tell me, Joseph, why did you quit the church? Did one of the other holy men make a pass at you?" His eyes darkened, and she surmised correctly that he didn't appreciate her repeated attempts at humor.

"I was surprised when Mary told me you were leaving the church." Surprised and angry. Fifteen years wasted. Fifteen years that by all rights should have belonged to her. Not that she thought along those lines.

Not anymore.

Studying the woman seated next to him, Joe knew he couldn't confide the real reason he had quit the priesthood. Annie would just toss it back in his face.

The fact that she'd never forgiven him for making promises, talking marriage, then bailing out on her after the baby died and joining the church was evident by the pinched look on her beautiful face—a face that had haunted him for more nights than he cared to remember, certainly more than a thousand and one.

Joe hadn't wanted to desert Annie. He'd fully intended to marry her and live up to his commitment. He had loved Annie then, still loved her now, and it hadn't been his intention to hurt her. But the baby's death had hit him hard, filling him with guilt and remorse.

He'd sinned against God and been punished for it. He had to atone for his sins. And so he had made the difficult decision to leave the one thing in life he loved above all else and dedicate his life to the church.

It had been a fitting punishment for a youthful indiscretion and the subsequent immature decision that had followed.

So how should he answer her question?

His reasons for quitting were varied. He no longer had the ability to make the sacrifices necessary to continue on in the role of priest. He'd lost his enthusiasm to change the world. He felt restless, unfulfilled. Lonely.

Celibacy was no longer an option.

The real reason Joe had quit was sitting next to him, taunting him with the clean, fresh citrus scent of her perfume, with her firm, tanned legs that seemed to go on forever. With a sassy smile and a pair of blue eyes that he'd fallen in love with a long time ago and could never forget.

He wanted Annie as a man wanted a woman.

And though he'd tried to pray her out of his system, the image of her, the knowledge of what they'd had together, wouldn't go away.

She'd been madly in love with him once, and he'd tossed

that love aside. Love should have counted for more. He should have been there for Annie, given her the love and support she needed.

Joe hoped it wasn't too late.

THREE

"Your health comes first;
you can always hang yourself later."

"Hiya, Pops! How's things hanging?"

Glancing up from the newspaper, Sid Goldman removed his reading glasses and shook his head at Annie. His irritation obvious, as was the affection shining brightly in his eyes for a daughter he had never understood, but loved nonetheless.

"Enough, already! You want I should call the police and have you arrested for having such a trashy mouth? What kind of daughter says such things to her father?"

Leaning over the royal-blue velvet rocker, Annie bussed him on the cheek, then grinned. "One who loves him." Her gaze flitted about the garishly decorated living room, which reminded her of a funeral parlor.

Her mother was into velvet in a big way, as evidenced by the paneled drapes hanging at the picture window and the three-piece sectional in front of it. An assortment of dark-walnut tables and overstuffed chairs completed the look only Morticia Addams and Gina Goldman could love.

Some people had early-American decor. Sid and Gina had early mortuary.

The entire house had been decorated in various shades of blue velvet and brocade, because Gina believed quality fabrics and expensive furniture were the mark of success.

And she wasn't about to give the Goldman girls a reason to criticize her. Not that Sid's sisters needed an excuse.

"Heard any juicy tidbits from the police scanner today? Any serial killers on the loose that I should know about?" She jerked her head toward the end table where the noisy police scanner—the bane of her mother's existence, and her father's pride and joy—rested like some rare museum objet d'art atop the crocheted doily her deceased grandmother had made.

"I should be so lucky." Her father leaned over to turn it down, but not completely off. After all, as Sid had pointed out many times before, you never knew when a triple homicide could happen. "The crooks are staying inside today. It's been quiet since I got home from the store."

Annie's dark brows knitted in concern. "You look tired, Pop. Are you feeling okay?" At sixty-two, Sid was over-weight, drank too much of the concord-grape wine he loved, and didn't exercise. He was a heart attack waiting to happen, and Annie worried for his health. Not that it did any good, because her father never listened to anybody's advice, including the doctor's.

"We had a big sale today. Women's bras and panties were half-off. Who knew those women were going to swarm over the merchandise like killer bees? I was busy all day. Now I feel tired. Nothing worse should ever happen." He picked up his glass of Manischewitz and sipped, heaving a contented sigh.

Sniffing the air like a bloodhound, Annie's frown deepened at the familiar odor. "Is that potato latkes I smell? Is Mom making those again, even after the doctor told you to watch your fat and cholesterol? I'm going to speak to Gina."

Annie had been calling her mother by her first name

since she'd been twelve and had latched on to the idea that she'd been adopted. Nothing her parents had said could convince her otherwise. Not even when it was said with ice cream and candy.

Sid blamed it on a stage she was going through. *"Annie'll grow out of it"* had been his answer to most everything in those days. But she never had, because it so infuriated her mother she couldn't resist doing it.

Annie was nothing if not perverse.

Sid shot his daughter a look of disbelief. "Are you crazy in the head? Of course she's making them. What does that quack Mankin know about what's inside my body? Does he look in? Can he tell if there's fat?" His face screwed up in disgust. "I pay Mankin good money and he tells me to watch what I eat? He's got cockamamie ideas, that one. Eat, schmeet. This you call a diagnosis? He should drop dead with that diagnosis."

"It's good advice that could save your life, so quit being stubborn and listen to Dr. Mankin. He knows what he's talking about."

"Now you sound like your mama. Don't be a *nudge*."

"Yeah, Gina nags but that hasn't stopped her from cooking what you want to eat. Fried, no less."

"You just want the latkes for yourself. You don't fool me. With the applesauce you'll eat them and never gain an ounce. *Oy!* To be young again." He patted his increased girth. "I used to be skinny. With old age doesn't come wisdom, with old age comes more fat and less hair."

Annie plopped down on his lap and kissed his balding pate. "You're still as handsome as ever, Pops. There's just more of you to love, that's all."

"And you, *maideleh,* have no fat." He circled his fingers around her thin wrist. "Like a bird."

"I haven't been a little girl for a long time, Pops." Though she loved it when he used the endearment. Sometimes she wished she were still a child. Life had been far less complicated back then, with only pimples and puberty to contend with. But she'd grown up fast, eager to consume everything life had to offer, digesting what appealed, and spitting out the rest.

"You're wasting away like those anorexic women on TV. You want to look like that stick Ally McBeal? The woman has no breasts! You should eat. How will you have healthy babies if you don't eat?"

The subject of babies always brought pain, and she forced a smile. She'd never told her parents about the child—Joe's child. She couldn't have dealt with their heartache and disappointment. She'd barely been able to deal with her own.

You never knew how important something was until you lost it.

"I'm not even married, Pops. You want me to go out and get myself knocked up? What kind of a father suggests that to his daughter?"

"One who loves her and wants her to be happy," he said, pinching her cheek. "Mama and I won't always be here, Annie. I don't want to see you end up alone."

"I won't be alone. I've got Mary."

He sighed. "She's married now and making her own family."

Yes, but they were still close and always would be, no matter what. Annie knew that in her heart. But she also knew that her relationship with Mary was bound to change somewhat. Now that she was married there'd be no more late-night phone calls to discuss Annie's disastrous dates and Mary's lack of them, no more marathon ice-cream binges and dirty joke competitions. She'd miss all that.

She already did.

"Who's married?" Annie's mother bustled into the living room, wiping her hands on a dish towel, and smiling happily when she spotted her daughter.

It wasn't hard to figure out from whom Annie had inherited her good looks. Gina Goldman was a very attractive woman, who was proud to admit she still wore a size ten, the same dress size as the day she'd married Sid.

She had graying shoulder-length black hair that was usually worn pulled back at the nape, which continued to be a bone of contention between mother and daughter. Annie wanted Gina to dye it "something dramatic," to cover the gray, but her mother argued that she'd earned every one of her gray hairs honestly, and wanted Sid to have a constant reminder of the sacrifices she'd made for him.

"I thought I heard your voice, Annie *mia*. You'll stay for dinner, no? I'm making a roast. Lou picked it out special for me. It's a beautiful piece of meat."

Lou Santini had had the hots for Mary not long ago, but her friend hadn't been interested in the butcher. Probably because Lou, who was closing in on forty, still lived with his mother, who was almost as overbearing and smothering as Sophia, if such a thing was possible. Unfortunately, it was.

Annie pitied the woman who married Lou, not because he wasn't a great guy—Lou was a mensch—but because his nightmare of a mother came with the package.

Annie and Mary had surmised long ago that Nina Santini and Sophia Russo were in reality twins who'd been separated at birth. The women were two peas in a pod, which is why they couldn't stand the sight of each other. Freud would have had a field day with them.

Annie rose to her feet. "I wasn't planning to stay, Gina. I

need to run by the restaurant and inventory the supplies, make sure everything's set for tomorrow." And maybe visit Joe. She knew he was still fixing up Mary's old apartment, and she was curious to see what changes, if any, he'd made. At least, that's what she told herself.

"It's Monday. Mama Sophia's is closed. Sit. Stay. Eat. Then you'll go by there. That Mary is lucky to have you working for her. Not many employees would be as hard-working and conscientious."

"My daughter learned responsibility from me," Sid declared proudly, a thoughtful expression crossing his face. He'd been toying with an idea for weeks. But he wouldn't speak of it to Annie just yet. The timing wasn't right. And as any successful Jew could tell you, timing was everything.

Gina heaved an Oscar-worthy sigh that even Meryl Streep would have been proud to claim. "I'm not sure how much longer I'll be on this earth, Annie," she said, covering her face with the towel, and making Annie wonder if she'd been taking drama lessons. "Who knows how many more dinners we'll share. My days are numbered. I can feel it. I'm not doing so good."

Father and daughter exchanged a knowing look, before Annie said, "You look fine to me."

"It's the makeup. It hides my sallow complexion. Just the other day I ran into Sophia Russo at Fiorelli's Bakery/Cafe. She told me I looked like one of the powdered jelly donuts Andrea had made that morning. I was so embarrassed and upset that I couldn't finish my bagel."

Sophia's insults weren't new. The woman was the Don Rickles of Little Italy.

"I've got such a pain in my back and side. I think my kidneys or gallbladder's diseased. I'm prone to stones, you know. Grandpa Johnny had gallstones."

"They're not hereditary, Gina. You can't get them because your father had them," Annie pointed out, though she knew she was wasting her breath. Her mother heard only what she wanted to hear. If Annie were to tell Gina she looked as if she had leprosy, that she would believe.

"I'm prone. Why, just last night I was running a fever."

"Ninety-eight point seven is not a fever," Sid told his wife, his disgust evident. "Stop talking yourself into illness. Tell her, Annie. Tell your mother it's not a fever."

"Oh, sure. A lot you know, Sid. I could have a cancer, or some other dreadful disease, and you wouldn't care. The only thing you care about is listening to that police radio. You've become a regular Sipowicz."

Come to think of it, her father did look a bit like Dennis Franz from *NYPD Blue*, Annie thought, only Sid was a few inches taller and much heavier than the actor.

"That's because there's always something different and exciting on the scanner. You sing the same old tune, day in and day out, like a broken record: *'I'm dying, Sid. I'm dying here.'* But you know what, Gina, you never do. You're still kicking."

"And you want me dead? Is that it?" With a sob, and an anguished look at her daughter, the distraught woman fled the room.

"Shame on you, Pops, for talking to Mom like that. You know how excitable she is." Only a caged rat on speed had more nervous energy than Gina Goldman.

"Then tell her to quit bustin' my chops with that sickness crap. The woman lives to kvetch. I'm sick of it." He rubbed his chest and winced. "She gives me indigestion. Now I won't be able to enjoy the latkes." He looked around impatiently. "Where the hell's that Maalox?"

Annie handed him the bottle of antacid she spied between the sofa cushions. "Come on, Pops. You know you love Mom."

"Of course I love her. Did I say I didn't love Gina? But the woman drives me meshuga. This illness stuff is all in her head. The one and only diagnosis Mankin got right.

"Her ailments are getting worse. I took her to the emergency room three times last week because she said she was dying. How do you die from gas, tell me that?"

Annie shrugged her answer.

"Do you know how much it costs to go to the ER? Plenty. Not to mention you're signing forms until they're coming out of your *tuchas*. *Oy!* I should have a dollar for every form I've filled out. I could be retired now."

"Maybe Mom needs to see a shrink. Sometimes after menopause a woman has problems."

"A head doctor? You think I'm going to pay for your mother to see one of those fancy, schmancy psychiatrists, so they can fill her already stuffed head with more crazy ideas?"

He shook his head. "No. What your mother needs is a hobby. She's got too much time on her hands. I told her to come to work at the store, like she used to when we were young and just starting out. And you know what she said?"

Annie was afraid to ask.

"She said I was cheap and wanted free labor. And that I should be ashamed that I wanted a woman her age to work like a slave. That's what she said." He punctuated his annoyance with a grunt. Sid could put a lot of feeling into a grunt.

"I'll talk to her."

"It won't do any good. I've tried. Nothing changes."

"Maybe you two should go on a trip, take a vacation."

"And leave the store?" He looked horrified at the thought.

Goldman's Department Store was Sid's lifeblood. He lived and breathed to sell outdated merchandise to old fogies who didn't have a lick of fashion sense. A few of his male customers still wore leisure suits from the 70s.

While in high school, Annie had worked part-time at the store and hated the place. She'd seen photos of Goldman's taken at the grand opening over forty years ago, and it still looked exactly the same.

No one would ever accuse Sid Goldman of being hip.

"I took Gina to a fancy resort in the Catskills last summer. She said the food made her nauseous."

Annie rolled her eyes in disbelief. "You took Mom to the Borscht Belt? No wonder she got sick." The Catskill resorts were full of old people, mostly Jews, who were taking their final fling before death. An exciting, fun-filled place, it was not.

"Maybe you could go on a cruise or take her to Jerusalem. You always said you wanted to visit the Holy Land. You could wail at the wall, walk in the footsteps of Jesus. It would be romantic." She tried to keep a straight face.

"Ha! A cruise. What can we do on a ship that we can't do in our own bed? Not that we do that much. Not anymore. They should make a pill for women, like that Viagra they've got for men who can't get it up. Now, there's some medicine your mother could use."

That was more information than Annie wanted. No child, no matter what age, should have to think about her parents having sex. The ick factor was tremendous.

She bolted to her feet. "I'll talk to Mom. See if I can find out what's wrong."

"What's wrong is that Gina's Italian, an Italian shiksa." Sid heaved a sigh. "Jews and Italians are a bad combination. I never should have married out. My rabbi warned me, my mother pleaded with me—God rest her soul—but did I listen? Did I pay the slightest attention?"

"I'm half Jewish and half Italian, and I didn't turn out so bad."

His eyes widened. "No? Look at your hair. Who in their right mind has blue hair? Only a woman with an identity crisis."

Or a woman who has Sid and Gina Goldman for parents.

Joe had just finished showering and was stepping into his jeans when a knock sounded at the door. Figuring it was the pizza delivery guy, he tunneled fingers through wet hair, combing it back as best he could, then reached for a shirt and hurried to answer the summons. He stubbed his big toe on a box he'd left sitting in the middle of the floor and bit back the profanity teetering on the tip of his tongue.

Hopping on one foot, he made his way to the door and opened it, his eyes widening in surprise and pleasure when he saw who was standing there. "Annie! I wasn't expecting you." The sight of her filled him with warmth.

Annie was dressed in tight black leather pants and a red knit top that did nothing to hide the fact that she wasn't wearing a bra. A large lump formed in his throat, matching the one forming below his waist. He swallowed, forcing his eyes and attention upward.

Annie wasn't expecting to be so affected by the sight of Joe's near-nakedness, either. It was obvious he'd just stepped out of the shower. The top three buttons of his 501s were undone, giving her a glimpse of olive skin and dark curly hairs. She raised her eyes to take in the wash-board flat stomach, the muscular expanse of his chest, lightly furred with hair.

Joe at twenty had been boyishly handsome, and had made her eighteen-year-old heart flutter madly. Joe at thirty-five was a wet dream come to life. And it had been a while since she'd done any *dreaming*.

She had grown bored with the dating and bar scene. Most of the men she met were only looking for one thing. And most of those couldn't carry on an intelligent conversation to save themselves. Sex and the single life were losing their appeal. She wanted what Mary had, to find someone to love and settle down.

She was tired of being alone. Tired of being lonely. But the thought of opening herself up to a man, making herself vulnerable, having her heart broken . . . She just couldn't deal with that kind of hurt again. So she kept her relationships superficial and her heart safe.

"I just got out of the shower," he said by way of explanation. His eyes followed hers to the waistband of his jeans, and he hastily buttoned them.

"I can see that. I was downstairs doing some last-minute things at the restaurant, and thought you might need some help unpacking." She hadn't intended to make the offer, but couldn't think of any other plausible explanation for why she'd dropped by unannounced that wouldn't sound contrived.

To be perfectly honest, Annie didn't know why she'd come. She tended to act on impulse and face the consequences later. Consequences like half-naked men who were sending her hormones into overdrive, like confronting feelings she thought dead and buried long ago.

Ushering Annie inside, Joe shut the door behind them.

"I just ordered a pizza. Thought you might be the delivery guy." Though no delivery person he ever saw looked as sexy, or had the power to turn his insides to rubber, as Annie. His heart was bouncing around his chest like a tennis ball; he moved his hand to cover it.

Of all the women in the world he could have chosen to love, why did he have to pick one that hated him?

"Good. I'm starving." She tossed her purse down on a taped carton. "Though don't tell your sister you ordered from the competition. Mary's very proprietary about Marco's pizza. If she finds out you've ordered from someone else, she'll think you're being disloyal."

"That's ridiculous. Why would she be upset? Mama Sophia's is closed, so I ordered from Uncle Luigi's, or what is now known as Pizza Perfect, since his death."

"Yeah? Well, try telling that to your sister." Her gaze moved around the room, taking in the organized chaos of cardboard cartons and scattered bits of newspaper that had been used for packing. Three long-sleeved, white dress shirts were draped over a halogen floor lamp, dimming the light somewhat, and creating a fire hazard.

Removing the shirts to a safer location, she said, "So where do you want to start? This place is a mess. Your sister would be horrified if she could see it." And Mary wasn't overly obsessive about neatness.

"How about the bedroom?"

His grin was altogether too sexy, and her heart started thumping, despite a cease-and-desist order to the contrary. "Very funny."

"No, I mean it. I've been so busy I haven't had time to make up the bed, and I'm getting tired of sleeping on the couch."

Great! Just what she wanted to do—spend the evening in Joe's bedroom. "You got linens?"

He pointed to a large box standing in the corner, marked "Bedroom" in black marker. "They're not fancy. I got 'em at Wal-Mart."

Pulling out the shrink-wrapped packages of sheets and pillowcases, Annie's brow lifted, and she couldn't contain her smile. "Well, well. Aren't you a surprise, Fa . . . Joseph. I didn't figure you for the satin sheets type."

Heat crept up his neck to land squarely on his cheeks. "I've always wanted to try them out. Figured this was as good a time as any." He'd forgotten all about the sheets he'd bought on impulse, part of his making-up-for-lost-experiences program.

She tossed him one of the packages. "This'll go faster if you help."

Following her into the bedroom, Joe positioned himself on the opposite side of the queen-size, brass bed.

"This bed brings back memories," Annie remarked.

"You've slept on it?" The image made him uneasy.

"Mostly reclined. Mary and I used to sit in here and discuss all kinds of weighty issues, like what to wear on dates, how our parents were driving us nuts, the stupidity of men, that sort of thing."

He was about to ask her about the last part, but then thought better of it. Annie had always been brutally honest, and she'd have no qualms about lumping him into that category, had probably already lumped him into that category. "Girl talk, huh?"

"Being a man must be boring. I mean . . . do you have anyone you confide in?"

"I used to confide in you, Annie."

Snapping the black satin sheet with a hard flick of her

wrist, she allowed it to float down onto the mattress and tried to ignore the pain stabbing into her breast. Smoothing out the creases, and her jumbled emotions, she replied, "I hardly remember those days."

"While I remember every moment."

Her gaze slid into Joe's, and she saw that he meant every word. She tried hard not to be affected. Infected. Joe was like a virus. Once you got him into your system, it was a slow, painful recovery. If you didn't die of a broken heart first, that is.

"Guess you've got too much time on your hands, then."

"Time has a way of putting things into perspective."

"Yeah?" She couldn't keep the animosity out of her voice. "It's also supposed to heal all wounds, and absence makes the heart grow fonder. But you know what? It's a crock. All of it." Fluffing the down pillows, she attempted to get her anger under control before she was tempted to bash him upside the head.

She wasn't sure what the penalty was for striking a priest, even a former one, but figured it had to be severe. Although it might be worth it.

Joe let the subject drop. "Thanks for your help with the bed." He pulled up the hunter-green and navy comforter, a housewarming present from his sister.

"Too bad you'll be sleeping on those satin sheets alone. They're really quite sensuous."

The image of Annie's white naked flesh sprawled on black satin had the power to make his mouth go dry, hardening both his resolve to keep his emotions in check, and certain *other* things.

"Who says I'll be sleeping alone?"

Her eyes widened, and she opened her mouth to reply, but a loud banging ensued just then, filling him with relief.

He wasn't up to matching wits with Annie just yet, knowing she'd had years to hone hers. "There's the pizza. Let's go eat. I can finish the rest later."

Joe's statement bothered Annie—priests, even ex-priests, weren't supposed to sleep around—but she refused to let him know that he'd thrown her a curve, pretending instead that she just didn't care. She *didn't* care, she told herself. Not much, anyway. "Fine with me."

The pie was an extra-large mushroom and sausage, loaded with extra mozzarella. It smelled delicious, and Annie's stomach grumbled, reminding her that she hadn't eaten since breakfast, and then only a bagel with a schmear of walnut-flavored cream cheese.

"You got any beer?" she asked over her shoulder, heading for the kitchen. Annie had spent a lot of time in this apartment, and was as familiar with it as her own.

"Yes, but it's not cold. Grab the bottle of Chianti off the counter. We'll eat in here. I don't feel like cleaning all the junk off the kitchen table right now."

Plopping down on the familiar cranberry-leather sofa, she placed the wine bottle, opener, and two clear plastic cups on the pine table. "Mary was really proud of this furniture when she bought it. I'm surprised she didn't take it with her."

"Mary took her glassware, cooking items, stuff like that, but Dan didn't have room in the condo for the furniture. She plans to take it when they eventually move into a house. In the meantime, she's allowing me to use it. But I had to swear on a stack of Bibles that I wouldn't scratch the finish or leave water stains." Reminded of that, he handed her a coaster.

Annie's throaty laughter tightened Joe's gut. "That sounds like Mary. So tell me . . . what are your plans now that you're no longer a priest?" She reached for a napkin and a slice of pie, hoping she sounded more nonchalant than she felt.

Joe shrugged, filling the cups with wine. "Obviously I need to find a job. Don't know what's available yet. I haven't started looking."

"You might try some of the restaurants." With one on every corner, they were the main attraction in Little Italy. "They can always use extra help with busing tables or washing dishes."

"And I can get a paper route, too," Joe tossed back, hating the reminder that he wasn't qualified to do much.

"No need to get defensive. You think I liked working at that sex hotline, having weirdos breathe heavy in my ear? But you do what you have to do to get by."

He sipped his wine thoughtfully, then asked, "Why'd you quit your job as a social worker? I thought you were good at it."

"I found it too depressing. The kids . . ." Four-year-old Nicole Brandon's cherubic face popped into her head, and she winced at the memory. Nicole had been physically and emotionally abused by her mother, and Annie had removed the child from the unstable, dangerous environment, placing her in protective custody. But Mrs. Brandon fought back in court, and a sympathetic judge had given the woman another chance. Nicole had died one week later of injuries sustained from another beating.

Annie heaved a sigh, hating the memories his question conjured up. "They were needy and sad. I wanted to help them, to do more, but the bureaucracy . . . It got to me after a while." She brushed away the depressing recollections and reached for her glass. "Of course, Sid's not happy that I tossed away four years of college to hand out menus."

Joe's look was empathetic. "I can relate. My mom barely speaks to me now, and Grandma Flora doesn't acknowledge my existence. I'm afraid they're still mad about my leaving the church."

His mother and grandmother weren't speaking to him and that was a bad thing? In Annie's opinion, Joe should be counting his blessings, not complaining. "They'll come around eventually. It's your life, and you have to do what's going to make you happy, which is why I quit being a social worker. I hated it."

"Oh, I intend to make myself happy," he replied. "You can rest assured of that."

A shiver slipped down her spine at his sly, self-assured smile, and she rose to her feet, suddenly eager to escape. "I'd better go."

"What's your hurry? Do I make you nervous?" He hoped so, because that meant she wasn't as indifferent to him as she pretended.

"Don't be ridiculous! Why should you make me nervous?" *Why, indeed!*

"I'm not safely tucked away in the church any longer, Annie. The rules have changed."

"I don't know what you're talking about, and I doubt you do, either." But she did, and she resented the hell out of him for bringing it up.

"I think you do. I think you know exactly what I mean."

"And I think I shouldn't have come here tonight."

"Why did you?"

It was a question she had no answer for—one she wasn't willing to face, at any rate. "I told you . . . I was working downstairs at the restaurant."

"You didn't bring a housewarming gift." His smile grew teasing.

Her expression was anything but. "I was fresh out of hemlock."

"Ouch!" He laid a hand on her arm, stopping her in mid-stride. "Do you really despise me that much, Annie?"

She hated the wounded look on his face, hated the fact that she'd put it there. But, dammit, what did he want from her? He was the one who had walked away. He was the one who hadn't loved her enough.

The memories renewed her determination to remain un-sympathetic. Anything else would be too costly. "For me to despise you would mean I cared, Joe. I don't. Not any-more. You chose to leave, to run away and hide, instead of supporting me after the death of our child. How could you profess to love and care about me, then turn around and join the church? I may only be half Italian, but I have a long memory, Joe. Maybe yours isn't long enough."

"Annie, please! I'm sorry. We need to talk."

But she merely shook her head. "There's nothing left to talk about. Nothing left of what we once had. You de-stroyed it, Joe. You. Maybe your God has forgiven you, but I never will." Picking up her purse, she walked out the door, not looking back to witness the devastation she'd wrought.

FOUR

"The truth is not always what we want to hear."

"So how's married life treating you? By the satisfied and oh-so-very-happy look on your face, I'd say you've been having some pretty erotic times with ol' Danny boy." Annie waited for her friend's inevitable blush, and she wasn't disappointed.

"I'm in love." Mary's smile was full of tenderness and happiness, and Annie felt envious, wondering if she'd ever feel that way about a man again. She doubted it. Even though she entertained thoughts from time to time about finding someone and getting married, she knew it wasn't in the cards for her.

Joe had been her life, her love. Every man she'd been involved with since had paled by comparison. Maybe she couldn't forgive Joe, but she couldn't fall entirely out of love with him, either.

"What can I say? Dan's everything I've ever wanted in a man. And you, Annie Goldman, are terrible to mention such a thing."

It was a workday, but they had several more hours until they were due back at the restaurant, and had decided to spend the afternoon at Mary's condo, catching up on the events of the past week. Marco had been left in charge of

Mama Sophia's while they were gone, which was likely to puff up the chef's already overinflated ego.

Stretching out on Mary's comfortable beige-leather sofa, Annie clasped her hands behind her head and grinned, looking not the least bit contrite. "I'm happy for you, *cara*. Truly. Dan's a great guy. I've always said as much. You were the hardheaded one who was afraid to commit, as I recall."

Mary heaved a sigh. "I wish you'd find someone to love, Annie. I want you to be happy, too." She took a bite of ham sandwich, talking around it. "You're not getting any younger, you know. It's time you settled down and got married."

Annie forced a smile. "Sadie, Sadie, married lady," she retorted, wondering what kind of perverse evil turned a sensible single woman into a matchmaker once she got married. Misery loved company was the only explanation she could come up with.

Been there. Almost done that. Never again!

"You're starting to sound like my father, and your mother, *cara*," Annie said, ignoring the way her friend blanched at the comparison. "I'm not worried about my future. If it happens, it happens. Besides, you know I like playing the field. I'm not anxious to tie myself down to any one man when there are so many to choose from." The explanation sounded hollow, even to her own ears.

Annie had created the I-don't-give-a-shit persona for herself and everyone believed it, including Mary, and including herself, most of the time. After her painful experience with Joe, she'd discovered it was much easier to leave a relationship than to be the one left behind.

Suddenly Mary's eyes lit with excitement, and she practically launched herself out of the chair, startling Annie.

Grinning from ear to ear, she blurted, "I've got something to tell you, Annie. I hope you'll be happy for me."

Not knowing what could possibly have the woman so wound up, Annie's brows knit together. Then, noting the glow on Mary's face, the joy in her dark eyes, she let loose a shriek. "Holy shit! You're pregnant. You're going to have a baby, aren't you?"

The tulle! It had to be the tulle.

Head bobbing, like one of those toy dogs displayed in car rear windows, Mary replied, "I did the test this morning. Dan doesn't know yet. I'm so excited. I can't wait to tell him. But I wanted you to be the first to know. Because . . . well, because we're best friends."

Smiling softly, Annie chose her words carefully. She didn't want to burst Mary's bubble, or seem unenthusiastic about the news. And though she was truly happy for her friend, she couldn't help the tiny spark of envy igniting in her breast. A baby. Mary's baby. Not Annie's. "I'm touched that you chose to tell me first, *cara,* but also confused. I thought you were taking birth control pills, that you wanted to wait to have kids because of the restaurant, Matthew's adjustment, and all that."

Matt's mother, who sounded like a real bitch, in Annie's opinion, had run off with her boy-toy aerobics instructor some months back, and no one, including Dan's son, had heard from Sharon Gallagher since. Which was probably fortunate for Mary, because there was no telling how much trouble the woman would cause if she came back into the picture.

"I was. I did. But you know how forgetful I am about taking medication. I must have missed a few of my birth control pills, because they apparently didn't work. And

Matt's already better adjusted than we expected, so there's no need to worry about him."

Smiling widely, Annie threw her arms about her friend and hugged tightly. "You'll make a fabulous mother, Mary *mia*. And, of course, I will make one hell of an aunt. We must have a toast." Her smile melted into one of concern. "But not with alcohol. Now that you're pregnant you mustn't drink. Got any apple or orange juice?"

Mary pulled a face. "Now you're starting to sound like my mother. God forbid! Speaking of which, Sophia will be so ecstatic when she hears about this baby, I'll never have another moment's peace. She'll be watching my every move." The realization had her paling. "Oh, God! What have I done?"

"It could be worse," Annie pointed out with a grin. "She could be living with you."

"What a horrible thing to say! Besides, Dan would never go along with that. He doesn't want Lenore living with us, so I doubt he'd welcome my mother. I'm just grateful Dad's still in good health, or I might have to overdose on chocolate cannolis."

Mary disappeared into the kitchen, returning a few moments later with two large glasses, filled with apple juice. "I hope you're happy," she said, shaking her head in disbelief. "This is hardly celebration libation."

Annie took the glass she proffered, and then touched it to her friend's, ignoring Mary's complaint. *"Salute!"* she said, then as an afterthought, *"Mazel tov!"*

"I never thought I'd see the day when Annie Goldman preferred apple juice to champagne."

"Tastes, like circumstances, change, *cara*. You should know that better than anyone." Sipping the fruit juice, Annie added, "I thought Dan's mother was still dating your uncle

Alfredo, the alleged Mafia kingpin of Little Italy." Mary's uncle enjoyed pretending he was a made man, though everyone in Little Italy, including the Russos, knew that wasn't the case. The man was a colorful character, if not a little eccentric.

"She is. They're actually very cute together. And my mother likes Lenore, despite her being Irish, which is a plus. Otherwise, the woman's life would be hell, as you know."

"You mean, like Dan's was for a while?"

"There's a saying: 'What doesn't kill you makes you stronger.' That's Dan and my mother. Fortunately, Dan knows how to handle Sophia. She's putty in his hands."

Annie had a difficult time believing that. Sophia Russo was like a granite boulder: unmovable, intractable, insufferable, pretty much all those "able" words.

"But enough about my mother. I want to hear what's been going on with you. Have you been dating anyone interesting?" Mary settled back, eager to hear all the juicy tidbits, and looked clearly disappointed when Annie shook her head to the negative.

"No?" Mary arched a disbelieving brow. Annie not dating anyone had always been cause for speculation. But the look she flashed warned Mary not to press, so the woman wisely changed the subject.

"So, what's new with your mom and dad? I feel like we haven't talked in a month."

"As I recall, Mary *mia*, we've chatted every night since you've been back from your honeymoon, either on the phone, or at the restaurant."

"I know, but it's not the same. And I miss you."

Annie squeezed her hand, her heart lightening somewhat. It helped to know their friendship was as important to Mary as it was to her. "Nothing will ever come between us, *cara*. Certainly not a mere man!" She grinned. "And now that you're going to have a baby . . . well, I intend to butt into your life even more."

"Good, because I'm going to need you to run interference for me with my mother. Sophia's likely to drive me insane. Not that she doesn't already." Mary threw her hands up in the air, clearly exasperated.

"Did I tell you she's been asking about my sex life? Can you believe it? I'm going to get her started reading romance novels. I think she needs the stimulation."

The image of Sophia reading a steamy novel brought a smile to Annie's lips, and she wondered if she shouldn't do the same with her mother. Reading about other people's problems might do Gina some good. And the love scenes couldn't hurt, either, judging from the remarks her father had made.

"I could use some help with my mom, too," Annie admitted. "Gina's obsession with her health is starting to get out of hand. She's making my dad nuts. He unloaded on me the other night, and I've never heard him talk that way about Mom before. Oh, I know Gina makes Pop crazy, but he usually lets it roll off his back. I'm worried all of this is taking a toll on his health. He doesn't look too good."

"I think your mom's lonely," Mary said, making swirling motions over her abdomen with the flat of her hand as she spoke. "With your dad at work all day she's got nothing and no one to keep her occupied."

Annie pondered her friend's words for a moment. "You may be right. Gina's been at loose ends since Mrs. Feldman moved to Florida. Those two did so much together— shopping at the mall, playing canasta on Wednesday afternoons, that sort of thing. But now Gina just stays around the house all day and watches TV.

"The other day she asked what we were serving for dinner at the restaurant, so I told her. And do you know what she said?" Mary's eyes widened in anticipation. " 'Is that your final answer?' she asks me, like on that millionaire show. *Oy!*" Annie rolled her eyes, making Mary laugh.

"You might consider a full-time companion."

"Like a live-in housekeeper, you mean?" Annie could hear Sid now: *"What would I want with strangers in my house? What am I, lonely?"* "That would never go over—"

"Like a dog," Mary interrupted. "Older people and pets are a natural combination. And the animal shelter is full of unwanted dogs and cats needing a good home." Mary's gaze fell on her stepson's cat, who was spread out on the sunny windowsill, next to her own.

"A dog! What a great idea. Why didn't I think of that? I'll check it out before I come to work this evening."

Mary propped her feet up on the coffee table, seeming quite pleased with herself. It wasn't often that she bested Annie in the idea department. "So tell me about your dad. You said he was sick?"

"Not sick, exactly. He looks tired, overworked. I'm worried about him. He doesn't listen to his doctor. And—" Annie's frown deepened, alarming the pregnant woman, who suddenly sat forward.

"What? What is it?"

"I'm not sure. Sid called this morning and said he wanted to talk to me about something important. We're having lunch at the store tomorrow. I'm afraid . . . worried that he's going to tell me that he's got an incurable disease or something." Annie and her parents didn't see eye to eye on many—okay, most—things, but the idea of losing one of them was unbearable.

She had made their lives miserable, with her unholy behavior and teenage rebellion. As a reckless adult with something to prove—to herself or to Joe, she wasn't really certain—she'd given them sleepless nights and plenty of reasons to worry. She'd gone through her "biker" phase, her "Madonna" craze, but through it all they'd remained supportive and loving.

"Don't be silly. You're jumping to conclusions. Yes, your dad has high cholesterol, but so does half this country. That doesn't mean he's going to drop dead. Stop worrying. That's my job. I'm the worrywart in this relationship, remember?"

"I guess you're right."

So what does Pop want to talk to me about?

"Joe tells me you stopped by his apartment the other night. Are you two mending fences?" Mary asked, looking hopeful.

The change in topic surprised Annie, serving to take her mind off her father, as it was meant to. It also unnerved her. "I helped Joe with"—no way was she mentioning the bedroom—"a bit of unpacking, that's all. Nothing's changed between us, so don't go getting any ideas."

"I got the impression from Joe that he wants things to change. Why are you so down on him? It looked to me as if you two had a great time at my wedding reception."

"I'd had too much to drink," she lied, knowing that her friend came from a long line of matchmaking Italians. Mary had been trained by the best, namely Sophia, and Annie had no intention of giving her an inch.

"It's obvious to everyone but you that whatever there once was between you and my brother is still there, smoldering.

One of these days when you least expect it—*Pow!*" Mary slammed her fist into her palm. "Human combustion."

"Well, in that case," Annie replied with an indulgent smile, "I'll be sure to carry around a fire extinguisher."

Feeling depressed, dejected, and wallowing somewhat in self-pity, a luxury he hadn't indulged in for years, Joe entered his sister's restaurant later that same afternoon to find the place empty, which shouldn't have surprised him. The luncheon crowd had dispersed quite a while ago, and Mama Sophia's wouldn't open again to serve dinner for at least another hour.

The lingering scents of garlic and onion permeated the large dining room. It was a smell he always associated with home and his mother's kitchen. Not that Sophia was cooking any meals for him these days. When it came to holding a grudge, the Capulets and Montagues had nothing on Sophia Russo.

Joe heaved a sigh, adding disappointment that Mary wasn't around to his growing list of negatives. He had been hoping to talk to his sister, ask her opinion about a few things, like what to do about Annie—he was still brooding over her harsh comments—and get some insight as to what he could do to fix the mess his life had become. In a nutshell: It sucked. And it hadn't taken him all that long to muck it up.

He turned to leave, halting in mid-stride when a familiar voice called out to him. "Hey, Joe! You haven't seen my wife, have you?"

Mary's husband entered the bar area from the kitchen, looking like the *GQ* man come to life, in jeans, gray polo shirt, and navy sports jacket. "Fine thing when a husband decides to surprise his wife and she's not even here," Dan complained.

"Guess my sister's in demand today."

"How's that?"

Joe shook his head, unwilling to enter into a lengthy explanation that would no doubt bore the poor guy. Annie was just one of his many problems. "I came by to see her, too," was all he said.

"Care to join me?" Reaching behind the bar, Dan pulled two cold beers from the refrigerator, then seated himself on one of the black leather stools. "It's Bud Light, in case you're worried about your waistline."

"I'm not." Joe crossed the room in quick strides, sitting down beside his brother-in-law. "I can use a beer after the rotten day I've had." He reached for the salty peanuts Dan placed before him.

Though he didn't know his new brother-in-law well, Joe liked Dan Gallagher. He had a terrific sense of humor, treated Mary as if she walked on water, and was a wonderful father to Matt. He was a welcome addition to the Russo family, something Joe's mother had finally come to realize, after putting the poor guy through hell.

"New job got you down? Mary said you were working construction." Joe's dust-caked jeans and boots made Dan thankful he worked indoors. Manual labor was not his thing.

"Was. I got canned today." Again. This was the second job he'd lost this week. Pulling on the cold brew, he slammed the long-neck bottle down on the bar, his frustration evident. "And it wasn't my fault. Not entirely."

Dan arched an inquiring brow. "Care to share? I've got the time if you need to unload."

"Sure." Joe heaved a sigh. "Why not?" Then went on to

explain, "I was on a remodel job, securing new aluminum siding to the back of a customer's house, and doing a pretty good job of it, if I say so myself." For a brief time, he'd foolishly entertained the idea that the construction job was going to work out.

"I happened to glance in the upstairs bedroom window to find a half-naked woman standing there. She smiled at me, quirking her finger, beckoning me to come inside. I was so stunned I pulled back, and—"

"Fell off the ladder?" Dan finished for him, chuckling at the disgusted look his brother-in-law wore.

"Nearly broke my neck, but I landed on top of a large boxwood bush and it cushioned my fall. Or else God was watching out for me. I'm not sure which one was responsible for saving my miserable hide."

"My money's on the Big Guy. You showed great restraint in not taking that woman up on her offer. Not many men who'd been celibate for as many years as you could have resisted such temptation."

Noting Dan's teasing grin, Joe finally smiled. "Just my luck to find some bored housewife looking for a dalliance."

Scooping up a handful of nuts, Dan sucked them out of his partially closed fist. "Most men would be flattered. Was she at least good-looking?"

"No, but she had big—" Joe caught himself just in time. "Never mind. You're married to my sister and shouldn't be asking stuff like that."

"I'm married, not dead. There's a big difference," Dan pointed out, sipping his beer, then wiping his mouth with the back of his hand. "So, what are you going to do now? Got any new jobs lined up?"

Joe shrugged. "I was hoping after the driving incident with the cement truck"—he'd accidentally dumped ten yards of wet cement on the front lawn of the wrong house—"that this job was going to work out. But I'm quickly forming the opinion that construction isn't for me."

"So find something you can do indoors."

"I can't afford to be choosey, Dan. I need to pay the rent. And most 'indoor jobs,' as you call them, require skills I don't have. I'm good in the abstract, not in the concrete, so to speak."

Joe looked distraught, and Dan wanted to help. "Mary's shorthanded here at the restaurant. She could use you as a part-time bartender in the evenings. That way, you could still look for work during the day."

Studying the variety of liquors and wine bottles lining the back wall of the bar, Joe felt even more uncertain. He had no idea what Chartreuse was used for. "It's been years since I tended bar, and then only during college fraternity parties. I'm not sure I'd remember what to do." And bartending wasn't a very dignified role for a priest.

You're not a priest! he reminded himself. And you're out of a job.

"Sure you would. It's like riding a bicycle, or having sex," Dan said, eyes twinkling. "It'll all come back to you. And you can't beat the distance to your apartment. You can walk to work."

Working for his sister seemed like a handout to Joe. He was the big brother. Mary shouldn't be forced to come to his rescue; it was supposed to be the other way around. "I don't know. . . ."

Sipping thoughtfully on his beer, Dan decided that his wife's brother needed a little shove in the right direction. "You'd be able to keep tabs on a certain lovely manager/ hostess if you worked here."

Annie. All of a sudden Dan's idea had merit. Being in

close proximity to Annie would allow Joe to work on their relationship, convince her that he wasn't such a bad guy after all, that things could work out between them.

He could swallow his pride if he had to.

He would definitely have to.

Annie would demand her pound of flesh, of that he was certain.

"Is this the technique you used to wear down my sister? Is that why she married you?"

The journalist grinned. "Mary married me because she fell crazy in love with me, and because I'm so damn good-looking that she couldn't resist my many charms."

Joe bit back a laugh. "Yeah. I figured it must've been something like that."

FIVE

*"The longest road in the world
is the one that leads to the pocket."*

Goldman's Department Store was located on Eastern Avenue, within walking distance of Little Italy, and about two blocks from St. Francis of Assisi's Catholic Church.

The small store had a predominately Jewish clientele, though the Italians in the neighborhood did patronize it on occasion. It carried just about everything, from underwear to outerwear, shoes, purses, and the ugliest array of costume jewelry Annie had ever seen, though as a child she'd been fascinated by it.

Knowing how she liked playing dress-up—Annie's sense of style had formed at an early age—her father had allowed her to sit on the floor behind the jewelry counter and play with the glittering rhinestones and faux pearls to her heart's content. Sid might not be the savviest businessman ever to come down the pike, but he was a mensch.

To say Goldman's was old-fashioned and out-of-date would be a major understatement. The storefront window still housed a "Support Our Troops in Vietnam" poster, which was faded and barely readable; a hideous man's white polyester suit that only John Travolta during his *Saturday Night Fever* days could appreciate; an odd assortment of Easter baskets from a past store promotion, their green-colored grass bleached white by the sun; a half-decorated plastic Christmas tree that Gina had insisted upon, though it bore the Star of David at the top to appease Sid; and a gold-plated bowling trophy with "1973" inscribed on it, though no one, including her father, could remember who had won the stupid thing or where it had come from.

The bowler's identity was a favorite topic of debate among the old-timers who frequented the store, which often resulted in a little friendly betting. The pool was now up to two hundred dollars, with no winner in sight. Annie believed that if anyone actually solved the mystery or won the money, the players involved would be devastated.

Staring in dismay at the eclectic, but ugly, display before her, Annie wrinkled her nose in disgust, wondering, not for the first time, who in their right mind would shop at her father's store. *Right mind* being the operative term. But she knew Sid Goldman had a loyal following; friends and neighbors who wouldn't dream of going anywhere else.

There was just no accounting for taste. Or lack thereof.

Horns honked as cars sped down the busy thoroughfare. A pair of older ladies walked by, pausing to stare strangely at Annie—she guessed it was the hair; people always stared at her hair—then moved on without saying a word, though the taller of the two women did look back, which prompted Annie to smile and wave.

She was still wearing that mischievous smile when she entered Goldman's a few moments later.

"You're late," her father accused when she stepped into the back room, where Sid kept his office, as well as the overflow stock.

There were certain scents Annie always associated with various stores: Victoria's Secret, where she purchased her lingerie, smelled of lavender and lace; Sears carried the distinctive odor of popcorn; and Goldman's was permeated with the smell of rotting rubber.

Mustiness and her father's store seemed to go hand in hand. Annie thought the smell was probably caused from the decaying rubber in the old-fashioned girdles he kept on hand for some of his die-hard customers.

Sylvia Greenburg claimed that a decent woman kept her girdle on and her gut in. Not that the contraption helped the overweight woman that much. Cats fighting inside a burlap bag pretty much summed up Mrs. Greenburg's look.

"I'm not late," Annie insisted. "I was standing out in front of the store, wondering why anyone who passed by that hideous display window would even come in here."

Sid stared at his daughter's tight, short, red skirt, the white see-through blouse with the dark bra visible beneath, and shook his head. "Now you're the fashion police? You dress like Madonna and you have the nerve to criticize what happens to be a Goldman's tradition? Nostalgia's a big seller. I'll have you know I get a lot of compliments on that window."

"From who? Escaped mental patients and blind people?"

Her father chose to ignore the snide remark and shoved a pastrami on rye, piled high with coleslaw, toward her. "I walked down to Little Italy and bought lunch from Santini's. They expanded; they've got a deli now." He placed a plastic squeeze container of Gulden's mustard in front of her. "The slaw's not bad, but your mother's is better. Eat in good health."

Annie's stomach grumbled at the delicious aroma, which made her mouth water. "Thanks!" She took a bite of the thick sandwich and heaved a sigh of pure pleasure. "Mmmm. Delish. This hits the spot."

Sid frowned. "You should eat more. Your collarbone sticks out. People will think we don't feed you."

Hoping to avoid another discussion of her weight, Annie decided to get right to the point. "You wanted to discuss something with me, Pop?"

"After we eat. I can't think on an empty stomach."

Like many men his age, Sid was big on order and routine. You didn't put the proverbial cart before the horse; you didn't talk business or other weighty matters until you fed your stomach. So it was written, so it was done.

"Where's Bullfrog? I didn't see him behind the counter when I came in." Bullfrog, as he was commonly known around the neighborhood, because of his puffy cheeks and bulging eyes, was Henry Grossmann, her father's long-time employee.

The overweight man was obnoxious, rude, and about as exciting as the outdated merchandise he sold. But that didn't stop him from hitting on every unattached female who strolled through the door, and Annie happened to be his favorite target.

"Henry," her father, who hated the nickname "Bullfrog," emphasized the man's given name, "went to the bank to deposit this morning's receipts. He'll be back soon."

"You mean you actually had customers this morning?" She cast disbelieving eyes through the open curtain, toward the main room, where racks of suits, slacks, dresses, and nightwear abounded. "This place is a tomb. Where is everybody? You know, like the customers?"

"Goldman's clientele is older, for the most part. They sleep late and shop in the afternoon. We're usually busier after lunch."

Annie thought the older folks might do better shopping while comatose. That way they wouldn't know the hideous stuff they were buying. "So what do you want to talk to me about? If it's about my hair color, I already told you—"

"If you want to look like the Energizer bunny, that's your business. But to be honest, I like it dark brown, the way God made you."

"Mr. Roy was in a pink mood today. I just didn't have the heart to say no."

"Mr. Roy." He made a face. "What kind of fruity name is that for a man?" Sid had little tolerance for homosexuals, though he kept his feelings carefully hidden. A retailer couldn't afford to discriminate, and Sid had no qualms about taking money from gay members of the community. Like so many closed-minded individuals, her father was an equal opportunity bigot.

"Mr. Roy is a wonderful friend. He's an artiste, like Marco Valenti—only he creates with hair, not food." She fingered her short mop of hair. "Besides, I like the Energizer bunny. He keeps going and going, just like *moi*." She smiled at the exasperated look her father cast her way.

Her hair color and style had always been a bone of contention between them. Sid was a traditionalist, like Joe, which was why, she suspected, that she liked being over the top. When she was younger her outrageous behavior was part of her rebellious nature; she rebelled against authority, her parents' moralistic attitudes, and society's rigid norms. As she grew older she found that she liked drawing attention to herself, thumbing her nose at those who thought she was weird or different. If there was one thing Annie despised, it was narrow-mindedness.

Joe had been critical of her behavior and mode of dress on more occasions than she cared to remember. And the fact that he disapproved gave her even more reason to flaunt her individuality.

Sid put a hand to his chest and rubbed. "Stop! You're giving me heartburn. Have some respect." He ignored her worried look. "I'm not getting any younger. I don't need the aggravation. I get enough at home."

Jumping to her feet, Annie said, "I knew it! There's something wrong with you, isn't there? What is it? Are you dying? Do you have cancer?" Tears filled her eyes.

Shaking his head in disbelief, Sid reached for his daughter's hand and squeezed, trying to allay her fears. "What is it with the cancer? Cancer, schmancer. I don't have any disease, except old age. Don't wish bad on me. I got enough trouble already."

Dropping back onto the chair, Annie breathed a sigh of relief that her father still had a few more years left, and composed herself. "I'm listening."

"I never had a son. But after you, why would I need one? You've been a good daughter, Annie. And you've got a good head on those bony shoulders of yours. I've been doing a lot of thinking lately, mostly about the future, and I want you to come work here at the store."

Annie's eyes widened. She thought she'd prepared herself for the worst possible news—her father's impending death—but nothing could have prepared her for the bombshell he'd just unloaded and dropped smack on her head.

He was grinning, acting as if he'd just presented her with the Crown jewels. She, on the other hand, was ready to hurl coleslaw.

"Work here? At Goldman's? You want me to work at the store?" She'd rather have her pubic hairs plucked out, one by one.

No way! Nuh-uh. Not a chance!

"Why so surprised? Surely you knew one day I'd have to leave the store to someone. You're my daughter. Who else would I give it to?

"A man takes pride in certain things: his work, his family. So I don't tell you very often how I feel. What am I, a woman? But I know what a hard worker you are."

Compliments didn't come easy to Sid, so Annie knew they were heartfelt. Her father's good opinion meant a great deal. Even though she was a grown woman, she would always be, to some extent, a little girl seeking his approval, as pathetic as that sounded. And it sounded pretty damn pathetic.

"Pop, I'm flattered. But it wouldn't be practical or wise for me to work here." They'd butt heads. Of that, she was positive.

Her comment had his eyes widening. "Why not? We don't see eye to eye on everything, but we get along good. And I'd give you a full partnership. You'd be half owner."

Her mouth dropped open. *A partner!* She couldn't believe her ears. Her father was offering her half ownership of the store? Now she was really worried about his health. Surely he had to be dying.

The old man wasn't exactly cheap, but he wasn't Bill Gates, either. Sid still changed the oil in the 1991 Cadillac he'd purchased used three years ago, though he could afford to take the car to Jiffy Lube, or one of those other quick-change places. Actually, he could afford to buy a new car every year if he wanted to, because Goldman's, for all its flaws and antiquated ways, made a respectable amount of money.

"You'd really make me a full partner?" There had to be a catch. She just hadn't figured it out yet.

"Didn't I just say so? Full. I'll have the papers drawn up,

so there's no doubt in anyone's mind, including yours. You'd be half owner of Goldman's Department Store."

Half owner of outdated merchandise and musty dressing rooms; male customers who wanted their inseams measured; overweight females who wore girdles like body armor and expected to fit into dresses two sizes too small.

Gee, why aren't I more excited?

The buzzer at the front door sounded, and she glanced toward it to see that Bullfrog was back. A reprieve about making a decision had just been handed to her; she took it with relish.

"I'm flattered, Pops. Truly. But I need time to think about it. This is a big step. And we'd have a lot of things to work out first." There was also the commitment she'd made to Mary that had to be considered. She wouldn't leave the restaurant, or her friend, high and dry.

He arched a graying brow, his expression wary. "Like?"

"Like I'd want equal say in how things are run around here. I'd want to be consulted on whatever decisions are made, even the minor ones."

Sid looked astounded, and just a little bit sick. "All decisions?" he asked, making circular motions over his chest with the flat of his hand, then finally belching.

"And, of course, I'd want the chance to implement some new ideas. I don't know what those are as yet, but the front display window would definitely receive a great deal of attention. That's nonnegotiable."

"You want to make changes?" He threw his hands up in the air. "*Ei! Ei! Ei!* How can you improve upon perfection, tell me that?"

Smiling inwardly at the horror reflected on his face, Annie rose to her feet and patted his hand, knowing how difficult the concept of change was for a man who still wore sock garters and suspenders. "You should think long and hard about this offer of yours, Pops, and I'll do the same. We'll talk again soon. And if you still want to do it, I'll give you my answer then."

He nodded in agreement. "Like I said, you've got a good head on your shoulders, Annie. You get that from me. Retail is in the blood. You think your mother's family, the Donellis, are as successful? They're good for nothings, the lot of them. Especially your aunt Lola; that woman's got a nut loose."

Fortunately Annie wasn't expected to answer the rhetorical question. She didn't like to be placed in the middle, forced to take sides between the Goldmans and the Donellis. There was good and bad in both families. Nuts, she'd discovered, grew as plentiful in Israel as they did in Italy.

"Good afternoon, Annie." Henry Grossman approached, a kiss-ass smile on his face as he attempted in front of her father to act like the gentleman he wasn't, though his eyes were bulging as he visually devoured every inch of her body. In Yiddish they called a man like Henry a *tuchas-lecker*. If his nose got any browner, he'd be mistaken for a bovine instead of an amphibian.

"Hello, Henry," she forced out, dismayed when her father excused himself and headed for the rest room. She fought the urge to call him back. Next to Sophia, Henry was her least favorite person.

"Well, well . . ." His eyebrows lifted in appreciation. "Don't you look good enough to eat." He wiped spittle from the corner of his mouth with a not-so-clean white hankie, then stuffed it back in the breast pocket of his brown herringbone jacket.

Annie tried not to gag. The man was drooling, for

chrissake! "You need to get a hold of yourself, Henry," she told him.

Obviously Bullfrog hadn't *croaked* in a while.

"Women like compliments. I pay compliments." With a pudgy index finger, he reached out to touch the material of her blouse. "Is that voile?"

Annie slapped his hand away. "It's *vile*, as in keep your vile hands to your vile self, toad face, or I'm going to let my father know what a pervert you are."

Henry's brown eyes widened. Well, as much as they could widen, being bulging and all. "Why do you deny what you feel, babe? You're hot for me. I can tell."

Annie couldn't help herself. She threw back her head and laughed until tears formed in her eyes. It was just too funny when Henry tried to act like a stud. It reminded her of the old *Saturday Night Live* routine with Steve Martin and Dan Ackroyd as the Czechoslovakian brothers—two wild and crazy guys.

"Have you been watching porn movies again, Henry? I think your imagination has gone into overdrive."

"Why not come over to my pad tonight and see my extensive collection? I've got *Deep Throat* and *Behind the Green Door*. They're classics, you know. We could . . ." the eyebrows rose again, "get it on." His upper lip and forehead were bathed in sweat, and she suspected by the way he rubbed both hands on his pants legs that his palms dripped buckets as well.

And they said pigs didn't sweat.

"As tempting as that offer is, I've got to scrub my toilets tonight, so I'll have to pass."

"I could come over and help you, then we could—"

"Hello! Earth to Henry. Do you get it? I'm not interested

in your porn, or in you. Now go find someone else to harass or I'll file a complaint with the pervert police."

He had the audacity to look offended. "If you don't want men noticing your long legs and large breasts, you shouldn't wear revealing clothes. Men get ideas."

Balling her hands into fists, Annie was seriously tempted to rearrange Henry's features. "What I wear is none of your concern. And if you say one more word, *Bullfrog*, I'm going to call my father over here and have you fired." She should have told Sid years ago that Henry Grossman was the biggest sex fiend ever to graduate from Lombard High. Well, there was also Sonny Brando to consider, she amended silently. But Henry was definitely the worst of the two.

The man smiled smugly at the threat. "I'm the best employee your father's ever had. He'd never get rid of me. And I doubt he'd believe you, at any rate. I'm always very well mannered around the female clientele. The older ladies adore me."

Knowing Henry as she did, Annie would bet money that he peeped into the ladies' dressing rooms. The disgusting man had voyeur written all over him. But she also knew the truth of his words. Sid thought Henry was a merchandising genius. That would be hysterically funny if it wasn't so damn pathetic.

It would almost be worth taking her father up on his offer, just to get rid of Henry. As half owner of Goldman's she'd have the power to fire the obnoxious man. Though she knew that Henry, for all his revolting habits, was good at his job, and to make matters worse, the customers liked him. And it wouldn't be very professional to allow her personal feelings to enter into a decision to can him. But it was sure tempting.

"Henry!" Sid shouted from the other side of the store, walking hurriedly in their direction, and looking totally pissed. Not an unusual occurrence by the look of trepidation on the sales clerk's face. "I don't pay you to stand around and kibitz with my daughter. Now get to work. There are swim trunks and brassieres that need to be priced and shelved. And make sure you put them in the right order this time, Mr. Upside-down!"

Annie could have hugged her father for his impeccable timing, smiling spitefully when the clerk's flaccid cheeks filled with color. "Run along, Henry." She made a shooing motion with her hands. "And don't try on too many of the bras," she said low enough for his ears alone. It was always disconcerting to find men with larger breasts than her own.

If the lethal look Henry shot her could have killed, Annie would be reclining at this very moment in one of the satin-lined caskets at Benny Buffano's funeral parlor.

"I'm glad you and Henry get along so well," her father remarked after the man left to do his bidding. "That'll make things easier when you're working here."

Annie forced a sick smile, adding another check to the minus side of the mental chart she'd been preparing since her father had made his partnership offer.

Entering the restaurant a few hours later, dressed sedately in a black skirt and white-knit shell, Annie had just seated herself at the hostess station, opening the reservation book to gauge the size of the dinner crowd, when she was approached by two of the waitresses.

Their eyes were bright, their cheeks flushed pink, which could only mean one thing: Fresh meat was on the premises. And she wasn't referring to the kind Marco kept in the freezer.

"Did you see the hunk behind the bar, Annie? Mary's hired a new bartender, and he's to-die-for." Francie Bella, the newest member of the wait staff, licked her bow-shaped lips. She was twenty-something and stacked, a young Sophia Loren lookalike. Annie thought Bella*donna* would have been a more appropriate name for the young woman; Francie was deadly on the men in her life.

"I get hot every time I look at him," the waitress admitted with a sigh. "I wonder if he's married. I sure hope not."

"You get hot every time you look at any man," Loretta Pazzoli reminded the man-hungry woman. Recently divorced from a philandering husband, Loretta was just starting to hate men a little less, and hadn't as yet started dating again.

"You know, there's something very familiar about that man," she said. Removing eyeglasses from her apron pocket, which she'd just started wearing for distance, Loretta let loose a gasp. "I was right!"

Noting the woman's horrified expression, the pitying look in her eyes, Annie got a sinking feeling in the pit of her stomach. Sliding off the stool, she walked to the doorway and peered into the restaurant, toward the bar, and then cursed inwardly.

Dammit, Mary! You couldn't leave well enough alone, could you?

Joe stood behind the bar, filling drink orders, and looking capable and relaxed as he chatted with the customers, who were mostly female, she noted. She was surprised by the spurt of jealousy burning in her chest when he laughed at something an attractive blonde said.

With his good looks and charm, the former priest would

not remain celibate for long. If, in fact, he still was. So why did that notion continue to rankle?

You know why, Annie, she told herself. You don't want him, but you don't want anyone else to have him, either.

"Do you know him?" Francie asked, her dark eyes bright with excitement. "You look as if you know him."

Turning back to face the woman, her voice filled with equal amounts of annoyance and impatience, Annie replied, "Yes, I know Joe Russo. He's Mary's brother, and I've known him since elementary school."

"Wow! And you're not sleeping with him? What a major waste."

"Shut up, Francie!" Loretta flashed her a warning look. "You've got a big mouth for such a short person. Come on. It's time to go to work."

Presenting the older woman a grateful smile, Annie said, "Great idea," then picked up a handful of menus and began to seat the arriving guests, trying to put Joe out of her mind, which was a lot easier said than done.

A short time later, Annie took her break and headed straight for the bar, drawn there like a magnet. Seating herself on the end stool near the kitchen, she watched Joe fill yet another drink order—Jim Beam on the rocks for a middle-aged gentleman. Beside her, wait staff dashed in and out of the revolving door, waving as they passed.

When Joe finally spotted her, he flashed her a smile that made her stomach tighten. She attributed her reaction to the calzone she'd eaten for dinner. "Hi!" he said, as if his presence at the restaurant wasn't the least bit out of the ordinary or unwelcome. "Can I get you something to drink?"

"Why are you working here, Joe?" Annie couldn't

disguise the annoyance filling her voice. "I thought you already had a job."

"How about a Coke?" he persisted. "You look tired and thirsty."

Heaving a sigh of defeat, she wondered why he always had to be so damn nice. Well, not always, she reminded herself. "Diet, and not too much ice. Thanks."

He fixed the drink, whispered something to the other bartender on duty, then moved down to where she was seated. Placing the diet drink in front of her, he leaned over the bar. "I had a job, but I was fired. It's a long story." And one he wasn't eager to relate again. "When Dan heard about my predicament, he mentioned that Mary was short-handed, due to a sudden increase in business, and could use another bartender, so he offered me a part-time job here. I'm working nights till I can find something else."

She almost breathed a sigh of relief that it was Dan, not Mary, who had unknowingly butted into her life. She didn't like thinking that her best friend would purposely betray her. "I wasn't aware you had any bartending experience."

Joe grinned, displaying those devastating dimples, and Annie tried not to notice how adorable he was when he smiled. "I've been serving up communal wine for years. This isn't that different. Plus, I bartended a bit in college. I was a little apprehensive when Dan first suggested it, but I've picked it right back up."

Feeling someone's gaze upon her, Annie looked down the long length of bar and saw the blonde Joe had been talking with earlier staring at them; she didn't look too happy.

The woman's interest in Joe was obvious—she was

practically salivating—her dislike of Annie evident. "Looks like you've already made friends."

Turning to look over his shoulder, Joe smiled at the customer, whose face brightened instantly, much to Annie's great annoyance. "That's Suzie. She's just broken up with her boyfriend, so I've been giving her a shoulder to cry on, along with a bit of advice. I think that comes under my job description as bartender confessor."

"You've always been good at butting into things that don't concern you," Annie said, wishing she hadn't sounded as bitchy as she felt. But dammit! He had no right being here, trying to pretend that everything was hunky-dory between them, especially after she'd gone out of her way to tell him exactly how she felt.

Joe picked up on her tone right away. "Is there a problem? Are you upset about my working here?" He reached for her hand, but she pulled back. No way was she going to let him touch her.

"I'm not thrilled with the idea, if you want to know the truth. I think it would be better for both of us if we kept our distance. We grate on each other, Joe, and I don't want Mary's business to suffer for it." At least the explanation sounded plausible. Sort of.

"And here I thought you were worried we might not be able to keep our hands off each other," Joe replied with a wink.

Splotches of color landed on Annie's cheeks. "Don't flatter yourself. I have no intention of going down that road again. It's a dead end, as far as I'm concerned."

"Well, then you shouldn't have a problem with us working together. I mean, it's obvious you don't have any interest in me as a man, right?"

"Didn't I just say so?"

"So what's the problem?"

"I—I guess I don't have one." He'd trapped her, and he knew it. She would not admit to Joe Russo that his presence bothered and aggravated her.

"Good." He glanced at his watch. "Guess I'd better get back to work before I get fired again."

"What a splendid idea. And maybe you should think twice about getting too personal with the customers. As manager, I don't recommend it. It could open the restaurant up to a lawsuit, or some other unpleasantness."

"You're speaking from a strictly professional standpoint, I take it?"

She slid off the stool, her professional demeanor firmly in place. "Of course. It's my job to make sure things run smoothly here."

Joe grinned, obviously not believing a word she said. "See you around, sweetheart," he said in his best Humphrey Bogart impersonation.

Annie sighed. How many times had they watched *Casablanca* together? How many little, inconsequential things did he know about her? Could he use against her to drive her wild, to break down the barriers she'd erected against him?

Too many.

It was time she made some life-altering decisions.

SIX

*"God could not be everywhere
and therefore he made mothers."*

"What the hell is that?"

Gina Goldman glared defiantly at her husband, ignoring the nasty tone in his voice as she clutched the soft mop of fur to her chest. "It's a dog," she flung back. "What does it look like? My daughter bought it. She cares what happens to me." *Even if you don't* was left unsaid, but hung in the air between them, making Sid's frown deepen.

"Annie sensed I was lonely and bought me a dog." The older woman smiled lovingly at her daughter. "She's a good girl, my Annie."

He turned from the cowering dog in his wife's arms to cast an accusing look at the "good girl," who had arms crossed, projected a mutinous look, and was obviously preparing to do battle. "Why did you buy that ugly thing? You know I don't like dogs, Annie. What is it, anyway? It looks like a dust mop."

"It's not ugly; it's a Shih Tzu from China," she replied, reaching out to pet the puppy. "And I didn't buy it. I got it from the animal shelter, for a small donation. The previous owner had to leave town and couldn't keep it.

"I figured Gina could use some company around the house, since you're at the store most of the day. You know," she raised her brows meaningfully, hoping he recalled their previous conversation, "to give her something to do."

He rolled his eyes. "*Oy!* I need this like a hole in the head."

Gina put the puppy down on the thick-piled blue carpeting. It ran straight to Annie's father, lifted his short hind leg, and peed all over Sid's highly polished cordovan wingtips.

"Stop, you *pisher*!" the outraged man shouted, pulling back his foot, and shaking it at the dog. "Shits on you! That's what they should call your kind of dog." He stared daggers at his wife and daughter, who were trying desperately not to laugh.

"Who's going to clean up this mess? Not me."

"Shame on you!" Gina scolded the puppy halfheartedly, rushing forward with the paper towels she carried in her apron pocket for just such an emergency. Licking her face fast and furiously, the dog seemed unconcerned with the havoc he'd wreaked.

Annie's mother blotted the carpet almost dry, then said, "Once he's housebroken he won't piddle in the house anymore. I'll put baking soda down to soak up the smell. You'll see; it'll be as good as new."

"By that time we'll need new carpeting. I don't want—"

Annie clutched her father's arm before he could finish. "I'm going to take the partnership you offered, Pop." Her last encounter with Joe had convinced her to put some distance between them. Working together in such close proximity, seeing him day after day, would only create problems. She couldn't afford to let her guard down. Not now. Not ever. "Before I accept, I've got another stipulation."

The surprised smile he almost produced vanished, replaced by a look of suspicion. "What now? I'm not playing that hippity-hoppity music on the overhead speakers, Annie. My customers would—"

"Mom gets to keep the dog." They'd discuss the music later.

Looking from his wife, who was kissing the dog all over his furry head and making cooing sounds he found disgusting coming from a grown woman, to his daughter's intractable expression, Sid knew he was fighting a losing battle. He rubbed the back of his neck. "There are laws against blackmail, but I don't have the strength to fight both of you when you gang up. You're giving me such a pain in— All right. The dog stays. But he'd better not crap in the house. And he's not sleeping on my bed. Is that clear, Gina?"

Though her mother smiled sweetly and said it was, it was plain that the woman was lying through her teeth. The dog yapped, and Annie guessed he knew it, too.

Kissing her husband's cheek, Gina whispered, *"Grazie, ti amo,"* and his expression softened somewhat. She then turned to her daughter.

"You'll stay for dinner." It was more command than question, and Annie knew better than to argue when her mother sounded so definite. Gina usually capitulated—living with Sid, you had to—but there were times, like now, when she felt strongly about something and dug in her heels. Her father called it putting on concrete shoes.

"We must celebrate the partnership of Goldman and daughter. It's a proud day in the family. I'm going to church later and make a novena. The good Lord needs to be thanked."

A nine-day prayer vigil! This must be a red-letter day. "Of course I'll stay," Annie said. At any rate, she figured her mother could use the moral support. Her father's bark was far worse than his bite, but he wasn't a man who liked surprises. And the fur ball was definitely an unwelcome surprise.

"Ha! I can hardly wait to hear what those miserable sisters of yours are going to say," Gina told her husband. "Esther believed that schlemiel nephew of hers would be brought in as your partner one day because you had no sons. The nerve of the woman!"

No one had ever disputed the fact that Aunt Esther and Aunt Golda had more chutzpah than most women and weren't afraid to display it. Annie suspected, though she'd never admit it to her mother, who would no doubt freak, that she'd inherited some of her brass from her father's side of the family.

"Esther can go peddle her fish elsewhere," Sid said. "I'd never bring that kid"—who happened to be forty-one—"into the business. Rudy's a klutz, and I already got one of those working for me."

Appeased by her husband's words, Gina indicated that Annie should follow her into the kitchen, to help with the spaghetti and meatballs she was preparing for dinner, unconcerned with the fact that her daughter ate Italian food five nights a week at the restaurant and could probably sing the aria from *Rigoletto*.

"So what did Mary say when you told her you were quitting? Was she upset?" Gina placed the as-yet-unnamed puppy in the brown wicker basket and told him to stay put. He gazed up at her with mournful eyes, whimpered a bit, then fell asleep quickly, tired out from his first day as a Goldman.

Annie could relate.

"Mary was excited for me," she replied, ripping the salad greens into small pieces before dropping them into the large yellow ceramic bowl. "Told me I couldn't pass up such a wonderful opportunity. She promised she would make everyone in her family, in the whole neighborhood, shop at Goldman's from now on."

Annie had broken down and cried at Mary's kindness and understanding, and at the thought of leaving her job at the restaurant, which she loved. And even though her startled friend had accused her of suffering from PMS, Annie didn't think being premenstrual had anything to do with her tumultuous feelings.

All the changes—Mary's marriage, Joe's reentry into her life, and all of the decisions she'd had to make of late—were turning her into an emotional mess. She'd always prided herself on being strong, and it wasn't easy to admit that she was fast becoming as vulnerable as the next person.

"I'm glad you'll be working with your father. He needs looking after. I worry that he's not taking care of himself. Sid eats like a horse and works long hours. He's not a kid anymore. But will he admit it?" She grunted her disapproval.

"Did you have a hand in Pop's decision? Was it your idea that he offer me a partnership?"

Her mother shook her head, filling the large stainless-steel pot with hot water, to which she added enough salt to cause a hypertensive stroke. "No. This was all Sid's doing. After you were born, and we found out that we couldn't have more children, your father began thinking along the lines of bringing you into the business, having you carry on the family name. He's always been proud of you, even though he doesn't say the words very often."

Annie was relieved that the partnership decision had been solely her father's. It meant he had faith in her abilities, that he trusted her. She wouldn't let him down. She would prove that she was business-minded and capable of managing the store and increasing profits. She was determined to make Sid even prouder.

"I'm glad we'll be working together. Pop's someone I admire. He's honest, fair-minded, and he has always treated me with respect, even though he doesn't usually agree with my decisions." It would be interesting to see if he agreed with the changes—innovative ideas had been percolating like crazy—she intended to make at the store. She rather doubted it.

Turning, Gina took her daughter's hands. "You've always followed the beat of your own drum, Annie *mia*. We knew that from when you were a little girl. I hated that you wouldn't call me Mama, but I got used to your ways. And now that I'm older, it doesn't seem so important. Though I'll make such a stink if my grandchildren don't call me Grandma."

Kissing her cheek, Annie's eyes twinkled. "It must be genetically inherent that all mothers want grandchildren. I promise they will—providing, of course, you have grandchildren." It was a safe promise at the moment, since she had no husbandly prospects on the horizon. Joe came to mind, but she pushed his disturbing image away.

Joe wasn't in any way, shape, or form husband material. Though she distinctly remembered the day she had told him about the baby. He'd been ecstatic at the prospect of fatherhood, so loving and supportive of her. They'd celebrated with a quart of milk and a dozen brownies he'd filched from his mother's kitchen. But, of course, all that had changed after the miscarriage.

"Go on with you." Gina waved away her daughter's doubt with a flick of her wrist. "I can't wait to spoil them rotten. I'll practice on the dog. What do you think we should call him? He's so cute."

Annie shook off the disturbing memories.

"I guess the first thing we should decide is whether he's an Italian or a Jewish dog."

"Oh, he's definitely Jewish!" her mother said emphatically. "Did you see the way he pissed on your father right off? Only a Jew would be so brazen. We Italians have more finesse."

Annie burst out laughing, and her mother joined in; soon the two women were holding their sides and howling.

"Did you see his face, Annie?" Gina could barely speak she was laughing so hard. "I thought Sid would burst a blood vessel when the dog tinkled on his shoes. You know how fussy your father is about his shoes."

She did know and had a hard time composing herself. "Pop called the puppy a *pisher*. That would fit, since he's little and does a lot of squirting."

"That's true. But I think I'm going to call him Bubbelah, or Bubbeh, for short. It's a much nicer term for someone you like. Plus, every time your father has to call him by that name, it will put a big smile on my face."

When you grow up Italian, the first thing you learn is that family is everything. The second: Buy a shovel, because the guilt that's piled on is likely to bury you.

Knowing this, Joe decided to take the coward's way out that Sunday afternoon and avoid his mother by entering his parent's home through the basement door, where he knew he would find his father tinkering with one of his inventions.

A retired electrician, Frank Russo wasn't the kind of man who could sit still and just enjoy his leisure time.

He always had to be doing something. And it was also a way for him to escape his wife's constant badgering and complaints about her ungrateful children and annoying mother-in-law.

To say Sophia and Grandma Flora were not the best of friends would be an understatement of major proportion. In fact, they barely tolerated each other most of the time. Joe thought of them as the "mutual aggravation society," though he couldn't quite decide which one should be president. Both were equally and immensely qualified.

"Hey, Dad!" Joe spoke loudly when he entered the basement, so as not to startle the older man, who was absorbed in some kind of mirror contraption. An Eddie Fisher 78 LP blared loudly from the ancient mahogany record player in the corner.

Turning to find his son descending the creaking staircase, Frank's face lit. "Hey, Joey! How you doing? Long time no see."

Joe wondered how old he'd have to be before his father quit calling him Joey. "What are you making this time?"

"It's a device to keep steam from clouding up the bathroom mirror. My heated toilet seat's a big hit. They're calling it 'The Bun Warmer.' Catchy, no? Anyway, I've decided to follow it up with another bathroom device." He wiped his hands on an oil-stained flannel rag that had once been Sophia's favorite nightgown.

"So, you been upstairs to see your mama?" When Joe shook his head, his father smiled knowingly. "Smart boy. I didn't raise no dummy." He motioned for him to sit down on the threadbare couch in his work area.

"Come. We'll share a glass of *vino* and you can tell me what you've been doing with yourself." Opening the royal-blue compact refrigerator left over from his son's college days, Frank pulled out a bottle of Lambrusco and filled two glasses with the hearty wine, handing one to Joe, who didn't bother to comment that red wine was usually consumed at room temperature.

You couldn't teach an old dog new tricks, as his mother was fond of saying, though Joe suspected it was more that you couldn't take New York out of a New Yorker.

"Is Mom still mad?" Joe asked. He'd been surprised when his sister had called to extend the invitation to dinner, the first he'd received in weeks.

The whole family usually gathered at his parents' home after church on Sundays to share a meal, noteworthy events, and gossip of the past week. The Russo women, no matter their age, loved to exchange the current rumors that were circulating around the neighborhood, and did so whenever they got together. Mary said it was a "woman thing." Like men never asking for directions was a "man thing."

"Your mama's slowly getting over her disappointment that you won't be the next Pope." Frank laughed, then stared strangely at his son's shirt, his eyes growing troubled, his smile disappearing.

"Something you wanna tell me, Joey? You know you can confide in me. Whatever you say will be left between us. I promise I won't tell your mother."

Brows knitted together, Joe wondered what his father was hinting at. "I don't think so, Dad. Everything's fine. Why do you ask?"

"You're wearing a pink shirt, Joey. I thought maybe you got something to tell me. You might want to . . . Whatta they call it? Come out of the closest."

Joe was so startled by his father's inference that he might be a homosexual, he could only stare in shocked silence for a moment. When he finally found his voice, he replied, "I'm not gay, Dad, if that's what you're worried about. Whatever gave you that idea?"

"Did I say I was worried? *Forgetaboutit!* I'm not worried. But I know a lot more about what's happening with the Catholic Church than your mother. I always said it was unnatural that priests couldn't marry. Even a man of God can be tempted to stray. Fifteen years is a long time to keep the horse in the barn, Joey boy."

Heat crawled up the younger man's neck. Joe and his father had always been close, but they'd never discussed things of a sexual nature. What he'd learned he'd learned on his own, through reading or experimentation. He preferred the latter, believing that practice really did make perfect. And as a randy youth, he'd practiced a lot.

Until, that is, he'd met Annie.

She became the only woman in his life, the one he wanted to be with, grow old with.

What had happened? How could he have allowed his fears, his guilt, to overrule his good judgment where she'd been concerned? How could he have left her alone to deal with the loss of their child?

Growing up with such a domineering mother had robbed him of a backbone, of the ability to take a stand and do the right thing. It had been easier, safer, to go along with his mother's insistence that he join the priesthood. She'd been pushing him toward it for years; Annie's miscarriage had given him the impetus to accede to her wishes, to take the coward's way out.

But something good had come out of his time as a priest. He'd learned to stand on his own two feet, to come out from behind his mother's shadow and be his own man. He'd learned to help others first, putting his own wants and needs second. He'd learned unselfishness and caring, and he'd learned what it meant to regret. To lose something he truly loved. That lesson had been the most painful of all.

"Connie gave me this shirt for my last birthday," he explained, pulling his thoughts together and staring down at the garment, but finding no fault with it. "I decided to wear it since she and Eddie will be here today."

Releasing a sigh filled with relief, the older man thought it wise to let the matter drop and quickly changed the subject. "So what have you been doing with yourself? You find a job you like yet?"

Joe shook his head, remembering the phone message he'd received on his answering machine from Bishop O'Fallon, about a position that would soon be available. He'd tried to return the man's call, but hadn't been able to reach him as yet, and he was dying of curiosity. But he had no intention of relating any of that to his parents, not until after he'd spoken to the priest. No sense getting their hopes up—or his, for that matter.

"I'm bartending part-time at Mama Sophia's and looking for work during the day."

"I was never in favor of you joining the church. That was your mother's doing," Frank admitted, shaking his head. "A man needs a trade. If you work with your hands, you'll never be out of a job." Leaning back in his chair, he sipped his wine, then added, "A man should be proud of his work."

"I don't think I'm cut out for manual labor, Dad. I'm hoping to find something else."

"You're a smart boy, Joey. I know it won't be long before you do." Frank cocked his head toward the basement stairs, where Sophia's announcement about dinner came floating down like a general's call to troops.

"Frank, the food's getting cold! Your mother is threatening to eat without us." The statement was followed by several colorful epithets hurled in Italian, then the door slamming shut.

"Drink up, son. It's time to face the music."

Joe blanched, and a sick feeling of dread formed in the pit of his stomach. "Is this a setup? Is that why I was invited over here?" He should have known. His mother wasn't the type to give up so easily. Not while she could still draw a breath.

"Let's just say your mama wants one more shot at changing your mind before she gives up. Personally, I'm relieved you're no longer a priest. I hated having to go to mass every Sunday. And I like Annie Goldman. I hope things work out for the two of you. She's a pistol, that Annie. And a looker. Even an old man like me can still appreciate a pretty face."

Joe wished he could have confided the truth about his and Annie's relationship, about what had driven them apart. But he knew he couldn't and wouldn't, especially to someone like his father—a man who always shouldered his responsibilities, a man who would have been disappointed to learn that the son he was so proud of had shirked his. "Annie hates me," he finally admitted. Saying the words, knowing they were true, filled him with sadness and a longing so great it made his heart ache.

"Don't be too sure, Joey boy. Women are like melons. You squeeze and squeeze, and when you find they're ripe, you take a bite. If you taste too early, the fruit is bitter, no? It's better to wait until the melon is sweet and juicy."

"Dad, if the melon doesn't ripen soon, that horse you spoke of is going to shrivel up and die in the barn."

* * *

"Well, look who it is—my son, the big shot."

Drawing a deep breath, Joe kissed his mother's cheek, still relatively smooth despite her age, and pasted on a smile. She was unarmed. A good sign. "Hi, Mom. Nice to see you, too."

He winked at his silver-haired grandmother, who waited impatiently to begin her meal. Grandma Flora ate her meals according to the clock, whether or not she was hungry. "I've missed you, *Nonna*," he said, bussing her wrinkled brow.

Reaching up, the old woman caressed his cheek and tears filled her eyes. "Your mama was mad at you, Joseph. She's not a nicea woman, your mama. Her heart isa filled with poison. But I'm glad you come here today. It'sa right you should be with your family. *La famiglia* isa everyting."

Grandma Flora cast her daughter-in-law the evil eye. "You should be ashamed, Sophia Graziano. Have you no heart? This is your son, flesh of your flesh, blood of your blood. You musta forgive him."

"Be quiet, old woman! You think my son doesn't know who is behind all the hard feelings?" She turned to Joe, unaware of the traditional Italian salute of displeasure her mother-in-law flicked at her.

"So how have you been?" his mother asked, giving him the once-over, which was done quickly, and not to be confused with "the look," usually reserved for enemies, or when conveying great displeasure. Sophia had both down pat.

"You look too thin. You haven't been eating." It was more statement than question. She tsked several times, then stared at his shirt. "You look much better in black, Father—" She choked up dramatically. "Joe."

"Quit bustin' the kid's balls, Sophia. He's not going

back to the church, so leave him alone. I'm tired of hearing about it. Now, let's eat."

"Uhh." Grandma grunted her approval.

"Where're Connie and Eddie?" Joe asked, grateful for his father's intervention. It was rare when Frank bucked his wife in front of the family. Rarer still when Sophia allowed it to happen. Frank might wear the pants, but his wife had firm control of the zipper.

Flashing her husband a look of promised retribution, Sophia replied, "Your sister called. They'll be late. Little Eddie has a soccer game and they're running behind."

"Soccer! Why don't they teach that kid to play bocci? An Italian kid should play bocci." Frank reached for the bottle of Chianti.

As Joe savored his first bite of spinach ravioli, he was gratified to know that few things had changed while he'd been persona non grata: His parents still fought, Connie continued to dote on her kids, and Grandma Flora loved him.

"Aren't Mary and Dan coming?" he asked

"Later," Sophia replied. "Your sister's hiding something. I can feel it. She was very secretive over the phone."

Well, if Mary was hiding something, his mother would worm it out of her. The Spanish Inquisition could have taken lessons from Sophia Russo. Harping, as his father called it, was an art form in his mother's experienced hands.

"So, are you still cozy with Annie Goldman?" she wanted to know, pinning him with "the look," and Joe groaned inwardly. He'd almost rather she'd asked about his returning to the priesthood. That explanation would have been much simpler.

"We work together at the same restaurant, so we see each other from time to time."

"I like Annie Goldman," Grandma Flora said, eager to play devil's advocate. "So she's Jewish. So what? The Jews suffered under Hitler like we suffered under that fat Fascist *bastardo*, Mussolini." She crossed herself, then bit into a piece of olive-oil-soaked bread, which promptly stuck to her dentures.

Unwilling to be drawn into one of his grandmother's bizarre political discussions, Joe changed the subject. "As a matter of fact, Annie is leaving the restaurant. Mary told me she's going to be working for her father at Goldman's Department Store." He'd been stunned by the news. And dismayed. The proximity he'd been counting on to bring them closer together had suddenly vanished, which was undoubtedly her plan.

Annie hadn't confided her plans to him, and that had hurt.

There'd been a time when they'd shared everything. The smallest victories and defeats: her election as homecoming queen, his failure to make the college debating team. Unfortunately that time had long since passed, and he had no idea how to recapture what they'd once shared. But he intended to keep trying. Somehow, someway, he intended to win her back.

Sophia's face brightened at the disclosure. "Really? Now, that's good news." When everyone turned questioning looks on her, she assumed an expression of innocence, explaining, "I mean . . . it's good that Annie will be working with her father. Sid Goldman is a fine man. He'll be a steadying influence. That girl's always been wild."

"They'll kill each other," Frank stated matter-of-factly, biting into his meatball, and pointing his fork at Joe. "Kids and their parents should never work together. It makes bad blood."

An Italian family without bad blood was a rarity, and Joe knew it. The Russos needed regular transfusions of outside influences to keep their bloodlines from becoming tainted with disharmony and dissension.

Blood might be thicker than water, but it could also clog your veins and choke the life out of you.

"Annie and her father get along very well. I don't think there'll be any problems between them," Joe replied.

"They're family. What could go wrong?" his grandmother asked, unaware of how prophetic her question was.

SEVEN

*"Charge nothing
and you'll get lots of customers."*

"You bought bathing suits instead of winter coats! Oy! You're supposed to be buying ahead for the next season. What the hell am I going to do with bathing suits when winter comes? And skimpy bikinis, no less! Goldman's customers are old and fat. Who's going to wear such things?"

With her father's condemning words ringing loudly in her ears, Annie pulled into the driveway of her town house and slammed on the brakes, wondering if it would be kosher to quit after only a few days on the job. She was tempted.

So she made a mistake. So what? It wasn't the end of the world. She'd just have to sweet-talk the manufacturer's rep into taking back the unwanted merchandise, that's all. Or maybe she could talk Donatella Foragi into buying some of it. For a senior citizen, Mrs. F had an unusual fashion sense. Spandex and flannel combinations were not out of the realm of possibility.

Annie expected to make some mistakes during her first week of work. Sid shouldn't and couldn't expect her to be perfect. Not without a little training.

"Tomorrow will be better," he'd said, trying desperately to convince himself of that, before downing half a bottle of Maalox, and taking refuge in his office. The look of disap-

pointment in his eyes had gnawed at her gut. And having to contend with Henry's smart-ass comments hadn't helped matters in the least.

Gigging for frogs had suddenly become an enticing idea.

"Tomorrow will be better," Annie vowed, unlocking the front door and letting herself in. Heading straight for the black-and-white-decorated bedroom—an ode to film noir— she kicked off her heels, shrugged out of her work clothes, tossing the skirt and blouse on the white wicker chair, before donning her shorts and sports bra.

Having decided that a workout was what she needed to clear her mind and get her spirit reenergized, she headed back to the living room stereo and dropped a Jerry Lee Lewis CD into the disc player, turning up the volume full-blast. She then began to exercise, and exorcise her demons.

Joe heard the loud music as soon as he stepped out of his father's silver 1958 Buick Roadmaster—the Sherman tank of automobiles—and onto the sidewalk in front of Annie's town house.

A union man to the core, Frank Russo was a firm believer in buying American, even if the car in question was a total piece of worthless garbage that belonged in the junkyard. To prove his point, the chrome-laden monstrosity kept idling, though Joe had turned off the ignition. The fact that the forty-three-year-old automobile was running at all was nothing short of miraculous.

A new car would be Joe's first purchase after the crisis center Bishop O'Fallon had hired him to manage was fully operational. He'd have to buy on credit—his salary wasn't large—but that was okay. He'd found a job that was going to suit him to a tee. Counseling troubled teens and young adults was something he was very qualified to do and enjoyed immensely.

The New Beginnings Crisis Center would be a new beginning for many, including himself. It was the answer to his prayers. Well, one of them, anyway.

Clutching to his chest the brown Bloomies shopping bag that he was delivering for his sister, Joe strolled up to Annie's front door.

If the mountain wouldn't come to Mohammed . . .

Joe knocked a few times, but it soon became obvious that Annie couldn't hear a thing above the loud music that was blaring like a 1950s rock-and-roll concert. "Annie!" he shouted, ringing the bell, then banging on the sidelight window. But there was still no response.

Trying the doorknob, he found that it turned easily in his hand, and frowned deeply. Annie hadn't bothered to lock the door. Didn't she know how dangerous it was to leave herself vulnerable and unprotected? Didn't she read the newspapers? Watch TV? A woman living alone couldn't be too careful these days.

Following the driving beat of the music, he entered the living room, to find Annie thrashing wildly to the strains of "A Whole Lotta Shakin' Goin' On." Her back was to him, her butt thrust in the air as she reached down to touch her toes, as if paying homage to Jerry Lee. It was difficult to tear his eyes away from the provocative sight.

"Annie!" he shouted, moving forward and tapping her on the shoulder to gain her attention, and divert his own. She screamed, bringing her arms up and flailing out at him, until she finally recognized who it was.

Cursing angrily beneath her breath, she bent over at the waist, palms on her knees, taking deep breaths to quiet her nerves and restore her oxygen level. "Are you crazy, sneaking up on me like that?" she said finally. "And what the hell are you doing in my house without an invitation?

Would you mind telling me that?" She doused herself with Evian water to cool off, and droplets of sweat and water rolled down her chest to lose itself in the tight bra, which barely covered her ample breasts. Her hard nipples poked through the damp material.

Joe remembered the feel of her, how her lashes fluttered when they kissed, her deep sighs of satisfaction after they'd made love. He remembered everything, a little too well. But Annie as a teenager was nothing compared to Annie as a woman.

The scent of her perfume enveloped him, and he swallowed with some difficulty before speaking. "I . . . I knocked. Hard. Several times." He stared as if mesmerized, taking in her bare midriff and skintight shorts.

Angry at the way his scrutiny made her feel, she glared back at him. "Why don't you take a picture? It'll last longer."

Her childish response would have been funny if he hadn't been caught with his tongue hanging out. "Mary asked me to run this over." He held out the bag, as if it were a peace offering. "She said you left some of your makeup and personal things in the restaurant's employee rest room, and figured you would want it." What he didn't tell her was that he had volunteered to come. He needed to see her again, to try and make things right between them.

Spying the box of tampons and various assorted eye shadows and blushers, she said, "I was going to come by later and pick them up. There was no need for you to go out of your way."

"You shouldn't leave your door unlocked, Annie. It's not safe. Be glad it was me who found you in a state of undress, not some maniac."

Squirting water into her mouth, she wiped her lips with the back of her forearm, eyes narrowing. "First of all, I'm not in a state of undress. These are workout clothes. And for your information, not that it's any of your business, I thought I had locked the door. I'm not stupid, Joe. I'm not asking to get raped, if that's what you're implying."

His face reddened. "Dammit, Annie! Quit trying to put words in my mouth."

She sighed. She didn't want to argue with Joe, she just wanted him to go. His nearness was unsettling, for want of a better word, or a more truthful one.

"Thanks for bringing my stuff. You want a cold beer?"

"No thanks. I'm working later. Just a Coke or glass of ice water will be fine."

She retreated to the kitchen, and his eyes riveted on her backside again. "Hurry up with that drink, will you?" he said, wiping sweat from his brow with the back of his hand.

Annie came back into the room and stared strangely at him, handing him the drink. "What's wrong? You look funny. Are you sick or something?"

"No!" He shook his head. "It's hot outside, that's all. Coming from the heat into the air-conditioning . . ." *Back into the heat that was Annie.* "I'll be fine in a minute." He gulped down his Coke, trying not to stare at her body, trying not to remember, which was difficult, since she was now sitting next to him on the couch.

"So how are things at Mama Sophia's? Anything new happening?"

At last a safe topic. "I suppose you already know, but we just got word that Mary's pregnant. Mom went nuts when she heard. You'd think it was the second coming of the Christ child."

Annie smiled, for she could well imagine Sophia's reaction. The woman made no secret of the fact that she wanted a grandchild. And not just any grandchild. Mary's sister, Connie, was pregnant again, but Sophia wouldn't be satisfied until she held one of Mary's babies in her arms.

"I'm thrilled for Mary. She and Dan are good together. They're lucky to have each other."

"Yes . . ." he paused meaningfully, "they are."

"I guess life is just a matter of choices. My choice is to remain single." She arched her back, noting how his eyes followed the movement, and smiled inwardly. It was just too good an opportunity to pass up.

God will punish you, Annie.

Yeah, I know.

"Would you do me a favor? My neck muscles are tight. Would you mind rubbing my shoulders and neck?"

"I . . ." The thought of touching her warm, bare flesh had him clenching his teeth, fists, and legs.

Scooting in front of him, she slid between those clenched thighs and could feel the prominent bulge. "I'd really appreciate it. You interrupted my workout, and I wasn't able to cool down completely."

When his hands moved to her neck and began a slow massage, goose bumps trailed down her arms. She bit her lower lip, trying to remember who was teasing whom. "Mmmm. You always did have great hands, Joe. That feels so incredibly good."

Her skin was like satin, soft and smooth. Joe tried counting to one hundred to take his mind off his barber-pole-size erection. When that didn't work he silently sang every verse he knew of "The Star-Spangled Banner."

Unfortunately, that didn't work, either. It was that verse about the rockets red glare and bombs bursting in air that finally got to him.

"Shall I take off my top?" she asked, looking over her

shoulder, to see him pale. "You know . . . to give you more access? It's not like you haven't seen everything I own."

"No!" He pushed her away from him and jumped to his feet, all in one motion, as if the fires of hell were nipping at his heels. "I'm late for work. I've got to go."

"You're not afraid of me, are you, Joseph?" she asked, tossing the words he'd spoken to her right back in his flushed face as she got to her feet and moved toward him.

When he reached the door he looked back. "You're a tease, Annie Goldman. And you're playing with fire. One of these days you're going to get burned."

Her teasing smile was gone, replaced by thin-lipped anger. "I've already been burned, Joseph. Remember? Burned big-time, as I recall, with no extinguisher to put out the flame."

"I'm sorry about what happened between us, Annie, about the way I left. I was young and stupid. Losing the baby tore me up inside. I couldn't deal with it."

"So you ran away and joined the priesthood, instead of sticking by me, supporting me? Was that your way of dealing with it? Don't expect me to feel sorry for you, Joe, because I don't. I had to deal with the loss of our child alone. I couldn't tell anyone about what had happened, not even my best friend, because you were Mary's brother, the man she looked up to and admired."

"I want to make things up to you, Annie." He stepped closer but she retreated, closing herself off.

"It's too late. Too much has happened."

"I still love you, Annie. That's never changed. And I think you still have feelings for me, too."

Her smile held no warmth. "Oh, I have feelings, all right: anger, resentment, distrust. Should I continue?"

He shook his head and sighed. "I'm not giving up this

time. I'm not that same selfish, frightened boy that you remember. I'm a man now, and I know what I want."

Annie watched him walk out the door, and a single tear trickled down her cheek. "You're too late, Joe," she whispered. "Fifteen years too late."

Linked arm in arm, Annie and her father stood in front of the vacant building next to Goldman's two days later, staring at the empty storefront, her face shining with optimism, his with trepidation.

"It's perfect, Pop. If we lease or buy the building adjacent to the store, we can add a hair and tanning salon. I've already spoken to my stylist, Mr. Roy, and he's agreed to open a second salon here at Goldman's. Just think of the clientele we would attract." Annie was excited about the possibilities, about bringing the store into the twenty-first century, and making a significant contribution to its success.

Sid made a face, apparently thinking, and not liking what he'd come up with. He rubbed his chin. "I don't know. It's a lot of money. I'm not sure how it would go over with our regular customers. Many of them are bald, including the women. If they want a tan, they can go to Florida."

His brows rose in question. "What's with the white hair? Now you're trying to look like an old woman? You think I want your Mr. Roy doing such things to my customers?"

She patted the back of her head. "Do you like it? Mr. Roy was going for a summer look. White reflects the heat. And from what I've seen of the old ladies who shop here, they could use his help, big-time.

"Besides, if we're going to survive with all the malls and department stores that are showing up everywhere, we need to attract a younger crowd, yuppies and puppies, who have lots of disposable income, and the credit cards with which to spend it.

"The salon is just the first of many ideas I've come up with. There're a lot more where that came from, Pops."

Fearful of that, Sid raised beseeching eyes skyward. "I guess it can't hurt to consider. Considering's not doing. This building's been vacant for a while, and it's an eyesore. It could be put to good use, I guess."

He was thinking aloud, and Annie thought that a very good sign. She squeezed his hand. "Then you think my idea has some merit?"

Her exuberance had him chuckling. "You're a smart girl, Annie. But I can't decide till I take a good look at the books. I'll give it some serious thought. We'll talk more about it later."

Just as they were about to reenter Goldman's, a sleek, black BMW pulled up in front of the vacant store, horn honking. Joe got out, much to Annie's great surprise, for she knew he couldn't afford such an expensive car. Wondering how he'd gotten his hands on it, she thought of his friend Suzie, then quickly pushed the disturbing idea away.

"Hello, Annie . . . Mr. Goldman." He came to stand next to them, all smiles and dimples, and smelling like sandalwood, as if nothing ugly had happened between them. The man was obviously in denial. "What are you two doing standing out here on the sidewalk? Are you thinking about redecorating the store window?"

Sid stiffened at the mention of the display window, which had now become his sacred cow. "Why? You don't like my tribute to the Vietnam vets?" He flashed a look of disgust. "What are you, unpatriotic? Young people have no respect."

"It's not that I don't like it. I just thought you might want to update it a bit, that's all."

Annie pounced on the opportunity to further her cause. "See, Pop, even Joe thinks it stinks. And he's been trained to be . . ." she glanced at the younger man, "honest."

He shifted his feet uncomfortably. "Now, Annie, I didn't say—"

Her father made a face. "You must make pretty good tips at your sister's restaurant to be driving such a fancy, schmancy car," Sid told the former priest.

Joe smiled at the disgruntled man, who had almost been his father-in-law and would be soon, if Joe had anything to say about it. "It's a loaner, Mr. Goldman. Sonny Brando is trying to entice me to buy it, by letting me drive it around town for a few days. Sure beats the heck out of the tank."

"What are you doing here, Joe?" Arms folded across her chest, Annie gave him a take-no-prisoners look. He had chutzpah, she'd give him that. Or else he was a glutton for punishment. "Have you come to purchase new clothes?" She admired the way his khakis hugged his long legs and derriere. But then, Joe would look good in sackcloth.

Sid laughed, wrapping his arm around his daughter. "A chip off the old block, huh? My daughter's always thinking about pushing the merchandise."

Shoving his hands deep in the front pockets of his khakis, Joe replied, "I do plan to purchase some clothing, but not right now. I've just started a new job, and I've come to check out the facilities. The Catholic Church has just rented the building next door to yours. I'm going to be heading up a crisis center for troubled youths."

Annie's face fell somewhere in the vicinity of her feet, then she and her father exchanged horrified looks before she said, "You're putting juvenile delinquents next door to my father's department store? Are you trying to run us out of business?"

"Not at all. Most of the teens I'll be counseling come from troubled homes, but they're not really bad kids. They're just in need of support and guidance, and I plan to offer that, help them turn their lives around."

"And you just happened to pick the building next to Goldman's?" Annie was furious. All her grandiose plans for a hair and tanning salon had just gone straight down the tubes, thanks to Joe. Was he purposely and single-handedly trying to ruin her life? Again?

Noting his daughter's hostility toward a man he had always found likeable, Sid said hurriedly, "I gotta get back inside." He cast disapproving eyes at the vacant building. "*Oy!* I need this like I need a hole in the head," he muttered before walking off.

"I didn't mean to upset your dad, Annie."

"You've upset everything, ruined my plans. Why did you have to pick this particular building? There are a lot of empty storefronts in this neighborhood. Eastern isn't exactly Fifth Avenue."

"I didn't pick it. Bishop O'Fallon did. Guess he liked the proximity to St. Francis. And the price was right, from what I gather. Why are you so concerned? I won't let the kids interfere with your business."

"I wanted the storefront for myself. We were planning to expand the store."

He rubbed the back of his neck, looking genuinely contrite. But then, Joe was good at contrition. "I'm really sorry. I didn't know. But even if I had, I couldn't have done anything about it. Apparently the Crisis Center has been in the works for some time. In fact, the church has the option to purchase the building, if the Center is a success."

"And you're heading it up?" There would be no "ifs" about the Center being a success. Joe was smart and determined; there wasn't much he couldn't accomplish once he set his mind to it.

Smiling a Judas smile, and looking quite pleased by the fact, he nodded. "I'll have help, of course."

As soon as those words were spoken, an attractive brunette in an expensive navy linen suit got out of her compact car and approached. Her smile was as gorgeous as the rest of her, and Annie felt suddenly inadequate. And Annie never felt inadequate, especially when it came to comparing herself to other women.

"Hi, Joe. Hope I'm not late for our appointment."

"Not at all. I just got here myself." Joe made the introductions, then said by way of explanation, "Angela's a lawyer. She'll be handling the legal end of things here at the Center, once we're up and running."

Annie returned the woman's smile, which seemed a lot more genuine than her own. "Nice meeting you, Angela."

"Annie's half owner of Goldman's," Joe explained. "If you need anything in the way of apparel, I'm sure she'll be only too happy to help."

"Ah . . ." The woman cast a disdainful look at the store-front window. "I do most of my shopping online, but thanks for the offer."

Things were just getting better and better, Annie thought. Her expansion plans had been ruined, thanks to Joe; a juvenile detention center was moving next door to the department store she was endeavoring to make upscale, thanks to Joe; and now Angela DeNero, who had Italian written all over her lovely face, and who would no doubt please Sophia to no end, had come into his life. Joe got credit for that one, too.

As Sid would say: Nothing worse should ever happen.

But, of course, it did.

EIGHT

"The constant friend is never welcome."

The brand-new, shiny red Cadillac convertible pulled to a halt in front of the Goldman residence, and Annie paled visibly as she caught sight of her cousin, Donna Wiseman, seated in the front seat, atop the white-leather upholstery, looking like Cleopatra riding her chariot. The hot July sun beat down, giving the woman's red hair the appearance of wild fire.

Annie squeezed her eyes shut, hoping the vision would disappear, but when she opened them again, Donna was still there, gazing into the rearview mirror, applying a fresh coat of lipstick, and admiring the vision reflecting back.

Annie was surprised her cousin didn't kiss the mirror. There were few people Donna loved better than herself.

Good God! First Joe confesses that he loves me, and now Donna. Life is cruel.

Dropping the blue velvet panel back in place, she turned to face her mother, who looked guilty as hell, and drilled her with accusing eyes. "What's *she* doing here? You didn't invite *her* for dinner tonight, did you? Please tell me you didn't."

Annie didn't bother to disguise the animosity in her voice. She disliked Donna "the prima donna" Wiseman.

The woman gave the term *Jewish American Princess* a bad name. She was spoiled, shallow, conceited, and believed the sun rose and set on her whim.

And those were her good points!

"Not exactly, dear. Your cousin's come for a brief visit. It seems things didn't work out with fiancé number three, and she's a bit despondent over the breakup. Your aunt Lola suggested she come here to sort things out. Lola thought it might cheer her up to be with family at such a difficult time."

The nerve of the woman! Lola was running a close second in chutzpah to the Goldman girls. "Why is Aunt Lola butting in? She doesn't get along with her daughter, so now she's trying to pawn her off on the relatives? Well, isn't that just like her?" The apple—in this case, Donna—didn't fall far from the tree.

"Lola's divorce from Lenny hit your cousin pretty hard."

Annie tried not to laugh. "Gina, Lola divorced Lenny when Donna was ten years old. She hardly knows the loser. He was more or less a sperm donor."

"Still, Lenny's her father. She shares his blood, and she gets cards from him regularly." Her mother's brows lifted. "Cards stuffed with money. He's been good about sending the money."

Lenny Wiseman worked as a blackjack dealer in Atlantic City, which was where Aunt Lola had met him. He sent his daughter money when the cards were hot, his winnings were big, and his guilty conscience needed salving.

Oh, did she forget to mention that Lenny was a compulsive gambler?

One of the few things Lola had done right in her life was to divorce the asshole.

"Lola's my sister. Family helps each other out."

"And because of that, and Donna's most recent screwup, we have to put up with the spoiled brat?" Rolling her eyes in disbelief, she started singing "Whatever Lola Wants, Lola Gets."

"Annie." Gina put a great deal of entreaty into that one word.

"Donna's never worked a day in her life. She has no idea of what living in the real world is like." Annie had serious doubts that her cousin knew that food and groceries came from the supermarket, and that they didn't just mysteriously appear on the kitchen table, dropped there by the grocery stork.

"I don't think Donna having three fiancés and getting dumped by each of them has been an accident or a coincidence, Gina. Who in their right mind would want to marry a woman so shallow?"

"It hasn't been easy for Donna growing up with Lola and her assorted male and female companions," her mother countered, arching a meaningful brow. "You know how eccentric your aunt is."

Eccentric wasn't quite the word Annie would have chosen to describe Lola. *Crazy. Insane. Wacko.* Those words suited her aunt much better.

The middle-aged woman—a former second-rate lounge singer by profession—fancied herself to be the next Ethel Merman. Lola thought nothing of standing up during family gatherings and belting out show tunes.

Annie distinctly remembered the time Lola had emerged from the bathroom one morning totally naked, save for the shower curtain she stood behind, singing "Everything's Coming Up Roses." Sid had taken one look at his sister-in-law and nearly fainted into his scrambled eggs.

Pulling the drapery aside once again, Annie gasped aloud. "My God! She's got massive amounts of luggage with her." Louis Vuitton, if she wasn't mistaken, had been stacked window high on the backseat.

Gina sighed. "She has a large wardrobe. I told Lola it would be all right if Donna stayed for a week."

"A week! Looks to me like she's here for the duration. She could go on a world cruise three times over and still not wear the same outfit twice. In fact, why don't we suggest it?"

"Now, Annie, be nice."

"And where's she going to stay? You're redoing the guest room, remember? Your old bedroom suite's been sold, and the new furniture you bought isn't supposed to be here for another month." Annie was getting a really bad feeling about this whole family-visit thing.

"I was hoping Donna could stay with you."

BOOM! There it was. The bomb had been dropped, and not too subtly. It was nuclear! When Annie opened her mouth to object, her mother placed a placating hand on her forearm.

Prepare for detonation.

"Please, Annie! I don't ask for that much. You and your cousin are about the same age. I'm sure you have lots of things in common." She thought quickly. "You're both single. And Donna dyes her hair, I'm sure of it. No one has hair that red.

"And you know how Aunt Lola and Donna drive your father insane. I'll never hear the end of it if she stays with me."

It was true. Sid thought Lola Wiseman was the devil incarnate, and Donna, who he considered a brainless piece of fluff, didn't fare much better in his opinion.

"And just when were you planning to tell me about this, *Gina*?" Annie uttered the name like a curse.

Her mother flinched and turned away, asking, "Is that a Coach bag she's carrying?" while doing her best to avoid the question. When she finally turned back to face her daughter, her cheeks were pink with embarrassment.

"I know how you feel about your cousin, but she's not a bad person. Donna has her good points." She thought a moment, and when none came to mind, said, "I think you could be a good influence on her. So she's a little self-centered, a little bit spoiled—"

"A little?" Annie's jaw unhinged. "You're kidding, right? And what good points does Donna have, besides long nails, designer outfits, and a daddy who gives her whatever she wants?"

"You're her cousin."

"Not by choice. And you're her aunt. Your rank is higher, so she should stay here with you."

"Don't make me beg, Annie," Gina placed a hand over her heart, then uttered dramatically, "I'm not feeling so good. I think I should go to the emergency room for an EKG."

"And I think I should go to the ER to have my head examined. I'll have them drill those little holes so I can look inside to see if I still have a brain." After a few agonizing moments, she said, "Oh, all right! She can stay. But only for a week. After that, I'm tossing Donna's skinny, designer-clad butt out the door."

Suddenly free of disease, Gina smiled widely. "Oh, thank you, Annie *mia*. You don't know how happy this makes me."

"Yeah. Well, I'm glad one of us is happy."

"You're a good girl, a wonderful daughter."

"What I am is a *schlemazel*!" If there was ever a sucker born, and an unlucky one at that, it was she.

"Well, Cousin Annie!" Donna said when she entered the house a few minutes later. "Don't you look *mature* with your white hair. Is it natural? As I recall, you are a few years older than me."

Annie managed a tight smile, wishing she could knock her cousin's straight, orthodontured teeth down her throat. Donna knew perfectly well that they were only three months apart in age.

Air-kissing Annie's cheek, the annoying woman moved directly to Gina, who she enveloped in a genuine hug of affection. "Hello, Auntie. It's so good to see you again. How have you been?"

Gina opened her mouth to respond, but Annie butted in. "No need to kiss my mom's ass, Donna. I'm the one you'll be staying with on this visit, so pucker up over here." She grinned at the woman's look of outrage, while her mother looked on, slightly nauseated.

"You haven't changed a bit, Cousin. Still as outspoken as ever, I see. I guess working in a low-class restaurant with all those crude people does that to a person." She tugged the hem of her white silk jacket, which Annie was positive was Armani. Her own black leather pants for which she had paid a small fortune suddenly felt like cheap vinyl next to Donna's designer duds.

"Oh, Annie's not working at the restaurant anymore," Gina informed her niece. "I guess your mother didn't tell you, but she's a partner now in her father's store. We're so proud of her."

"Really?" The woman's green eyes—the result of contact lenses—widened. "How convenient that nepotism still works. Is Goldman's where you buy all of your clothes?" Giving Annie a quick once-over, she made a face of distaste, an indication that she found Annie's wardrobe lacking.

"I thought the whole Madonna craze went out after she gave birth to her baby. That Englishman she married is *soooo* good-looking. I never could understand what she saw in Sean Penn. He's not handsome at all."

"And I should care about all of this because . . . ?"

"Don't you watch *Entertainment Tonight*?" Donna asked, horrified by the thought that her cousin was somehow missing out on the very best that life had to offer, as if Annie had committed an act of high treason, or broken one of the commandments: Thou shalt not miss an opportunity to glean gossip from mindless television programs.

What was next, Annie wondered, *The Secret Sins of Gilligan's Island*?

"I mean . . . how do you follow what the celebrities are doing, if you don't watch it every night? *Access Hollywood* isn't nearly as informative, though sometimes I watch E! on the cable channel."

"I don't give a damn what celebrities do or don't do. I have a life of my own. I don't need to live vicariously through someone else's."

Was the woman a voyeur, or what?

Still wearing the massive diamond that fiancé number three had given her, Donna waved five lethal-looking nails in Annie's direction, as if to dismiss her objection altogether. "Hollywood and New York City are where it's happening. They set the trends for fashion and everything else." Her smile was condescending. "No wonder you're not up on the latest—"

"Donna!" Gina interrupted, noting how her daughter's hands had clenched into fists. Apparently Annie had never forgiven her cousin for pulling the heads off her favorite Barbie dolls. And then there'd been the incident where Donna had stapled shut the leg openings on all of Annie's underpants.

"Why don't you come into the kitchen and let me show you the newest member of the Goldman family? I have a new puppy."

Donna wrinkled her nose, clearly unimpressed. "Does it smell? Does it bite? Will it scratch and tear my pantyhose? These are Donna Karan, and they're very expensive."

"No, but if you get too close, he might scratch your eyes out," Annie cautioned. "Bubbeh's been trained as an attack dog, and he doesn't like to be disparaged by animal-hating celebrity groupies, who—"

"Here we are." Gina cut her daughter off in mid-insult, flashing her a look that said she'd better keep quiet if she knew what was good for her. "This is my Bubbeh."

The little dog awoke at the sound of his mistress's voice and started yapping, then bolted straight for Donna's feet, lifted his leg, and pulled a "Sid" on her, which is how Annie now referred to the dog's penchant for peeing on everyone's shoes. The puppy was particularly fond of expensive shoes, which was why Annie had been spared, thus far.

Staring down at her feet with a horrified expression, the distraught woman exclaimed, "My shoes! My shoes! These are Ferragamo."

"Now they're drenched Ferragamos." Annie couldn't suppress her delight or smile as she leaned over to pick up the puppy and kiss him on the head. "*Tsk, tsk.* It's such a bitch to clean suede. And those looked new."

Donna glared but remained silent.

"You've just earned your first dog biscuit, Bubbeh baby," Annie whispered in the dog's ear when the other two women moved toward the sink. He responded by licking her cheek, as if to say, "I don't like her, either."

Joe studied the young woman seated across from his battered oak desk and sighed inwardly. Tess Romano was not going to be an easy teenager to counsel. Not many were. But in her case, with alcoholic parents, and a question of abuse that hadn't been verified, she would be difficult to reach. She had a mouth on her that spewed forth garbage like an out-of-whack disposal, and a protective wall around her heart that would take a long time to breach, if that was even possible. At this point, Joe had his doubts.

But he sensed Tess was a good kid at heart. He'd read her case file and knew that at one time she'd been a straight-A student with a lot of potential. But that had changed over the past few years. Circumstances being what they were, he could certainly understand her rebellious behavior. He understood, but he didn't condone.

Tess had been arrested several times, mostly for petty crimes, like breaking curfew and performing acts of vandalism at the high school. Nothing he and his friends hadn't done as kids—he and Murray Abrahms, now a district court judge, once dumped Jell-O into the high school swimming pool as a senior prank—but times were different now, authority figures much less tolerant, and Joe and Murray hadn't been caught.

Tess wasn't a criminal, just a troubled kid who needed to turn her life around; Joe intended to see that she did.

"Spit the gum out, Tess." He held out his hand, his hard-edged expression brooking no refusal. "I can't understand a word you're saying while you're smacking that gum like a cud-chewing cow."

She smiled spitefully. "Maybe that's because I didn't say anything." She chewed a few more times, just to prove she could, then spit into his hand. Gum and saliva slipped through his fingers, and he reached for a tissue, not bothering to react to the childish act of defiance.

With some of these kids, defiance was all they had left.

"We'd better get a few things straight, Tess. You either succeed in this program, or you'll end up in a juvenile detention center. Your parents aren't capable of taking care of you any longer. We're going to have to find someone else to foster that responsibility." And he knew that wouldn't be easy. Kids Tess's age, who shared similar backgrounds, were usually difficult to place.

The teenager shrugged. "I can take care of myself. I've been doing it for years." She brushed dark, matted hairs out of equally dark eyes. Sad eyes that had seen too much for a sixteen-year-old. Eyes that held fear. The overhead fluorescent lights illuminated just how young and frightened the girl really was, despite her show of bravado.

"The law says differently. Would you like me to call Miss DeNero over so she can explain your legal position to you?"

Tess glanced across the large room, toward the lawyer's desk. "You humping her or what? I've seen the way she looks at you, like she could eat you for dinner. Can't blame her. You're pretty good-looking, for an old guy."

Anger washed through Joe, but knowing that Tess was purposely trying to goad him into losing his cool, he fought hard to keep his temper in check. "My mom used to wash my mouth out with soap when I said something she didn't like." Sophia also used a big wooden spoon. His mother, unlike Joe, had no problem with corporal punishment. "I thought you were too old for that sort of thing, but maybe not."

She ignored the threat. "Got any smokes? I'm dying for a cigarette."

"There's no smoking allowed anywhere in this building. And I'd better not catch you smoking off-premises, either, young lady. You understand?"

"This place is a dump. I thought the Catholic Church was rolling in dough. How come they didn't give this place any of it? Figures. They think we're all a bunch of dumb kids, and they don't want to waste their money on us."

Joe had to agree. The place wasn't anything to brag about. But they had only been open for two weeks, and hadn't yet received all of their funding, though he doubted the money would be spent on enhancing the appearance of the place. A new computer was in the budget, but the cast-off office furnishings would have to remain.

"The Center is supported mainly by donations from the parishioners of St. Francis and by various Catholic charities in and out of the area. We do the best we can with the budget that's allotted us. The furniture's used because that's all we can afford right now. And if you'd take your feet off it, the stuff would last a lot longer."

Unfolding her legs, she moved her dirty tennis shoes to the floor. "I didn't ask to be brought here. I'd rather go to jail."

"No, you wouldn't. Trust me on that." He'd heard of cases where young women like Tess were raped or sodomized, sometimes by other kids, sometimes by guards, and he would do everything in his power to prevent that from happening.

Joe took his responsibilities seriously. No one on his watch was going to fail, especially Tess.

"Gina, you've got to come over here and get Donna! She's driving me nuts," Annie pleaded quietly into the phone to her mother. Not that her cousin could hear their conversation, with the television blaring so loudly that Annie could hardly hear herself think.

"Bring me a diet drink, will you, Annie?" Donna shouted from the living room. "And put lots of ice in it."

Annie ground her teeth before baring them like a rabid dog on the edge.

"Now, Annie, we've already talked about this, the three other times you called," her mother said. "Just tell Donna to clean up after herself. I'm sure she's more than willing to do her fair share of the chores."

Uh-huh. Sure. Whatever.

"I've tried that. The woman's a slob. Her room looks like a nuclear bomb exploded in it. I can't live like this, Gina. She's making a shambles of my town house. The board of health is going to condemn it soon." The once neat abode looked like Hurricane Donna had swallowed it whole then spit it out, like yesterday's garbage. There were dirty dishes everywhere: on the coffee table, beneath the cushions of the couch, and she'd even left some particularly nasty egg-encrusted ones in the linen closet, which Annie had found—thank God!—this morning.

Her home was a prime target for cockroach infestation, which would go nicely with the pig she currently had living with her. If all else failed, she could rename the place "Animal Farm."

"I've got to go," her mother said, the alarm in her voice ringing through loud and clear. "Bubbeh is chewing up one of your father's shoes. Oh, God! They're Florsheim! Stop that!" she shouted at the dog. Then, "I'll see you and Donna tonight. Don't forget . . . be here by six. You promised to arrive before your aunt Lola, so you could protect me from your father's wrath. You know how much he dislikes my sister."

Annie heaved a sigh. "We'll be there, Gina. Don't worry. I already told Sid I had to leave an hour early. He didn't ask why."

"You're a good girl."

Yeah, right, Annie thought, hanging up the phone, and wondering why she always allowed her mother to manipulate her. Gina definitely had a passive-aggressive type personality. She didn't shout, she didn't cry, she just persisted until she got what she wanted.

Maybe I'll be rewarded in the next life, because I sure as hell am not getting any perks in this one.

"Hurry up with that soda, will you? Don't you want to watch *Regis*? It's coming on, and Whoopi Goldberg is today's cohost. Did you know that she dumped that guy she was dating?"

"I'm already late for work," Annie shouted back. "I

don't give a damn about Whoopi, get your own soda, and for chrissake, clean up after yourself! I'm not your maid."

Silence greeted the outburst, right before the volume on the TV increased. So furious that smoke almost poured from her nostrils, Annie was about to march in and give her cousin a piece of her mind when the doorbell rang.

"You're damn lucky, Donna Wiseman!"

Trying to work the hoop earring wire through her earlobe as she hurried to answer the summons, she gave serious thought to packing her bags and leaving the country for an indeterminate length of time.

She was contemplating the pros and cons of that tempting idea when she pulled open the door to find Joe standing there. He was the last person she'd expected to see on her doorstep, and her heart gave a funny little lurch that surprised her. "Hi!"

He smiled sheepishly, rocking back on his heels. "I'm sorry to stop over here so early, Annie. I was on my way to work, and—"

"Come in," she interrupted. She had no time for lengthy explanations or apologies, or feelings she didn't want to feel. Think of Joe as the enemy, she told herself. But that concept was just too difficult to employ. "I've only got a few minutes before I have to leave. Do you want coffee?"

"Sure. That'd be great." He glanced around the room and his forehead wrinkled. "What happened? Did you have a burglary? How come the TV's so loud? You want me to turn it off?" He made a move in that direction.

"Follow me into the kitchen and I'll explain." While Joe seated himself on a stool at the breakfast bar, Annie filled two cups with French roast and went on to tell him about her unwelcome and aggravating houseguest.

His eyes widened. "Donna? Isn't she the one with the mother who—"

"The very same. Aunt Lola will be at my mom's tonight for dinner, and Sid doesn't know. *Oy vey!* There's going to be hell to pay, and I'll be the one caught in the middle."

"I guess this isn't a good time to ask a favor of you, then, is it?"

Drowning in his warm brown eyes, she sighed and turned toward the refrigerator, trying to refocus on the question, and wondering why this man had such a hold over her.

"To be honest, it's not. But I don't think there's going to be a good time until I can get rid of my cousin, so you may as well let me have it."

"One of the kids I'm counseling at the Center needs a part-time job and a place to stay temporarily." Annie swallowed her groan. "Tess Romano is a good kid, but she's carrying a lot of baggage. Her parents are alcoholics, and she's kind of wild, and . . . well, Tess reminds me of the way you were at sixteen, Annie. She's wild and unpredictable, but basically deep down where it counts she's good and decent.

"I'd like to place her with someone who might understand what she's going through. Someone to whom she can relate."

"Someone like me, I take it?" she said, wondering why God was dumping on her, big-time.

I didn't really want to fornicate with a priest. I was only joking. Lighten up, will you, Big Guy?

Joe smiled ruefully. "I didn't know about your cousin staying here when I thought about asking you for help. It might be more than you can handle right now. You look kinda crazed at the moment."

Annie's first instinct was to say *"Hell No!"* She didn't need another complication in her life right now. Joe was complication enough. Donna had already overstayed her welcome, and she didn't appear to be all that anxious to leave. But maybe if Annie brought someone else into the house, someone who might make her cousin just a bit uncomfortable . . . A troubled teenager with her own nasty habits might just be the ticket to get Cousin Donna out of her house and her life.

"Crazed doesn't come close to what I'm feeling at the moment, Joe. Isn't there a lot of paperwork involved with this sort of thing?"

Joe nodded. "But it won't be a problem. Angela's a pro at getting things like this done quickly."

"I'll need some time to think it over. Can I drop by the Center tomorrow and give you my answer then?"

With a smile that made her heart do a flip-flop, he reached for her hand, squeezing gently. "That'd be great, Annie!" He pushed off the stool. "I'd better go. I'll be late for work if I don't. See you tomorrow, okay?"

" 'Kay," she said, watching him walk out the door and missing him already.

Sap! she told herself, wondering if people really did change, if second chances in life were possible, if things really could work out between her and Joe.

And if they could, do I really want them to?

"Annie, have you left yet? I'm still waiting for my soft drink."

What was the penalty for murdering your cousin? she wondered. Surely no jury in the world would convict her. Not when she could claim justifiable homicide.

"Annieeee!"

Grabbing her purse, Annie headed out the door, resisting the temptation to stuff slightly moldy salami down her cousin Donna's throat.

NINE

"A table is not blessed if it has fed no scholars."

"Things have gone from bad to worse," her mother whispered frantically as soon as Annie stepped into the front hallway of the Goldman residence, with Donna in tow.

Mahogany-framed photographs of various Goldman and Donelli ancestors stared down from their respective perches, looking like the lineup for the FBI's Ten Most Wanted. Gina raised her hands in supplication, rolling her eyes as she tried to convey to her daughter the seriousness of the situation.

"We've got big trouble."

"Hi, Auntie! Is my mom here yet?" Donna seemed totally oblivious to the drama going on around her. "I wore waterproof tennis shoes, just in case your dog decides to get frisky; they're Easy Spirits." She looked inordinately proud of herself.

Nodding absently, Gina forced a smile. "That's nice, dear. Your mother's in the living room with my father. Why don't you go in and say hello? Annie and I will be right in. We need to discuss a few things first." Taking the hint, Donna left the two women alone.

"Grandpa Johnny's here, too?" Annie asked, wondering why that was a problem. She adored her seventy-five-year-old grandfather. He had an amusing story for every occasion, and a discerning eye that still appreciated the sight of a pretty woman.

Giovanni Donelli, whom everyone called Johnny, had been a stud in his younger days. Still was, if you believed some of his more colorful tales. His was one of the photos hanging on the wall. Jet-black hair and deep-brown eyes, Johnny had been a hunk in his youth, not that he wasn't still handsome. But his black hair was now frosted white, his olive skin covered with character.

The old ladies in the neighborhood found Grandpa Johnny quite to their liking, and he had no trouble getting dates to go ballroom dancing, which was his favorite pastime.

"Is that what you meant about things going from bad to worse," she prodded, "the fact that Grandpa's here?"

Gina smacked her forehead. "I wish it was only your grandfather. Your father called a few minutes ago to tell me that his sisters are coming for dinner tonight. They'll be here any minute." She crossed herself, as if she were preparing to ward off evil. Annie thought that if Gina had a crucifix handy, she'd be waving that around, too.

"Where's Sid? How come he's not home yet?"

"At the store. He said he'd be a few minutes late. Something about a delivery of nasty underwear."

Uh-oh, Annie thought, wishing she would have been on hand to receive the delivery of the revealing undergarments she had ordered for the women's department. Thongs were not something her father would understand—Mrs. Foragi in a thong did give one pause—and she didn't want Henry, the pervert, messing with the merchandise. He'd probably be tempted to try something on.

"I didn't have the nerve to tell him about Lola and Pop. He's going to be mad, that's for sure."

Sid being pissed was just a fact of life. Everyone knew that he lived in a perpetual state of pissiness. "They're your family." Annie patted her mother's hand reassuringly. "You have every right to have them to dinner. Act like nothing's the matter. We'll get through this just fine. You'll see."

"What? Now you're Miss Optimistic? Did you hear what I said? The Goldman girls are descending. Like the wrath of God, they'll swoop down and cause trouble, spreading their malicious ways. . . . I feel nauseous."

"Come on, Gina! You're being overly dramatic." So what else was new? Her mother hurled at the drop of a hat. "They're just a couple of old women who get off on starting trouble. They're not the devil's spawn, so lighten up. You've got your family here to act as a buffer."

Suddenly from the other room came a loud, exuberant rendition of "I'm Gonna Wash That Man Right Outta My Hair," as only Lola could sing it.

So much for buffers.

A car backfired several times, and Annie went to the door's sidelight window to look out, pulling back the white sheers. A 1969 Ford Fairlane in mint condition graced the curb in all its blue and white ugliness. "Aunt Golda and Aunt Esther are here. Either that, or we're being invaded by the Munsters."

Her mother groaned. "I should have taken an enema, cleaned out my system. That always makes my mind more settled."

Annie was tempted to tell her mother that an enema wasn't going to help someone who was as full of shit as she was, but she didn't think Gina was in the right frame of mind to fully appreciate her humor just now. Pity, because a sense of humor was a definite requirement to survive in the Goldman family.

She opened the door to let her father's sisters in. Funny, she never thought of them as her aunts, but always Sid's sisters, or the Goldman girls. They weren't the type of women you could wrap your arms around and hug. For one thing, they were both immensely proportioned; for another, the scowls they perpetually wore were forbidding, even to someone as thick-skinned as Annie. No one had ever accused the Goldman girls of being sweet and cuddly.

"Well, I see you're still a shame and a disgrace to your poor father," Aunt Golda said, her gaze roving over Annie's apparel in an insulting fashion, her frown deepening the crags in her fleshy cheeks.

The woman wore an ugly black-silk shirtwaist dress with an ecru-lace collar that even a dead person wouldn't be caught buried in, and she had the nerve to criticize Annie's clothing? Annie bit back a retort.

"Maybe now that you're working with your father," her aunt added, "you'll be able to buy some new clothes. You think a doctor or attorney is going to marry a woman who dresses so suggestively?"

Hearing what sounded like her mother's knees knocking in the background, Annie sucked in her anger, forcing out what could almost pass for a smile. "Hello, Aunt Golda, Aunt Esther." She refused to say it was nice to see them.

Their respective gazes flew over Annie to land squarely on Gina, who almost recoiled at the impact. "What's the matter? Didn't our brother tell you we were coming?"

Esther shook her head at Gina's bilious expression. "Are you sick again? It's that rich Italian food you eat. Too much starch, too much fat."

Gina stiffened, whether in outrage or palsy, Annie

couldn't be certain. "Of course Sid told me. We're happy you could come." She turned to her daughter for moral support. "Aren't we?" It sounded more like a question than confirmation.

"I know I'm ecstatic," Annie finally replied when Gina's fist plowed unobtrusively into the small of her back.

"Everyone's in the living room. Come in. We'll have a glass of wine, eat some nuts, schmooze a bit, while we wait for Sid to get home."

Esther patted the large mound that passed for her stomach. "I was noshing all day. I'm not hungry."

"Sid's not here yet?" Golda tsked several times and went into combat mode. "My brother works too hard, and for what? So you can buy these fancy furnishings and live high off the hog?"

Annie could never figure out how a Jew, or someone married to a Jew, could live off a hog when pork wasn't considered kosher.

"Maybe you should take pity, settle for less, so he can get home at a decent time. Are you trying to kill him?"

Aunt Esther agreed, which was not surprising, for she rarely disagreed with her older sister about anything. "Your husband's not a young man. You should take care, not be so demanding. A wife needs to accept her situation. Of course, you're *gentile*—," she spit the word out as if it were an anathema, "and not versed in the Jewish way." Her eyes held a wealth of condemnation.

Noting her mother's high color, Annie clasped Gina's clammy hand and pulled her forward. Being half Jewish, Annie got only half the amount of shit dumped on her head as did Gina. And the Goldman girls used a big shovel.

"I can use a glass of wine after the hectic day I've had at the store. How about you, Gina?"

Having already been apprised of Annie's exalted position at the store, and not liking it one bit, Esther sneered at the younger woman. "It's not right that a woman should take bread out of a man's mouth, especially a family man. A woman should stay home and have babies. The Torah is very specific about such things."

"Is that before or after she gets married?" Annie couldn't help asking.

Her mother sucked in her breath, then started giggling like a hyena on methamphetamine. "My Annie is such a comedienne. She keeps Sid and me in stitches."

Annie was thinking of keeping her mother in a straitjacket and her aunts in a cage.

And then there was Lola, who was dressed in a skintight pair of leopard pants with matching tank top. Black ankle boots completed the ensemble. Somehow on Lola, the outfit worked. It was sort of Wonder Woman meets Tarzan. "Hey, Aunt Lola. Nice threads."

The older woman grinned, rushing across the room to envelope Annie in a bear hug. "You get prettier every time I see you, sweet cheeks. God, what I'd give for that figure. Did you see her boobs, Donna? Her mother tells me they're real, not a bit of silicone. I would kill for boobs like that. Mine are starting to knock against my knees." She laughed, then reached for a handful of cashews.

Donna, who was used to her mother's offbeat sense of humor and didn't appreciate it, at any rate, failed to respond; instead, she retreated to the opposite side of the room.

Grandpa Johnny winked at Annie and smiled. "*Bella, bella.* My Annie, she's a pretty girl, no? And smart." He then turned his charm on the Goldman girls, who were still wide-eyed and gasping at Lola's outrageous remarks.

"Ah, who do we have here? This cannot be Golda and Esther, can it? I haven't seen you two girls since my daughter's wedding to the merchant." Grandpa Johnny always referred to Sid as "the merchant," or sometimes "the tailor," "the ragman," or whatever insulting clothing-related appellation he could think of.

Johnny winked at the younger of the two women, whose cheeks filled with color. "Do you still like to dance, Esther? If I recall, you had some very fancy footwork. Agnes de Mille could take lessons, no?"

Aunt Esther dancing? Now, that would be something worth seeing.

At the question, Golda's head snapped around so fast, Annie thought she might be doing a scene from *The Exorcist*. She half expected green slime to start oozing from Golda's mouth. "What does the old man mean by that?"

Grandpa Johnny stiffened. "Hey, watch who you're calling an old man. I don't need no pills to get it up. You want I should prove it? Come on. Let's go into the bedroom. I'll show you who's old."

Lola threw back her head and howled. Annie bit the inside of her cheek to keep from doing the same. Gina clutched her chest, about to have a mild myocardial infarction, while Esther's face flushed bright red before she replied, "We danced at the wedding, that's all. It's not a crime to dance, Golda."

"A gentleman never kisses and tells, right, Esther?" Johnny winked at the embarrassed woman, who suddenly developed an urgency that sent her rushing straight to the bathroom.

"You should tell your father to keep his nasty tongue to himself, Gina. I don't want my sister's reputation stained. Someone could get the wrong idea."

"I already got plenty of ideas. Your sister's a hot number."

Annie chuckled at both her grandfather and aunt's absurd statements. It was unlikely anyone gave a fig if Esther or Golda *shtupped* their hearts out, except perhaps for Golda, who had apparently appointed herself Esther's protector. Lucky Esther.

Moving across the room, to where her cousin sat enthralled in front of the tube, Annie felt a tad guilty about leaving her mother at the mercy of the old ladies. But she figured she'd be more hindrance than help, and Gina still had Lola and Grandpa Johnny to run interference, if the need arose.

If the worst happened, and her mother needed rescuing, Lola could perform a number from *Gypsy*. That was always good for at least twenty minutes.

"Sit down, Annie," Donna insisted, her eyes bright with excitement as she yanked on the pant leg of Annie's jeans. "The E! channel's going to make some startling revelations about the death of Marilyn Monroe."

"You mean there's something we don't already know? I thought Robert Kennedy and his cronies were the ones who had done poor Marilyn dirty."

"That's never been proven."

"Why do you like watching all this crap? You've got the best drama going on across the room, and you're sitting here watching this. *Oy!*"

"I find it's more interesting to live in a fantasy world. I haven't had much luck in the real one." She flashed her ring finger. "Especially with the men I was going to marry."

Annie reclined back against the sofa and tucked her right leg beneath her. "Did you love any of them?"

"Well, of course I did, silly. Sort of. I mean—all three

had gobs of money. And my mother always says that it's just as easy to fall in love with a rich man as a poor one, which makes perfectly good sense if you think about it. And they treated me nice, bought me expensive things, and took me on trips."

"Why depend on men at all, Donna?" Annie knew first-hand you couldn't. "You should go out and make a life for yourself, get a job, an apartment." *And get out of mine while you're at it.*

The woman's green eyes widened, as if she'd never before considered the possibility. "A job? But what would I do? I've never worked before. I have no skills. Like Blanche Dubois, I've always relied on the kindness of strangers."

"Yeah? Well, look how she ended up." That gave her cousin pause.

"You're attractive, reasonably intelligent"—okay, that was a stretch, but these were desperate times—"and you can speak English, a real plus in this day and age." Donna'd be a shoe-in as a cabbie. "Those are marketable skills."

"That sounds like an awful lot of work," her cousin replied. "Actually, it sounds just awful. It'll be a whole lot easier just to find another man. I've got good looks, a great figure. It shouldn't be too hard. And in the meantime, I'm enjoying my stay with you. It was so sweet of you to take me in. I feel like we're bonding already, don't you?"

Bonding? As in bondage, strangulation, asphyxiation?

Yeah, they were bonding, all right.

"Being independent is the best thing in the world, Donna. I would never want to be dependent on anyone, man or woman. You can't count on anyone but yourself. Remember that."

"But Mama said—"

"Mama said there'd be days like this. . . ."

Annie rolled her eyes. "Times have changed. Women aren't useless pieces of window dressing anymore." Which reminded her that the display window at Goldman's still needed fixing. "A woman should make a contribution."

Donna mulled over her cousin's words, then, not liking what she was hearing, pushed out her lower lip. "I think you're just trying to get rid of me, Annie, that's what I think. Well, it won't work." The redhead crossed her arms over her chest. "Aunt Gina told my mom I could stay with you for as long as I wanted because I'm family."

Annie fought hard not to lose her cool. She doubted Gina had said any such thing, though she didn't doubt for a moment that Lola had. Her aunt usually said whatever was convenient.

"Whatever Lola wants, Lola—"

Yeah, right.

Though she hated to do it, it was time to bring out the big guns. Getting rid of Donna was like trying to rid your house of cockroaches. It was pretty much an impossibility. "It's going to get a bit crowded in the apartment in the near future. I'm thinking about letting someone else move in with us."

Obviously not convinced that this wasn't just another ploy to get rid of her, Donna instantly grew suspicious. After all, Annie had made it quite plain that she wanted her to leave, though Donna just didn't understand why. Much to Annie's great dismay, Donna loved living with her. No, Cousin Donna was definitely in no hurry to leave Little Italy.

"Who's moving in? A man or a woman?" she asked.

Annie hedged. "I'll let you know after tomorrow. I'm meeting a friend who has a friend in need of a place to stay.

Of course, I immediately thought of that extra twin bed in the guest room. The more the merrier, right?"

The woman looked genuinely distraught. "But I've got my suitcases on that bed! And there's no more room in the closet. It's a very small closet. You should really think about getting it made bigger. I don't know how you manage."

Annie shrugged and rose to her feet. "Guess you'll just have to fold those expensive designer outfits of yours and shove them under the bed for the time being. It's really going to be tough on the Versaces."

Donna gasped aloud. "You're evil!"

Annie smiled. "Well, it does seem to run in the family."

Joe glanced at his watch, then out the window, but there was still no sign of Annie. Where was she? She had said she'd come by the Center to give him her answer about taking Tess in, but it was now 5:45 P.M. and she still hadn't shown.

Maybe she didn't want to do it and was too embarrassed to tell him. Maybe he shouldn't have asked it of her. It was a great deal of responsibility, and Annie had a lot on her plate at the moment, what with her new job, her cousin, and all.

And they still had unresolved issues—issues that needed to be talked out. Until everything was brought out in the open, feelings explored more fully, nothing would change between them.

He hoped she showed. Not just for Tess's sake, but for his own. He had something important to ask her, and he desperately wanted to see her again.

Needing to take his mind off the fact that she might not be coming, he sharpened all the pencils on his desk, and then did Angela's as well, glancing at his watch once again. Four minutes had elapsed.

Still no Annie.

He paced to the rear of the room, then back to the front window, counting his steps as he walked across the speckled linoleum—two hundred twenty-seven.

Still no Annie.

He went into the rest room, splashed water on his face, combed his hair, and checked his teeth. He looked pretty good, if he said so himself. Annie had always complimented his straight, white teeth. She'd had orthodonture; his were natural.

Still no Annie.

He was about to give up when the front door suddenly swung open and there she was, slightly out of breath, her face flushed, from hurrying, he assumed. She looked beautiful, and his heart ached at the sight of her.

Love, he'd discovered, wasn't quite as thrilling when it was only one-sided.

Joe noted that Annie's hair was no longer white. In fact, the color almost looked normal. It had been a long time since he'd seen her hair a rich chestnut color, and he wondered why she'd changed it so drastically. Normal had become drastic, as odd as that seemed.

"Hi!" she said, tossing her purse on his desk. "Sorry I'm late. I couldn't get rid of the last customer. Mrs. Koontz must have tried on twenty-five girdles before she finally bought one. *Oy vey!* Stuffing her into that rubber was a nightmare. I don't know how Sid's done it all these years."

"No problem," he said, trying to sound nonchalant. "I was just catching up on a few chores that needed doing."

Annie seated herself on the chair fronting his desk, crossing her long legs. Joe perched on the desk's edge and admired the view. "Thanks for coming by. I assume you've made a decision about Tess Romano?"

She nodded. "I've given Tess's situation a great deal of thought, and—"

"You've decided not to do it? That's okay. I—"

"That's not what I was going to say."

He looked somewhat surprised. "Oh?"

"As I was saying, before I was so rudely interrupted, I've given Tess's situation a lot of thought. Admittedly, some of my reasons are purely selfish . . . well, most actually . . . but I've decided to let Tess come and stay with me, temporarily, of course, provided I've been approved as a caretaker. And I'll give her a job at the store, as well." Tess might prove very useful in deciding what type of clothing she should purchase for the younger generation of shoppers.

"You've been approved." Joe's smile was filled with relief and gratitude, and something else she didn't want to ponder. "And I'm very grateful. You don't know how much this will mean to Tess, what a positive effect it'll have on her life." He moved to take the chair next to her.

"I wouldn't be too sure about that. I'm not exactly a perfect role model, and there is Donna to consider. The woman's a slob, and she's obsessed with television. Tess is likely to pick up all of her bad habits, as well as a few of my own." Annie didn't have the heart to bring up Sid's flaws and spoil Joe's good mood.

"You are a good role model, Annie," he insisted. "Quit trying to sell yourself short. You're smart, hardworking, and you've got a generous heart. I don't think anyone could ask for more than that."

Annie swallowed, touched by his words. "Th . . . thank you. I didn't know you felt that way. I thought— Never mind."

"What? That I dumped you because you were different, that you didn't fit all of the acceptable norms?" That was partially true. Annie's nonconventional manner of dress and behavior had worried him at the time. His family, save for Mary, would have been a major obstacle to their getting married. But even that hadn't been the deciding factor. Upon reflection, it all seemed so stupid now, such a waste.

He rose to his feet and began to pace. "That wasn't it, not really. I was consumed by my own selfish needs, by guilt. I'd gotten you pregnant because I hadn't used protection. Then when the baby died, I felt God was punishing me for what had happened. I guess I went a little crazy. I thought if I joined the church, the way my mother had been pressuring me to, I might atone for my sins. I can't even begin to explain all my reasons for behaving the way I did."

"Oh, Joe . . ." Annie noted the pain in his eyes, and she swallowed with some difficulty. He'd never explained his feelings so eloquently before. Or maybe he had, and she just hadn't been listening.

But she couldn't deal with his self-recriminations right now. Not on top of everything else she had to contend with. "Let's not discuss this right now. I'm not up to it." And she needed time to think.

He looked disappointed. Confession was, after all, good for the soul. "All right. We'll table this discussion for another time. But sooner or later we need to hash this out."

"But not now."

He nodded, and she rose to her feet, relieved they weren't going to get into another discussion about their failed past relationship. She needed to put it behind her. She hoped they could still be friends; it was apparently what he wanted.

And she had finally come to the realization that it was what she wanted, too.

"I'd better get going. Will you be dropping Tess off this evening?"

He shook his head. "I'll wait till Saturday, so you'll have the weekend to adjust to each other. I need to talk to Tess again, let her know what will be expected of her."

"She's not into drugs or anything, is she?" For all her liberal ways, that was the one thing Annie wouldn't condone.

"Not that I'm aware of. Tess isn't really a danger to anyone but herself."

"All right, then. We'll expect you on Saturday."

As she reached the door, Joe sucked in his breath, letting it out slowly. "Annie, wait! Before you go, there's something else I want to ask you."

"Something else?" Disappointment stabbed her breast as she jumped headfirst into the wrong conclusion. "I should have known when you were saying all those nice—"

"My brother-in-law Eddie's birthday party is Friday night," he interrupted. "I was hoping you might come with me." When she hesitated, he added, "We could discuss Tess, maybe go over a few strategies. What d'ya say?"

A date with Joe? She had just made up her mind to be friends, and now he was asking her out on a date?

She couldn't. She shouldn't. But . . .

It would be a break from Donna. A whole evening of not having to watch television with her cousin babbling on about every actor's sex life, which aging actresses had had face-lifts, how much money each was paid for their work. Julia Roberts was leading the pack with twenty million.

Donna was a regular encyclopedia of knowledge when it came to movies and movie stars. She knew all the behind-the-scenes stories, all the sordid little details that no one else cared about.

Annie had decided that if she ever became a contestant on *Who Wants to Be a Millionaire*, Donna was going to be her lifeline in that category. She'd use Joe for religious questions, her father for geography and Judaism, Mary for cooking, and Dan for sports. Gina, she would line up for medical diseases. Her mother was, after all, an expert.

"Well?" He took another deep breath. "Would you like to go? It starts at eight. I think it's going to be a lot of fun. Connie always throws a good party."

Annie hesitated. Accepting Joe's invitation would open a door she wasn't prepared to walk though. And yet, she really wanted to say yes. "Are you sure you want me there? What about your mom? Isn't Sophia going to be there?"

"I can't live my life for my mother. I tried that once, and it didn't work out. Now I'm living it for myself. And yes, I want you there, with me."

She sighed, still unsure. But she knew Mary and Dan would probably be there, which made the decision a teensy bit easier. "All right. I'll go."

"Would you mind driving? I had to turn the Beemer back over to Sonny. But I can borrow my dad's Buick, if you'd rather not."

She almost laughed. They'd gone on quite a few dates in Frank Russo's silver Buick Roadmaster, spent many an evening parked in some dark, secluded area, reclining on the roomy, red-leather, rolled-and-tucked rear seat. "I'll be at your apartment by seven-thirty."

"Great. And Annie, thanks!"

"Don't thank me yet. You're still going to have to contend with your mother, and it could get ugly," she said as she waltzed out the door, wearing a big grin on her face.

Joe wasn't sure if she was pleased about the date, or by the idea that his mother was going to go ballistic when she saw whom he had brought to Eddie's party. Knowing Annie, it was the latter.

TEN

"The devil comes to us in our hour of darkness,
but we do not have to let him in.
And we do not have to listen, either."

At precisely 7:30 P.M. on Friday evening, Annie arrived at Joe's apartment, dressed to thrill. The tight, black, thigh-high knit dress that shrouded her body like a second skin made the former priest realize just how long he'd been celibate.

Too long, *waaay* too long!

It was going to be a frustrating night.

"Are you ready to go?" she asked, seemingly unaware of the effect she was having on him, though her eyes held a mischievous sparkle.

"You look incredible!"

"Why, thank you, Joseph," she said with a soft smile, stepping over the threshold into his apartment and leaving the seductive scent of Possession behind to torment his senses.

"You don't look so bad yourself." The deep blue pull-over sweater brought out the color of his dark eyes—eyes that were staring back at her with unconcealed lust. Annie very nearly toppled over on her impractically high, but very sexy heels.

Comfort and practicality always placed second when it came to achieving a look. Tonight she had dressed to entice, to give Joe a glimpse of what he'd been missing all these years, and to play the role his mother had always cast her in: the seductress from hell.

Dangling the car keys in front of him, she asked, "Would you like to—?"

"Yes . . . I would!" His eyes burned bright as he grabbed the keys out of her hand, not allowing her to finish the sentence, but there was no need. They both knew where his thoughts were centered. The sexual attraction between them was strong; it hung in the air like thick humidity on a hot summer's night, almost smothering in its intensity.

Things didn't get any cooler in the car, despite the fact that the air-conditioning was on full-blast. Joe wasn't able to keep his eyes solely on the road while driving to his sister's house in the Baltimore suburbs. Instead, his gaze kept drifting over Annie's legs, up the enticing expanse of thigh that her dress failed to cover. It didn't take much imagination to know those firm thighs would be as smooth as silk when he touched them.

If. If he touched them. There were no guarantees in this relationship, he reminded himself. A date was a first step, not the completion of a marathon.

"I know this is a stupid question, but what does a woman wear under a dress that's so . . . so formfitting?" He regretted the question as soon as it left his mouth. Was he suicidal? A masochist? Or just plain dumb? Because he couldn't seem to stop himself. "I noticed you aren't wearing any stockings."

Annie's dress had ridden up to an indecently high point. More indecent than even Joe could imagine. "It's much too hot for pantyhose. And if you must know, I'm not wearing anything under this dress. I hate panty lines and . . . well, it's just not a dress made for underwear."

Joe's gaze flitted to her breasts, down her legs, then up to her face, all in the space of a heartbeat, his imagination revving into overdrive. Just then, the stoplight in front of them turned red, and he slammed on the brakes. "Dammit, Annie! You shouldn't tell a man a thing like that while he's driving. I almost crashed your new car. I could have killed us both."

"Well, you asked. And besides, how was I to know you'd be affected by what I wear or don't wear? This is our first"— she didn't want to say *date*—"outing in a very long time. If what I'm wearing offends you, I'll just—"

Pulling over to the curb in front of his sister's two-story brick house, he cut the engine and turned to face her. "It doesn't offend me. It excites me, if you want to know the truth. I haven't . . . I haven't *dated* anyone in a very long time."

"Oh," she said. "I forgot. Well, in that case I guess I'll just take your reaction as a compliment and leave it at that."

But Joe wasn't about to leave it at that. He'd become single-minded and obsessed about the fact that Annie wasn't wearing any underwear, that other men were likely to notice, and about the fact that she had a body made for sin, and he had just turned into the world's biggest sinner!

Connie opened the door and faltered momentarily when she spotted Annie at Joe's side. But she was too nice a person and too good a hostess to be unsettled for long.

Genuine warmth filled her voice. "Annie! Welcome! It's nice to see you again. I've missed you at the restaurant. Things aren't the same without you."

"You're looking radiant, Connie," she told the pregnant

woman, whose belly was softly rounded. Joe's youngest sister was a little farther along in her pregnancy than Mary, and Annie felt a twinge of envy.

Though having a child was something she tried not to think about, the one she'd miscarried was always there, in the back of her mind, in her heart. Deep down she wanted a baby.

"Hey, sis! Are we early or late? There's hardly anyone here." Joe glanced over her shoulder into the empty living room.

Mary walked up just then, wearing a big grin on her face. "Maybe they heard a former priest was coming and decided to stay away." Sidling up next to Annie, she wrapped her arm about her friend's waist, and bussed Joe on the cheek, her brow arching in speculation. " 'Bout time you two got together. I'd about given up hope."

Annie shot her friend a warning look. "Now, don't start, Mary."

"Yeah, peanut, lighten up, will you?" Joe said, though there was a big grin plastered on his face. "You'll scare Annie off, and it took all of my persuasive powers to get her to come here tonight." And a few dozen prayers.

"Come inside," Connie directed the couple. "There's plenty of wine and food. The disc jockey is still setting up, but it shouldn't be too long before we have music."

Gazing at her older brother, Connie smiled. "No one ever comes to a party on time, Joe. Except for Mom, that is. She and Pop are in the family room, helping out with the kids. Eddie got called in to the hospital, so we'll have to start without him."

"That's too bad," Annie said, grateful she wasn't married to a doctor. The hours they worked were awful, not to mention Eddie's specialty—proctology—left a lot to be desired. No way would she want to be referred to as "Mrs. Butt Doctor."

"I'm glad your mom's busy with the kids. Maybe now she won't notice my presence." Fat chance of that. There wasn't much that escaped the nosy woman's attention.

Joe's sister Connie waved off her objection. "Trust me, my mother's bark is worse than her bite. Don't worry about it."

Yeah, but Sophia was like a Great Dane and a pit bull rolled into one, Annie was tempted to point out.

"Connie's right," Mary said, though she didn't sound nearly as confident as her sister as she tugged Annie farther into the house. "Let's have a glass of wine, shall we? You look like you could use some." When Annie frowned, she added, "I'll have a glass of sparkling cider. Satisfied?"

"Is Dan here?" Annie asked.

"He's in the back room, watching some sports show." Mary's smile was indulgent. "Some party animal, huh?"

It wasn't long after that the large living room, with the massive stone fireplace and vaulted ceiling, filled with people, becoming quite crowded and noisy. Even though most of the furniture had been removed to make room for the dancing, it was still elbow-to-elbow and difficult to hear conversation over the loud music.

Eddie Falcone had a lot of friends, who apparently had no problem celebrating his birthday without him.

The buffet table was loaded with all kinds of delicious-smelling Italian dishes; garlic and oregano perfumed the air with their pungent aroma. Many Annie recognized as Marco's signature dishes; Sophia, who was an excellent cook in her own right, had furnished some of the others.

"Mmmm. These deviled eggs are to die for," she told Joe. "Do you know who made them? I'd love to get the recipe." Now that she had finally learned to cook, thanks to Marco's not-so-patient tutoring, she was actually enjoying the process.

She licked her fingers, one by one, and Joe's stomach knotted into a tight little ball. "Connie made 'em. They're her specialty. She feels a bit overshadowed with her cooking, because of my mom and Mary, but she's a very good cook.

"Here," he handed her a small plate filled with dumplings, "try one of these. My sister made them, and they're very tasty. I think she calls it a knish, or something like that."

Staring at the small potato dumplings, Annie burst out laughing, holding her sides to keep from doubling over.

"What's so funny?"

"What you've just handed me are called knishes. *Knish* is the Yiddish term for . . ." she lowered her voice, and he bent down to listen, "vagina."

At first he thought she was kidding, but when her expression remained sober, his cheeks stained a deep crimson. "Oh."

"It's an easy mistake to make if you're not Jewish. My aunt Lola found that out the hard way at a party my parents gave for Sid's rabbi. She went up to the man holding a plate of the dumplings and asked him, pretty as you please, if he'd like to taste her knish. My father overheard the comment and rushed over, trying to explain to the shocked rabbi that Lola was Italian, and didn't know what she was talking about. But the poor man was out the door and halfway down the street by then."

Joe threw back his head and laughed, and the sound sent shivers of awareness slithering down Annie's spine, like hot fudge over ice cream. He looked good enough to eat, and Annie's hunger was building.

"Shall we get something to drink? I think I can use a little fortification after making such a stupid mistake," he said, and she was only too happy to agree. Enough alcohol would dull her senses, which were presently in an over-heated, overload mode.

Two hours and many glasses of wine later, Annie was feeling no pain. In fact, she was feeling quite extraordinary, which was why, when Sophia bustled in after putting her grandchildren to bed, Annie hardly took notice.

Unfortunately, Joe's mother locked on to her with the accuracy of a stealth bomber. "Did you come here with my son?" She crossed her arms over her ample chest, obviously prepared to do battle.

Annie saw no reason to lie. "Yes. I'm enjoying the party very much. How about you?" If Sophia had been enjoying herself, it didn't show by the pinched expression she presented. A clam had more animation.

Her eyes narrowed to match her lips. "My son will never marry you, Annie Goldman. He finds you exciting, because you are a dangerous woman. You lured him away from the church, from God, as Eve did to Adam, but he'll come to his senses soon enough. Joe needs to find a nice Italian girl, someone more like himself. You are too fast for my son."

"On the contrary, Mom, I think Annie is just right for me," Joe said, stepping between the two women, and wrapping his arm about Annie's waist in proprietary fashion. "And despite what you choose to believe, she didn't lure me away from anything. I'm old enough to make my own decisions." The look he shot his mother was border-line lethal, his voice dripping ice. "Don't presume to speak for me again in the future. I won't stand for it. Do you understand?"

"But, Joe!" Sophia looked confused and hurt that her son would speak to her in such a fashion. As an Italian mother, she had license to interfere, like James Bond had license to kill. When Sophia took aim and fired her best shot, she usually hit her target. This time, however, the ammunition exploded in her face. "Surely you cannot be serious about—"

"That's enough! I won't have you butting into my business or insulting my friends, especially someone I care about."

Someone I care about. For Joe to admit such a thing to his mother . . . Could it be true? Did he really love her, as he professed? She found it hard to believe that any man, including Joe, would spend fifteen years pining over her.

Though hadn't she spent that long pining over him?

"It's all right, Joe," she said, trying to keep peace be-tween mother and son, though she had no idea why. Sophia wasn't likely to appreciate her efforts. "I'm sure your mother didn't mean anything by her comments."

His mother cast her a disparaging look, gave a loud har-rumph, turned on her heel, and stomped off in the opposite direction, muttering comments about ungrateful children who didn't listen to their mothers.

Pain and disgust pinched Joe's features. "I'm sorry, Annie. My mother can be such a—"

She squeezed his arm. "Sophia's had you all to herself for a long time, Joe. She's still not used to the idea that you left the church. And you know your mother and I have never seen eye to eye on anything, so it's easy for her to blame me for things she doesn't understand. I don't mind."

"Well, I do. No one is going to talk to you like that, especially a member of my own family." He intended to have a talk with his mother, get a few things straightened out. He would not allow her to interfere in his life, the way she had interfered in his sisters'. Nothing would come between him and Annie again. Not his mother, and certainly not his own stupidity.

"Don't start a feud over it. It's not worth it. They're your family and are entitled to their opinion."

Clasping her hand in his, he pulled her into the crowd of dancing couples. "Let's dance. That's what we came here for, to enjoy ourselves, right?"

"Really?" She swallowed her smile. "And here I thought we came to discuss Tess Romano. Or was that just a ploy to get me to go out with you?"

He flicked the end of her nose and grinned, "Guilty as charged. I'd much rather hold you in my arms and dance than talk business." To demonstrate, he pulled her close, enveloping her in his embrace. "Unchained Melody" played on, and Bill Medley's deep, soothing voice sang of hunger, and touching, and long, lonely time.

Annie soon forgot about everything but the man who was holding her tight. The man who was worming his way back into her heart. The man she had never quite fallen out of love with.

Annie had had way too much to drink and she knew it. She was still hopelessly in love with Joe and didn't know what, if anything, she could do about it. She'd began imbibing more than she should, hoping the liquor would bolster her immune system and make her somehow resistant to his powerful allure.

It hadn't.

She wanted Joe in the most elemental way a woman wanted a man. But based on past experience, and the painful lessons she had learned, Annie was doing everything in her power to resist her natural inclinations.

"I think you've had a bit too much to drink, babe," Joe said, dropping her car keys back into his pocket. "I'll make some coffee. I don't want you driving home in this condition. In fact, you may as well spend the night here."

Even through her alcohol-fogged brain she was horrified by the suggestion. Spend the night with Joe? That didn't seem like a real smart idea, not with the amorous way she was feeling. "No! I'm fine." She shook her head, then wished she hadn't. "I just have a slight headache." If one could call a banging kettledrum slight. "Make the coffee. I'll be all right. I just need a good dose of caffeine."

Joe was intoxicated, too. But not by alcohol. Annie's nearness made him drunk with love. He needed her, wanted her, but he wasn't the type of guy who took advantage of an inebriated woman. He went into the kitchen and made a full pot of coffee, extra strong, though what he really needed to take off the edge was an ice-cold shower.

When he returned, Annie was sprawled on the couch, feet propped up on the coffee table, head resting against the back of the sofa. She made an enticing picture. But he was in this for the long haul, not just a one-night stand.

"Here's the coffee," he said, placing the tray down on the table and pouring her a cup. She didn't move a muscle. "Drink this," he ordered, sitting down next to her.

"You're so sweet to take care of me like this, Joseph."

Annie's hand settled on his thigh, and he sucked in his breath, keeping a close watch on those inquisitive fingers.

"You've always been considerate. When you're not being a bastard, you're really a very nice man."

He couldn't help but smile. "I think you're drunk and need some coffee. It'll help sober you up."

"I don't want to sober up. I like feeling the way I do." She squeezed his leg. "I feel tingly, tingly all over. Do you?"

"Annie . . ." He clasped her hand when it made a move toward his crotch and brought it to his mouth for a kiss. "I always feel tingly when I'm around you, but now is not the right time for any of that. I won't take advantage of your condition."

Suddenly she turned, wrapping her arms about his neck, and pressing her body into his. Her nipples were rock hard; he could feel them stabbing into his chest. "Kiss me, Joe. Kiss me like you used to. I always loved it when you kissed me senseless."

Gently he tried to disengage her arms. "Annie. Sweet, sweet, Annie. You're killing me. We've got to stop before things get out of hand." He had fifteen years worth of love and lust to share with this woman. But now was not the time. Not when she was so vulnerable.

When they finally came together he wanted her to be one hundred percent willing and two hundred percent aware of with whom she was making love. He'd waited this long for Annie; he could wait a little longer. He loved her with all his heart and soul, and he wanted their time together to be perfect.

"Kiss me. Just one kiss and then I'll behave."

Gazing into blue eyes dark with passion, he felt himself being pulled under. "Promise? You'll stop after one?"

She nodded. "Promise."

Taking her head between his hands, he lowered his mouth to hers, and at the first touch of his lips meeting hers, Joe knew he'd come home.

Did Annie feel it, too? This sweet familiarity, the feeling that even though so much time had passed, they had never really been apart.

Parting her lips with the tip of his tongue, he delved in. Their tongues mated furiously, thoroughly, sending shock waves of desire between and through them.

Fifteen years of pent-up desire was transmitted in that kiss, and Annie felt it down to her toes. And certain other places! "Mmmm. You always were a good kisser, Joe." She gazed into his eyes and heaved a deep sigh of longing. "Just one more, for old time's sake."

Joe was weakening; he couldn't take much more. "No! I . . ."

Annie became the aggressor, straddling his lap, and he became instantly aware that the only thing between their bodies was his good intentions and the thin fabric of his clothes. "Kiss me, Joe. I need you to kiss me."

"God, Annie!" But he couldn't resist when her tongue was doing wonderful things to his mouth, and her fingers were inching beneath his shirt to explore the soft mat of hair on his chest.

Reaching down, he smoothed his hands over her buttocks, hearing her deep moan of satisfaction. She wiggled against his erection, making it clear what she wanted.

"Take off your clothes. You're wearing too many clothes."

"Annie," he soothed. "I don't think—"

"Don't think. Just act! I need you, Joe."

Easing her down onto the sofa, he lowered his head to

her breasts, nibbling the hardened nipples through the stretchy fabric, while his hands made magic.

Floating in a wonderful cloud of pure pleasure, Annie was on the brink of obtaining the ultimate fulfillment, when Joe's romantic whispers finally penetrated the sensual haze surrounding her. She stiffened in mortification when she realized what she was allowing him to do.

Suddenly stone sober, and aware of everything that was happening, Annie knew damn well who was to blame. And it wasn't Joe. "Stop!" she said, pushing against his chest. "Please, stop!"

The two most difficult words she had ever spoken and Joe had ever heard came crashing down on them like a thunderous rock-slide. He stopped at once, rolling off of Annie, and turning his back to allow her some privacy while she straightened her dress.

Joe was breathing as hard as she, his face flushed, as he ran impatient fingers through his sweat-dampened hair.

"Oh, God! I've got to get out of here." Annie searched the floor for her shoes, totally mortified by what had just happened. What *she* had allowed to happen. My God! She had begged for it, begged for Joe to kiss her, touch her.

And Annie never begged. Certainly not for sex!

How could she ever face him again?

Handing Annie the spiked heels he found beneath the sofa, Joe wondered fleetingly how anyone could walk on such spindly shoes. "Don't be embarrassed, babe. I'm not."

"Of course you're not. You're not the one who made a complete fool of himself. That was me."

"You didn't do anything wrong. What happened would have happened sooner or later. You know that."

"That's debatable," she said, wishing the floor would open up and swallow her whole. Joe was being too nice about everything. Damn him! "I'm sorry. I drank too much and got carried away. You shouldn't put any meaning into what happened here tonight."

God! What if he thought . . . Don't go there now, Annie.

His smile was achingly sweet as he reached out to caress her cheek. "You just don't get it, do you, Annie? Tonight doesn't change anything for me. I—"

"Don't say it!" She shook her head adamantly. "Don't say another word. I've got to go home." She held out her hand, palm up. "I need my car keys, please."

"Are you sure you're okay to drive? If you're not, I can drive you home, or you can spend the night here. I'll sleep on the couch."

"I'm fine. I just need to get home." Home to safety, sensibility, and sleep, endless sleep.

"May I kiss you good night?"

She almost sobbed. "I don't think that's a very good idea." It was a very bad idea, actually, because they would most likely end up in bed. And sleep was the furthest thing from either of their minds at the moment!

"Thanks for taking me to the party. I—" Annie rushed out the door before she could finish. But then, there wasn't anything left for her to say.

Joe watched her go, a bemused expression on his face. His groin was throbbing like a son of a bitch, his blood pumping through his veins like a raging geyser, and he'd never felt happier in his life.

Whether she knew it or not, whether she would ever admit it or not, Annie was still in love with him. And it gave him a definite advantage.

Joe was not the kind of man to use seduction and games to win a woman over. But with Annie he was going to pull out all the stops. He would win her back. Nothing or no one would stop him.

And as everyone knew, he took his vows very seriously.

ELEVEN

*"If one person tells you
that you have an ass's ears,
take no notice.
Should two tell you so, procure a saddle."*

"Hey, you two doing the dirty, or what?"

With only a cursory glance at the two new arrivals standing in the foyer of her town house, Annie headed straight for the kitchen and coffeepot without saying a word.

First things first. And caffeine ranked heads and shoulders above fresh-mouthed teenage girls and mortified ex-priests.

Of course, Annie had far more reasons to be mortified than did Joe after what had happened last evening, but she was nowhere near being able to deal with that yet.

She had spent a sleepless, frustrating night lying in her cold bed and wondering why she had lost control. She never lost control. Control was her middle name.

Returning a few minutes later, she found Joe and a sullen Tess Romano still standing in the same spot where she'd left them. Not far away was her cousin, holding up the wall and looking tired and confused, as only Donna could. Dragging herself out of bed to answer the doorbell had been a major feat for the woman. She rarely emerged from her bedroom until noon, and then it was usually under protest.

"You shouldn't walk around with your ass hanging out

like that," Tess said, commenting on Annie's current state of undress. She wore a ragged gray University of Maryland T-shirt over a black teddy, and ancient denim cutoffs, which covered her ass, and then some. "Joe here's gonna get himself a big ol' hard-on if—"

Joe's large hand came down to clamp over the girl's even bigger mouth. "Sorry," he apologized. "Tess doesn't think before she speaks." The girl squirmed in his grasp, and he finally let loose, but not without shooting her a warning look.

"Hey, no need to get physical!" Tess turned her attention on Donna, who remained propped against the wall, still half asleep. "Who's the creature with the big, ugly hair? Jesus! Red ain't your color, lady. I haven't seen hair that ugly since my mom made me watch reruns of *The Golden Girls*."

Suddenly awake, Donna's eyes popped open, then narrowed. "Why, you . . ."

Annie bit the inside of her cheek to keep from laughing. Unless she missed her guess, Cousin Donna would be packed and ready to go before dinnertime. "Donna, I'd like you to meet Tess Romano. She's going to be working part-time at the store and staying here with us, for the time being."

Horrified, Donna covered her mouth, as if to hold back the bile that rose suddenly to her throat. "I've got to share my room with that foul-mouthed little—"

"Hey! I didn't ask to come here, lady, so don't start raggin' on me." Tess turned to Joe. "Come on. I'm not wanted here. Let's split."

"This is my cousin, Donna Wiseman," Annie said, purposely ignoring the girl's comment about leaving. She was more concerned with the resignation she heard in Tess Romano's voice, the sadness reflected in her eyes, despite her show of bravado.

She'd met many girls like Tess while involved with social services. Too many unloved, underappreciated souls who were lost, and she'd lost the strength, the capacity to guide them.

Annie had never considered herself a quitter, but she had finally come to the realization that the change she'd hoped to effect in the system wasn't going to happen in her lifetime. Maybe fear did undermine good intentions, as Joe had said. It was something for her to think about.

"Donna's not used to sharing, so don't pay her any attention," she told Tess. "You're welcome to stay here, as long as you play by my rules."

What those rules were, Annie had no idea—she didn't live by many hard and fast ones herself—but she was sure she could come up with something to suit a teenager. Sid had rules for every occasion—not that she'd ever obeyed any of them—and she could borrow some of his, if need be, making it up as she went along.

"Tess, remember what we talked about?" Joe cautioned the young woman. "I expect you to get along and listen to Annie. She'll be your temporary guardian, so you're to do what she says. Do I make myself clear?"

The girl shrugged, clearly unhappy about the recent turn of events. Annie couldn't blame her. It wasn't easy being dumped—or dumped on, for that matter. And she suspected that Tess had been dumped on a lot during the short span of her life.

Annie could relate, which was why, even though she loved Joe, she intended to keep that wall she'd erected around her heart firmly in place.

Joe had already filled her in on Tess's so-called family life with alcoholic parents. Listening to some of what she had endured, Annie had felt even more grateful for the loving home she'd had while growing up. Of course, at the time she hadn't really appreciated it. What teenager did? But now as an adult she could see that Sid and Gina, for all their quirks, squabbles, and odd ways, had been, and still were, heads above many other parents.

"Yeah. I guess," the girl replied reluctantly.

"Good. Then I'll leave all of you to get acquainted. I'll call you later, Annie, to see if you need anything."

Joe flashed a rakish smile that said more clearly than words that he remembered every detail of their night together, and seemed inordinately pleased about the whole turn of events. Annie's face flushed an uncharacteristic red, and her heart began beating a John Philip Sousa march.

Damn you, Joe, for making me want you again!

"Man, is he hot for you!" Tess told Annie after Joe had shut the door behind him. "I thought for sure he was gonna jump your bones right there in front of us."

"What a horrid child!" Donna said, plopping down on the sofa, and casting the girl an evil look that would have made Buffy the Vampire Slayer proud. "I don't know what I've done to deserve this."

Ignoring her cousin's oh-woe-is-me attitude, Annie decided not to take issue or overreact to Tess's too-accurate-for-comfort observations. Her own vast experience with trying to annoy adults told her that Tess wanted to get a rise out of her. She decided that rather than criticize or rebuke, she would employ other methods to bring the girl around.

"Well, I am pretty irresistible, after all," she said, trying to keep a straight face. "Put me in a room with a man for five

minutes and I'll have him drooling and begging at my feet."
Tess's jaw unhinged, then realizing she'd just been had, the
corners of her mouth lifted.

"I can see that happening. Your hair's really cool, and
you're pretty hot, for an older woman. Are your boobs real?"

Not the least bit offended, Annie smiled and wrapped an
arm about Tess's shoulders, relieved when she didn't pull
away. The girl needed love and attention, and Annie had no
problem providing that. A little TLC would go a long way
with a child like Tess. "Very. Come on. Let's go make
breakfast. I'm starving. Do you like waffles?"

Donna stared at her cousin as if she'd lost her mind, then
launched herself off the sofa, rushing forward, arms akimbo,
and pink peignoir flying behind like Superman's cape. "You
can't be serious about letting this juvenile delinquent stay
here! She's liable to kill us both in our beds while we sleep.
You know I need a full eight hours, and I won't be able to
sleep a wink with her in the house."

Tess's eyes narrowed at the self-centered woman. "I'll
take you out first, Miss Wiseass, so I don't have to listen to
your big crybaby mouth." Her eyes fell to Donna's feet.
"Where'd you get those shoes? They're totally gross."

Donna's hands balled into fists, as if she was ready to
strike someone. Of course, she would never actually hit
anyone, because it might damage her perfectly manicured
nails, which she had done every week at the salon, along
with her perfectly coiffed hair.

"These are not shoes." She glanced down at the pink satin slippers trimmed with white ostrich feathers. "They're
mules, for your information. Very expensive and very chic.

"And how dare you speak to me like that, you, you—"
she threw her hands in the air "—bad person!"

"Mules for a Wise*ass*. That fits."

And so it began. . . .

Sid stared first at the new part-time employee, then at his daughter, both of whom sported multiple earrings in each of their ears, and shook his head in disgust. "What's the matter, one hole in your ear is not enough? You want to look like a pincushion? I don't like this new fashion. Ears are for listening, not for poking holes."

He belched. "I got gas. Are you happy now that you gave your father heartburn?" he asked Annie.

"Hey, Mr. Goldman!" Tess said, smiling at the older man, whom she'd taken an immediate liking to. "You should really think about fixing up this place. No offense, but it's pretty lame. I don't think any of my friends would shop here."

He arched a brow. "And that's a bad thing? I got enough trouble without attracting teenyboppers. I don't want bubble gum all over the merchandise and floor. That I can do without, Miss Smarty Pants." His nickname for Tess. Sid had taken one look at the girl and had seen her potential. She reminded him of Annie. Smart, but not a good dresser.

"Annie told me you were trying to get more business," the girl said with a shrug. "No skin off my teeth."

"Now everyone's a critic." Sid turned to find his daughter smiling. "I see you've been brainwashing the help."

"No need to, Pop," Annie said. "Tess can see for herself how outdated Goldman's is. She agrees that we need to make some changes. We spent most of last week trying to come up with ways to do that."

They actually worked well together as a team. Once Tess figured out that Annie wasn't buying into her hard-ass,

I-don't-give-a-shit routine, which was fairly similar to Annie's own, she began to soften a bit. Tess had never had a sister, and, except for Mary, who was the closest thing she had to one, neither had Annie, and that was as good a description of their present relationship as any.

The young woman hadn't opened up to Annie as yet about her parents, the life she'd lived before coming to stay with her, but Annie felt it was just a matter of time before she did.

Something her parents had always been successful at was keeping the lines of communication open, and Annie intended to do her best to follow their example.

Sid grew immediately suspicious about the changes Annie mentioned. "No more bikinis! Or that skimpy underwear you bought. Disgraceful! Old man Moressi almost had a heart attack when he saw what we were selling. He thought they were slingshots and was going to buy one for his grandson."

Annie swallowed her smile. "That skimpy underwear, as you call it, has completely sold out. Or haven't you noticed?" His eyes widened in surprise, and she added, "The ladies who shop here might be old, but they're not dead. And the men don't seem to mind seeing their wives or lady friends in something other than cotton underpants.

"Benny Buffano just purchased a black lace teddy for Mrs. Foragi. Of course, for his wife, he bought white cotton briefs." The undertaker and Joe's landlady had been having an on-again, off-again affair for years. Everyone in Little Italy knew about it, including Mrs. Buffano, who periodically packed her bags and went to New York to visit her children.

Donatella Foragi had once bragged that she and Benny

had had sex in the back of the undertaker's hearse, along-side the dead bodies, which only served to make Annie realize that they weren't the only "stiff" things present.

Sid clutched his chest. "Don't tell me any more. I'm tasting acid."

"Underwear should serve many purposes," Annie pointed out, remembering that she had said the very same thing to Mary before her first date with Dan. Of course, at the time her friend had looked like a poster child for Playtex.

"You could get a serious injury from wearing those thong things," Sid replied. "I don't want your mother buying any. Gina's got enough problems. Next thing you know, she'll be wanting to visit Mary's brother-in-law, the proctologist."

"You know what they call a Jamaican proctologist, Pop?" Sid shook his head. "Pokémon."

His lips twitched. "Very funny. Now you're a comedienne."

The two females exchanged grins, then Annie said, "Getting back to the changes we intend to make, Tess and I are thinking about putting up a Web site. You know, on the Internet? We could take orders through our Web page, then ship the merchandise out. I think it would increase sales and give us more visibility in the community. A lot of people shop online now. It's not just a fad anymore."

Sid rubbed his chin contemplatively, knowing Annie spoke the truth. But she could tell he wasn't sure if he wanted to enter the new millennium; the old one was much more comfortable, less complicated, and more to his liking. "What's this going to cost me? I'm not made of money, you know."

"I'll do it for free, Mr. Goldman," Tess volunteered, eager to please Sid, though he was gruff and set in his ways. But he had been kind and caring to the troubled teen, always asking if she needed money or candy bars, and Annie suspected that no one had been kind to Tess in a very long time.

"I learned how to do Web-site design in high school. But I'll need a computer and the software to go with it."

"Ha! I knew there was a catch."

"The store should have a computerized system anyway, Pop," Annie reasoned. "The way we've been working is antiquated. If we had a computer, we could track our inventory and sales. I bet it would cut down on overordering or purchasing the wrong type of merchandise." Annie knew that if ideas were presented in such a way that could save her father money, he was always more receptive to them.

Reaching into his pants pocket, Sid withdrew a small container of chewable Maalox and popped a few. "I'll look into it. But no promises."

"Come on outside, Mr. Goldman, and see what Annie and I are working on." Tess's face glowed with pleasure and a sense of belonging. "The display window is starting to look really cool."

"When did you do it? It looked the same as it always did this morning when I came in."

"We've been working on it all day, Pop. We wanted it to be a surprise."

Sid hated surprises, like Bubbeh pissing on his shoes. Who in their right mind named a dog Bubbeh, for chrissake? he asked Annie at least once a day.

Staring in shock at the naked mannequins, Sid's eyes

widened and his mouth fell open. "Who knew dummies had breasts? Since when do they have breasts?" He stepped closer to the window to get a better look, not bothering to mention that they had nipples, too.

Amused by her father's reaction, Annie replied, "The ones they sell now are anatomically correct, including the males." His eyes widened even farther. "I ordered a few for the store. Don't worry, they won't remain naked for long. I intend to dress them in something very chic."

"Chic sounds expensive. And I don't want those male and female dummies too close together. This is a respectable place."

"Designer labels will cost more to stock. But they will also bring in more profit. I've done my homework; the markup on the merchandise is incredible."

"What's with the fall leaves? I'm dying here from the heat and humidity, and you're giving me leaves."

Baltimore could be brutal during the summer months, and having fake trees with autumn leaves didn't make it any cooler, but they were pretty. Sid still liked the Vietnam poster, and wanted to know where they had put the bowling trophy, but Annie had no intention of telling him. It was safe was all she would say when he asked.

"Time to start pushing the fall merchandise," she told him. "People will be thinking 'Back to School' before you know it. It would be nice to lure some of the Inner Harbor shoppers here. I'm going to put some ads in the paper, and Tess and I have been toying with the idea of having a fashion show, though we haven't worked out the details as yet."

"A fashion show? Not with those half-naked models like you see on TV?" He threw his hands up in the air. "This is a respectable place. I got a reputation in the community."

"Don't worry, Pop. It'll all be done very tastefully when the time comes."

"Is this a private viewing, or can anyone join in?" Joe sauntered up to stare over Tess's shoulder at the window. "Made a few changes, I see. Very nice." He flashed Annie a smile that said he knew she'd been avoiding him. She frowned before looking away.

"Sure, Joe. Come look at the naked women. My daughter's brought nudity to Goldman's. Forty years we had no nudity, now we got nudity. It's a shame and a disgrace.

"*Oy!* I gotta go get some lunch. I'm starting to feel nauseous."

"Yeah, naked boobs sometimes do that to men, Mr. Goldman," Tess told the horrified man, whose face crimsoned instantly.

"You remind me of someone, you know that, Miss Smarty Pants?" he said to Tess, before turning to stare at his daughter accusingly, then stalking off down the street.

"Guess I'll go grab some lunch, too, Annie, if that's okay with you," the younger girl said. "Donna's making me meet her at Santini's for lunch. She's afraid to go there by herself."

Annie's brows drew together. "Why? Lou's a very nice man."

"I think maybe she had a run-in with his mother last week. The crybaby's paying me five bucks to meet her, so I thought I'd go and earn the extra cash. Though I should have charged her more, since she's such a pain in the butt to hang out with."

"Remember what we talked about, Tess," Joe said patiently. "Respect goes both ways in a relationship."

"Oh, man! Not another lecture. Annie says you preach so much because you used to be a priest."

"Tess and Donna tolerate each other, Joe," Annie explained. "It's the best we can expect for now." The young girl flashed a grateful smile, and Annie winked back, waving Tess on her way.

"Don't be late coming back. We still have to finish the window."

"I won't, Annie Fannie. See ya."

"Annie Fannie?" Joe arched a brow and smiled. "Sounds like you and Tess are bonding. I'm happy to see that. I'm still a bit bothered by her attitude toward adults, though I think that will improve over time and with more counseling."

"You need to tread lightly with her, Joe. If you push Tess too hard, you'll just cause her to rebel even more. I'm speaking from experience here. If you recall, I was something of a brat while growing up."

He nodded, and there was a definite twinkle in his eye. "I recall you were good at pushing buttons and getting yourself into trouble. Which is why I wanted you to be the one to help Tess. I think she can relate better to you. And I'm afraid that I come across as preachy. Hard habit to break."

"Tess and Donna will find their own way. Besides, my cousin isn't the easiest person to get along with." Understatement alert!

"Did you come by here to discuss Tess, or was there another reason?" Annie asked.

He followed her into the store. "I need to buy a new suit, some pants, a few shirts. Thought you might be able to help me out."

"Henry usually waits on the male customers, but he's off today. My dad will be back soon, though, if you want to wait."

Looking about, Joe discovered that there wasn't another customer in the store. "I'd like you to assist me."

"I . . ." She clutched the edge of the counter, not wanting to indulge in such an intimate act. Picking out clothing for a man was . . . well, wifely.

"What's the matter?" His smile was full of challenge. "You're not afraid to help me because of what happened last week, are you?"

"Of course not! Don't be ridiculous." She had no intention of allowing him to get the best of her, even if she had to lie through her teeth. Last week had changed things, even if she hadn't wanted them to.

"That's good. Shall we get started?"

Like a lamb to slaughter, she led him to the rack of men's suits. "What color did you have in mind?" she asked, keeping her voice and demeanor very professional.

"I'm partial to blue." He gazed into her eyes, drowning in their intensity.

"Blue?" she asked dumbly, as if he were speaking a foreign language. *Concentrate, Annie!* "I assume you mean navy blue. What size suit do you wear?"

"I'm not sure. It's been a while since I've bought anything new."

She removed a tape measure from her skirt pocket. "Turn around. I'm guessing you're a forty-four long. But we'd better make sure." She brought the tape to his shoulders and stretched it taut across the impressive width, then down the length of his arm.

"If you're buying a suit, you'll probably need to have the pants altered. The waist is going to be way too big." Tape in hand, she wrapped her arms about his midsection, resisting the urge to hug him. Joe was immensely huggable.

"I was right. You've a thirty-four waist, and the pants on a forty-four suit are much bigger. Weight lifting has made your thighs and biceps more muscular, but it hasn't increased your waistline."

"You sound pretty knowledgeable." He was impressed that she'd learned so much in such a short time, but he wasn't surprised. Annie was much too smart for her own good.

"I'm a fast learner, and Sid is a slave driver." The pride she saw reflected in his eyes made her insides go mushy. "You'd better go try on the suit. If you like it, we'll need to mark it for the tailor, so he can make the necessary alterations. The pants don't come cuffed."

Joe grinned at the way her cheeks filled with color. It took a lot to make Annie blush. "Guess you'll have to measure them, then, won't you?"

Annie bit the inside of her cheek, dreading the prospect. "Guess you'd better hope I'm not holding a pair of scissors in my hand when I do."

Joe was still chuckling when he came out of the dressing room. "Where should I stand?"

She was tempted to tell him exactly where he could go, but she didn't. Instead, Annie pointed to the raised platform in front of the triple mirrors. "Stand still with your legs slightly spread."

"You're giving me ideas, babe."

Gasping aloud, Annie nearly dropped the chalk she was holding. "What kind of thing is that for a priest to admit? Shame on you, Joseph Russo!" But damn if her insides weren't tingling again.

"I'm no longer a priest. Just a man in need of a good . . ." he heard her sharp intake of breath, "suit."

Kneeling at Joe's feet, she pulled the tape up the inside

pant leg to his crotch, being very careful not to get too close to his more *susceptible* parts, and praying he didn't move even a fraction of an inch. "You've got a long—"

"Why, thank you!"

"Inseam," she finished, gritting her teeth. "Now behave, or I'll make you wait for my father."

"Yes, ma'am," he said, unable to keep the smile out of his voice.

She finished chalking the measurements of the pants legs and moved to the waistband, drawing the pants out with her forefinger. "You've got room enough in here for two."

"I'm game if you are. The dressing rooms are nice and cozy."

The idea of them naked together in one of the dressing rooms, taking each other's measurements, and God knew what else, sent a hot flush spreading over her entire body, as she turned to stare stupidly in their direction. She blinked several times to dispel the image. "We'd probably end up on the front page of *The Sun* if we engaged in anything so . . . so . . ."

"Delicious? Wanton? Incredibly satisfying?"

"Inappropriate. Bullfrog's probably got a video recorder hooked to each one of those rooms."

At the mention of Henry Grossman, Joe's smile faded. "Still as perverted as ever, I take it?"

"Some people never change."

"And some do, babe," he whispered, drawing Annie into his embrace and caressing her back, encouraged when she didn't resist. "Have dinner with me tonight. I've missed you."

The admission touched her, and she had missed him,

too. The distance she'd tried to put between them since that unfortunate, but stimulating, episode at his apartment hadn't worked. She thought about him every waking moment, while lying in her bed at night, eating her breakfast, taking a bath. Especially when taking a bath!

Knowing that he was within walking distance of the store was the most torturous temptation of all, because she had to restrain herself from running over to the Crisis Center and throwing herself in his arms.

She gnawed her lower lip. "I don't know . . ."

"I promise to behave myself."

"You're not the problem!" she blurted, and then wished she hadn't spoken her thoughts aloud.

He arched a dark brow. "Are you trying to tell me I'm irresistible?"

"If we're going to start seeing each other again, Joe, then we're going to have to lay down some ground rules. We're not the same people we were fifteen years ago. I'm not the rebellious, starry-eyed teen I once was, and you need to discover who you really are and what you really want

"I think we need time to rediscover the new and hopefully improved versions of Joe Russo and Annie Goldman."

"You mean, we need to become friends?"

"Yes, that's exactly what I mean. Friends, not lovers."

He could live with that. For now. "I agree. What time shall I pick you up?"

"You've got wheels?"

He smiled sheepishly. "Just the Buick." He'd purchased a slightly used, fully loaded Mustang convertible, which he'd gotten for a great price, but hadn't finished the financing on yet.

"A stroll down memory lane, huh?" She grinned. "How

about seven? That'll give me time to shower, change, and settle any squabbles between Tess and Donna before we go."

"How is life with Donna, by the way? Or shouldn't I ask?"

She grimaced. "I'm thinking of moving in with your mother. Does that answer your question?"

TWELVE

*"A person who gets used to telling lies
will always be enticed to falsehood."*

Chester's Crab House was little more than a hole in the wall, located in an old brewery in Fell's Point, overlooking the water. The Formica tables were old, the wood-planked floor less than spotless, but it had always been one of Annie's favorite places to dine out. And the rapturous look on her face, as she cracked open a steaming Maryland blue crab, seemed to indicate that some things hadn't changed. Not her passion for crabs, at any rate.

"If you looked at me the way you're looking at the crustacean, I'd be a happy man," Joe said.

"If you tasted this good, I might." Realizing what she'd just said, Annie reached for a glass of water and gulped greedily, hoping her face wasn't as red as it felt.

His grin was totally lascivious. "How do you know I don't?"

Not willing to touch that question with a ten-foot pole, she quickly changed the subject. "Thanks for bringing me here tonight. The crabs are delicious. Just like I remembered." She had been tempted to come to the restaurant many times over the years, but couldn't bring herself to do it. Not without Joe. Chester's had always been special to them. It was where they'd had their first "official" date, where Joe had taken her before the homecoming dance.

"How are your crab cakes? You haven't eaten very much of your dinner."

"I'm having too much fun watching you eat."

Pounding another crab with a wooden dowel, she cracked it open, using her fingers and nails to pick out the juicy white meat. "How are things going at the Crisis Center? Is Angela still working there?" She knew the answer, but wanted to get Joe's reaction. The pleased smile he wore made her ill.

"Angela's great with the kids. I don't know what I'd do without her. She's got a mind like a steel trap. Remembers every detail about every kid."

Annie tried not to feel jealous or spiteful, which was difficult. Angela DeNero was everything Annie was not: conventional, modest in demeanor, a success in her profession, and most of all, she was warm and friendly to Joe. They were far better suited than she and Joe were to each other, though Annie had absolutely no intention of telling him that.

"How nice. I guess you're enjoying your new position as head honcho, huh?"

"I enjoy working with the kids, and trying to make a difference in their lives, though sometimes it's frustrating. But I think I'm well suited for the job, and I intend to stick with it."

"Do you miss the priesthood?"

He ran the tines of his fork over the baked potato, making trails in the sour-cream topping, his expression thoughtful and somewhat sad. "Sometimes. I had mixed feelings about leaving. I'd devoted so much of my life to the church, hoped I would make a difference in the lives of those I touched, but my heart was never fully engaged. I wasn't giving all of myself, and that wasn't fair to the church, God, or my parishioners.

"I know now that I made the right decision. The priesthood couldn't give me the one thing I wanted above all else."

Crab juice dribbled down Annie's chin, and she dabbed at it with a red-checked napkin. If he'd only come to that realization years ago, they might have had a chance to . . . *Don't go there, Annie. It's over.* But was it?

Hiding behind a flip rejoinder, she asked, "Which is what, sex?"

"You."

Choking on the sliver of crabmeat she'd just swallowed, she reached for her water glass again. "Are you trying to kill me, or what? You shouldn't say stuff like that while I'm eating." But his response had been worth dying for.

"Why not? It's true. I made a mistake all those years ago. If I could go back, I'd change every decision, every moment since the death of our child."

"So you've said. But it's too late to go back. We can only go forward."

A kernel of hope sprouted in his chest, and he leaned forward. "Are you saying you want to? Go forward, I mean."

She sighed. "I'm saying . . . I don't know. Maybe."

"Well, that's a start." He decided not to push. "So tell me, how do you like working at Goldman's? Are you and your dad getting along okay?"

"I like it much more than I thought I would. I've got a purpose in life now—trying to bring the store into the twenty-first century. So far I'm enjoying myself, though I can't say my dad is all that enthusiastic about the changes

I'm making. He has a hard time dealing with modernization. But knowing I have a stake in the business makes me determined to win him over to my way of thinking."

"Tess seems to be doing much better. She seems happier, much more settled, since moving in with you," Joe said. "She talks nonstop about you, your father, and the store, during our counseling sessions."

Annie smiled, happy she'd made a difference in the girl's life. "Tess has been a tremendous help at the store. She's up on all the latest fashion crazes, and doesn't mind voicing her opinion, even when I don't ask for it. I enjoy having her around; we get along just great. And my parents are wild about her."

"And what about Donna? Any change there?"

She made a face. "I know you were once a priest, but let's not hope for miracles, okay? Suffice it to say, Donna and Tess barely tolerate each other. They get along about as well as Henry and I do, which is to say, not at all."

"Has Grossman been a problem? Because if he has, I want you to tell me."

"What are you going to do—beat the crap out of him, like you did when I was in high school?"

Joe smiled, remembering the time he'd come upon Henry in the high school parking lot, harassing Annie and some of her girlfriends, and how he'd blackened his eye when he'd overheard him making crude remarks to them. "Ah, the good old days. I hadn't thought about that incident in years."

"Bullfrog still makes comments. And I know I could fire him. But why bother? I can handle him. And Sid likes Henry, or tolerates him, at any rate, so . . ." She shrugged, picking up another crab, the juice dribbling over her fingers before she licked them.

Watching Annie devour the crabs was doing torturous things to Joe's mental well-being, and he was having a difficult time concentrating on their conversation. "Ah. Right. Bullfrog. I don't want that bag of wind talking to you like that. Guess I'll have to come over there and have a little talk with Henry, set him straight about a few things."

Annie laughed. "Are you trying to defend my honor, Joe? Because . . . well, that ship has sailed." She could tell he was bothered by her honesty, and added, "Although your offer is sweet, I'm perfectly capable of defending myself, both verbally and physically. I know karate, so if Bullfrog gets out of line . . . chop, chop." She made a motion with her hand. "Frog legs."

"Should I be scared?"

"Are you intending to get out of line?"

"Definitely," he replied, his sexy smile full of promise.

Distracted, Annie dropped her fork to the floor with a clang, arousing the attention of the patrons seated nearby. She'd forgotten how powerful an aphrodisiac Joe's smile was. She'd forgotten a great many things, like how considerate he could be, how interested he'd always been in what she had to say. How his kisses made her toes curl downward . . .

Wiping her hands on the napkin, she took a moment to compose herself. "Hell, yes, you should be scared, especially after promising to behave. You do recall our earlier conversation?"

"I have behaved. We made small talk over dinner. I've kept my hands above the table at all times. And I haven't had any lustful thoughts about you for at least," he glanced at his watch, "fifteen seconds. I thought I was doing pretty good."

She shook her head and smiled. "I can see that you and celibacy aren't a happy match."

"I take a lot of cold showers."

"I usually work out my frustrations with exercise." And there was also hot fudge sundaes and strawberry short-cake, when things got really difficult.

"Seems like a waste of water and energy to me. We should combine our methods of relieving tension. Not that I'm suggesting anything inappropriate, of course."

His erotic grin belied that statement, and Annie reached for the menu, squirming restlessly in her chair before signaling for the waitress. "I'm having dessert."

Joe's eyes widened. "You're kidding. How can you still be hungry after all the crabs you just polished off?"

"I just am, that's all. Suddenly I've got a humongous craving for a hot fudge sundae. Care to join me?"

Annie's cheeks were slightly flushed, her eyes too bright, and Joe smiled knowingly. "Only if we use gobs and gobs of whipped cream. I like to lick it real slow, swirl it around my tongue, and then . . ."

"Make that four scoops of vanilla, please!" Annie blurted to the waitress. "And hurry!"

Annie opened the door to her town house and turned to face Joe, who was standing on the porch, right behind her. "I had a nice time tonight. Thank you."

"Nice enough to invite me in?"

She took a moment to weigh the consequences, then said, "I guess it's time we talk."

In the living room, she took a seat on the sofa, motioning for Joe to sit in the wing chair opposite her. She needed to keep her distance, her perspective. She'd spent fifteen years angry at this man, blaming him for everything that went wrong in her life, whether justified or not. Forgiving him was not going to be easy.

"Annie . . ."

She held up her hand. "I know you're sorry for what happened between us, Joe. And I know it took a lot of courage to admit what you did was wrong. But I just can't forget the past like nothing happened. You hurt me. You said you loved me, told me we'd get married, and then you left. Do you know how that made me feel, Joe?

"I blamed myself for losing the baby. Did I eat something wrong? Did I exercise too much? Not enough? And then you left me, confirming my belief that I really must have been at fault. That somehow I had caused the child to miscarry."

Her words made him blanch. "God, Annie, I'm sorry! I never blamed you. I was devastated by what happened. I felt guilty for getting you pregnant in the first place. In my mind I had brought this down upon us and was being punished for going against God's wishes. I know it sounds stupid and archaic, but I was raised to believe in atonement for one's sins. At that point, I'd had twenty years of Catholic guilt laid upon me."

Tears trickled down Annie's face. "You abandoned me, Joe, just when I needed you the most."

"I know, and I've never stopped blaming myself for such a selfish and cowardly act."

She went on as if he hadn't spoken, as if the words she'd kept bottled inside for all these years were finally bursting out of her, like some hideous alien creature from a science fiction movie. "How could I compete with God, Joe? How could I lure you back from the arms of the church? How could I make you love me as much as you loved God? If you'd left me for another woman, maybe I would have understood, been able to fight, but . . ."

He moved to the sofa and drew her into his arms. "I love you. I've always loved you, Annie. If I could take all the hurt away, I would. But I can't. All I can try to do is make up for what I've done. Please forgive me."

"Oh, Joe, I . . ." She nestled against his chest, unable to say the words: that she loved him. It was too soon, her feelings too raw. She needed time to sort it all out.

"Tonight is a new beginning for us, Annie. I'm not asking for a commitment. Just say we can see each other, see where things lead."

She chewed her lower lip. "I don't know."

"Please, Annie. I won't screw it up this time. I promise."

"We'll take things slow? Get to know each other all over again? I don't want to make another mistake, Joe."

He nodded. "You're in charge. We'll do things your way."

She smiled through her tears. "Really? I like the sound of that."

"Good, so do I."

The following Sunday afternoon, and two days after their first "real" date, Annie decided that since Joe was having dinner with his family, she would take Gina up on her offer, and had brought Donna and Tess over to the Goldman house to eat.

The ability to experience a normal—okay, sort of normal—family life was good for Tess, who hadn't had much of one, and it gave Annie a chance to talk to her mother about her cousin, who was still driving her crazy.

Leaving Tess and Donna alone in the living room, squabbling over the remote control, Annie entered the kitchen to find her mother standing over the stove, wooden spoon in hand, stirring up a batch of chicken soup—her father's favorite. Gina often prepared several nights' worth of dinners at one time and froze what they weren't going to eat right away.

"Hey, Gina! We're here."

Bubbeh, who'd been napping in his wicker basket, rushed forward to greet her, tail wagging and yap, yap, yapping to beat the band. "Well, will you look at you, you little rug rat. You've grown so much since the last time I was here." She bent down to pick up the pup, who showed his appreciation by licking her face.

"The dog eats like a pig. He's like your father, hungry all the time." Gina kissed her daughter's cheek, then the dog's nose, before turning to the task of preparing the manicotti. She began to fill the soft tubes of dough with ricotta cheese, placing each one in a glass baking dish.

"I love manicotti!" Annie said, stomach growling. "How long before we eat?"

Her mother smiled knowingly. "Like I don't know how much you like manicotti? It will be a while before we eat, though. Your father wants to cut the grass first. He's out back with that damn electric lawn mower he bought from Frank Russo. It's supposed to mow the lawn by remote control, but it mowed my gladiolas instead." She shook her head in disgust. "That's what happens when your father tries to take the easy way out.

"So . . . are you still dating Joe?" Gina said, changing the subject quickly and catching Annie off guard. "Have you gone out with him again?"

"I had dinner with him the other night."

Gina's brow shot up. "Oh?"

"We're taking it nice and slow, so don't go giving me any ohs and ahs, okay?"

"Slow is good. Why should you rush things? How does his mother feel about the two of you dating again?"

Annie shrugged. "Sophia hates me. That won't change. And I don't know if she's heard yet that we're dating." Probably not, because a black hand hadn't been painted on her door, and she had yet to find a horse's head placed in her bed.

Gina clasped her hands together. "I'm so happy for you, Annie. You and Joe belong together. It was meant to be. All these years . . . I knew someday it would happen. You can't go against fate."

"That remains to be seen." Though Annie had to admit, things looked promising. She and Joe had done a lot of talking over the past couple of days, not only about their past, but about a great many things, and found they had a lot more in common than they'd previously thought. Besides their mutual attraction, they shared similar beliefs on social and political issues, and adored the same movies, books, and television programs. It was uncanny.

She was comfortable being with Joe, when he wasn't making her feel all nervous and tingly inside, which was most of the time. She felt like a giddy schoolgirl all over again.

"You shouldn't worry about Sophia. The woman is sick in the head. Look how she almost ruined Mary's life. Joe won't allow that to happen." She poked herself in the chest. "*I* won't allow that to happen."

Setting the dog down on the floor, Annie pulled out a chair from the table and sat, leaning toward her mother. At the moment, she had more pressing problems to discuss than Sophia Russo.

"You've got to get Donna out of my life," she told her mother, barely above a whisper. "She was only supposed to stay a week, and now I've got a permanent roommate. And I happen to like living alone." Tess didn't count, because she was only a temporary visitor, unlike Donna, who seemed to have set down taproots.

"I spoke to your aunt Lola just the other day, and she begged me to have Donna stay with you a little while longer. Lola thinks your influence is helping Donna. She's seen a change for the better in her daughter."

Uh-huh. Right! The only person it was helping was Lola, who had always been good at shirking her responsibilities. She'd dumped on Gina a number of times, which is why, Annie suspected, Lola was not Sid's favorite person.

"Donna and Tess fight all the time. Just this morning they had a huge shouting match over one of Donna's blouses that was supposedly stolen. Donna accused Tess of stealing it, which, of course, she denied. It got rather ugly."

Her mother's voice filled with concern. "So what happened? Did the blouse turn up?"

Annie made a face of disgust. "Of course it turned up. It was under Donna's bedspread. She never hangs up anything, so losing it among the linens didn't come as a big surprise to anyone, except my dear cousin. In true Donna fashion, she refused to apologize, saying that Tess had probably hidden it there just to annoy her."

"Oy!"

"Exactly. Can't you please let her live here with you, Gina? You've got the room, and the patience to deal with her. I've reached the end of my rope. And I don't think a self-absorbed, selfish woman is a very good role model for Tess."

Looking both sympathetic and apologetic at the same

time, Gina reached out and covered Annie's hand. "I wish I could, *cara,* but your father has already warned me not to make the offer. He likes peace and quiet when he comes home from work. And he holds it against Donna that she's my sister's daughter. It would create all kinds of problems for me if I went against his wishes."

"Maybe I should be talking to Pop instead of you."

"It won't do any good. His mind is made up."

And Annie knew once Sid's mind was made up, that was it. Talking to a brick wall usually had better results.

Damn Aunt Lola for pissing off her father!

"What's everyone doing in here?"

As if conjured up by their conversation, and Annie's dark thoughts, Donna appeared, entering the kitchen through the swinging door that led from the dining room. She glanced at the dog, which was now fast asleep, down at her navy-and-white spectator pumps, then stepped farther into the room, figuring it was safe for the time being.

"Nothing, dear," Gina said, not daring to look at her daughter. "Just talking. How are you? You've put on a little weight, I see. That's good. I like to see a girl who isn't afraid to eat."

Face paling, Donna looked down at herself. "Do you think so? Annie's a good cook, and I have been eating more than I should, but I don't want to get fat. My mother says men don't like women who let themselves go."

"Nina Santini tells me you've visited the butcher shop and deli a couple of times," Gina remarked, eyes brimming with speculation. "You must like their food a lot, no?"

The redhead's cheeks filled with color, and Annie smiled to herself. "I think Donna likes Lou more than the food. Isn't that right, Donna?"

"Oh, Lou Santini's handsome enough, I suppose," her cousin conceded, "in a rough, uncivilized kind of way."

Who was she kidding? Lou was very good-looking. He had biceps resembling ham shanks and a chest that made Arnold Schwarzenegger's look anemic. Lou was a weight lifter, but unlike Joe, the butcher was borderline fanatical about it.

"Handsome is as handsome does," Annie's mother said in true Forrest Gump fashion. "The important thing is that Lou's a piece of bread. And when his mother drops dead— I don't wish her ill, but she's a very unpleasant woman — he's going to be rich."

"Really?" Donna was visibly impressed.

"Nina's a miser. She never spends money unless she has to. I bet the mattresses in their apartment are loaded with cash; I don't think she trusts banks. Nina Santini's probably got the first buck she ever made. God knows she doesn't spend it on the furnishings in their apartment above the store."

"I don't think Mrs. Santini likes me very much," Donna admitted, unable to believe that such a possibility could actually exist. "When I go to the meat counter to place my order, she pushes Lou out of the way and invents something for him to do. She always waits on me herself. It's obvious she's doesn't want me talking to him. Though I can't imagine why. I've always been very pleasant."

Fawning. Ingratiating. Sickeningly sweet. Annie decided Donna should have a doll named after her: Kiss-Ass Barbie.

"The woman is controlling," Gina said. "Whoever marries Lou will be earning every penny of the money he inherits from his mother, that's for certain."

"You thinking about marrying Lou, Donna?" An intriguing idea began swimming toward the surface. If Donna married Lou . . . Hmmm. Annie may have found a way of getting her cousin out of her house and, more importantly, out of her life.

But poor Lou! He was such a nice man . . . and to stick him with Donna, the prima donna . . . Could she really do that to someone she liked? Annie smiled thoughtfully.

Glancing down at the huge, glimmering rock still adorning her left hand, Donna grew thoughtful. "I always find it best to keep my options open." Nose in the air, she turned on her heel and walked from the room.

Staring after her, Annie almost pitied her cousin. Almost, but not quite. It was time for Marjorie Morningstar to enter the real world and get a dose of reality. And Lou's mother was about as real as they came. "Nina Santini will chew her up and spit her out for dinner," she remarked, rising to stand next to Gina. "Donna's too soft to go up against Lou's mother."

Gina stared in the direction her niece had departed and smiled knowingly. "I wouldn't be too sure of that, Annie. Donna is a lot smarter than you give her credit for. And she can be charming when she puts her mind to it." Admittedly, that wasn't very often, but the girl did have her moments.

"Yeah? Well, how come she never charmed Sid, tell me that. You'd think after all these years she would have been able to win Pop over, if she's so damn charming."

"Probably for the same reason you haven't been able to charm Sophia Russo," her mother pointed out, making Annie's face flush red. "Some people are just naturally rude and nasty. I hate to say it, but your father is one of them."

"So how come you married Pop, if you think he's so nasty?"

"You should know the answer to that better than anyone, Annie *mia*. Because I love him. Can't live without him. So Sid's driving me to an early grave. So what? I'll be happy until I get there. Such is life, no?"

"So what you're telling me is that true love is a death sentence?"

Great. Wonderful. Just what I wanted to hear.

Gina shrugged. "I guess you could say that. But there's a lot of good that happens before you die. A lot of tears and joy and happiness. You take the good with the bad. And if you're lucky, it all works out."

Smiling with a great deal of indulgence, Annie wrapped her arms about her mother and hugged. Gina's view of life was honest and simplistic; she admired her for that. "I hope you never become a marriage counselor, Gina. The divorce rate is high enough."

"What? What did I say?"

While Annie digested her mother's cooking and sage advice, Joe was fighting the urge to scream at Sophia, stomp out of the house, and disappear from the face of the earth. The interfering woman had invited Angela DeNero to dinner without first consulting him.

"Isn't it nice that Angela could come to dinner today, Joe?" Sophia said. "She's Italian, you know? A good Catholic girl." As far as Sophia was concerned, that was better than the *Good Housekeeping* seal of approval.

His mother's delighted mission-accomplished smile said all Joe needed to know—Angela DeNero had been chosen as *the* bridal candidate.

Swallowing his anger, he said, "Of course I know. Angela and I work together. We're *friends*." He emphasized the word. "And with a name like DeNero, I don't think she's going to be mistaken for a German."

"That'sa good, because we don't like Nazis around here." Grandma Flora explained to the startled guest, "Joe's been dating a Jew, and Sophia doesn't like it. She's gotta poison in her heart, my daughter-in-law. Such a burden on an old woman. I won't last much longer, living in the same house with her. And her cooking is not so good."

Flashing her mother-in-law a warning look, Sophia smiled apologetically at the newcomer, who was looking rather perplexed by the whole conversation. "Don't mind Flora. She's a little . . ." she lowered her voice, twirling her finger round and round her ear, "crazy in the head, if you know what I mean. I like everybody. Okay, so I'm not too crazy about the Nazis, or most of those Irish people, but I'm fine with just about everyone else. And you're Italian, so you shouldn't worry. Just forget what the old woman said."

Grandma Flora harrumphed loudly.

Picking up his wineglass, Joe downed the ruby liquid in one gulp, then smiled apologetically at Angela, who shrugged, as if to say: *Don't worry. It doesn't matter. I understand.*

"Why don't you show Angela around the neighborhood, Joe? We've got a little while before dinner. I'm sure she'd like to stretch her legs and work up an appetite. And it's a beautiful day. The sun is shining, the birds are singing. . . ."

What was there to see in the neighborhood, besides concrete sidewalks, out-of-date stores, a multitude of restaurants, and other ugly houses like his parents'? Joe wanted to ask, but didn't. The sun was shining, but there was close to one hundred percent humidity, making the air oppressive. The birds were singing, true, but they were also dive-bombing everyone who walked down the sidewalk, and had barely missed Joe when he arrived.

"Would you like to go for a walk, Angela?" he asked to be polite, shooting his mother a look of his own and receiving a smug smile in return.

"I'm from a big Italian family, Joe," Angela said once they were standing outside on the sidewalk and out of earshot. "Your mother's motives are perfectly clear, but don't worry, I've got a steady boyfriend up in Boston, so her matchmaking efforts won't get very far."

Joe almost breathed a sigh of relief, but knew Sophia would never be dissuaded by something as insignificant as Angela having a boyfriend.

They strolled down the street as they talked, looking in the storefront windows, smiling and waving at neighbors, most of whom Joe had known his whole life. "My mother doesn't approve of Annie," he confided. "She's trying to set me up with someone she feels is more suitable, namely you."

"Well, I'm flattered. But what's she got against Annie Goldman? She seems like a lovely young woman. And it's obvious you care about her."

"It is?" Joe smiled ruefully. "I guess it is rather obvious. I've never tried to hide the fact that I'm crazy about Annie, except when I was in the priesthood."

"Guess a priest having a girlfriend wouldn't have gone over too well with the Bishop, huh?"

"Annie and I have a history. Sophia thinks she's a bad influence."

"So tell your mom to butt out. You're a grown man, and old enough to make your own decisions about your love life. For heaven's sake, Joe! Why do you put up with it?"

"I have told her, believe me. I've told her many times.

But Sophia doesn't listen. You'd have to know my mother to understand what I'm up against. She's like a tidal wave that just keeps coming and coming, until she's either drowned you or swallowed you whole.

"Don't get me wrong, I love my mom. But she's too controlling, too opinionated, too . . . Italian!"

"Then ignore her. She'll give up after a while."

"Annie said the same thing."

Angela grinned. "Smart woman, your Annie."

Taking the lawyer's hand, Joe squeezed it in thanks.

From the window, Sophia's smile broadened as she caught sight of the couple, who looked awfully cozy in her opinion. "I knew it! I knew they'd be perfect for each other."

Across the kitchen, Frank shook his head and frowned. "You should be ashamed, Sophia. Quit spying on them. First you try to run Mary's life, and now Joe's. What's the matter that you can't see the boy's in love with Annie Goldman? If you weren't so blinded by your dislike of the woman, you'd see they're perfect for each other."

Turning from the sink, Sophia stared at her husband as if he'd grown two heads. "The Goldman girl is no good for him, Frank. Everyone knows that she runs around like a *puttana*. She's wild, that one. Look how she dresses and dyes her hair all those terrible colors."

"You dye your hair," he pointed out, but she ignored the comparison.

"As his mother it's my duty to protect Joe. God put me on this earth to watch out for him."

"Joe's a grown man, not a baby anymore. Leave him alone, or you're going to lose him with your interfering ways. Wasn't it bad enough that you pushed him into becoming a priest?"

"He wanted that."

Frank snorted. "Yeah. Every young man wants to be celibate for his whole life. You can't live his life for him, Sophia, so quit trying."

"A lot you know," she insisted, ignoring her husband's warning. "Angela DeNero is perfect for him." She clasped her hands together and shook them. "A lawyer, Frank! Can you imagine? And she's Italian. Like should marry like; it's what God intended."

"*Forgetaboutit!* Your daughter just married an Irishman, and the world hasn't ended. Dan's a good guy, and Mary's lucky to have him.

"Listen to how you sound. You're obsessed with running your children's lives. It's time you stopped." He banged the flat of his hand on the Formica countertop. "I want you to stop butting in! Do you hear me?"

Sophia rarely cried, but she had tears in her eyes now. Frank rarely raised his voice, never shouted at her, but he was shouting now.

"They're all I have left, Frank," she said barely above a whisper.

Wrapping his arms about his wife's thick waist, he rested his chin on the top of her head, his voice once more tender. "You have me, *il mio amore*. Why can't that be enough? There was a time when it was."

Sophia didn't know how to answer her husband—the man she'd been married to for over forty years. She loved Frank, and knew he loved her. But he didn't need her, not like her children and grandchildren needed her.

Frank had his inventions, his bocci . . . his mother. Sophia had only her children. They were her full-time vocation, her passion in life.

And Frank was a man. He could never understand what

it meant to be a mother. A mother nurtured, loved, and protected. And when a child veered off course, like Joe, it was a mother's job to steer him back.

Sophia was positive she was doing the right thing. One day Joe would thank her for showing him his mistakes.

A mother knew these things.

THIRTEEN

"Love is sweet, but tastes best with bread."

Donna peered into the front window of Santini's Butcher Shop/Deli and breathed a sigh of relief. Lou Santini stood behind the counter, cutting up something that looked suspiciously like the hind end of a cow—she shuddered at the thought, grateful it wasn't Eloise he was butchering, and even more grateful that his annoying mother was nowhere to be seen.

She'd dressed carefully for her trip to the deli this afternoon. The raw silk, shocking-pink pantsuit had cost her—well, to be perfectly honest, it had cost her father—a small fortune, but it made her eyes look impossibly large, which was worth any price, in her opinion.

Donna believed in always looking her best, and expensive designer clothes just seemed to fit better than those purchased off the rack. Plus, a woman had only so many tools at her disposal in an effort to be beautiful, and Donna liked to take advantage of every single one.

Moving quickly to the meat counter, and hoping Nina Santini wouldn't suddenly materialize, she studied the neat rows of steaks, pork, and lamb chops, the piles of chicken, and the slices of assorted cheeses, then cleared her throat, smiling at the handsome butcher when he turned around to greet her.

"Hi! Remember me? Donna Wiseman—Annie Goldman's cousin. We met a week or two ago." She had a terrible time remembering dates. "I'm staying with Annie, for the time being."

He glanced down at the enormous ring on her finger, at the wild mane of red hair that had been tamed into a neat 'do, gave a careful perusal of her very adequately proportioned figure, then shrugged, seemingly unimpressed.

"Yeah. I remember."

Damn! Why hadn't she remembered to take off the damn ring? No wonder he was put off.

"What can I get for you?"

Good thing he hadn't asked what he could *do* for her, because she'd already come up with about fifty suggestions, none of them G-rated. "What would you suggest?" Donna smiled again, batting her eyelashes a bit. Men, she'd found, were simple creatures who liked that sort of thing.

All but Lou Santini, apparently.

"You got something in your eye, or what? I had a cousin once who had astigmatism. He blinked all the time. Drove me nuts. Maybe you should get that looked at by an eye doctor. I've got a cousin who does that kind of work. I can give you his card."

Donna's cheeks filled with color. So much for the come-hither stare. "Thanks. But I think it's just mascara."

"So you want some suggestions for lunch? Well, the pastrami on rye is very good. Mama makes the coleslaw; she's an excellent cook, my mama. Also, the sausage with peppers and onions, or the meatball sub smothered with mozzarella. Or, if you're watching your weight, like the rest of the women in the neighborhood, I can make you a chicken Caesar salad."

"I don't diet," she said imperiously. "I eat sensibly, so I can eat whatever I want, when I want, and I don't gain weight. Well, except I may have gained a pound or two since living with Annie. She cooks a lot of Italian dishes, and they can be very fattening."

His dark brow shot up. "What's wrong with Italian? You don't like Italian?"

Italians certainly took their food seriously, much more so than did Jews, Donna decided. "I love it! That's the problem."

He gave her another once-over. "Don't look like a problem to me, but if you want to get in shape, you could always come down to the gym and work out. I lift weights at Gold's Gym. You could stand to firm up those arms a bit. Your breasts look pretty good, though."

At his outrageous remark, Donna's jaw unhinged; she stared blankly at him, before finally remembering to shut her mouth.

What kind of insensitive clod was Lou Santini? The men she dated didn't comment on her arms, or her breasts— especially her breasts!—unless it was to pay a compliment. They were gentlemen, something that couldn't be said for the butcher—a man who spent his days hugging sides of beef, a man whose mind had been frozen by spending too much time in a meat locker.

Lou Santini might be eye candy, with his black hair and brooding eyes, but he wasn't at all what Donna was looking for in a man. "I have to go," she told him. "Please cancel my order. I forgot that I'm supposed to meet my aunt at Goldman's in just a few minutes."

"I don't think so."

Her eyes widened. "What?" She was starting to get irritated. The man had practically insulted her, and now he

was calling her a liar. Which she was. But he didn't need to
know that, for heaven's sake! What was he, the Amazing
Kreskin, or something?

"Your aunt Gina's standing out in front of the store,
talking to Sophia Russo. Looks to me like they're arguing
instead of talking, though. Guess your aunt must have forgotten your appointment, too."

Donna began to stammer, and Lou broke into a grin.

Mercy, but the man was good to look at!

"You shouldn't lie, you know," he told her. "It's not polite. Your face gets all red and blotchy when you lie. And
you never got around to ordering, so there's nothing to
cancel."

Inhaling deeply, nostrils flaring slightly, Donna drew herself up to her full five-foot, six-inch height, and clenched
her fists. "Did anyone ever tell you, Mr. Santini, that you are
very rude and outspoken? Obnoxious, even? It's no wonder
you're almost forty and not married."

He threw back his head and laughed, and damn if he
didn't look like one of the Baldwin brothers: Alec, she decided, only Lou had a much better body than the movie star.

"Well, it looks like you won't have that problem, Donna
Wiseman, judging by the size of the rock on your finger.
It's real, isn't it?"

She fought the urge to hide her hand. "Of course it's
real. And I no longer have a fiancé. Not that it's any of your
business."

"What's the matter? He didn't like that sharp tongue of
yours and took off?" His smile was sexy as hell. "Not that
a sharp tongue doesn't come in handy from time to time,"
he added with a wink. *"Capice?"*

Donna understood very well, and gasped, then turned
on her heel and fled, barely acknowledging her aunt, who

had stopped arguing long enough to greet her, and doing her best to ignore the sound of male laughter that followed her out the door.

"I'm telling you, Gina Goldman, that my son is not interested in your daughter. In fact, he's seeing someone else. A fine young woman—a lawyer—by the name of Angela DeNero. She's Italian. And more importantly, she's a good Catholic."

Gina's glare was about as bright as the hot sun beating down on the macadam. "I know all about how you tried to fix Joe up with his coworker. A lousy trick, in my opinion. Did you really think he would fall for it, Sophia? It's my daughter your son loves." Annie had been furious when Joe had confided what his mother had done, and she'd acted a little bit jealous, which was a good thing. Maybe Sophia had unwittingly aided Gina's cause to see the young couple married.

Sophia shook her head. "I'm not going to stand out here in the hot sun and argue with you any longer. My ankles are starting to swell. If you want to live in a dreamworld, it's your business. I have lamb chops to buy." Pushing Gina aside, she entered Santini's with the same determination the Allied forces had when they took the beaches of Normandy. Gina followed her in.

Gazing longingly at the enticing mound of pink pork chops, Annie's mother licked her lips, and released a sigh of yearning. Because of her husband's religious beliefs, pork wasn't allowed at their table, and Gina missed it. Sometimes when they went out to dinner, she would order pork chops or a pork loin, but not very often, because Sid frowned when she ate it, and that took all of the enjoyment out of the meal.

"I'll have four of the lamb chops, Lou," Gina said, placing her order. "They look especially nice today. And Sid's just crazy about your lamb chops."

"Give me four, too," Sophia said, not to be outdone. "My Frank likes them as much or more than her husband." She lifted her chin toward Gina.

Gazing at the two combatants, the butcher heaved a sigh. "Sorry, ladies, but there are only four lamb chops left. I can give them to one of you. You'll have to decide between you which one gets them. We'll have more tomorrow."

Sophia glared daggers at Gina. "You only ordered those chops because you heard me say I wanted them. In all fairness, they should be mine."

"What? Are you nuts? I was intending to buy chops all along. Why do you think I came here? It certainly wasn't to stand outside in front of the store and argue with you about things you know nothing about."

Crossing her arms over her chest, Sophia stated emphatically, "Joe will never marry Annie! Now give me those lamb chops."

"I wouldn't be too sure of that."

At Gina's smug expression, Joe's mother knew a moment of unease. "What makes you so certain?"

"Because in my heart I know they belong together, and always have. True love comes around only once, and it grows stronger with time."

"Bah! What nonsense! You talk like a teenager. Be practical, Gina. Your husband wants this match about as much as I do. He's a Jew. What would he want with another Catholic in the family?"

"Sid wants Annie to be happy. Unlike you, he thinks of his child's happiness first."

The remark, so similar to the one her husband had made,

stung Sophia like a thousand pinpricks. "Annie is too wild for Joe. He needs someone more settled, someone with a good head on her shoulders."

"Is that so?" Gina's hands went to her hips, and she glared. "Who? Someone like you? Is that what you're thinking?"

"A son could do worse than to look for a wife who has many of the same qualities as his mother. Isn't that right, Lou?" She turned toward the butcher, knowing he had a close relationship with his mother, which probably qualified him for sainthood. Nina Santini was not an easy woman to be around.

Lou's eyes widened, and then he shrugged, not eager to enter into a disagreement with two of his best customers, not to mention the mothers of two of his good friends. "A son should love his mother—"

"See?" Sophia's chin rose.

"But that doesn't mean he should marry a woman like her," Lou finished before disappearing into the back room.

"See?" Gina tossed back. "And everyone knows Lou is crazy about his mother."

"Well, that should tell you something. This discussion is over." Sophia threw her hands up in the air. "*Madonna mia disgrazia*. Keep the lamb chops, keep your daughter. I have errands to run."

"Mark my words, those two will be together," Gina shouted after the woman.

Sophia turned at the door. "Over my dead body!"

"That can be arranged," Gina said beneath her breath, then looked back to the meat counter to finish her shopping.

After a great deal of soul-searching and listening to endless recounts of the "Mad Mothers Marathon," which the eager residents of Little Italy were only too happy to relate, ad nauseum, regarding the fight Annie's mother had had with Sophia Russo at Santini's two days before, Annie had gone home, dialed Joe's number at the Crisis Center—before she could chicken out—and had invited him to spend the weekend with her at the beach. Alone. No mothers. No cousins. No teenagers. Just the two of them.

After several moments of stunned silence, he had accepted, and she had made arrangements with a whining, but nonetheless guilt-ridden, Donna to look after Tess; for Gina, also wracked with guilt, to cover for her at the store; and with Marco to pack her a romantic, transportable dinner for two, which could be eaten on the shores of Cape May, New Jersey, or in a dimly lit room at the bed-and-breakfast, whichever worked out best.

If their mothers were going to fight over them, then they might as well give them something to really battle over: Annie and Joe, alone together for a weekend, in a romantic Victorian inn, frolicking half-naked in the surf. The stuff dreams and wars were fought over.

But getting back at their mothers wasn't the real reason she had suggested the trip. She wanted to be alone with Joe. Taking things slow, she'd discovered, was highly overrated, and making her nuts. She wanted to be held in his arms and made love to. The kisses and caresses they shared were pure torture. She wanted more. She wanted it all.

"I wouldn't want to be at your house when Sophia hears the news of our weekend together," Annie said, rolling down the car window to let the fresh ocean breeze in. She inhaled deeply. They were only a few minutes away from their destination, and she was eager to reach it.

This weekend tryst with Joe wasn't an impulsive gesture, as Mary had suggested the night before.

"You're going away to have sex with my brother?" The pregnant woman had looked positively flabbergasted.

"Not sex, exactly, but that will probably happen. Why are you upset? I thought you were anxious for us to get together. We've made inroads into our relationship. I thought it was time to take things to the next level and see what develops."

"I'm not upset. I'm happy," Mary said, looking uncertain. "You two belong together. But I don't want you to get hurt, Annie. For all your tough posturing, you're vulnerable where my brother is concerned. I want you to be sure, to think this weekend through. Don't do this just to get back at my mother."

Annie threw back her head and laughed. "Trust me, Mary *mia*. I would never have an affair just to irritate Sophia. I hope you give me more credit than that."

Mary reached for her hand. "You care about Joe, don't you, Annie? Maybe even love him?"

Her face revealing little of what she felt, Annie hid behind a flip remark. "Of course I care. I always care about the men I have sex with."

And that's all Annie would admit to. Though she knew deep down where it counted that it had always been Joe.

"Let's not talk about our mothers this weekend, okay?" Joe said, drawing Annie's attention back to the present. "I'd rather keep our families out of the time we have together." His hands were gripping the steering wheel and sweat beaded his forehead and upper lip.

"All right. That's fine with me. You know, if I didn't know better, I'd say you were nervous. Are you sure going away with me is something you want to do? We can always go back. I won't be offended or get mad or anything." Though she would be disappointed.

Being intimate with Joe again was something she'd thought a lot about over the years. Would it be the same between them? They'd always been so compatible in bed, but things could have changed.

Maybe she had rushed things. Maybe he wasn't ready. Maybe he would read more into this weekend than she was ready to concede.

Catching sight of the quaint blue gingerbread-trimmed house that was the Blue Marlin Inn, he pulled into a parking space at the curb in front and cut the engine. "Are you crazy? Do you really think I don't want to be here? I admit, I'm nervous. Think about it, Annie. I haven't been with a woman for fifteen years. Hell, I don't even know if I can remember how to do *it*."

"Oh, is that all?" She leaned toward him, caressing his cheek, finding Joe's nervousness sweet and refreshing. No macho moves to impress, no stupid come-ons to talk her into bed. Joe was honest, and she hadn't met many honest, tell-it-like-it-is men in her lifetime.

"Don't worry, Joseph. It'll all come back to you. Instinct has a way of taking over." With a smile that held promise of things to come, she exited the car and headed up the sidewalk.

Tossing his overnight bag onto the bed of their cozy guest cottage, Joe walked to the large bay window and looked out. The cerulean, sunlit sky was dappled with fluffy, cottonlike clouds and the surf was choppy, whitecaps breaking over the shoreline. "Looks like we've got a nice view of the ocean from here." The bathroom door opened just then, and he turned, his mouth dropping open.

The view had just improved dramatically.

Wearing two teeny scraps of red material that were supposed to pass for a bathing suit, Annie stepped into the bedroom. "Like it? I ordered these suits without Pop knowing about it. For some reason he has a thing against thongs." She spun around and heard Joe's gasp.

"You're wearing too many clothes," she told him. "Why don't you change, and we'll go for a swim."

"I can think of a few things I'd rather do right now besides swim," he said, noting the way her lush breasts nearly overflowed their confines. "You're not going out in public in that, are you?" She would likely cause a small riot. She was a beautiful, sexy woman. And she was all his, for the weekend, at least.

"I am. Unless, of course, you'd rather go skinny-dipping instead." She grinned at his shocked expression.

Joe grabbed his bag off the bed. "I'll be right back."

"Aren't you going to strip for me?" Annie made a face of disappointment. "It would be like my own private viewing of the Chippendales."

Her teasing mood dissolved some of his nervousness and made him smile. "I'll strip when you lie down on that bed and decide to quit teasing me."

"Did I tell you that this swimsuit has a special feature?"

"Hopefully it expands when it gets wet, and covers your entire body."

She shook her head. "It turns transparent in the water."

"No shit!"

Annie laughed, for Joe rarely swore. "No. I just wanted to gauge your reaction."

"I've got an erection the size of a California redwood, and you want to gauge my reaction?"

Glancing down, her eyes widened. "Why, Joseph! I'm impressed."

"Hold that thought, babe. I'll be right back."

"Hope you brought roomy swim trunks or you might have a wee bit of trouble getting into them."

He pulled her into his arms and kissed her, then said, "Getting out of them is the only thing I care about. Once I get you in that bed, we're going to stay there for a very long time."

They found a relatively secluded beach and Annie spread out their towels. Overhead, seagulls cavorted like gliders before the sun, and waves washed the shore in gentle slaps.

"Care to go for a swim before we have lunch?" She placed the picnic hamper on the towel to keep the sand out of it.

Lunch? They had to eat lunch, too? "I'm hungry, but not for food."

Smiling seductively, she removed her cover-up, and Joe glanced around to make sure no one else could see the sexy unveiling. "You should be arrested for indecent exposure. That swimsuit is a lethal weapon," he said, following her into the water, and wondering how he was going to survive the next hour.

"*Oooh!* The water's freezing."

"Thank you, Lord!" Joe muttered beneath his breath, counting on the cold water to shrink his ardor.

Annie had always been a strong swimmer, but so was Joe, and it didn't take him any time at all to catch up with her, as she cavorted through the water like a playful, sleek porpoise.

Wrapping his arms about her waist, he pulled her close. "You're driving me wild, Annie." And then he kissed her.

It was a long, slow kiss, and if Annie had been standing, she probably would have fallen flat on her face from the sheer pleasure of it. Responding in kind, she pressed into him. "Mmmm. I take it you're happy to see me."

Groaning, Joe palmed her breasts, heard her soft moan, then insinuated his thumbs beneath the small bit of fabric and began to rub her nipples in circular motions. "I can't wait much longer to have you, babe. Can we skip lunch and go right to dessert?"

Her deep throaty laugh was filled with sensuality and promise. "I think that can be arranged. But why wait? Let's make love right here, right now."

Joe was used to Annie's impulsive nature, but his eyes widened nonetheless at her suggestion. "In the water? What if someone comes?"

"I was hoping for that, Joseph, weren't you?" She untied the top of her bikini and draped it around his neck, baring her breasts to his view, pleased to see his eyes light with admiration, then darken with passion. "I might need this later."

Reaching for her, he began an achingly slow massage of her breasts, then bent his head to fill his mouth, licking the swollen nipples. She tasted of flowers, salt water, and woman. "This is better than taffy," he murmured, his fingers moving down her sides to her thong and lowering the material.

Annie moaned, rubbing against his magical fingers, seeking and searching for that elusive moment of pleasure. She slipped her hands down the front of his swim trunks to find him hard and pulsing, then released his member from its confines, guiding it toward her. "I want you, Joe. I want you so badly!"

Joe plunged into her like a man possessed, and she cried out in satisfaction, wrapping her legs around him and pulling him into her.

With his mouth firmly fastened on hers, he dove farther in, riding her as the undulating movement of the water and their frenzied motions carried them to climax.

"Oh, my God!" Annie said when her heartbeat had slowed enough for her to speak. "I thought I was going to drown. But what a wonderful way to go." She felt wonderful, totally replete. Happy. Very happy. "You certainly haven't forgotten a thing."

"It didn't last long enough," he whispered, kissing her again. "I want to take our time. Savor it."

"I do, too. But not here. Suddenly I yearn for a comfortable bed and cool, clean sheets."

He helped her back into her swimsuit. "I don't plan on getting any sleep tonight, and neither should you."

Suddenly he felt overcome with emotion and swallowed the lump in his throat. "That was so perfect, Annie. I—"

"Sssh." She covered his lips with her fingertips. "We've got plenty of time to make up for. Let's not waste it by talking."

They made love several more times that afternoon, then when the sun began to set, turning the sky a brilliant pinkish hue, they stopped to dine on cold chicken and pasta salad from the picnic basket Marco had prepared. Joe remarked that he had never eaten dinner naked before, while Annie merely smiled, placed several chunks of watermelon on her abdomen, and told him to try some dessert.

It was dark outside when Joe flipped on the lamp beside the bed to see what time it was. "It's nearly nine," he remarked, astounded that he was still able to function, though he wasn't about to complain. He hadn't felt so wonderfully fulfilled in years.

Annie leaned over and toyed with his ear, making the hair on his neck and arms stand at attention. "Are you trying to tell me that you'd rather watch television than make love with me again? I must be losing my touch." Her hand slid down his abdomen, and he sucked in his breath, his sex rising to belie her comment.

Turning toward her without saying a word, he kissed her full breasts, drawing her pebble-hard nipple into his mouth, first one, then the other, then moved lower, placing feathery kisses on her stomach and abdomen, until his tongue reached the juncture of her thighs. "You're so beautiful, Annie," he said, before dipping his tongue inside to taste her.

Gripping the sheets, Annie writhed against the delicious onslaught, bucking against his mouth as his tongue performed an erotic dance. A few glorious, mind-altering moments later, she tensed, then released, crying out in climax.

Kissing his way back up her body, Joe reached her lips and kissed her tenderly, and she could taste her musky scent on him. It was sensual and erotic.

She'd had sex with other men, but she'd never been as intimate, never made love, as she had with Joe.

Annie's heart was ready to burst with love for this man. She wanted to tell him how much she loved him, but she held back, past fears making her cautious.

Joe didn't have the same reservations.

"I love you, Annie. I always have and I always will. I know you don't want to hear that, but I do love you."

Joe had made similar avowals before . . . before he left. And a man who'd been celibate for as long as Joe had no doubt confused lust with love.

It was understandable. They had always been compatible in bed, and fifteen years was a long time to wait to satisfy one's curiosity. Not to mention oneself.

Annie loved Joe, always had, and probably always would. But could she trust him? That was the biggest question. And she just didn't know the answer.

FOURTEEN

*"Time and words can't be recalled,
even if it was only yesterday."*

"I've been hearing rumors, Annie. About you and the priest."

Annie plopped down on the sofa next to her father and sucked in her breath. This was not a conversation she wanted to have, now or anytime in the future. Her father still thought of her as a child, and though she was pushing thirty-four, that little detail didn't seem to matter to him.

Jewish fathers were far worse than Jewish mothers, in her opinion, not that she'd ever had a Jewish mother, but still, she'd heard things. Jewish mothers were said to be over-protective and smothering. Sid was not only overprotective and smothering, he was well-meaning, which meant he wasn't just an ordinary meddler, but was righteous—at least in his own mind—about his reasons for meddling. The only person she could compare him to, loath though she was to do it, was Sophia Russo.

"His name is Joe, Pops, and he's not a priest any longer. I think you know that."

"The customers who shop at Goldman's like to gossip. I almost punched Henry in the mouth when he tried to tell me that you and Joe Russo had gone away together last weekend. Not my Annie, I told him." Sid patted her cheek, seeing the little girl again, and not the grown woman.

"You know I never interfere in your life," he continued, and Annie fought the urge to roll her eyes, "but a woman has to be careful about her reputation. Reputation is very important, especially in retail."

She nearly laughed. Her reputation had been in shreds for years. Whether the rumors that circulated from time to time were true or not—the one about her starring in a porno flick was her favorite, and had probably been started by Bullfrog—everyone preferred to believe them.

Was her father just now noticing?

"Don't get stressed-out over stuff Henry tells you. He's come on to me a few times, and I rejected him, so it's likely he's just trying to start trouble between us."

Digesting that bit of information, Sid's eyes narrowed dangerously, which didn't bode well for Henry. Her father didn't like the help getting familiar, and Sid had always kept a professional distance between himself and his employees. That Henry had designs on his daughter was cause for termination, or extermination.

"So it's not true that you and the Russo boy spent the weekend together?"

"Oh, it's true, all right. Joe and I are sleeping together." Though in reality they did very little sleeping. But then, sleep was terribly overrated. Her heart rate accelerated every time she thought about how good they were together, in and out of bed.

Sid shot off the couch like a turbocharged, fuel-injected rocket, his face reddening in anger. "He's plucked you!"

"Plucked?" Annie's brow wrinkled in confusion. "Is that a Jewish euphemism for the other word?" Before he could answer, she said, "Listen, Pop, I'm thirty-three years old, and I've been plucked,"—Or was she a pluckee? She didn't really know—"as you call it, for a very long time.

"At my age, if I didn't have sex, you'd accuse me of being a weirdo or a lesbian. Now, admit it. Isn't it better that I'm having sex with a man, rather than a woman?"

He looked at his daughter as if she'd grown two heads—two blond heads. Annie was doing platinum these days. "Where the hell are my antacids?"

She grabbed the bottle of chewable Maalox off the coffee table and handed it to him, worried at how purple his face was getting.

"That explanation is supposed to make me feel better? I'm going to kick that boy's *tuchas* when he comes here tonight. Joe Russo's got a lot of chutzpah coming over here to eat my food so soon after plucking my daughter."

Annie did roll her eyes that time, at her father's false bravado. Sid was such a softy he made Bambi look fierce. "You are not going to kick anyone's butt. You're going to smile, be polite, and ask Joe if he'd like more potato latkes.

"I'm a grown woman, as much as you hate to admit it, and I've got to live my own life." When her father's frown deepened, she added, "Come on, Pop, be reasonable. Surely you know I have been having sex since I was a teenager."

Grasping his heart, Sid fell back on the couch. "Stop! You're killing me with your honesty. A man can vomit from so much honesty. I knew you were different, that you liked to dye your hair those weird colors and dress like a rock star, but—"

"Do you love me any less because I'm not a virgin? You're not one, either, and I don't hold it against you."

He threw his hands up in the air, a look of disbelief on his face. "Such a fresh mouth. Do you want I should call the police? *Oy!* It's no wonder I've got heartburn, living with you and your mother."

Which brought up another question.

"Does your mother know about you and Joe Russo?"

Annie shrugged. "I suspect she does, but she's never come right out and asked me." Gina was much too savvy for that. And Annie suspected that her mother was hoping Annie and Joe would end up in bed together.

"I wish I hadn't."

"Me, too. Discussing sex with your parents is the ultimate nightmare. It never serves any purpose." Other than to make the parents crazy or suicidal.

Annie wondered if Sophia had taken the news as *well* as Sid. She hoped so.

"So what now? Are you and the Russo boy going to get married?" her father wanted to know.

Annie wanted to know why parents always asked if "I do" was involved, like it was some fait accompli. "We're not that far along in our relationship, so don't bring up anything about marriage, okay?"

"You sleep with him, but you're not that far in your relationship?" Her father muttered a few choice words in Yiddish beneath his breath. "I don't understand you young people. Where's the commitment? The responsibility for your actions?"

"I take birth control pills. That's being responsible." Joe had offered to use a condom, but she'd said no, figuring anyone who'd been celibate for as long as Joe had must be free of disease. And she'd wanted nothing to come between them, especially that first time.

"How can a man of God do such a thing? He's supposed to be above all that. He should burn up!"

"Joe's a man, same as you. The instinct to mate is part of our genetic makeup."

"Mate, shmate! What about marriage?"

The doorbell rang just then, and Annie was saved from answering. She saw Gina heading for the front door. Wrapping her arms around Sid's shoulders, she looked at him beseechingly. "Joe's here, Pop. It would mean a lot to me if you were nice to him. I know you like Joe, so nothing that's happened should make you feel any differently."

"Are you crazy in the head? There's been plucking. How can I get around that?"

"You want grandkids someday, you'll get around it. You can't get grandkids without a little plucking and *shtupping*."

"Where did you hear such a word?"

She smiled. "From you. Now smile and put on your best customer face. We have company."

"*Oy!* And your mother thinks she's the one heading for an early grave." He raised his eyes heavenward. "See? See what I go through? A man should be blessed in his old age, not cursed with problems and a daughter who's got garbage in her mouth."

"Look on the bright side, Pop. I may make it to the altar without a walker. Stranger things have happened."

Joe sensed something was amiss the minute he walked into the living room of the Goldman residence. Gina was all smiles, hugging and kissing him, like he was some long-lost son, but Annie's father was quite a different story.

Sid just glared. And when he wasn't glaring he was frowning and mumbling under his breath, something about growing like an onion with his head in the ground. From the old man's lethal look, Joe surmised that it was his head Sid was ready to plant.

"How's business, Mr. Goldman? Annie tells me you've

been busy, that her ad campaign to reach young shoppers is working."

The older man's graying eyebrows rose, his fierce expression firmly in place. "I'm surprised you two have had time to talk about such things."

Annie shot her father a warning look, her mother a pleading one, then brought Joe a glass of the Manischewitz wine her father was so fond of, leading him to the sofa to sit beside her. "You look very nice tonight," she said, earning a soft smile.

"This is some of the stuff you helped me pick out. I bought everything at Goldman's," he told Annie's father, hoping to soften up the old man.

It didn't work.

"So you've got good taste," Sid conceded. "Is that supposed to make a father feel better when he learns that his daughter's been—?"

"Sid!" Gina started babbling Italian curse words at her husband.

"Pop!" Annie shouted, and Sid finally shut up, though continued to mumble beneath his breath. Nothing flattering, Joe was certain.

Annie's cheeks were flushed bright red. Gina, in contrast, had turned deathly pale, and suddenly Sid's comments made sense to Joe. Annie's father knew about their weekend together. No wonder the old man was upset. He could hardly blame him. If some man had been messing with his daughter, there would be hell to pay, that was for certain.

He wondered if Sid owned a gun.

Of course, Joe wasn't just messing with Annie. He had every intention of marrying her. He just had to figure out how to convince her of his love. No easy feat, with someone as guarded as Annie had become.

He was about to offer up an explanation to Annie's father that he hoped would appease him, smooth things over, so to speak, when Annie latched on to his hand, saying, "I want to show you how big Bubbeh's grown," and pulled him out of the room. Joe felt a measure of relief, as well as a great deal of guilt.

"You looked as if you were about to confess," she told him. "That wouldn't have been a good idea, Joe. Save your confessions for church. Sid's Jewish, remember?"

"But your father's upset. I need to talk to him. Perhaps if I explained the way I feel about—"

She shook her head. "It's too soon. Besides, my sex life is not a topic of discussion for the dinner table. It's bound to give everyone, including me, indigestion."

He pulled her into the darkened hallway and wrapped his arms around her. "I've missed you. Are you coming over tonight?"

"My, my, but you certainly have turned into an oversexed creature, Joseph." She kissed his chin. "Not that I mind, you understand," she said. "But I can't come over tonight. Tess and I are going over the plans for the fashion show that we're having next week at the store.

"Would you like to participate? You look almost as good *in* your clothes as you do *out* of them."

"Don't make me drag you into that coat closet and have my way with you, Annie. I doubt your father would like it very much."

She started laughing at the idea of Sid finding them in such a compromising position. No amount of Maalox would cure her father's acidic reaction to that. "He said you plucked me. I felt like a naked chicken."

Joe swallowed his smile. "Are you sure you don't want me to square things with your dad? I should take responsibility for—"

She covered his lips with her fingertips. "Just kiss me, then we'll go in to dinner and pretend everything is hunky-dory."

"Annie!" Sid shouted from the other room. "What are you two doing? Come and eat. It's time for dinner. Bring your friend. I don't want him wandering around the house by himself."

"See? He's already calming down. He called you my friend."

Joe did not look appeased. "He thinks I'm going to steal something. We'd better go in."

Annie shook her head. "Uh-uh. Not until you kiss me. And I want to feel it all the way down to my toes, and then some, so make it good."

"But what if your father comes looking for us?"

Joe looked so disturbed by the possibility that it made Annie laugh. "I'm thirty-three, Joe, and you're two years older than me. Do you really think I care if my father sees us kissing?"

"Does he own a gun?"

Annie shook her head. "No." She pressed herself into him. "But it feels like you're carrying one in your pants pocket."

"Damn, Annie! This isn't funny. I'm walking around with a .357 Magnum between my legs, and you're making jokes. What am I supposed to tell your father?"

Swallowing a grin, she arched a brow. "That you're a member of the NRA?"

* * *

Joe leaned back in his swivel chair and studied the young man seated across the desk from him. Nick Gennaro had made great strides in the last year. The fatherless teen was no longer on cocaine, and no longer a problem for his over-anxious mother.

He had taken Nick under his wing while still a priest at St. Francis's, and had done his best through counseling and caring to turn the boy around. He'd become his part-time father, brother, and full-time friend.

"So how's the job at Santini's going? You still able to keep up with your studies okay? You need to study hard, Nick, if you're going to get into college next year." Although he probably sounded like a broken record to these kids, he couldn't emphasize enough the importance of a college education and how difficult it was to be accepted into a good school if you didn't have excellent grades.

"I have been, Fath—I mean, Joe." The young man shook his head, smiling ruefully. "Not sure I'll ever get used to you not being a priest, but I like having you for a full-time counselor. Mom's really psyched about it. She thinks you walk on water."

Lena Gennaro had been so grateful to have someone help get Nick straightened out that she still sent Joe cookies and other confections on a regular basis, as a way of thanking him. Joe had gained five pounds over the last year, despite his regular workout sessions at the gym.

"How's the peer pressure been at school? Do you still feel the need to fit in, or have you worked out those issues?" Peer pressure is what got Nick into drugs in the first place. Joe had tried to build up Nick's sense of self-worth by urging him to excel in his studies and find friends who were not on their way to a life of crime.

"I have new friends. Some are kinda nerdy—they've

always got their face in a book, or in front of a computer screen—but they're nice guys. We have a lot of fun together.

"Don't worry. I don't intend to mess up again. Miss DeNero said if I keep my nose clean," he smiled at the pun, and Joe rolled his eyes, "she'll have my record purged, so I can start over with a clean slate."

"Miss DeNero is a smart lady."

"Yeah, and she's hot, too." Nick raised then lowered his eyebrows a few times.

The kid was too handsome for his own good, Joe thought. He'd be a real heartbreaker in a few more years. "So I've been told on numerous occasions." His mother had not given up on him and Angela getting together. Not only would they have beautiful babies, she had promised, as if she had the inside track, but they would be brilliant, maybe geniuses, because Angela was a lawyer.

Joe knew his mother's stock in the neighborhood would increase tenfold if she were to bag a lawyer for her son, after landing a doctor for her youngest daughter. The medical and legal professions were highly respected in his community, because with the degrees came money and prestige. No self-respecting Italian turned down that combination. The priesthood was the only thing that could trump them.

"I noticed there's a new girl working next door at Goldman's," Nick said, not bothering to disguise his interest. "Do you know her?"

Joe smiled inwardly at the eagerness in the boy's dark eyes. "I do. Tess Romano's working part-time at Goldman's and living temporarily with Annie Goldman."

"I've seen her hanging around here. Is Tess Romano one of your kids, too? She's not into drugs, is she?"

"Yes, she's one of mine. And no, she's not into drugs. But I really can't say much more about Tess's situation without breaking a confidence."

"Maybe I'll go next door and introduce myself. She's pretty cute. Of course, that Annie Goldman, now she's really something. Man, if I were only a little older—"

"Well, I'm glad you're not, or else we might be fighting over her."

Nick laughed. "So that's how it is, huh? Lucky man."

"That's how it is. And luck has nothing to do with it. I've worked very hard to win Annie's affections." Not that he'd succeeded entirely. There was still the issue of trust to contend with. Annie didn't trust him. She thought what he felt for her was lust, even though he'd told her countless times that he loved her, was crazy about her. And though they'd made sweet, passionate, earth-shattering love, she'd never uttered the words he longed to hear, never given herself over to him completely.

"So maybe I'll go and give this Tess Romano a try. See if she'll like to go out with me."

"You'll have to pass muster with Annie first. She's very protective of Tess. They've grown close these past few weeks. And, Nick, I expect you to behave like a perfect gentleman if Tess agrees to go out with you. Understand?"

The boy nodded solemnly, saying with a teasing smile, "Hey, I've been enrolled in the Joe Russo charm school. How can I fail?"

"It's clear that you haven't met Annie Goldman yet."

"So? How did it go?" Donna asked as soon as Annie walked through the doorway. Annie's cousin was painting her fingernails Passion Pink and watching *Jeopardy!* She had just applied the last coat of lacquer and was holding her hands out to admire her handiwork, wiggling her fingers and blowing on her nails to dry them more quickly.

Annie knew her cousin was asking about the much-anticipated Goldman's fashion show—the disastrous fashion show that could have almost been called X-rated. Actually, her father, who'd been quite upset at the whole turn of events, had called it that, among other things. None good.

Who knew Sid had so many Yiddish curse words at his disposal?

At Joe's urging, she had used several of the boys from the Crisis Center as models, many who already worked for her as stock clerks. Toward the end of the show, which had been going wonderfully up until that point, two of the boys—Raymond Rosario and Billy Rothstein—decided to pull a Mark Wahlberg by exposing their Calvin Klein underwear for the audience to see. Only they didn't just show a bit of their waistband. No, these clowns dropped their jeans and exposed the white cotton briefs beneath.

The clientele of Goldman's Department Store was not ready to see teenage boys in their underwear. Most of the elderly ladies, and a few of the gentleman, had covered their eyes and run out of the store. Some had even climbed on top of their folding chairs, as if they had seen a mouse. It would have been funny, if it hadn't been so damn humiliating.

She and Tess had worked very hard on the show, and had wanted to impress Sid in the worst way.

Well, perhaps they had accomplished that.

Joe had been apologetic, but she hadn't been in any mood to listen to him, or her father's continued rantings, for that matter, and so had left as soon as the ordeal was over.

"You don't want to know," she finally told her cousin.

"It was a complete disaster." Annie explained what had happened, and Donna's eyes widened in disbelief.

"I wish I'd been there," the redhead said with unconcealed envy. "Not much exciting's happened since I moved to Baltimore. I could have used a—"

Annie's tone dripped ice. "Not funny, Donna. I'm very upset right now, and I don't need your smart-ass comments at the moment." Henry's had been bad enough.

The redhead clicked off the television, a true indication of how wounded she was feeling. "I wasn't making fun, Annie. Honest."

With a shrug, Annie plopped down on the sofa and heaved a sigh. Sid was disappointed in her; she was disappointed in herself.

"Where's the kid?" Donna asked, suddenly aware that the teenager wasn't around. "How come Tess didn't come home with you?"

"She has a date to go to the movies with Nick Gennaro. She promised to be home by ten. And Joe vouched for the boy, who seems very nice." They actually made quite a cute couple, reminding Annie of how she and Joe had been at that age, which had propelled her into an hour-long discussion of why a woman shouldn't have sex until she was married. Tess had hung on her every word as if it were gospel.

Mary would have laughed herself silly had she known Annie was giving lectures on safe sex and the joys of abstinence. It was such an un-Annie-like thing to do.

"And you actually believe Tess will be home by ten? Do you think it's wise that you allowed her to go out with a boy we don't know? And who is this guy she's seeing, anyway? I just don't like the sound of it."

"You're certainly very protective of Tess, all of a sudden. I thought you didn't like her."

Donna took a moment to answer. "Tess is okay. I'm learning to adjust to having her around."

As Annie had learned—make that endeavored to learn—to adjust to having Donna around. Not that she ever would. Taking a cocktail napkin, she wiped up the onion-dip mess her cousin had spilled all over her glass-and-brass coffee table. The sour cream smeared into ugly streaks, and Annie fought hard to keep from screaming.

"Well, that's high praise coming from you, Cuz."

"I never had a sister, so it's kinda fun having Tess around. When she isn't being a pain in the butt, that is."

Annie let that last remark slide. "I see you've been to the butcher shop again. I noticed three steaks in the freezer when I checked this morning."

"I sent Tess to Santini's when she came home from school yesterday. I'm never stepping foot in that store again. Those people are rude. The son is as bad as the mother, if you ask me."

"No one's as bad as Lou's mother. Well, except for Sophia Russo. She's twice as bad. So tell me what happened."

"Nothing. I just decided that Lou and I have nothing in common, and that we don't suit each other at all."

"I didn't know he had asked you out, so how could you form that opinion?"

The woman's cheeks filled with color. "He hasn't. But a woman can form an opinion about a man's character without going out on a date with him."

"I see." Though she really didn't, but feared her cousin's explanation would be too convoluted and lengthy. "And have you had any luck finding a job this week? You did promise to start looking, remember?"

Donna's embarrassed blush didn't bode well. "I . . . I didn't actually get much job hunting done this week, Annie. I'm sorry. I know I said I would, but something came up."

"Donna . . ." There was a wealth of warning in that one word, and her cousin shrank back against the cushions.

"I intended to start looking, really I did, but then I glanced in the *TV Guide* and found out that *Roots* was being aired all this week in the afternoon. Well, you know how long the miniseries is, and I couldn't very well miss an episode. *Roots* is, after all, a very important contribution to television history, it being the highest-rated miniseries of all time."

Only Donna would have that information at her finger-tips. "Are you trying to tell me that you haven't seen Kunta Kinte and the gang before this? I find that hard to believe."

"Well, of course I've seen it, silly. But it was just too good an opportunity to pass up. And it's not like I really need the money. I told you that."

Counting silently to ten, she was almost afraid to ask. "And that's because. . . ?"

"Daddy sends me money every month. I've been paying my fair share of the expenses, you know that."

Annie shook her head at her cousin's denseness. How on earth could she get through to the woman? Make her see that her parasitic life wasn't healthy?

"What are you going to do, Donna, if your daddy decides to cut you off without a red cent one of these days? God forbid, but the man could die suddenly. Have you thought of that?" Obviously Donna hadn't, because her face paled.

"You have to find gainful employment and start supporting yourself. It's the only sensible thing to do."

"What a horrible thing to say, Annie Goldman. If I wasn't afraid that it would bring him bad luck at the blackjack table, I'd tell my daddy what you just said. He'd be furious, I can promise you that."

Her cousin obviously had her low-life father up on a pedestal, and Annie didn't have the energy at the moment to burst her bubble. "Never mind. Just remember your promise to look for a job come Monday morning."

"Okay. I just need to check one thing," Donna said, reaching for the *TV Guide*, and Annie's eyes narrowed.

"Donna Marie Wiseman, I'm warning you!"

FIFTEEN

*"Don't judge a man by the words of his mother,
listen to the comments of his neighbors."*

Joe had just pulled the key out of the door and jiggled the
brass knob to make sure his apartment was locked securely
when his landlady stepped up behind him and tapped him
on the shoulder. He nearly jumped out of his skin.

"Mrs. Foragi!" he said when he could finally speak over
the lump in his throat.

The woman smiled up at him, having no idea that she
had just taken ten years off his life, or not caring, if she did.
Dressed in what Annie called Mrs. Foragi's carpenter
outfit— cotton plaid shirt, baggy jeans, and leather tool
belt with matching boots— Donatella Foragi looked like
an ad in *Popular Mechanics*.

Joe's landlady owned the building and enjoyed doing
her own repairs. She was pretty good at it, too. Frank was
impressed with the woman's ability to glaze a window.

"I hear you're taking Annie over to your sister's house
today for dinner," she said, munching on a slice of pizza.
Mrs. Foragi was rarely without food in hand. It never failed
to amaze Joe that his landlady could wield a hammer,
knock in a nail dead on center, and continue to eat without
missing a beat. It was a true measure of manual dexterity.

"You're a brave man, Joe Russo."

"Who told you that, Mrs. Foragi?" Joe didn't gossip,

and he didn't appreciate anyone else speculating on his personal life. Residents of Little Italy didn't need the *National Enquirer*. Not when they had people like his mother and landlady dishing dirt like human steam shovels.

"No one had to tell me. It's all over the neighborhood." She waved her arms, as if to embrace the entire city. "People are placing bets on how long your mother can keep her mouth shut before tearing into Annie Goldman. I have ten dollars that says it will only take five minutes. Let me know if I win."

Joe had been dreading this afternoon's dinner, even before Mrs. Foragi's comment. When Mary had called, asking him expressly to bring Annie to Sunday dinner— she wanted to show off the nursery she and Dan had just finished for the baby—he'd been tempted to say no. But it was hardly an invitation he could refuse, and he wanted Annie with him, even though he knew she had no desire to see his mother.

Sophia would no doubt be garbed in unrelenting black, the traditional bereavement attire of all Italian women. She was definitely going through another period of self-imposed mourning.

He suspected his mother knew that he and Annie had been intimate, though she'd never come right out and asked him. But she had taken to dressing up like a crow, and her rosary beads had been clicking at breakneck speed, a sure indication. In contrast, his father had done a lot of winking and backslapping, as if to say, "That's my boy!" but he'd never asked, either, assuming his son was following in his macho footsteps.

"To satisfy your curiosity, Mrs. Foragi, Annie and I will be attending Sunday dinner at Mary's house, and I'll be sure to tell her you said hello."

Reaching up, she patted his cheek, and Joe hoped she didn't have tomato sauce on her hand. "I like your sister, Joe, but I'm crazy about Annie Goldman. She's a stitch, that one. I hope you follow your heart and don't let your miserable mother tell you how to run your life.

"We get few enough chances at happiness during our lifetime, which is why I hang on to a married man. I'm going to hell. I know that. But it'll be more fun there anyway. You be sure not to toss your happiness away, you hear?"

Touched by the woman's words, Joe leaned down and bussed her flaccid cheek, being careful to avoid the mozzarella plastered there. "Thanks, Mrs. Foragi."

Her eyes twinkled. "If only I was a few years younger, I'd give that Annie a run for her money." Donatella winked at him.

He smiled to be polite. "I've got to be running along now. I'll give Annie your good wishes."

"You do that. I got work to do anyway. I can't stand around all day yakking about your love life."

Joe was still thinking about the strange conversation he'd had with his landlady when he picked Annie up a few minutes later.

"I'm nervous as hell about this dinner today," she confessed, sliding into the beige-leather bucket seat of his Mustang. The red sundress reached her knees—a first, so he figured she was trying to make a concession for his family. Her short blond hair was gelled and spiked, looking rather futuristic. "Are you sure your mother isn't going to kill me?" she asked, and Joe couldn't contain his grin.

"You weren't so concerned when I thought your father had a gun and was going to shoot me on sight."

"Yes, but everyone knows Sid's bark is worse than his bite, and your mother is just plain—"

He arched a questioning brow, as if daring her to continue. "Yes?"

Fortunately she wasn't that stupid or insensitive. "Opinionated," she answered smoothly. Annie didn't think Joe wanted to hear what she really thought: that his mother was mean, nasty-tempered, and impossibly rude.

How could he not notice?

"We'll only stay as long as we have to," Joe promised. "I'll make up some excuse to leave early."

"Just be careful what you say, Joe. I'd rather have your mother screaming at me all night than hurt my best friend's feelings. Mary is very excited about having her family over, and showing off the new nursery. This is the first dinner she's given since she's been married and she wants everything to be perfect."

Leaning over, he kissed her lips. "You look beautiful, and you're very sweet, do you know that? No wonder I love you so much."

Heat blossomed in her cheeks, her heart started pounding loudly in her ears, and she fought against the feelings his words elicited. "Stop saying that! You're in lust, not in love."

"I think I know the difference, babe."

"Well, just don't say it anymore, okay? I've got enough to deal with at the moment."

Most women would be ecstatic if the man they were sleeping with confessed his love.

But not Annie.

Oh, no, she took it as a personal affront, something that had to be "dealt" with. Joe bit back a sharp retort, reminding himself that he'd promised to give her time. After all, he'd been the one to mess things up. He'd have to be the one to set things right again.

But did it have to take forever?

It was a gorgeous summer day, with nary a cloud in the sky. The bay was full of boats, the Inner Harbor area bustling with tourists and shoppers. On any other day they would have been chatting about the renewal going on in the area, how long the lines at the National Aquarium had been lately, but not today. Today they were silent, lost in their thoughts of what was to come, now, and in the future.

Both Annie and Joe felt vastly relieved when the Gallagher's town house finally loomed in front of them.

"Annie! Joe!" An exuberant Mary held her arms out wide. "I'm so glad you could come. You're the first ones here. Connie will probably be late. She's always late." Mary ushered them into the living room, where Dan was waiting with drinks and hors d'oeuvres.

"Look how big I'm getting." She turned sideways, so everyone could see her protruding stomach, which in reality wasn't very big at all. "Dan says I'm still not fat enough to be wearing maternity clothes, but I went out and bought a bunch of new stuff. One of the benefits to pregnancy, no?"

Annie, Joe, and Dan exchanged amused smiles, then Annie said, "You look beautiful, *cara*. Being pregnant agrees with you." Mary's face glowed with happiness and contentment, and Annie fantasized briefly about how she would look carrying Joe's baby. Lately those kinds of thoughts kept popping into her head, and it was all Joe's fault. All his "I love you"s were starting to tear down that wall she'd constructed.

"You wouldn't think so, if you could see me puking up

my guts every morning," Mary said with a grin. "Dan gets sick every time I do and throws up, too."

"Well, isn't that sweet of him?" Annie's smile grew broader as Dan's complexion grew redder. "So how are the plans for the new restaurant coming?" she asked him. "Have you finalized them yet?"

"We're sticking with the sports theme idea, and we're going to open it in Little Italy. I think it'll go over well there. I want to create a publike atmosphere, where people feel comfortable ordering beer, watching their favorite sports programs on a wide-screen TV, and maybe playing a game of darts with old friends."

"Sounds great," Joe said, impressed with his brother-in-law's vision. "When's it going to open?"

"I've gotten the ball rolling, but not for a while. I've been busy at the newspaper, and Mary's got her hands full at Mama Sophia's, so we're taking our time with it. And we need to find just the right person to hire as manager. Hey, you're not looking for a job, are you?"

"Joe's very happy at the Crisis Center," Annie said, butting in before Joe could answer. "He's wonderful with the kids, and more importantly, he's needed there. I'm not looking, either, not that you asked," she added with mock indignation. "I'm quite happy working at Goldman's, thank you very much."

Wrapping his arm about her waist, Joe squeezed. "Thanks for the vote of confidence, babe."

Mary and Dan's brows shot up simultaneously, and they exchanged meaningful looks.

"Dan, why don't you show Joe the new herb garden we just planted out back, while I show Annie the nursery," Mary suggested.

Wondering why it was so quiet—the TV wasn't blaring, like it usually was—Annie glanced toward the stairs. "Where's Matt? I thought he'd be excited to see his aunt Annie. The kid's crazy about me."

"True. But he's staying with Dan's mother, in Gaithersburg," Mary explained. "Lenore wanted him to spend a few weeks with her before school started again. We thought it would be good for Matt to get that special kind of attention only a grandmother can provide, especially with the new baby coming. We don't want him to be jealous of the baby, or feel slighted in any way."

"Mary's a good mom," Dan said, kissing her cheek before handing his brother-in-law a beer. "Come on, Joe. Let's go outside and leave the ladies to their gossip."

Once the back door slammed shut, Annie pulled Mary up the stairs and into the nursery, closing the door behind them. "And what kind of specialized attention am I going to receive from your mother today?" she asked, her voice filled with uncertainty. "I hope coming here wasn't a huge mistake, Mary. I don't want to cause any trouble for Joe. You know how much Sophia dislikes me."

Mary clutched a Winnie the Pooh bear to her chest. "Ma knows you and Joe spent a weekend together. She came right out and asked me. I didn't see the point in lying. Sophia might as well know that you're a couple. Maybe that way she'll get off Joe's back about marrying Angela DeNero."

Annie's lips slashed into a thin line. "She's still trying to pawn Joe off on Angela? Guess I don't measure up to a lawyer."

"Stop it, Annie! You have a college degree, same as Angela. And you're the one my brother loves, not Angela DeNero, in spite of everything my mother's tried to do."

Annie rolled her eyes in disbelief. "Not you, too, Mary.

Oy vey! Joe thinks he's in love with me, and maybe he is. But I'm not ready to make a commitment. I . . . I'm just not ready."

"Good Lord! You're starting to sound like me. I was afraid to commit, but I took a chance, at your insistence, I might add. When are you going to realize that Joe's the best thing that's ever happened to you?"

The best and the worst, Annie thought, and promptly changed the subject. "Oh, this nursery is just so adorable," she declared, looking around the gaily decorated room. "I love the bunny border, and the way you've sponge-painted the walls this cheery lemon yellow. And look at this mobile over the crib. I just love it. You've done a fabulous job, Mary *mia*."

"I'll let you borrow everything when you get pregnant," Mary said, "providing your stubbornness doesn't make you too old to bear children."

Annie made a face. "Quit lecturing me, will you? You're ruining my appetite. And it smells like eggplant Parmesan, unless I miss my guess."

"Why should I? You lectured me every single day about my sex life, or lack thereof, and you were right. I was in a rut, living under my mother's thumb. If you hadn't made me see that I could lose Dan . . . well, we may never have gotten married."

"My situation is entirely different than yours was." She wished she could confide in Mary, but Joe was Mary's brother, her idol, and Annie didn't want to say anything that might ruin their relationship.

"You can lie to yourself, Annie, but you shouldn't lie to your best friend. I knew you when you were still flat-chested, and you've never been any good at it, anyway. You love Joe. I can see it in your eyes every time you look at him. So quit pretending otherwise."

"So I love him." She shrugged. "So what? You think that's going to change things? I might love him, but I don't trust him not to run off and leave me again. I can't go back to that point in my life. It hurt too damn much."

"Then go forward, for crying out loud. Joe's not the same man now that he was then. Give him some credit. Sure, he made a stupid mistake, thought you both were too young to get married, and that his calling was with the church. And don't forget my mother was pressuring him to join the priesthood. And no one can put the pressure on like my mother, as you know."

"I'm not forgetting anything. It would never work out between Joe and me. Too much has happened. Besides, your mother would never approve. Could you picture her reaction if Joe announced that he was marrying 'Satan's Handmaiden'?" Sophia's favorite nickname for Annie.

"As *Nonna* is fond of saying, Bah! Sophia didn't like the Irish, either, remember, and she's welcomed Dan with open arms. It's disgusting the way she fawns over him. I think she's convinced herself that he has Italian blood in his lineage."

The doorbell rang, then the front door opened a moment later, and Mary's mother called out, "Mary, where are you? You invite people for dinner and you don't answer the door. What way is that to treat guests?"

"Keep quiet, Sophia!" Grandma Flora spoke out next. "Leave the *bambina* alone. Always with the yelling. You give an old woman a headache."

"And you give me a pain in the butt."

"Vaffanculo!" the old woman said.

"Uh-oh," Mary murmured, her brows lifting appreciably.

Annie merely grinned, saying, "In the immortal words of Sherlock Holmes, the game is afoot."

"No shit, Sherlock!"

Locking arms, the two women headed back downstairs to the living room, where Annie knew the enemy was waiting, and it wasn't Moriarty.

Sophia took one look at the blond woman and her lips thinned immediately. "I see you've got another new hair color, Annie Goldman. Isn't your true color good enough? Why must you always make with the strange colors? A woman should blend, not stand out like a sore thumb."

"I could ask you the same question, Sophia Russo," Annie retorted in kind. "I don't think that red color is natural, or am I mistaken?" Mary's mother looked like an older version of Lucille Ball, but without the gorgeous gams.

"Sophia dyes her hair because she doesn't want people to a know thata she's an olda woman like me," Grandma Flora said, then began to chuckle, the sound bearing a marked resemblance to a rusty lawn mower.

"*Madonna mia disgrazia.* Keep quiet, old woman! You talk too much."

But Grandma refused to be silenced. "She's vain, my daughter-in-law. But I don'ta think that'sa why you make all the pretty colors with your hair, is it, Annie? I think you like to make life interesting, colorful. *La dolce vita,* heh?"

Smiling fondly at the old lady, Annie winked, wondering if Mary's grandmother had psychic abilities. Annie's hair color was as mercurial as her moods. It was different, and she liked being different. What was the harm in that? "Something like that, *Nonna.*"

"I'm told you are sleeping with my son," Sophia said to Annie, her lips pinched tight. "It won't do you any good. Why buy the cow when you get the milk for free?"

"Ma! Be quiet," Mary said, looking totally mortified. "It's none of your business what Annie and Joe do. They're adults, and you should butt out. Besides, the dairy thing is getting pretty old."

Entering the house just then, Frank began to laugh. "You want your mother to butt out? That's not going to happen in this lifetime." He waved at the young woman, "Hello, Annie," then added to no one in particular, "I'm going outside to join the men. I hear them talking out back." He beat a hasty retreat before his wife could arm herself.

"My husband's a coward. He says what he says then runs off like a scared rabbit."

Flora glared at her daughter-in-law. "My Frank's a saint, Sophia Graziano! He's too good for you."

Annie decided the conversation was going well. No one had been murdered as yet, and Sophia had been momentarily rendered speechless, always a plus—thank you, Grandma Flora!—which gave her the opportunity to speak. "As Joe's mother, you're entitled to your opinion, Sophia, but you should know that we care about each other, and that we have for a very long time."

The red-haired woman crossed beefy arms over an ample chest, jutting her chin out. "Like marries like. You're not Italian."

"I'm half. And who said anything about marriage? I don't believe it was even brought up. I certainly didn't bring it up."

Joe's mother would not be dissuaded, nor was she placated by Annie's assurances. "I bet your father's upset. He's a practicing Jew, and I'm sure he doesn't approve of your running around with my son. I don't like that sort of behavior, and neither does the church." She crossed herself, saying, *"Ció rompe il mio cuore."*

This breaks my heart, Sophia had said, believing the young woman wouldn't understand, but she understood only too well. Annie was tempted to make a cross with her fingers and hold it up to her, just in case it worked on interfering old women, as it supposedly did on vampires.

"Sid's a father," Annie tried to explain. "Parents have a right to be upset when their children grow too old for them to lecture. But my father knows better than to interfere." It was a small lie, but a necessary one. Actually, if Jews were awarded medals for meddling, Sid Goldman would have won the gold. She didn't dare look at Mary, who was probably staring back at her with her mouth hanging open wide enough to catch flies.

"Annie's a smart girl," Grandma Flora told her daughter-in-law. "You should listen more and not talk so much." But Joe's mother merely grunted in disapproval.

Deciding it was time to change the subject, Annie tried a different tack. "I've learned how to cook finally, and I was wondering, Sophia, if you would give me your banana bread recipe? It's one of my favorites." She caught Mary's surprised expression, and thought she saw a hint of pleasure in the older woman's eyes, before Sophia shuttered them closed.

"I give it only to family."

"Whether or not you want to admit it, I've been part of your family since I was a kid."

"That's true, Ma! Annie and I grew up together," Mary pointed out, a pleading note in her voice.

"So? You think that makes you sisters? It takes more than that to be a Russo. We got tradition in this family."

If Sophia started dancing around like Topol from *Fiddler on the Roof* and singing "Tradition," Annie was going to leave. Her generosity extended only so far, and it had just about reached its limit.

Outside, Dan had just handed Joe and Frank a cigar. "I don't smoke, but I thought I'd practice for when Mary has the baby."

"A good idea, Dan," Frank said, peeling off the wrapper and lighting up. "So, you got any more of that wine to go with this? Nothing like a glass of *vino* to drink with a good cigar." He puffed several times, looking quite impressed. "These Cuban?"

Dan shook his head. "Cuban cigars aren't allowed in the United States, Frank. They're considered contraband."

"Too bad. Those Communists know how to make a good cigar."

Glancing toward the back door, Joe asked the two men, "What do you think's going on inside? Do you think Mom's laid into Annie yet?" He heaved a frustrated sigh. "I'd better go in and make sure everything's okay." Though inside was the last place he wanted to be, he didn't trust his mother not to be rude.

Frank puffed contentedly on his cigar, then wrapped his arm about his son's shoulder. "The girl is holding her own, Joey. I listened outside the window for a few minutes before I went in, and I'm telling you, she's good. It's best to let Annie handle your mother. I think Sophia has met her match."

Joe and Dan exchanged startled looks, neither of them believing such a thing was possible.

"Annie doesn't believe that I love her," Joe admitted.

"She's afraid," his father said. "You give her more time. Soon she'll come around to your way of thinking. Every woman wants to be married, whether or not they admit it. Annie's no different. And I know her father would approve of the match. Sid Goldman's told me several times that he worries his daughter will end up alone."

"But I'm worried Mom won't ever accept Annie into the family. I'd hate to have to choose between them, because Mom will come out the loser."

"Your mother can be handled. Trust me, Joey. I'm speaking from experience."

"I'm sure you remember how difficult it was for me to convince your sister to marry me," Dan said, hoping to reassure his brother-in-law. "But I was persistent, and eventually she caved. Although, I must admit that I'm pretty damn hard to resist." He winked at the skeptical man. "Sophia adores me now, so I must be pretty good, huh?"

Joe finally let loose a smile, small though it was. "I'm not giving up. But I wonder how long it will take before Annie finally admits that she loves me. I know in my heart she does, so why won't she say the words?"

"If a man could read a woman's mind, Joey boy, he'd make himself a billion dollars." Frank blew smoke rings into the air. "It's the biggest mystery going. They say one thing and mean another." The older man shook his head. "I've been married to your mother for forty-three years, and do you think I'm any closer to understanding what makes her tick? *Forgetaboutit!* It's not going to happen, I'm telling you.

"It's like that book . . . you know, the Venus one that tells you how different men and women are from each other, like we needed a book to know that." He threw his hands up in the air. "*Pleeease*. That guy's rich now, because everyone believed he knew the answer. But I'm telling you, boys, only God knows the answer, and He's not talking.

"*Forgetaboutit!* Let's have more wine."

Joe hugged his father, feeling very close to him at that

moment. They hadn't had a lot of father and son talks while he was growing up, but the old man was trying to make up for it now, and Joe appreciated the effort.

"You know, Dad, you're pretty smart for an old guy."

Frank threw back his head and laughed, then said with a wink, "How do you think I've stayed married to your mother all these years, Joey boy?"

SIXTEEN

*"A man is not honest simply
because he never had a chance to steal."*

"What do you mean, there are three Armani suits missing from the rack? Are you sure you counted correctly? Maybe you're confused."

Henry Grossman stared back at Annie, stiffening in insult, and trying to draw himself up to his full five-foot, eight-inch height. It didn't help. As far as she was concerned, he still looked like a Butterball turkey.

"I'm not confused," he stated, bulging eyes narrowing. "I've worked here long enough to know how to do inventory. Six suits came in yesterday, and I hung them on the rack. This morning there were three. I checked the computer and we didn't sell any. They're gone, and your father's not going to be pleased."

That was the understatement of the year. When Sid found out, he was going to be royally pissed, and she knew whom he would blame. "I'll recheck the computer inventory," Annie said. "Maybe there's a glitch, or maybe Tess racked them in the wrong place." The young woman had been moony-eyed over Nick Gennaro ever since their date, and not concentrating on her work as she should. But Annie, who remembered what it was like to be young and infatuated, hadn't called her on it, preferring instead to give her some slack, despite Sid's direction to the contrary.

"That's what happens when you hire druggies and psychos because your boyfriend recommended them. You've got Tess working the cash register, and those boys back in the stockroom. Bad things were bound to happen. And now they have."

The smug look on Bullfrog's face infuriated Annie. She counted to ten, trying to keep her temper in check. If she ever unleashed it against this man . . . well, she just didn't want to go there. Murder was not out of the question. "I resent what you're implying, and I think you should keep those kinds of comments to yourself.

"The kids from the Crisis Center have worked here for weeks with no problems whatsoever." Except for the fashion show, but she wasn't bringing that up again. Joe had put Raymond and Billy on restriction, so the matter was settled, as far she was concerned. "I see no reason to disparage, suspect, or place blame on anyone until we know exactly what's happened to the merchandise." For all she knew, Henry might have had something to do with its disappearance. The man was a master at causing trouble, and she wouldn't put it past him to have hidden the missing garments.

Henry shrugged, making his neck look even larger, if that were possible. "Suit yourself. But the old man's going to be double dosing on his Maalox if this doesn't get straightened out soon. And I'm telling you right now, I'm not taking the blame."

"Until we figure out the problem, I don't want you mentioning any of this to my father, do you understand? There's no sense upsetting him for no reason."

Licking his lips suggestively—did frogs actually have lips?—he rubbed his hands together in anticipation. "I might be able to be persuaded, if you agree to go out with me. You know you want to. I've seen how you lust after me when you think I'm not looking."

"I'd rather be lashed to a pole and whipped with a wet noodle."

Bullfrog's eyes lit. "*Oooh*. Kinky. That can be arranged."

Trying not to gag, Annie turned away from the human amphibian and headed toward the rack of women's suits. She counted them again, then proceeded to the men's department and searched through those racks as well, to see if perhaps they'd been put in the wrong place.

No such luck.

Tess approached just then, her smile melting at the concerned expression Annie wore. "What's the matter? You look worried about something." The kid was intuitive, she'd give her that.

Tess had just returned from her counseling session with Joe, and Annie thought she looked like a different girl from the one who'd come to stay with her all those weeks ago. Her long dark hair was neatly fastened in a ponytail, and she now paid more attention to her dress and makeup, using her salary and ten percent store discount to purchase clothing items other than jeans and tank tops. The long red skirt and white knit top she was wearing looked adorable, showing off her blossoming figure to perfection.

Tess's attitude had improved dramatically, as well. She was beginning to understand that her parent's drinking problem had little to do with her and everything to do with their own mental state and illness. The teenager had made great strides in the past few weeks, and Annie was very proud of her.

"Hi, kiddo!" Annie said as she came around the clothes rack to stand next to her. "I am worried. We're missing three of the Armani wool suits we just got in on the last shipment. Do you know what might have happened to them?"

Tess shook her head. "No. But hey, do you think Henry might have done something with them? Sometimes when he really gets lazy he shoves the merchandise in a drawer, or stuffs it in an empty dressing room, so he won't have to put it away. I don't mean to be a snitch, but this sounds kinda serious."

Annie's eyes darkened. "It is serious. Thanks for telling me. And don't worry, I won't let on to Henry that you've said anything. I'll just keep a sharper eye on him from now on."

The slug. She'd always known Henry was lazy, though he went out of his way to look industrious whenever Sid was around. But she'd seen him loafing in the stockroom when he should have been inventorying merchandise, and taking extra bathroom breaks, for God only knew what purpose! She wasn't going there, either.

"Good, 'cause he gives me the creeps."

"He hasn't touched you, or said anything suggestive, has he?" If that disgusting pervert had made one move toward Tess, she was going to call the police. Then she would fire him.

"No, nothing like that," the young woman replied, and she let loose the breath she was holding. "He's just gross when he eats, and he's always reading those nudie magazines when he thinks no one's looking. Henry's been pretty nice to me, so I probably shouldn't have said anything. I don't want to get him in trouble."

Wrapping an arm about Tess's slender shoulders, Annie squeezed. "You know you can always come to me if you've got a problem, right? I don't care what it is. I promise I won't get mad. We'll take care of it. No matter what."

"Yeah, you're not like Donna. She's always yelling at me when I borrow her clothes. She went ballistic this morning when she couldn't find her cashmere sweater. As if I'd want to wear that ugly thing."

"Donna's very territorial. I think it would be better if you borrowed my stuff instead."

Tess's gaze went from the tight-fitting black leather pants to the bright-blue silk blouse Annie had knotted at her waist, and she shook her head. "No offense, but I don't think Joe would approve of me dressing like you. You're older, so you can get away with it, but I'd just look like a teenage hooker."

Unsure if she should be insulted—for some strange reason, she suddenly felt insecure—Annie wondered if people thought she looked like a hooker. Only it wasn't "people" she was concerned about, just one person's opinion. "Did Joe say I looked like a hooker?"

"No way. Are you kidding? His eyes practically bulge out as far as Henry's whenever you walk into a room. Joe's just conservative and parental when it comes to the kids he works with."

"Do you think I look like a hooker?" Annie couldn't believe she was actually worried about what someone else thought of the way she dressed. She never had before. But things were different now. She was a partner in the store, and there was Joe to consider. "Maybe my hair's a little over the top. What do you think?" She knew Tess would give her an honest answer. They had that kind of trusting relationship now.

"I love the way you look. Don't change a thing. If you were to dress like the rest of the world, you wouldn't be Annie. Besides, like I said, Joe thinks you're hotter than chili peppers, and they're pretty hot."

Annie winked, feeling somewhat relieved. "Thanks, kiddo!"

"You're welcome." Tess smacked her gum. "So how we gonna hide this mess from your dad? I sure don't want Sid breathing down my neck when he finds out there's merchandise missing."

"Oy vey!" was all Annie could manage to say.

Annie had been thinking about the missing suits throughout the workday. She was still thinking about them when she entered her town house later that evening, to find Donna's note on the kitchen table.

The woman's handwriting was barely legible, but Annie finally deciphered that Donna and Tess had gotten tired of waiting for her to get home from work and had gone to the movies, and then out for a pizza. They'd promised to bring back a pie, which was good, because Annie was starving and the idea of cooking for herself just didn't appeal.

Annie hadn't expected to be so late, but the missing merchandise bothered her, and she'd stayed after closing to conduct another search, which this time had included the stockroom and dressing rooms. Unfortunately, she hadn't found what she'd been looking for.

Eventually she was going to have to tell her father about the missing merchandise, and she was dreading that day and intended to put it off for as long as possible, knowing he would be disappointed. Again.

A knock on the door interrupted her musings. Tossing Donna's note in the trash, she went to open the door, thinking it might be Joe. Hoping it was Joe. She needed him right now, needed his calming presence and levelheadedness. Needed his strong arms wrapped around her.

For a long time Annie had convinced herself that she

didn't need anyone, that it was better to handle things on her own and not ask for help. Relying on someone—Joe—had proven painful and futile, and she hadn't wanted to open herself up to that kind of pain again. There was risk in getting close to someone. Risk, disappointment, and heartache. Her trust had been shattered.

She was just starting to believe in love again and was finally coming to realize that having someone to share things with was so much nicer than being alone.

Opening the door, Annie's eyes widened, and then filled with concern when she saw the forlorn expression on her best friend's face. "Mary," she said, wondering what she was doing out at this time of day. Usually Mary was either at the restaurant, or at home, cooking Dan's dinner. "What's the matter? You look like you've been crying. Are you feeling okay?" Annie's stomach clenched. "There's nothing wrong with the baby, is there?"

Please, God! Don't let it be that.

Mary shook her head, and Annie breathed a sigh of relief. "The baby's fine. I'm the one who's the basket case."

"What's wrong, kiddo? You look like you've lost your best friend. You haven't. I still adore you."

From her purse, Mary pulled out a letter and held it up. "This arrived in today's mail for Dan. It's from Sharon, his ex-wife."

"Oy vey!" She had a bad feeling about this. "Come in, *cara.* Do you want a glass of milk, or maybe some juice? I doubt there's much of anything to eat. Donna consumes food like a human vacuum cleaner and barely gains an ounce."

Mary forced a smile. "I used to say the same thing about you, Annie. It's so aggravating to watch you eat tons of food and stay as slim as you are. Some of us aren't that lucky."

"Luck has nothing to do with it. I work out," she replied, knowing of her friend's aversion to exercise. Searching through the cupboards, she discovered a package of Hostess cupcakes that Donna had no doubt been hiding from Tess; they were the chocolate kind Mary liked. "Here," she said, handing her the package and watching her eyes light up. "I figure you need this more than my cousin does."

With an eagerness that would have put a six-year-old to shame, Mary tore open the cellophane wrapper. "You're a lifesaver. I've had this humongous craving for chocolate ever since I got that damn letter in the mail."

"So what else is new? You crave chocolate whenever you get upset, and most times when you're feeling just fine." It was an addiction Mary had never been able to conquer. Annie had never craved chocolate or sweets, even as a kid, so she had a difficult time understanding her friend's all-consuming need for it. Now, bread, that was a different story. Give her a loaf of warm Italian bread and a pound of butter and she was good to go.

Annie plopped down on the kitchen chair next to the pregnant woman. "So what does the letter say?"

"Sharon Gallagher wants Matt back. She's planning to sue Dan for custody, according to her not-so-veiled threats. Thank God Matt is with Lenore, so that bitch can't get her hands on him. I'm so upset, Annie."

"But she'll never win. She abandoned the kid and ran off with her aerobics instructor, leaving Dan to raise Matt. From what you told me, the woman never even attempted to get in touch with her son. She's unfit to raise a child." Reaching out, she covered her friend's shaking hand and squeezed, trying to offer what comfort she could.

"Sharon Gallagher will *never* win, Mary," Annie said again, more emphatically this time. "The courts won't award custody of a child to a woman like that. Why, you've got people who will testify against her. Matt's teachers, his pediatrician . . . They can say how distraught he was after his mother abandoned him. And the judge will ask Matt whom he wants to live with."

Mary spoke with her hands as much as she spoke with her voice, and as agitated as she was, she was waving them around like a whirligig. "That's all true, and I'd like to believe what you say. But Sharon had legal custody of Matt before she took off for parts unknown, and she's remarried now . . . to a lawyer." She made a face of disgust. "Plus, in spite of the way he was treated, Matt loves his mother. He may want to go back with her."

Noting the pain in her friend's eyes, Annie shook her head. "I don't believe that for a second, and neither should you."

Mary heaved a sigh. "It seems Sharon dumped the aerobics guy in favor of Mr. Money Bags. She's frying bigger fish, and now all of a sudden she's feeling maternal and wants her son back home to live with her. My guess is that she's trying to impress Clarence Darrow."

"What does Dan say about all this? I know he must be upset, but surely he intends to fight back."

Mary hesitated a moment, then stuffed the rest of the cupcake in her mouth before replying in a garbled voice, "I haven't told him yet."

Annie's jaw unhinged. "What?"

"I didn't have the heart. Dan's been working such long hours, trying to get the restaurant off the ground, and his job at the paper has him stressed. And with the new baby coming . . . well, I just couldn't tell him something like this over the phone. And I was too upset to go down to *The Sun*. I plan to tell him as soon as I get home, but I wanted to talk to you about it first."

"Jesus!" Annie shook her head in disbelief. "We are a pair, *cara*."

Mary's brows knit together. "What's that supposed to mean?"

"We've had some theft at the store, and I'm too much of a chicken to tell my father about it. Though I think your news is much worse."

"Great. I'm glad I can be of some consolation."

"I guess neither one of us has ever been very good at confronting our problems head-on," Annie said.

"Well, I know I haven't, but I thought you were better at it. You always seemed to be."

"I'm good at solving other people's problems. When it comes to my own, I suck. I want my father to be proud of me, and now he's going to think I'm nothing but a screwup."

And she had no idea what she was going to do about Joe. She was afraid. For the first time in a very long time, Annie Goldman, fearless, reckless, risk taker, was afraid—of love, life, and the pursuit of happiness.

"At least you might find the lost merchandise before Sid discovers it's missing." Mary glanced at her watch, her frown deepening. "I've got about twenty minutes to think about what I'm going to tell Dan when he gets home." With a sigh, she rose to her feet. "Guess I'd better get going."

"You have to tell him the truth, *cara*. When Dan reads the letter, he'll know just what to do."

"Hello?" Mary's eyes widened in disbelief. "Are you

forgetting that we're talking about a man? Since when do men know what to do in a crisis?"

Wrapping her arm about her best friend's thickened waist, Annie kissed her cheek, conceding that she had a good point. Men were usually worthless in crisis situations.

Sid was the perfect example. When his mother was dying of cancer, he had been too distraught and overcome with grief to function properly, and it was Gina who became the rock he leaned on. She'd also been the one to make the old woman's funeral arrangements when she'd died, and had kept everything running smoothly at Goldman's Department Store in her husband's absence. When push came to shove, Gina had put aside her many maladies and had risen to the occasion. Of course, Sid had conveniently forgotten all that.

Men were not only miserable during difficult situations, they had terrible memories, to boot.

"Good luck," she said finally. "And keep me informed. If there's anything I can do to help, call me, understand?"

"Of course. I plan to call even if there's nothing you can do. By the way, do you know the name of a good lawyer? Someone competent, whom you trust?"

Annie thought for a moment, and then went to fetch her purse. "As a matter of fact, I do." Searching through the contents, she pulled out a business card, and handed it to Mary, whose eyes widened when she read it.

"Angela DeNero! You're sure you want me to contact her? My mother will nominate the woman for sainthood if she wins the custody case."

"Joe trusts her, and that's good enough for me. Besides," Annie's brow lifted, "she's practically engaged to some guy in Boston. I think we're safe from Sophia's matchmaking."

Mary didn't look convinced. "If you're sure . . ."

"I want you and Dan to have the best representation possible, *cara*. And I think Angela's it." She hoped so, anyway, because Mary and Dan could not, and would not, lose custody of Matt, not if Annie had anything to say about it.

Joe arrived at Annie's house an hour after his sister departed. She was so glad to see him that she launched herself into his arms as soon as he stepped through the doorway. "Thank God, you're here! I've had the most miserable day."

Thrilled that Annie was happy to see him, but concerned by the haunted look on her face, Joe wrapped his arms about her and kissed the top of her head. It wasn't often that she let her vulnerability show, and he was glad she trusted him enough to lean on. "What's wrong?" Taking her hand, he led her to the couch and pulled her down on his lap.

"I hardly know where to begin. Mary was just here. Have you heard about—?"

He nodded. "My mother called just before I left. She's gone ballistic. Sharon Gallagher better stay out of her path or she'll end up in the hospital."

"For once I approve of your mother's hot temper. You don't think Dan and Mary will lose custody of Matt, do you? It just wouldn't be fair." But no one knew better than Annie that life wasn't always fair.

"There's always a chance, Annie. Nothing's ever one hundred percent certain in these situations. But I don't believe they'll lose. They've got too much going for them. Character counts in cases like this."

"I gave Angela DeNero's card to Mary and told her to call her. You told me once that Angela had handled child custody cases like this before, so I think she'll be a big help to them."

Joe's heart squeezed, and he drew her close and kissed her. For Annie to put aside her own . . . well, insecurities, for want of a better word, where Angela was concerned—thanks to his mother's machinations!—and place Mary's welfare above her own . . . "Thank you."

Smiling softly, she kissed him back. "You're welcome."

"Is Mary's problem the only thing bothering you?" he asked, sensing there was more she wanted to talk about.

Heaving a sigh of frustration, she snuggled against his chest, seeking the comfort she knew she would find there. "We've got merchandise missing from the store, expensive merchandise, and I'm afraid to tell my father. Sid's going to freak when he finds out. And he'll think I'm incompetent. Hell, maybe I am. I don't know."

Joe tipped up her chin with his forefinger and looked into her eyes, noting uncertainty and vulnerability. "You're smart, Annie, and your dad knows it. Why do you think he brought you into the business? No one would ever accuse you of being incompetent. These things happen for a variety of reasons. I'm sure he's had losses over the years. That's just part of being in business."

He was being so sweet, so supportive, Annie felt like kissing every inch of him. "God, you're making me hot!"

Joe arched a brow. "But I haven't done anything yet, except hold you. *Yet* being the operative word. I've been thinking about you all day, babe."

"You believe in me, and that makes me feel really good and really hot. Let's make love." She glanced at the watch on Joe's wrist. "We've got at least two hours before Donna and Tess get home." She began to unbutton his shirt.

"That's the best offer I've had all day." He smiled softly,

then eased Annie down on the couch and untied her blouse, pausing with a frown. "No way those pants are coming off without a fight. They look glued on."

Annie wasted no time shimmying out of the black leather pants and tossing them aside; the blue blouse followed. "No problem. Now, get naked and make love to me. I need you, Joe."

"I need you, too, babe, more than you'll ever know." Removing his clothing as quickly as he could, Joe covered Annie's body with his own, thinking how unbelievably lucky he was to have such a sweet, sexy, uninhibited woman in his life. "You're beautiful, Annie, inside and out." He caressed her cheek tenderly. "I love you, and I'm never going to stop saying it. Someday you might actually believe me."

"Kiss me. Make me believe. I want to believe that everything you tell me is for real this time."

"Believe it." His mouth covered hers hungrily, and he thrust his tongue deep inside. Annie met him stroke for stroke, returning his kiss with reckless abandon, and trying to communicate what she was reluctant to say with words: She loved him. Had always loved him. Would always love him.

Joe's mouth traveled a delicious dance down her neck and chest, pausing from time to time to taste the inside of her arm, her ear, and settling on her breasts. Unhooking the front of her bra, he pushed the material aside and moved to her swollen nipples, tonguing them as his fingers moved beneath the elastic of her panties to explore the heat between her thighs.

"Oh, God!" She moaned. "Take them off! Take them off!"

He had just started sliding the silky material down her legs when the phone rang.

Annie's moan was replaced with a groan. "Whoever that is is going to be murdered."

"Let it ring," he whispered, placing feathery kisses over her satiny skin. "You don't have to answer it."

The phone kept ringing, and with every shrill chime Annie's guilt multiplied. It was the Italian Catholic part of her, she knew. Squeezing her legs and eyes shut, she wished now she had unplugged the damn thing.

Placing her hands on Joe's shoulders, she sighed with regret and said softly, "I have to answer it, Joe. It might be Tess or Donna. They might have had car trouble, or worse. I'd never forgive myself if something happened to them. And neither would you."

Pulling back, he nodded. "You're right," he said, then reached for the portable phone on the coffee table and handed it to her. He watched the color drain from her face as she listened. "Annie, what is it? What's wrong?"

Hanging up the phone, she reached for him. "It's the security service from the store. We've had a break-in."

SEVENTEEN

*"Light is not recognized
except through darkness."*

"It looks like a hit-and-run, Miss Goldman. They smashed the display window and took everything that wasn't nailed down. There's no sign of the thieves. I imagine they're long gone by now."

Staring at the nearly empty display window, Annie's hands went to her face, and she felt like crying, but she resisted the urge, knowing it would do little good at this point. She was actually more angry than anything else.

She and Tess had worked hard on the window, getting the decorations for the fall season just so, picking out the right clothing to display. They'd been very proud of the results. And now this.

What was she going to tell Tess? The girl was sure to be disappointed. And worse, what was Annie going to tell her father? The expensive mannequins, not to mention the designer clothing they'd worn, were missing.

Of course, to look on the bright side, at least Sid wouldn't have to look at naked dummies any longer.

"You said on the phone that my father had been called?" An unfortunate occurrence, since she needed time to figure everything out. But she had a feeling that, despite what the Rolling Stones had assured her, time was not on her side.

"Yes, ma'am. That's correct. We called Mr. Goldman as

soon as the alarm sounded," the young, freckle-faced security officer replied, sounding sickeningly efficient, and looking almost adult in his navy blue uniform. She figured he needed about four more years before he looked like a real adult.

"We located Mr. Goldman at the hospital emergency room," Tom—embroidered on his shirt—Flannery explained. "He's on his way here now with Mrs. Goldman."

Standing on the sidewalk next to Annie, listening to the exchange, Joe latched on to her arm, his voice filling with concern. "Do you think something's happened to your mother? Do you want me to drive you to the hospital?"

"No, that won't be necessary. But thanks." She had spoken to Gina on the phone shortly before Joe had arrived at her town house, so she knew her mother hadn't been feeling well, at least in her own mind. "Gina's fine. This is one of her regular visits to the ER. Did you know the hospital's thinking about naming a wing after her because she's spent so much money there?" She tucked her tongue in her cheek, watching Joe's eyes widen a fraction.

"You're kidding, right?"

"You bet." She explained, "Gina told me her stomach hurt, and that she probably has abdominal cancer, either that or adhesions. My mother's very big on adhesions, you have to understand."

"Are you sure she's not really sick? You know, like the boy who cried wolf so many times no one believed him when he really needed them to."

"Yes, I'm sure. But it's sweet of you to worry. Gina's getting better about her hypochondria. The visits to the ER are getting less frequent. But still, every once in a while she feels the need to go, to make certain she isn't dying, so my father takes her there. I'm beginning to think she likes the attention she gets from Sid during those times. Despite all his complaining, he's very attentive toward her.

"If you want to worry about someone," she told him, "worry about me. My father's likely to kill me when he sees that the expensive merchandise I insisted on ordering is gone."

He started to say something, comforting, no doubt, but her father's car pulled up just then, and Sid and Gina got out. Annie reached for his hand and squeezed. "I'm so glad you're here." Joe's calm in the face of adversity was so reassuring; she needed to draw from that now.

"You'll be fine," he whispered, and she smiled gratefully at him.

His expression fierce, Sid stomped up to the broken display window and threw his hands up in the air. "Hoodlums! They've robbed us!" He turned to the security officer. "Why am I paying you good money? The criminals came to my store and robbed me anyway. What do I look like, a schmuck?"

"I'm sorry, Mr. Goldman. We responded to the alarm as quickly as we could, but the perpetrators were already gone when we got here. I explained all of this to your daughter."

"It's true, Pop, he did."

Sid turned to face Annie. "What did they get? I don't see those naked dummies anymore. Please tell me you removed them from the front window."

"I wish I could, but they were stolen, along with two Perry Ellis men's suits and a Donna Karan dress."

Grabbing the sides of his head, he muttered a few choice Yiddish words beneath his breath. "We're going broke with all this fancy, schmancy designer stuff you brought into the store. I knew it was a mistake. We got a catastrophe here."

Annie sent Joe an I-told-you-so look.

"Now, Sid, be fair." Gina came to stand by her daughter. "You told me yourself that Annie has increased sales with her choice of merchandise."

The younger woman's eyes widened at that. Sid had never passed on any compliments to her.

"That was before we were robbed. This changes everything. We've become targets for criminals looking to fence expensive merchandise. Before, when we had regular labels, nobody cared. Now we got theft."

"I'm afraid it's worse than that, Pop."

"Worse? How can it be worse? Did someone die?"

"Three Armani suits from the fall collection are missing from the inventory," she explained. "I've searched the entire store but found no trace of them."

Sid grabbed his chest. "Stop! You're killing me. I'm dying here." His gaze shifted to his wife. "I might not make it until the rabbi comes. Don't forget, Gina, seven days for the shivah."

With a look of exasperation she had perfected over the years, Gina placed her hand gently on her husband's arm and admonished, "Instead of worrying about dying, Sidney Goldman, you should be asking Joe to help you board up the window, until we can get it fixed in the morning."

"I'll be happy to help, Mrs. Goldman," Joe answered before Sid could say anything. "I'm sorry about the break-in. I hope you have insurance to cover the loss."

"First the plucking and now this. Thieves in the night." He cast Joe a dirty look, and it was clear that he wasn't referring to just the break-in, then said to his wife, "We are living under a cloud, Gina. A cloud, you hear me? I got no luck that isn't bad. *Oy!* An unlucky person is a dead person."

"I'm sure these are just isolated incidents, Mr. Goldman," Joe offered, hoping to ease the older man's anxiety.

Sid glared back at him. "What are you, a kibitzer? I got problems and you're giving me platitudes."

Wrapping his arm about Annie's waist, Joe pulled her close to his side. The protective gesture wasn't lost on either of the Goldmans, especially Gina, who was smiling widely.

"I don't think you can place blame on anyone, Mr. Goldman," Joe said, his voice filled with equal amounts of determination and understanding.

"Hmph!" Sid flashed his wife a bilious look. "We'll see."

Unfortunately, the incidents were not the isolated events Joe had predicted. In the following week, three more men's suits were lifted, and a carton of ladies' nightwear was stolen from the back room.

Sid had gone from angry to despondent, then back to angry again. "This has to be an inside job," he told Annie the following Monday morning over coffee and bagels. "We're missing too many pieces of merchandise for it not to be."

"Do you think it might be Henry? I've never trusted the man." Though she hated to accuse anyone without proof. The man was revolting, a sex maniac . . . but was he a thief?

Sid's eyes rounded. "What? Are you meshuga? The man's been with me for years. Just because you two don't get along, that's no reason to accuse him of robbing me blind."

"I'm not accusing anyone, Pop. I just asked for your opinion." Annie sipped her coffee, wishing she were back home in bed—wishing she were anywhere but here, having this discussion. She was beginning to suspect that retail wasn't in her future, after all.

"You want my opinion? I'll give it to you. You brought hoodlums and delinquents into the store, and now we got merchandise missing. That's my opinion."

The accusation hurt, but she wouldn't give him the satisfaction of knowing how his words wounded. "You've been listening to Henry." She wasn't surprised, just disappointed. After all, Bullfrog had been putting one over on her father for years.

"Henry's right. We had no trouble before those kids came to work here. Now we got theft and vandalism. Don't get me started on the nudity."

"Well, maybe you should accuse me, too, Pop. After all, you had no theft until I came to work here."

Dismissing her comment as ridiculous, he patted her hand. "You, I trust. Your judgment . . . that could use a little work. But I'm not saying this is your fault entirely, Annie, only that the kids might be taking the stuff when no one is looking, and selling it off. You know how kids are. They use drugs. They need money."

Annie was rendered speechless by her father's accusations. To condemn the kids without proof was unconscionable. Okay, so she'd done it to Henry, but that was different. He was a pervert. "Are you lumping Tess into that category, too? I thought you liked her."

Sid took a moment to answer. "I do like Tess. She's a nice kid. A smart-mouth, like you, but a good kid. I don't think she's part of this."

"Pop, I don't know what to say. I've never heard you

speak so judgmentally before, especially without a shred of evidence to back you up."

"Be reasonable, Annie. There's more than coincidence at work here; even you have to admit that. And don't forget the horrible mess those boys made of the fashion show. They exposed their *tuchases* to my customers."

"They weren't naked, Pop. There was no nudity."

"No? Three of my best customers are afraid to shop here now. They're afraid of what they might see when they come into my store. Two weeks ago Mrs. Frobish bumped into one of the naked male mannequins—I won't tell you where, but she almost fainted. She hasn't stepped foot in Goldman's since. We'll be broke before Christmas."

"But why would Mrs. Frobish faint? She's married. Surely she's seen a p—"

"Don't say it." He held up his hand. "There are some things a father doesn't want to talk about with his daughter. And besides, it's very doubtful Mrs. Frobish has ever seen her husband naked."

Annie's eyes widened. "Really? How absurd."

"We're dealing with different generations here, Annie. You can't expect older people to behave the same way you young ones do."

Well, if Gina hadn't seen Sid's *merchandise* in all the years they'd been married, then maybe that's the reason they were having trouble in the bedroom. Annie felt like telling her father that, but didn't want to embarrass him. Sid and sex just wasn't a good conversation.

"Do you think I should quit, Pop? Maybe if I was no longer working here at the store, these sort of incidents wouldn't happen."

"Quit? What? Are you nuts?" He threw exasperated hands in the air. "You're half owner of this store, and you've got a responsibility to it. Quitting is not an option. We've got to get to the bottom of this thievery and find out who's behind it."

"And how do you propose we do that?"

"To start, I think you need to talk with Joe, ask him about the possibility of . . . well, you know."

"Joe? But I'm not convinced the kids from the Crisis Center have anything to do with this."

"You've got to separate business from personal, Annie. As part owner of Goldman's, you've got to ask tough questions. Maybe you won't like the answers. I don't know." He pushed himself up from the chair. "Time to get to work. We've got to sell what merchandise we got left." He paused at the curtain. "You coming?"

"In a minute. I've got to think this through and decide what I'm going to do."

"Think, schmink. That doesn't get the work done."

Annie heaved a sigh, wondering if her father was right about Joe's kids. She had entertained the same idea, as unappealing as it was, but couldn't quite bring herself to believe it might be true.

But what if it was? What if the some of the kids had been behind the trouble they'd had of late? She couldn't just dismiss the possibility out of hand. She had a responsibility to the store; her father was right about that.

There was only one thing left to do. She would talk to Joe, ask if he thought such a thing was possible. No doubt he wouldn't appreciate the questions, but it was business. Surely he would understand.

"Hey, Miss Goldman!"

Paul Parducci waved as she stepped into the Crisis Center that evening. He was one of her stock boys, and she liked him. But was he a thief? She couldn't bring herself to think so.

The Center was empty, for the most part. Everyone had gone home for the day, including Angela, it appeared. Her desk had been cleared of any paperwork.

She'd wanted to talk to the woman about Mary and Dan's custody situation, get her opinion on their legal position where Matthew was concerned, but she supposed it was better to wait and let them handle things their own way.

Smiling, she waved back at Paul. He looked as innocent as a spring lamb. None of the kids who worked at Goldman's seemed capable of committing crimes, in her opinion. "Hi, Paulie. Is Joe around? I need to talk to him. It's kind of important."

"Sure. I'll get him." He brushed back a cowlick, and she was reminded of Opie from *The Andy Griffith Show*. "He's in the kitchen, making another pot of coffee."

Joe and his coffee. The man was addicted to caffeine. Not that she should talk. Annie couldn't function without two cups in the morning.

Joe was smiling as he approached, looking awfully sexy in his blue jeans and black T-shirt, coffee mug in hand. "I wasn't expecting to see you this early. Figured you had your hands full with your dad, and all that." He kissed her cheek. "But it's a nice surprise. You want to go get something to eat? I'm about finished here."

"Um, that would be nice. But first, there's something I need to talk to you about."

Perching on the edge of his desk, he offered her the chair in front, but she preferred to remain standing. "What about? You look upset. Did something else happen?"

"I'm going now, Joe," Paul called out, diverting the

couple's attention momentarily. "See you tomorrow, Miss Goldman," he added before disappearing out the front door.

Annie took a deep breath. "I feel terrible about mentioning this, Joe." She hemmed and hawed a bit, then finally swallowed her nervousness. "I think we need to face the possibility that some of the kids from the Center might be involved with what's been happening at the store."

His eyes widened. "Are you serious? You think some of the kids are to blame?"

"I know it's hard to believe, but . . . well, stuff didn't start happening until after they started working at the store, and we've got to face the fact that some of them might be involved. I don't want to believe it, Joe. Really I don't."

"But to accuse the kids without proof, Annie. That's not like you. I realize they make easy targets, because of their pasts, but to think that they might have stolen from you, and without one shred of evidence to back you up. I'm disappointed you would think such a thing." Joe knew he was being unreasonable, but he just couldn't help himself. Annie's lack of trust in the kids, in him, hit him where it hurt: his pride.

The wounded look he flashed went straight to her heart, creating a dull ache. "I'm not accusing anyone, Joe. Just raising possibilities. I have a responsibility to Goldman's. I'm a partner. I made the decision to hire the kids. And I'm the one who has to find out if they're involved, which is why I came to talk to you. I thought we could have a rational discussion about this. Who knew you'd be so defensive?"

But Annie knew very well that Joe was loyal to a fault. When he believed in something—someone—he went to the mat.

"This is more than just about the kids stealing from you, isn't it, Annie? This is about trust. Something you have little of. I knew you were a skeptic, but I never thought you would doubt me, or the kids. But then, why shouldn't you? You've never believed that people can and do change.

"Do you think because the kids were once in trouble that they can't grow beyond that stage of their lives? Do you think because I was once stupid and immature and left you that I haven't changed for the better?"

"No. That's not what I think at all. I—"

"You don't believe me when I tell you I love you. You don't trust me not to walk out the door and leave you again. Admit it. You'll never say that you love me, because to do so would make you weak and vulnerable. You might actually open yourself up to getting hurt again.

"Well, join the club, babe. I opened my heart to you, and you've ripped it out of my chest with both hands." Walking away from her, he crossed to the window and looked out at the enveloping darkness.

Rooted to her spot, Annie's feet felt as leaden as her emotions. She couldn't have moved if she'd wanted to. "Joe, please! I'm just trying to get to the bottom of things at the store. I don't distrust you. I—"

Say it, Annie. Tell him you love him now, before it's too late.

"No?" He whirled to face her, hands shoved deep in his pants pockets. "Then why do you hold back? Why haven't you told me how you feel? For crying out loud, Annie, we've been as intimate as any two people can be. And still you won't let me in. You expect to be let down. You're waiting for it to happen. Maybe you want it to happen, so you can feel you were right about me all along."

There was some truth to his words, and she choked on

them, and her unshed tears. "I'm sorry," she whispered, but Joe was having none of her apology.

"I suppose you think Tess is in this so-called teenage theft ring, too."

She shook her head adamantly. "No. I don't. I've never believed for one second that Tess is involved, and neither does my father."

"Well, isn't that a relief? Should I offer thanks now, or wait in case you change your mind?"

"You're not being fair."

No, he wasn't, but he couldn't seem to stop himself. The floodgates had opened, and every feeling, every thought he had held in was pouring out. "I'm not the one making false accusations. That would be you."

"How do you know they're false? Where's your proof?"

He patted his chest. "Here. That's where. In my heart I know those kids would never steal from you. They like and respect you and your father. Do you think they have no loyalty, no feelings, no appreciation that you gave them a chance when no one else would?" He tunneled frustrated fingers through his hair and heaved a sigh.

Annie was stunned by his outburst. "I don't know what to say. I didn't come here to hurt you or the kids. I just want to get to the bottom of things and find out the truth."

Moving toward her, he reached for her hand and placed it over her heart. "The truth you seek is here. Trust is more important than love, Annie. Without it a relationship can never survive. Any kind of a relationship. Think about it. Maybe someday you'll figure it out before it's too late."

The phone rang, ending their difficult conversation, and Annie ran for the door, not daring to look back to see the hurt, disappointment, and sadness on Joe's face. Not willing to let him see the tears on hers.

* * *

Joe watched Annie leave and felt like the biggest idiot in the world. She had every right to question him about the kids, to seek his counsel. And instead of discussing the problem rationally, he'd gone off on her, like some irrational, crazed lunatic.

Real professional, Joe!

He'd made all sorts of claims about the kids' honesty, without knowing for certain if they were true. Some of the older boys had stolen before, and had served time at the juvenile detention center. But he was positive that even those kids had turned themselves around, finding it hard to believe that any of them would be involved.

Maybe that's because if they are, Joe, you'll end up a failure. Useless. You'll have to admit that your counseling and guidance might not make a difference.

He'd told Annie not long ago that he wouldn't screw up again, let her down. But he just had. Was he cutting and running again? Was he taking the easy way out, instead of facing the truth?

"You're a first-rate asshole, Joe Russo. You just let the best thing that's ever happened to you walk out the door. So, what are you going to do about it?"

Reaching into the pocket of his jeans, Joe pulled out the small gold crucifix he always carried. "Pray," he whispered, hoping someone a lot smarter than he would have the answer he sought.

EIGHTEEN

"As we live, so we learn."

Gina hadn't seen her daughter cry since she was eleven and Tony Marconi, her elementary school classmate, had refused her invitation to attend the fifth-grade Christmas dance.

Fortunately, Annie was no longer pining over Tony, who now weighed close to three hundred pounds, had six kids, and worked as a garbage collector. Not that there was anything wrong with that, but . . . well, a garbage collector wasn't quite as impressive as being a priest, or even an ex-priest, like Joe. That took someone very special.

But Annie was crying now, pining over that special someone, and her heart-wrenching sobs tore at Gina's heart. "Annie, stop! Please. You'll make yourself sick." Gina moved to sit down beside her at the kitchen table. "I'm sure Joe's just upset. He'll come around eventually. You'll see."

Wiping her runny nose on the sleeve of her expensive red silk blouse, Annie shook her head. "No, he won't. I haven't heard from him in over a week." She'd hoped that by now Joe would have gotten over his pique and called or visited her. But he'd kept his distance. Apparently he was still fuming over their discussion about the kids' possible involvement with the store theft.

Well, that was just too darn bad. She had every right to question him. Some of the kids had been in trouble before. Joe was just being too overprotective, too unreasonable, and too ridiculous for words. Why couldn't he see that?

Tess was going out of her way to avoid talking to her, too. She'd heard from some of the kids about Annie's suspicions involving the store, and had confronted Annie, and Annie had no choice but to relate what she suspected.

"How could you think I stole from you? I'd never do a terrible thing like that. I thought we were friends. I guess I was wrong."

"You're not wrong, Tess. We are friends, and I've never thought any such thing," she tried to explain.

"You think some of the kids from the Center are behind the trouble. I work there, so I guess that makes me guilty, too."

"My father and I trust you implicitly, Tess. You must believe me."

Shaking her head, the girl wore her betrayal like a plate of armor. "I thought we had a special relationship, Annie, like sisters, almost."

Oh, Tess, Annie thought, feeling utterly miserable, we are like sisters.

Gina clasped Annie's hand, worry lines creasing her brow. "I know your father is behind this, and I'm sorry for that. But Sid has a volatile nature and always speaks before he thinks. The man should have been born an Italian."

Annie sighed. "Pop was right. I had to put the store first. Joe is being unreasonable about this. He's letting our personal relationship cloud his judgment. Even if it's eventually proven that the kids had nothing to do with it, the subject still had to be broached."

"Do you think they're responsible?"

She shrugged. "I don't know. I hope not. Most of the kids are really sweet."

"Even sweet kids get into trouble, *cara*."

Annie's startled gaze flew up to meet her mother's. "What are you saying? Are you saying you think they did it?"

Shaking her head, Gina replied, "No, I don't think that at all. But I do think there's an ongoing problem, and you're going to have to find out the truth. Until you do, you'll never be able to put this behind you. It will remain like some big cancerous tumor between you and Joe, eating away at your relationship."

With Gina you always got medical analogies.

"But Joe doesn't need or want proof," Annie said. "He trusts those kids implicitly."

"Are you forgetting, Annie, that Joe was once a priest? He looks for the good in people, and that's wonderful. He's certainly nothing like his mother." She wrinkled her nose in disgust. "But you've got a different burden to bear. You're part owner of the store and, as such, you did the right thing by confronting your suspicions; or maybe they were your father's suspicions, that doesn't really matter now.

"Also, if the kids under Joe's supervision are involved, he's going to feel responsible, that he failed in some way."

"I hadn't thought of that."

"I'm not saying Joe was wrong to stand up for those kids, but you weren't wrong, either, *cara*."

"He made some terribly hurtful comments. I'm not sure things will ever work out between us." Figures, just when she thought they would, this had to happen. Another tear trickled down her cheek, to land on the table. Bubbeh, lying beneath, whined in sympathy, then army-crawled his way over to place his head on her foot.

"I love him, Gina. I really love him. What am I going to do? Everything's such a mess."

"Then you must make it right. But first, you must take care of the business at hand. Joe is not going anywhere. He's in love with you." At Annie's look of doubt, she added, "Yes, he's hurt right now. But as I said, he'll get over it."

"I wish I could believe that."

"Believe it. A mother would never lie about such things. Now, you must concentrate on fixing matters at the store, so your father won't make everyone around him miserable, namely me. The man is a master at that."

"I'm not sure what you expect me to do about the theft. It's been difficult catching the culprits involved. They continue to steal. And though we've tried to remain vigilant, we can't watch every square inch of the store every second of the day."

"I have a cousin who specializes in surveillance work."

As the possibilities began to unfold before her, Annie's heart rate accelerated, then dropped. "Gina, we're not related to any private detective."

"No? Louie installs security devices for a living. You can get one of those video cameras that watch everything and have it installed in the store. That way you'll know exactly who's responsible.

"I've tried for years to talk your father into installing them, but you know how old-fashioned he is. Not to mention cheap. After we put in the burglar alarm, he didn't want to spend the money on the other. I bet now he wishes he'd listened to me."

Straightening in her chair, Annie gazed at her mother as if she'd just discovered the cure for PMS, and smiled for the first time in days. "You're a genius, Mom! I can't believe Pop didn't listen to you. I can't believe I didn't think of this myself."

Gina's mouth fell open, and suddenly her eyes filled with tears. "You called me Mom."

"*Oy vey!* I wouldn't have, if I'd known it was going to upset you."

"Don't be silly. I'm not upset. I'm happy." She clasped her hands together. "I've been waiting for this day. The good Lord works in mysterious ways."

"Because I called you Mom?" Annie was totally confused. Not an unusual occurrence when dealing with her mother's convoluted way of thinking.

"It's a sign that we're getting closer."

"But we've always been close. At least, I've always thought so. I love you, you know that."

"But you never call me Mom, or Mother, always Gina."

"If it means that much to you, I can start."

"Would you?" her mother asked, her face suffused with pleasure. "It would make me so happy."

"Why didn't you say something before this, if it bothered you so much?"

"I didn't want to push. I thought maybe you needed time to come to terms with our relationship."

Annie rolled her eyes. "As if my life isn't complicated enough right now."

Kissing her daughter's cheek, Gina said, "I'll get Louie's card. It's in the junk drawer somewhere." She moved to the bank of drawers and began to rummage through the one designated for "things," finally pulling out a small white business card from among the mess of nails, rubber bands, and other assorted items that didn't have anywhere else to live. A house could not survive without a junk drawer, Gina always said, and Annie wasn't inclined to argue, since she and everyone else she knew had one just like it.

"Here it is." She handed the card to her daughter. "Louie's very good at what he does. Myra Shertzer caught her husband in," her eyebrows raised meaningfully, " 'the act' with another woman. Thanks to Louie's spying techniques—the man is a regular James Bond—she's getting a divorce from the no-good bum.

"Thank God your father isn't like that. Of course, men your father's age don't have as much interest in sex, like when they were younger. It's a burden to bear, but a wife does what a wife has to do."

That's not what Sid had implied. Not by a long shot. It was obvious to Annie that when it came to things of a sexual nature, her parents were on two different wavelengths. Actually, they were on two different planets. Good thing their cosmic energies had collided at least once, to produce her.

Deciding not to interfere—she had enough problems of her own at the moment—she replied, "Thanks, Mom!" returning her kiss. "I'm going to call Louie right away."

"Tell him I said hi. And Annie, everything is going to work out. You'll see. Remember, I love you."

"I love you, too, Mom," she said, and Gina burst into tears again.

"Didn't I tell you Annie Goldman was the wrong girl for you, Joe? A woman must have faith in her man, trust him, like when your father burned my ass with that toilet seat invention. Did I complain? Did I criticize?

"You didn't listen to your mother, and now look what's happened."

Joe shot Sophia a murderous glance that had her taking a step back. "I still don't want to listen, so drop it."

Just the mention of Annie's name made his heart twist painfully and his stomach tie up in knots. He hadn't seen her in over a week, but her image was burned into his brain, his heart. He'd started to call her a dozen times or more, but his pride held him back.

He missed her, and it was damn painful.

Sophia threw her hands in the air, looking at her husband and mother-in-law for support. Though God only knew why, because she wasn't likely to get any. "What? What did I say? I'm only trying to help. Be happy you found this out before you got serious. Now you can find a nice Italian girl—a good Catholic girl—and settle down, have children. It's for the best. You'll see I'm right."

"Be quiet, Sophia!" Frank finally interjected, looking up from his newspaper and scowling fiercely at his wife. "Can't you see the boy is hurting?"

Having had his fill of family closeness for one day, Joe grabbed his leather jacket off the back of the dining room chair. "I can't stay for dinner, Mom. Sorry, but I've got to go." He cast an apologetic glance at his father, who nodded in understanding.

"But, Joe, it's almost time to eat. I made a nice rib roast—it's choice—and there's baked ziti, just the way you like it, with lots of mozzarella."

"See what you did, Sophia Graziano? You've pushed your only son out the door." Frank's mother grunted her disapproval. "You never learn, no matter how old you get. *Stupida.*"

"Is that true, Joe? Are you upset at your mother, the woman who gave birth to you, the woman who worries about you from morning till night? I couldn't live with myself if I thought that. I might as well drop dead this instant." She clutched her heart dramatically.

"Good," Flora said, then picked up her crocheting, adjusting her thick-lensed glasses.

Knowing it was pointless to argue or to try to reason with her, Joe bussed his mother's cheek. She wasn't about to change her ways at this late date. She was only content when she was trying to run his life, which was most of the time. "I'm not mad at you, Mom. I've just got things to do. I'll call you later, okay?"

"Mad? Why should you be mad, Joseph? I tell only the truth. As your mother it's my job to look out for you. I've made sacrifices. I—"

Sophia was still wearing that perplexed look on her face when Joe pulled the front door shut tightly behind him and walked into the cool evening air. He took a deep breath to ward off the feelings of mother-induced suffocation, then traversed the short distance to his apartment, while trying to make sense of everything that had happened between him and Annie.

For most of his adult life he had pondered the problem of Annie Goldman. What to do about Annie had become the question that had burdened him from morning till night, through fifteen years of priesthood, and a whole lot longer than that, if he counted back to the beginning.

He'd loved her, then left her, and then fallen in love with her all over again. Not that he'd ever stopped loving Annie. But this time it was a mature love, an all-consuming I-want-to-be-with-you-the-rest-of-my-life kind of love.

But despite his love, Joe knew that he hadn't made any headway into breaching the wall she'd erected around her heart. She was determined to keep him at arm's length, and—dammit to hell!—she was succeeding.

Annie's accusations about the kids had bothered him. But it went much deeper than that. She distrusted people, him most of all. He thought he had convinced her of his love, about how good things could be between them, if only she'd give them a chance.

But he realized now that their relationship was hopeless. She would never give her heart to him, trust him. And as he'd so recently told her, there could be no future without trust. Until she could open up her heart totally and completely, until she could learn to trust with every molecule and cell in her body, they couldn't make their relationship work.

"Dammit, Annie! Why do you have to be so stubborn?" *Why do I have to love you so much?*

Trudging up the steps leading to his apartment, Joe ignored the noise coming from Mama Sophia's, and had almost reached the top landing when a soft voice he recognized only too well called out to him.

"Joe, wait!"

He looked over his shoulder to find his sister approaching with a determined look on her face, and he fought the urge to groan aloud. At any other time he would have been happy to see Mary. But not now. Now he needed to be alone, lick his wounds, and figure out how to live in a world that didn't include Annie.

"Have you and Annie made up yet?" she wanted to know, breathing in deeply. "Man, these steps are a lot harder to climb than when I lived here."

Joe looked down to find that her feet were swollen, due to the fact that she'd been standing on them for most of the day. "I don't want to talk about Annie. I've had enough of that discussion for one evening."

"Ma's been ragging on you, huh?"

He unlocked the door and she followed him inside. "Of course. Has the woman ever had an opinion she didn't voice? What's happened is all for the best, didn't you know?" He let loose a string of epithets, and Mary's eyes widened; Joe rarely swore.

"Joseph Russo, shame on you. Even though you're no longer a priest, you shouldn't take the Lord's name in vain."

He knew she was right, but . . . "Sorry."

"Don't apologize to me. I think you need to go to confession and unburden yourself. You've obviously got some demons you need to exorcise." Her smile grew mischievous. "Maybe you should pay Father Damian a visit. He did wonders for Linda Blair."

"Very funny. And that's strange talk coming from you, peanut. I practically had to hog-tie and drag you into the confessional."

Mary lowered herself onto the sofa, running her hand over the smooth leather. "I just love this furniture. You're taking care of it, right?"

"Why are you here?" As if he didn't know. "Not that I mind you visiting, but don't you have a restaurant to run? It sounded like the place was packed."

"Annie's miserable. You're even more miserable. I think you're being a pigheaded, stubborn fool."

Dark eyes widened. "I'm your brother. How can you take her side in this? Blood is supposed to be thicker than—"

"Please." She held up her hand. "You're starting to sound like Ma. Just hear me out, and then I'll leave you to your misery. It's obvious you're wanting to brood."

His cheeks reddened at her accurate assumption, and he folded his arms across his chest. "Go on."

"I realize you were hurt by Annie's questions about the theft. She told me all about the conversation you and she had regarding the missing merchandise and the kids. But you have to realize where she was coming from, Joe. She didn't want to believe the kids were involved, but she's got a father who is very much like our mother. Need I say more? And Annie takes her responsibilities to the store very seriously. And you know damn well that some of those kids you're coddling have been in trouble with the law before.

"What was she supposed to do? Just forget about it?"

"What about her responsibility to me?" He shook his head. "I don't blame you for defending her, Mary. Annie's your best friend. But I love her, and she . . . well, never mind."

"She loves you, too. Can't you see that?"

The kernel of hope sprouting in his chest was reflected in his eyes. "Did she tell you that?"

Her voice softened. "Not in so many words, but you'd have to be blind and stupid not to see it. It's written all over her face."

"My vision is twenty-twenty, and I haven't seen any such thing. Annie's never forgiven me for leaving her all those years ago. She never will. I've about reached the end of my rope where she's concerned. I'm tired of trying to convince her I've changed.

"I was immature and selfish when we were first involved, I admit that. But I was young and so was Annie. I'd like to think that I've grown up, become responsible for my actions, learned to face up to problems instead of running from them."

"Why do I suddenly get the feeling that there's more going on here than a teen romance that suddenly soured?"

"Because there is. But I'm not going to discuss it with you. What happened between Annie and me is personal, and it's going to stay that way. Suffice it to say that Annie still doesn't trust me, and leave it at that."

Mary shook her head. "I can't believe such impossible, mule-headed people surround me. You love her. She loves you. Enough said.

"Besides, it's time for me to get back to work." Mary stood, a weary look on her face as she clutched her brother's arm. "Think things through, Joe, before you make a rash decision that you'll regret. Your future and Annie's may depend on it."

In the space of two heartbeats she was gone, leaving Joe feeling more miserable than he had before she'd arrived. "And they call women the weaker sex!"

Standing shoulder to shoulder in the Goldmans' living room, Annie and her father watched the videotape roll, and witnessed Raymond Rosario and Billy Rothstein shoplifting merchandise from the racks of Goldman's Department Store. As thieves went, they were quite good and very professional.

Joe is going to be upset was Annie's first thought. She didn't want to be the one to tell him that he had a couple of rotten apples in his orchard.

"Those little bastards!" Fist raised in midair, Sid shouted at the television set—a Zenith he'd purchased over twenty-five years ago. There was no remote control; but then, Annie's father always said that you could get a lot of exercise by getting up to switch channels.

"I'm going to have them arrested."

"Well, that'll be a lot easier than what I have to do," she replied, dreading her upcoming confrontation with Joe. "I need to talk to Joe about this before we proceed, Pop. He has a right to know what's going on."

Sid rubbed his chest, noting his daughter's deepening frown of displeasure. "Why are you looking so down in the mouth? We caught the thieves. Soon the police will arrest them and everything will be back to normal. You should be happy, not wearing such a face."

"How can I be happy when two of Joe's kids are involved? He's going to be devastated. He's going to blame himself."

"Why should Joe blame himself? It wasn't his fault. Don't be silly. Everything will be fine, you'll see." Her father didn't look the least bit upset, but Annie wasn't surprised. It was all in a day's work to him.

"Joe's been counseling Ray and Billy for weeks, thinking he's made a difference, and now when he finds out what they've done . . ."

"*Oy!* I see your point. So, you're going over there to tell him?"

Annie grabbed her purse off the coffee table. "Yes. Give me thirty minutes to talk to Joe, then call that detective in charge of our case and let him know what we discovered."

"I hope you can smooth things out with Joe, Annie. I know how much you care. And, well . . . I like him, too. For a *shaygitz*, he's not too bad."

"Yes, I care."

"Joe's a mensch. Not that you asked, but if he wants to make an honest woman out of you, you've got my blessing."

Annie's smile filled with love for her father. It was difficult to be angry when she knew he cared so deeply about her. Sure, Sid had his faults—plenty of them—but he was a good husband and father, and his heart was always in the right place.

"Joe's not the only one who's a mensch, Pop. See you later."

Joe was alone in his office when Annie entered the Crisis Center a short time later. Head bent over a sheaf of papers, he was nibbling on the end of a pencil, looking studious and totally adorable. Her heart caught in her chest.

She cleared her throat and he looked up, eyes widening in surprise. And then he smiled, a warm friendly smile that said he was happy to see her, and she breathed a sigh of relief. "Annie!"

"Hi, Joe. I hope I'm not intruding or anything." She moved toward his desk.

"You're not intruding. Hell, I've wanted to call you, started to a dozen times."

"So why didn't you?"

He look chagrined. "Because I'm an ass."

"I won't dispute that opinion."

"I shouldn't have overreacted about the kids, Annie. And I'm sorry. I know you have issues with trust, and . . ."

"Two of the kids were behind the theft at the store, Joe," she blurted. "We caught Raymond Rosario and Billy Rothstein on videotape. I wanted to tell you before the police are called."

He blanched. "I don't believe it!"

She stiffened. "Would you like to see the tape?"

"I'm sorry." He shook his head. "I mean, how could I have been so blind, so stupid not to have seen what's been going on right under my nose?"

She'd had a feeling he'd react that way. "Don't blame

yourself, Joe. Pop and I had no idea, either, and we worked with Ray and Billy every day. They were good. Very good."

He plowed frustrated fingers through his hair. "I guess I owe you an even bigger apology."

She smiled softly. "I guess we owe each other an apology, but this is neither the time nor the place to make them. And I need to tell Tess. She needs to hear this from me. Why don't you come over to my place tomorrow night for dinner and we'll talk. Really talk. I think it's time."

When she entered the town house a short time later, Annie was relieved to find Tess home alone, watching television. She didn't turn around at the sound of the door closing, and Annie knew she was still upset with her.

"Hi, Tess! What are you watching?" Reruns of *The Brady Bunch*, from the looks of it.

"What do you care?"

Placing her purse and keys on the hall table, Annie moved to the couch to sit beside the young woman. "I do care, very much. And I'd like to talk, if you have a minute."

With a shrug of her shoulders, Tess clicked off the TV and turned to face Annie, her expression guarded. "What about? Donna's not here. I didn't take anything from her room, if that's what she said. I'm not a thief."

Annie moved to wrap her arm about the girl's shoulder; Tess stiffened, but didn't move away. "I know that. And I'm sorry if I made you feel bad about yourself. I never meant for any of this to rub off on you. But I had a responsibility to the store, to my father. I hope you can understand that."

Tess's eyes widened. "You don't think I'm a thief?"

Annie saw the relief in the teenager's eyes. "I never

thought you were, sweetie. And I'm sorry you misunder-
stood. We caught the boys who stole the merchandise. It
was Ray and Billy."

"Ray and Billy! Oh, wow! Guess they're in big trouble.
I'm not surprised, though. Those two were always getting
themselves into stuff they shouldn't have." Tess smacked
her gum a few times, and Annie realized she'd miss that
sound and a whole lot more when Tess finally moved into
her permanent foster home.

"I guess they're going to learn a painful lesson. Too bad
they had to learn it the hard way."

"Is Joe really upset?"

Annie nodded. "Yes, but I think he realizes that there
wasn't anything he could have done to prevent what happened." At least, she hoped he realized that. "Do you want
to have dinner at Mama Sophia's tonight? I think we can
both use an evening out."

Tess's eyes lit. "Okay. I'm starving. And, well, I was
kinda hoping we wouldn't have to eat Donna's cooking."
She made a face. "It's pretty gross."

Amen to that. "Speaking of Donna, where is my cousin?"

"She went shopping. Donna's got more clothes than she
knows what to do with, but said she needed a new fall
wardrobe, that last year's just wouldn't do at all." Tess
mimicked her inflection perfectly.

Donna buying new clothes was certainly nothing new. The
woman had never met a sale or a credit card she didn't like.

"Well, I don't think we should let Donna have all the
fun. What say after dinner we hit the mall and do some
shopping ourselves?"

"Cool." Tess flung herself into Annie's arms. "I love
you, Annie. I'm so glad we're friends again."

Annie hugged her tightly, and a lump formed in her throat. "Same here, kiddo. Now let's go do some serious damage to my VISA card."

NINETEEN

"You can't dance at two weddings
at the same time;
nor can you sit on two horses
with one behind."

"Something smells delicious," Joe said, taking his place at the small, cloth-covered table in Annie's kitchen, which had been set with colorful red and green plates, wine-glasses, and candles. He sniffed the air again. "Let me guess . . . manicotti or cannelloni."

Smiling, she retrieved the spaghetti and meatballs she had slaved over all day, setting the large pasta bowl in the center of the table. "Nothing that fancy, I'm afraid. Don't forget, I'm still learning the fine art of Italian cooking, though I'm much better than I used to be, thanks to Marco."

Mary's chef had taught her well and had even compli-mented her lasagna. Would wonders never cease? You could have knocked her over with a feather when the short, pompous man had deigned to bestow his blessing upon her cooking. It could only be compared to receiving a dispen-sation from the Pope.

Filling their glasses with deep red Chianti, she sat down, holding her breath as he took the first bite. She knew it wouldn't be as good as what he was used to—Mary and Sophia were excellent cooks, and Joe had been spoiled by their expertise—but she hoped he liked it anyway.

Eyes wide with pleasure, he made several contented

sounds, then said, "Excellent. Some of the best spaghetti I've ever had. And the meatballs are quite good, too."

Even if he was lying through his teeth, Annie was thrilled that he'd paid her such a lavish compliment, and she smiled happily. "I heard the way to a man's heart is through his stomach. Guess that's true."

"That's one theory." The sexy smile he flashed made her heart go into triple time. "But there are others."

Though she hated to spoil the moment, Annie knew it was time to get things straightened out between them. "I'm glad you came tonight, Joe. There are things we need to talk about, things I need to say."

"Sounds ominous."

Fearing a massive attack of indigestion, Annie said, "Let's eat first, then we'll talk. My father thinks it's very bad for digestion to mix serious conversation with eating. Most of the meals I ate at home were spent in silence."

"Really? That's the exact opposite of my family. You couldn't eat a meal in silence if you tried. I'm not sure such a thing exists in an Italian family. Nothing like a good fight or two to get the juices flowing.

"Food fights were pretty common during dinner at our house. Connie pelted me alongside the head once with a meatball." He grinned at the memory of how furious his mother had become, especially after Grandma Flora joined the melee and began tossing pieces of bread around the table.

Annie laughed. "My mother tried to make dinner conversation, because that's what she was used to in her family, but my father made it clear that wasn't his way, so she eventually gave up. We did a lot of communicating with eye rolling and smiles, though."

Easing back in his chair, Joe studied Annie as she talked. She was dressed very casually, in jeans and a loose-fitting red sweater, and he liked the fact that she wasn't dressed to seduce her way around their problems, as she had been other times. He'd come to learn that she wore her suggestive clothing like armor, to protect her vulnerable side.

He wasn't sure, however, why her head was covered in a scarf that had been tied up like a turban. "Is that a new look? I don't recall ever seeing you in a hat or a head-piece before." Annie liked flaunting her outrageous hair colors. He suspected it was her way of thumbing her nose at society.

Her face reddened, and she reached up self-consciously to pat her head. "Ah, there was a little accident today at the beauty parlor. You might call it revenge of the hair follicles."

"Don't tell me. You're bald." He was kidding, but then noting the horrified look on her face, his teasing smile melted

"Not exactly, but my hair did break off kinda short, so I decided to cover it up."

"Are you going to wear a scarf until it grows out? That could take months, and I like seeing your hair."

Noting that Joe was finished eating, Annie pushed away from the table and stood, grabbing her glass of wine before heading for the living room. "I haven't decided yet. I guess I was waiting to see your reaction."

"It's that bad, huh?"

Once in the living room, she removed the scarf, and Joe stared wide-eyed at first, then smiled. "It's short, but it's not ugly. I like it."

Her jaw unhinged. "You do? You must be crazy. I look

like I've just had radiation treatments. I almost killed Mr. Roy. I left the beauty parlor with a towel wrapped around my head. I was totally mortified."

"Well, at least it's your natural color, or close to it."

"*Oy vey!* It started out purple, but it was the wrong shade, sort of lavender, so Mr. Roy decided to try again, and that's when my hair revolted. He was finally able to darken it enough so I didn't look totally weird." Not totally. Just mostly.

Noting the tears she tried valiantly to hold back, Joe smiled softly and pulled her into his arms. "It's not that bad, babe. And it'll grow out. Why, by next week it'll probably be almost back to normal."

"Ya think? I kinda doubt it."

He kissed the top of her head. "So you'll start a new fashion trend. You're good at that."

She looked up, saw the sincerity and kindness in his eyes, and caressed his cheek, feeling so much in love it was disgusting. "You're a good man, Joe Russo. I'm not sure I deserve you in my life, but I love you. I've loved you for a very long time. I was just too afraid to admit it. You hurt me, and . . . well, I'm just Italian enough to hold a grudge."

Pure joy poured out of his smile; he hugged her tightly to his chest. "I love you, too, Annie. It seems like I have forever, and I want to spend the rest of my life with you. I want us to have babies, and grow old together, and—"

"Babies?" Her face lit with wonder at the possibility of having a child . . . Joe's child. "You want to have a baby with me?"

"I want that more than anything. Maybe the baby we lost wasn't meant to be. It wasn't the right time for us. But it is now. I want to have lots of babies with you. And I wouldn't mind starting on the project right now, this very minute." He kissed her passionately. "I'm so crazy in love with you, Annie Goldman. Will you marry me?"

Annie, who hardly ever cried, who used to think that showing emotion was a sign of weakness, who thought that being comforted was the ultimate uncool, covered her face with her hands and began to bawl like a baby.

Deep heart-wrenching sobs tore from her body, tears streamed down her face in a river of emotion, and Joe grew panicked by her unorthodox display of sentiment. "Annie, I'm sorry. I didn't mean to upset you. If you don't want to get married, I—"

Her head shot up. "What? Are you crazy?" She thumped his chest with her fist. "Of course I want to marry you. A woman's entitled to a little crying jag when she gets a marriage proposal. Didn't your mother ever explain that to you?"

Shaking his head, he smiled, amused by her reaction. "Sophia neglected to mention that part."

At the mention of his mother, Annie stopped crying instantly and trepidation replaced her joy of moments before. "Sophia." She breathed the name as if it were an evil omen, then sucked in her breath. "Your mother is not going to be happy about this, Joe. She doesn't like me, and she certainly doesn't want me for a daughter-in-law. We are doomed before we begin."

Kissing the top of her head, he said, "You handle me, babe, and let me handle my mother."

"Mom!" Annie called out, marching into her parents' home the next evening to give them the news of their engagement, Joe following close on her heels.

She inhaled deeply the scents of cinnamon and nutmeg

and knew Gina had been baking apple pies. Her delighted stomach grumbled in response, even though she and Joe had just finished eating dinner at Mama Sophia's a short while ago.

Mary had been ecstatic when told the news of their impending marriage, and had promised not to breathe a word until they'd had time to make the announcement to their respective families.

"They're probably in the living room watching TV," she explained when no one answered. "Sid's a big fan of *Wheel of Fortune*. He thinks Vanna White's hot."

"Vanna's a little too plastic for my taste," Joe said, nibbling the back of Annie's neck. "I prefer a softer, tastier type of woman."

"Stop that and behave! We have important business to discuss." But she was dreamy-eyed when she said it, and Joe grinned.

They entered the living room, stopping short at the sight of Annie's parents kissing on the sofa like two love-starved teenagers. They were really going at it, as evidenced by Joe's strangled sound.

"Damn!" she heard him mutter.

"Mom? Dad?" Eyes wide with disbelief, she turned to find Joe's grin as wide as hers. "Well, well. Still waters really do run deep."

"Annie!" Her mother's face flushed red when she spotted her daughter and Joe, and pushed out of her husband's embrace. "We weren't expecting you."

Sid readjusted his clothing and cursed colorful epithets under his breath. "What? You don't knock anymore?"

Annie wondered which one of her parents had been taking the extra vitamins. They must have been potent little devils, she decided. "That's obvious. Shall we come back later? We don't want to intrude."

"Stop with your fresh mouth," a red-faced Sid told his daughter, motioning them in. And to Joe: "Come. Sit. Parents are entitled to kiss," he added at Annie's teasing grin.

"What brings you out this evening?" Joe opened his mouth to reply, but Sid just kept on talking. "It's nice to see you two made up. Thank God, because my stomach couldn't take much more of my daughter's moans and groans. The woman kvetches worse than her mother. Who knew it was possible?"

Annie's grin couldn't be contained. "Joe and I did more than make up, Pop. He's asked me to marry him."

With a startled scream, Gina flew off the sofa to embrace her daughter. "Oh, Annie, that's wonderful!" She molded Annie's head between her hands and kissed her soundly on the lips, then threw her arms around her future son-in-law and kissed him, too.

"You've made an excellent choice, Joe. My Annie's a good girl, a wonderful daughter. You won't be sorry." She then kissed the tiny gold cross she always wore around her neck and offered a silent prayer of thanks. Annie decided it was directed to St. Jude, the patron saint of hopeless causes.

Sid stared thoughtfully at his daughter. "You look happy. Bald, but happy. I don't care for the new hairdo. It looks like something one of those punk people would wear. In my day punks were hoodlums, now they're fashion mavens. *Oy!* What's this world coming to? First dummies with breasts, now punks."

"It's not a new look, Pop; it's a mistake," Annie informed him.

He shook his head in disgust. "I'll say. So, I'm assuming

you said yes to Joe's proposal." He gazed down at his daughter's hand and frowned. "Where's the ring? You can't have an engagement without a ring. I got a reputation. What will people think if you have no ring?"

Embarrassment turned Joe's face red. "We haven't picked one out yet, Mr. Goldman. It was sort of a spur-of-the-moment proposal. But we plan to go shopping for a ring first thing Monday morning."

"You'll come to my store instead. I'll give you a ten per-cent discount on whatever ring you choose. We got a nice selection. I keep the good stuff in my office safe. You look over the merchandise, then let me know what you decide. It's an important decision, but at ten percent you can afford to splurge a little."

Arms folded across her chest, Annie's brow shot up, and she leveled a disapproving gaze on her father. "Ten per-cent? I don't think so, Pop."

The older man threw his hands up in the air. "*Oy!* Such a tough bargain my Annie makes. I forgot she's not only a big shot now, she's a partner. Okay, twenty-five. But no more. I got to make a living."

Joe and Annie exchanged amused glances, and then Joe said, "Thanks, Mr. Goldman! That's very generous of you."

"I only got one daughter. No one calls Sid Goldman cheap." Except the Goldman store employees, but he wasn't going there.

Gina wiped tears of joy from her eyes. "Oh, Sid! I'm so happy."

He put his arm around his wife and grunted. "Of course you're happy. Your daughter is getting married. I'm the one who has to pay for it. It'll probably put me in the poorhouse."

"You've been saying that for years, Pop," Annie teased,

knowing her father claimed entry to the poorhouse at least once a week.

"Fresh mouth. So what kind of wedding are we talking about? Jewish, right? Of course, you'll both have to convert. I'll talk to the rabbi right away. You're circumcised, aren't you?" he asked Joe, though it had no bearing on the matter at hand, and the younger man's mouth dropped open.

Annie giggled at Joe's mortified look.

"Stop!" Holding her hand up like a frenzied traffic cop, Gina shook her head adamantly. "They must be married in the Catholic Church. Joe was a priest, not a rabbi. How can you even think they'd get married in a synagogue, Sid? Stop speaking such nonsense."

"Catholic! What? Are you crazy?"

All eyes landed on Annie, who sucked in her breath and prayed for divine intervention. When none was forthcoming, due in part to the fact that Sid and Gina had pissed off God, she said, "We haven't discussed the actual arrangements yet." And she was already dreading the ordeal. There would be two sets of parents to appease—two sets of very opinionated parents. It was an impossibility, as far as she was concerned. "I'll let you know when we make our decision." She clutched Joe's hand for moral support and squeezed.

"I haven't told my parents yet," he added, "so we're waiting to make the official announcement."

Now it was Gina and Annie's turn to exchange a look of trepidation.

"I don't think your mother is going to be too crazy about the idea, Joe," Annie's mother said, worry wrinkling her brow. "Not to say anything bad about Sophia, but she has very definite opinions about my daughter. None very good.

There could be problems." Her expression said there'd better not be.

"Another Italian Catholic. Of course she's opinionated. It's part of their nationality." Sid shook his head, then said to Annie and Joe,

"*Mazel tov.* I think you two will need all the luck you can get."

TWENTY

"Parents can give a dowry, but not good luck."

Cowering on the Russo's front porch, Annie wrapped her arms about herself and shook her head at Joe's insistence that she accompany him inside. There was a stiff autumn breeze blowing that had nothing to do with why she felt chilled to the bone.

"You go first. When the coast is clear, call me. If you don't come back, I'll know Sophia murdered you. No sense in both of us dying young."

Joe smiled in understanding. "You're being silly, Annie. My mother's going to be thrilled that I'm getting married. It's all she's talked about since I left the priesthood."

"Yeah, but not with me. Never with me. She wanted you to marry Angela. Angela not Annie. Remember?"

His hand on the brass knob, he started to push open the door. "I love you. That's all that matters. Now quit being a wuss or you're going to spoil your image."

"That was all a ruse. I'm not really that tough."

Wrapping his arm about her waist, he kissed her cheek. "You're actually quite soft, babe, and I want to explore that a bit later. But now it's show time."

"Okay. But if your mother attacks me, I'm suing."

* * *

"Joe!" Sophia rushed toward the front door when she heard it open, but skidded to a halt when she saw who had accompanied her son.

"Hello, Annie Goldman."

Forcing a smile, Annie reminded herself that this glowering woman was soon to be her mother-in-law. It was a hideous thought at best. Immediately, the old Ernie K. Doe song came to mind. *"The worst person I know . . . mother-in-law . . ."* "Mrs. Russo. Nice to see you again."

"You'll stay for dinner, Joe? I made plenty. Annie Goldman can stay, too, if you want," she said, though the invitation was less than cordial. Cannibals extended more warmth.

"I want." He winked at Annie, who was counting to ten under her breath, and then decided she'd better go all the way to twenty.

They followed Joe's mother into the garlic-scented kitchen, where Frank and Flora were seated at the Formica table, sharing a glass of before-dinner wine.

Joe had been hoping for a private audience with his mother, just in case she went off the deep end and started saying rude things; he didn't want Annie to be embarrassed. But it looked as if he was destined to speak before the entire family, because Connie walked in just then and was followed by Mary. Dan had remained outside to toss the football around with Matt.

Once everyone had gathered around the table, Joe cleared his throat, drew Annie close to his side, and said, "We've got an announcement to make. I hope everyone will be very happy."

Sophia clutched the back of a kitchen chair for support, her knuckles turning as white as her face. "What kind of announcement?" she asked cautiously, barely able to breathe.

"Joe and I are getting married!" Annie blurted, surprising herself and Joe by letting him off the hook. "He's proposed and I've accepted."

Joe smiled at her. "That's right," he added before anyone—his mother—could say anything. "I love Annie, and I want to spend the rest of my life with her."

There were several moments of stunned silence as everyone in the room digested the announcement, then turned to look at Sophia, who had now lowered herself onto the kitchen chair and was clasping her chest.

"My heart! My heart! I think I'm having an attack. Call an ambulance."

Sophia's reaction was no more than Annie and Joe had expected, so they remained rooted in their places. Even Frank failed to take action. Grandma Flora merely smiled at the possibility of her daughter-in-law's impending demise.

Finally Mary moved forward. "Now, Mom, you know the last time we went to the ER the doctor said you had the heart of a nineteen-year-old." When the older woman didn't dispute that fact, Mary turned to Annie and Joe, kissing each one in turn on the cheek, and smiling widely.

"Congratulations! I'm so excited for you. I can't wait to tell Dan. It's about time you two got hitched."

"It sure as heck is," Connie agreed, rushing forward and embracing the couple.

Frank, who was smiling wider than Julia Roberts, held up the wine bottle. "Let's have a toast to celebrate this happy occasion." He didn't dare glance at his wife, whom he knew would be casting daggers at him.

"I'ma very happy for you, Annie and Joe," Grandma Flora claimed, her eyes filled with tears of joy. "I hope you will be as happy asa I wasa with my Sal. He wasa good man, God rest his soul."

Annie let loose the breath she hadn't known she'd been holding, thinking all was well, until she saw Joe's mother stand, heard her say, "Excuse me. I'm not feeling so good," then watched her disappear from the room. Her heart fell.

"I'll go see what's wrong," Mary said, but Joe shook his head, his face a mask of determination.

"No. I'll go. I think we all know what's wrong, and I'm the one who needs to fix it."

Annie clasped his arm. "Remember to keep your temper, Joe, no matter what she says. They're just words, and words don't matter. Sophia's your mother, and she loves you."

"I likea this girl," Flora said, admiration glittering in her eyes as she watched Joe quit the room in search of his mother. "She reminds me of me."

Annie and Mary couldn't help grinning at each other.

Joe found his mother in the master bedroom, sitting on the edge of the bed, her face covered by the apron she always wore around her waist. "Mom, can I come in?" he asked from the doorway.

"Why do you ask? You didn't ask before you went and made your engagement to Annie Goldman, so why should you ask now?"

Sitting down beside her, he clasped her hand, as she had clasped his so many times over the years, to comfort, to pray, to encourage when he needed a swift kick in the pants and a boost of self-confidence. Sophia loved him, and he knew that, so his words were gentle when he spoke. "You want me to be happy, don't you, Mom? You want me to find the happiness in life that you found with Dad?"

Gazing into his eyes, she patted his cheek. "Of course I do, Joe. You're my firstborn, my son, and I love you. But

Annie Goldman . . ." She heaved a deep, disappointed sigh. "She's not the girl for you."

"She is, Mom. I love Annie more than I've ever loved anything or anyone, including God."

Sophia sucked in her breath and made the sign of the cross quickly, so Joe wouldn't be struck down where he sat. The walls of the room were covered with religious pictures and icons—the eyes of Jesus followed wherever you moved—so the former priest's immortal soul was relatively safe.

"You mustn't say such things. That's blasphemy, Joseph. God will punish you if you talk that way. Did you learn nothing as a priest?"

"I'll take my chances where God is concerned. He's much more forgiving than some people I know, much more understanding."

Her lower lip trembled. "You speak to your mother this way?"

"I know when you married Dad that you did it against Grandma Flora's wishes, Mom. She didn't want you for her son, just as you don't want Annie for me. But Dad went against her wishes and married you anyway, because he loved you, and wanted to spend the rest of his life with you, just as I want to spend the rest of mine with Annie.

"We love each other. And we're going to get married, with or without your blessing. I hope it will be with, because I don't want to have to choose." He hoped he'd made himself clear, because if his mother didn't accept Annie as his wife, then . . . well, he just didn't want to go there right now. Just thinking about a break with his family was painful. They had faults, but he loved them, warts and all.

Considering the full import of his words, Sophia soon realized that she was being given an ultimatum. She was a stubborn woman, but not a foolish one. "What about children? Annie Goldman doesn't strike me as the kind of woman who would want to start a family."

"What you don't know about Annie could fill a book, Mom. She's crazy about kids, wants at least three, maybe four. We talked about it last night."

Her eyes lit at the news, and she said, "That's good." Then her expression softened somewhat. "It shows the girl has good sense. And I know Annie works hard. I've been hearing reports around the neighborhood about how she's been making changes at Goldman's Department Store. It needed changing, let me tell you that. That display window was a disgrace."

Joe felt encouraged by her comments. "Annie's smart. In fact, she reminds me an awful lot of you." Sophia stiffened at the comparison. "She's stubborn, opinionated, but very loving. And she's turned into an excellent cook. Annie cooked dinner for me the other night. Spaghetti and meatballs." But the dessert was the best part, Joe thought, smiling to himself.

Sophia's brows shot up, and it was clear she was surprised by the revelation. "When did all this come about? Where was I, not to see these changes?"

"People do change, Mom. I've changed, and so has Annie. Actually, it would be better to say that we've grown, matured, become adults."

Pushing herself off the bed, Sophia walked to the window and looked out. Dan and Matthew were playing catch on the front lawn, and though she smiled at the sight, she worried about their future. She worried for all her children and grandchildren. As a mother and grandmother, that was her job.

A moment later, her mind made up, she turned. "If

Annie Goldman makes you happy, Joe, then I won't stand in your way. In time I can learn to like her. It won't be easy, but . . ." At Joe's admonishing look, she said, "You say she wants lots of children?"

"Thanks, Mom." Kissing her cheek, Joe rose to his feet. "Come on. Let's go back and celebrate with the others. This should be a happy occasion for everyone."

"You go, Joe. I'll only be a second. I've got something I want to do first."

Hoping it didn't have anything to do with drowning herself in the toilet bowl, he cast her a puzzled glance, then nodded before quitting the room.

A few minutes later Sophia emerged, looking poised as she entered the kitchen, though a bit uncertain when she came to stand before her future daughter-in-law. Everyone in the room held a collective breath, including Annie.

"There's something I want you to have, Annie Goldman." She glanced at her son, and then softened her tone, "Annie." Reaching into her apron pocket, she withdrew a piece of paper and handed it to the startled young woman.

Surprised by the gesture, Annie unfolded it and her eyes filled with tears as she read it. Mary and Connie gasped, until they heard her say, "Thank you, Sophia. You've made me very happy."

"It's nothing. I should have given it to you a long time ago."

"I take it that'sa not your walking papers she'sa giving you," Grandma Flora told Annie, casting her son's wife a suspicious look.

Sophia glared at her mother-in-law. "Keep quiet, old woman! Can't you see I'm trying to have a conversation with Annie? You're lucky you won't have a mother-in-law like mine," she told Annie, who decided to remain silent and fought the urge to roll her eyes.

Coming to stand beside his fiancée, Joe gazed down at the paper she held in her hand. Written in Sophia's distinctive handwriting was a recipe, and his brows drew together in confusion. "It's a recipe for banana bread," he stated to no one in particular.

Mary squealed, realizing the importance of the gesture. "Ma, I'm so proud of you," she said, patting her protruding belly. "And this baby is proud of you, too."

Sophia's face flushed the same color as her tomato sauce. "*Madonna mia disgrazia!* My sauce is boiling over," was all she said, but she was smiling when she winked at Annie and Joe.

"The shower invitations are almost done, Annie. And I've put a pot roast on the stove to cook."

Annie stared at her cousin in disbelief, wondering if the aliens Donna was so fond of watching on *The X-Files* had replaced her cousin with someone from another planet.

Marjorie Morningstar had turned into Martha Stewart when no one was looking.

The thought of eating another of Donna's homemade meals was enough to make Annie gag, but she didn't, because she knew it had taken a lot of effort on the woman's part to open a cookbook and follow the recipe's directions.

Been there. Done that.

"Thanks. Hope it's as good as those enchiladas you made the other night."

"Do you really think they were good? I think maybe I put a little too much cinnamon in the sauce."

Annie clutched her stomach, remembering, and was glad that Donna's back was turned. "I heard from Henry

Grossman that you two had a lunch date at Santini's the other day. Is that true?"

"It wasn't really a date. We met at the deli and had a conversation over a turkey sandwich. He asked me to the movies, and I accepted. Henry seems to be a very nice man."

Annie's eyes widened, but she kept her opinions to herself. Maybe there was more to Henry than met the eye. She hoped so. "You've got a good heart, Donna," she said under her breath, surprised that her cousin had consented to go out with the man. Actually she was surprised that anyone would consent to go out with Henry. But, in all fairness, she knew he was making an effort to change.

He hadn't said one suggestive thing to her these past few weeks, which was nothing short of a miracle. She supposed the engagement ring she sported might have had something to do with that. Henry walked on eggshells around Joe, having apparently never forgotten the high school parking lot incident.

"What?"

"I said I hope you have a good time."

"Well, it's better than sitting home alone. Now that Tess is dating Nick, and you and Joe are over at his apartment all the time, I feel a bit left out," her cousin admitted.

"Why don't you invite Lou over for dinner?"

Donna stiffened in her seat. "Never! He insults me every time I go into the butcher shop. Why, just the other day he laughed at my faux leopard jacket. Can you imagine? The man has no taste in clothes. And he flirts outrageously with every woman who walks through the door. I saw him hit on Mary just yesterday, and she's pregnant. The man has no shame at all."

Annie grinned. "That's just Lou's way. And for someone

who professes no interest, you sure do spend a lot of time at the butcher shop."

"We have to eat, don't we? And Santini's has the best cuts of meat. And besides, now that you're so busy with the wedding preparations and all, I decided to help out a bit more. I cleaned up my room, I'll have you know."

With jaw unhinged, Annie strode closer to her cousin and looked at her intently. "Are you sure you're the real Donna Wiseman, and not some impersonator sent to take her place?"

"Of course I'm sure, silly." Suddenly Donna glanced at the clock on the wall and bolted from her chair. "Oh, my God! I nearly forgot." She rushed into the living room and Annie followed, wondering what was the matter.

"What is it?" she asked, watching Donna pick up the remote.

"It's time for *Entertainment Tonight*. They're doing a big story on Russell Crowe. He's such a hunk. Did you see *L.A. Confidential* and *Gladiator*? Mmmm. That man is hot."

Listening to her cousin wax poetic over her favorite television program, Annie smiled in relief, saying, "Yeah, you're the same old Donna, all right," and joined her on the sofa.

Mary Hart and Bob Goen were actually starting to grow on her, and Annie found that frightening.

TWENTY-ONE

*"No marriage contract
is made without a quarrel."*

Staring down the long length of the Russos' dinner table to where Joe's father was seated, Annie smiled at the charming older man, whom she had come to adore. He was kind and funny, and always had a good story to share. In a lot of ways, Frank reminded her of Grandpa Johnny.

Winking at her, he bent his head to hear something Grandma Flora was whispering. From the way he began to laugh, Annie figured the old woman had said something pretty funny. Which wasn't unusual. Grandma was a stitch.

Annie decided that becoming a Russo wasn't going to be quite the ordeal she had anticipated. Even Sophia was starting to warm up to her a bit, especially after she passed the woman's pop quiz on child rearing. Of course, Annie knew once Joe's mother and the rest of the family learned of the wedding plans they'd made, that was likely to change.

Gina and Sid, dressed in their Sunday finest, and seated across from Annie and Joe, waited impatiently for Sophia to reappear with the main course. They had already waded through antipasto, minestrone soup, tortellini, and two bottles of Chianti, and were feeling no pain at the moment, judging by the dazed looks on their faces. As she was quickly learning, being part of the Russo clan for even a short period of time could be very overwhelming.

303

"Your mother's a very good cook, Joe," Gina commented, for want of something more interesting to say.

The conversation up to that point hadn't been exactly scintillating. Sid hadn't wanted to chat during dinner, as was his usual custom, and had grunted most of his responses to the questions Frank and Sophia posed. When they couldn't get much out of the taciturn man, they finally gave up and turned to each other, speaking of inconsequential things that concerned their family.

"Here we are," Sophia declared, bustling back into the dining room, carrying a large white ceramic platter with something that looked suspiciously to Annie like a pork roast. She groaned inwardly as she noted her father's outraged expression and kicked Joe beneath the table. It was the kind of kick that said, "I don't know what to do now, so I hope you do."

"This is one of my family's favorite meals, so I made it special for you," Sophia told the Goldmans, beaming as she set the meat on the table before them. "Tradition is very important to Italians, and making a nice roast for Sunday dinner and on special occasions is one of them."

"It . . . it looks delicious," Annie's mother said hesitantly, nudging her husband beneath the table in response to his muffled curse, all the while smiling politely.

"It's pork!" Sid declared, not bothering to mince words. "I'm a Jew. I don't eat pork."

Sophia looked as if the man had lost his mind. "What do you mean, you don't eat pork? Everyone eats pork. It's the other white meat. And it's got a nice apple-wine gravy, and—"

"The man said he doesn't eat pork, Sophia," her husband told her, trying to communicate with a lift of his brows that she should shut up. *"Forgetaboutit."*

"Mom," Joe interrupted, trying to explain, "the Jewish religion doesn't allow for eating pork. They believe pork to be unclean, as it comes from pigs."

"Unclean?" Her brow wrinkled in confusion. "But I bought it at Santini's. Paid a good price. It's very clean. It was wrapped in butcher paper and everything.

"Don't be silly. Eat the pork, Sid. You'll see. It's good for you."

Annie's father glared at the bossy woman. "I don't eat pork. It's not permitted."

"You want some more wine, Pop?" Annie offered.

"Annie and I have decided on our wedding plans," Joe tossed out, hoping to ease the tension, though he knew what he was about to say would only create more problems.

"Did you book the church?" "Did you make arrangements with the rabbi?" Sophia and Sid asked, one after the other, and then turned to stare daggers at each other.

"Joe and I have decided on a nonsectarian wedding, so we won't be getting married in either religion." When all four parents opened their mouth to protest, Annie added quickly, "But we'll be incorporating elements of both religions into the ceremony. We've talked it over with Reverend Kelly, the clergyman who'll be officiating. He's agreed that our circumstances are a bit unusual."

"But that won't be a real wedding," Sophia declared, looking distraught. "And he sounds like an Irishman. Is he Irish? No offense to Dan, but those Irishmen are a bunch of drunks."

Annie's father nodded. "No, it's not real. You should be married in a synagogue."

Gina cleared her throat. "If getting married in a nondenominational church is what Annie and Joe want, then that's what they should have. We all need to butt out, including you, Sid." Her husband grunted but said nothing.

"Good for you, Gina Goldman!" Grandma Flora said. "Everyone is forgetting whose wedding thisa is. The *bambini* should have whata they want, no?"

"Gina and my mother are right." Frank avoided his wife's hostile look. "The kids should decide what they want. It's only fair."

"Fair, shmare, I'm paying," Sid pointed out.

"But—" Sophia began.

Annie held up her hand to forestall both arguments. "This is the only way we could come up with a solution. If you don't all agree, we're going to elope, and then there will be no wedding."

Gasping aloud, Joe's mother crossed herself, and this time, Grandma Flora followed suit. "No wedding." Joe's mother breathed the words as if they were an anathema. "That's sacrilegious. We would have to move out of the neighborhood after such a disgrace. Frank, tell her." But her husband remained quiet; not so Annie's father.

"Eloping's not a bad idea," he said, leaning back in his chair and contemplating the situation. "It could save me a bundle. I'll throw in a honeymoon to the Catskills if you decide to elope."

Annie didn't bother to hide her frustration. "Pop! We're getting married in a church. I've already picked out my dress."

"You have?" Gina's face lit with excitement. "When can I see it?"

"After we all come to an agreement about this wedding," Joe said in a voice filled with finality.

A moment of silence ensued, then Sid and Sophia looked

at each other, came to a decision, and finally nodded. "All right," they agreed in unison.

"I can get the Paisans to play for the wedding," Frank offered. "They did a good job at Mary's wedding. And they come cheap."

"My sister will sing during the wedding ceremony," Gina said. "Lola's got a beautiful voice. She used to be a lounge singer, you know."

"If you like screeching tires," Sid added. "Is she going to wear clothes or come naked? I don't want—"

While the parents and grandparent carried on the conversation about the wedding, Annie and Joe slipped from the table as unobtrusively as possible and ventured outside to sit on the front porch.

"Well, that went pretty well," Joe said, wrapping his arm about Annie's shoulders and taking a deep breath of the crisp autumn air. "We survived with our hides intact. Not a bad day's work."

"Day ain't over yet, holy man," Annie said with a wink, then kissed his chin. "I love you, Joe Russo, but I've decided that we should just forget this whole wedding thing and elope. It'll be a whole lot easier."

He met her suggestion with a horrified look. "Do you have a death wish? Because my mother would never forgive us if we did such a blasphemous thing, and neither would yours, for that matter." Sid, however, was another matter. All he could see were dollar signs.

"But it's going to be a nightmare, Joe! You've heard them. They can't agree on anything."

Drawing her into his arms, Joe kissed her. "Let's go to my place, get naked, and make love."

"But, Joe! That's not going to change things. That won't keep your mother from cooking pork, my father from being rude . . . and, oh, God, Aunt Lola from singing. I'm not sure she even remembers anything except 'Everything's Coming Up Roses.' How can you even think about making love at a time like this?"

"Because I think it'll make both of us feel a whole lot better than the alternative."

"Which is?"

"Going back inside and listening to our parents argue some more."

She jumped up. "Good point. I'll race you."

They were laughing when they reached Joe's apartment. Mrs. Foragi was going up the stairs just ahead of them, and stopped to shake her finger in chastisement.

"I don't want any lawsuits. People who run up the stairs fall and break their necks."

They didn't respond, just kept on laughing, and the older woman let herself inside her apartment and banged the door loudly with a harrumph, but not before saying, "Lovebirds." She made it sound like a curse. She and Benny had broken up again, and Donatella was not a happy woman at the moment.

"I'll probably be evicted now," Joe said to Annie. "See what you've done?"

She smiled. "Who cares? We've already decided to live at my town house. It's much bigger than this apartment." She began stripping out of her clothes, dropping them as she walked toward the bedroom, and Joe followed behind like an eager puppy.

"Who gets to use the shower first?"

Joe's grin was lascivious. "I thought we'd share."

She looked down and grinned. "My, my, Joseph. Aren't we impatient?"

After a frenzied bout of lovemaking, Annie finished showering and toweled off. "Sex in the shower isn't safe. I thought I'd impale myself on—"

"As I recall, you did."

"The faucet," she finished, dropping her towel at Joe's feet, and heading for the bed. "Care to join me?" She asked the question as if in challenge. "Of course, if you're too tired . . ."

"You're insatiable, woman! How many times in an hour do you think I can pleasure you? I'm not as young as I used to be."

"It's only been twice, and I couldn't relax standing up."

With a naughty grin, he said, "Oh, well, then," and scooped her up into his arms, carrying her to the bed and dropping her unceremoniously onto the center of it, then climbing on top of her. "I'm a big believer in relaxation, babe." Covering her mouth with his, he kissed her passionately, mapping every inch of her body with his hands, until she was writhing beneath his touch and moaning loud enough for Mrs. Foragi to hear.

"Do you think sex is this good for everyone, Joe?" she asked, then, not waiting for his answer, demanded, "I want you inside me now. I'll die if you don't hurry."

Joe entered her quickly, and she matched him stroke for stroke, as they climbed the road to fulfillment. When they reached their climax simultaneously, she cried out, "I . . . love . . . you."

"I love you, too, Annie. Always have, always will."

"Promise?"

"Promise."

"Even when I'm old and fat? Will you love me then, too?"

He kissed her tenderly. "Even then. Though I doubt that

will ever happen with as much exercise as you do. And the amount of sex we have certainly burns up a lot of calories."

She heaved a sigh of pure contentment. "I guess we'd better have a church wedding. I've never told anyone this, but I've always wanted to be married in a church, wearing a white dress, with Mary as my maid of honor."

"So you're traditional, after all, huh?" He kissed her again. "You always surprise me."

"Mmmm. I wouldn't say traditional. My wedding gown is a bit unorthodox."

"It's the differences that make me love you all the more, Annie Goldman soon-to-be Russo."

She smiled and patted his face. "Hold that thought, Joseph. I have a feeling it's going to be put to the test very soon."

"What exactly does this wedding dress look like?" he asked with some uncertainty.

But Annie only smiled, before kissing him again.

TWENTY-TWO

"Life is the greatest bargain:
We get it for nothing."

It was white.

It was tight.

It was short.

And man, was it hot!

Eyes bugged, tongues wagged, lips pursed, and brows raised when Annie Goldman marched down the aisle on the arm of her father to the strains of—what else?— "Everything's Coming Up Roses."

The curtain was up, the lights were lit, and Lola Wiseman, dressed in red sequins and sporting a white feather boa any stripper in Atlantic City would have been proud to claim, hit every high note and a few off the musical scales as well.

"That woman should have her tongue ripped out," Sid whispered to his daughter, eyeing his sister-in-law with distaste, and making a face of displeasure. "She sounds like a cat in heat."

"Ssh! Someone might hear you," Annie murmured, smiling and nodding in acknowledgment at the curious but familiar faces as she headed toward Joe, who stood handsomely at the altar in his traditional black tuxedo.

She recalled the last time she'd seen him standing at the altar, at Mary's wedding, and she smiled at how far Father What-a-Hunk had traveled—all the way to her bed and now back to the altar, only this time he was standing next to her. She was one lucky woman.

Annie had waited eons for this day and would not allow anyone to ruin it, including her father, who was now counting heads and mentally calculating how much the reception at Mama Sophia's was going to cost him.

Marco had been honored that Annie had chosen him to prepare the wedding feast, and had actually cried over her inclusion of his signature dish, Saltimbocca à la Valenti.

Trailing behind Annie were Mary, Donna, and Tess, wearing slightly more conservative garb, due to Mary's pregnancy, Tess's age, and Donna's insistence that she wouldn't be caught dead wearing a thigh-high dress in church. Annie had no such reservation.

Their dresses were black satin, backless, sleeveless, and very chic. They wore matching elbow-length gloves. The entire bridal entourage looked like Diana Ross and the Supremes come to life. All that was missing was— No, wait! Lola had just started singing "Baby Love."

Annie thought Joe's mother was going to have an apoplectic fit, her face was so red. Gina's was, too, but mostly from crying.

"What kind of bridal outfits are those?" Sophia whispered to her husband. "Annie's dress is too short." Crossing herself, she made a quick apology to the Almighty, who stared down from the cross very disapprovingly, in her opinion. "Those girls are going to freeze, with their backs sticking out like that. And why is that woman singing a rock-and-roll song? *Mama mia!* Doesn't anyone else notice these things but me?"

Frank was too busy looking at the woman in question to pay his wife any attention, until Sophia's elbow jabbed into his side, and he grunted. "Annie's aunt has quite a set of lungs on her."

"Her bosoms are hanging out of that dress. It's indecent. A disgrace. And if you don't stop looking at them, I'll bash you over the head with this hymnal." Sophia was dressed in conservative blue, as befitting the mother of the groom.

"I'm not dead, Sophia. A man can look."

"Yeah? Well, he can also die," she told him.

In the pew across the aisle, Gina, dressed in cream satin and lace, dabbed her eyes with a hankie and tried bravely to hold back tears, but was failing miserably. "My Annie looks so beautiful," she said to no one in particular, smiling at her daughter and husband, who had just reached the altar.

The only thing that would have made Gina even happier would have been the inclusion of Bubbeh as ring bearer. She had suggested using the dog, and though Annie had considered it, Sid and Joe had vetoed the idea.

A *chuppah*, or wedding canopy, had been constructed to shelter the couple, as was Jewish custom. Joe and Annie joined hands, and the minister, who was bearded, wore sandals, and looked like a throwback to the sixties, began to recite scripture in a deep, melodious voice.

"You look gorgeous, babe, like a princess," Joe whispered.

"So do you. You don't think it's too much?"

"Where did you get the hair extensions?" Annie's short-cropped hair was now shoulder length, due to the wonders of science and an innovative Mr. Roy.

"I've decided to grow my hair out, and I thought it would look better long with the rhinestone crown I'm wearing." Annie had decided to give Queen Liz a run for her money.

Reverend Tom, as he liked to be called, cleared his throat and stared meaningfully at the couple until they quit talking. "Dearly beloved . . ."

"Your daughter looks like she's in the Miss America pageant. What's with the crown?" Sid shook his head, but he was dabbing his eyes. "The girl's got style. Whose, I'm not sure, but she looks beautiful. Like her mother." He kissed Gina's cheek, noting how pale it was, how clammy her hand felt, and suddenly felt sick himself.

"Oh, Sid, I'm so happy. But I'm feeling nauseous."

Her husband's face whitened to the color of his dress shirt. "Not here, Gina. Don't you dare throw up in church. Your daughter will never forgive you, and neither will I."

"Do you think I might be pregnant?"

"I should drop dead at this very minute if you are. Now, be quiet. Our daughter is getting married."

"They wrote their own vows," she whispered.

"Like I couldn't tell."

"Do you, Annie Goldman, promise to love and cherish Joseph Russo, to keep your hair color natural, to never, ever wear a thong bathing suit, for as long as you both shall live?"

The church filled with laughter, and Annie nodded solemnly, saying, "I do," then winked at the man she had given her heart to all those years ago.

"And do you, Joseph Russo, promise to love Annie Goldman, to never, ever leave her, no matter what, to share in the household chores, and to make love to her at least once a day, for as long as you both shall live?"

"I do!" Joe said loudly and emphatically to a resulting chorus of cheers and applause.

"Lotsa *bambini* are coming, I tink," Grandma Flora

said with a big smile, ignoring her daughter-in-law's reddening face.

Sophia clutched her rosary beads tightly and began reciting fast and furiously.

"I now pronounce you man and wife. You may kiss the bride."

By stomping on the glass, another Jewish tradition, derived from the Talmud, Joe signaled that the ceremony was at an end. Everyone shouted *"Mazel tov!"* Annie's aunt Lola began to sing the "Ave Maria," and the bride and groom made their way out of the church.

Holding hands, Annie and Joe hurried to the waiting limousine that Sid had hired to take them to the wedding reception, only Annie had different ideas.

"What do you say we skip the reception?" Annie suggested once she'd settled back against the black leather seat. "I'm not all that hungry. And I'm tired of smiling at people I barely know."

"Fine with me," Joe said. "But our parents are going to kill us. You do realize that, don't you?"

"Mary's going to explain everything and make our apologies."

Joe's eyes lit with suspicion. "What have you two been cooking up?"

Annie smiled, studied the lovely gold band and diamond ring on her finger, and said, "It's time to get the honeymoon under way, Joseph. Remember the promise you made at the altar? Well, I'm holding you to it."

He grinned. "It'll be an easy one to keep, babe. So, what did you have in mind? Shall we check into a hotel and spend our honeymoon there, or go back to the town house and pack our bags?"

"The bags are already packed and in the trunk of the

limo." His eyes widened, and she explained, "We're running off, Joe. Just the two of us. No parents. No relatives. Just you, me, and two round-trip tickets to an isolated island, where visitors can roam around naked, if they want. It'll be like that TV show *Survivor*, but without the million bucks." She slid the glass partition back and said to the driver, "Take us to BWI Airport, please."

"Well, aren't you just full of surprises?"

"You don't know the half of it, Joe." Pulling the privacy curtain closed, she smiled seductively and said, "I believe we've got at least thirty minutes before we get to the airport."

Joe laughed, thinking that life was never going to be dull with Annie in it. "Annie, Annie, Annie. I don't know what I'm going to do with you. You're a whole lot of woman for a mere man to handle."

"There's only one way to handle a woman like me," she said, removing the studs from his shirt and kissing her way down his chest. "Just love me. Even when I make you nuts and you want to throttle me, just love me."

"I do love you, Annie. And I'm going to spend the rest of my life proving it to you."

She wrapped her arms around him and grinned. "Oh, good. You can start right now."

He kissed her breathless, then said, "The pleasure's all mine, babe."

"Mmmm. And to think I used to believe weddings were terribly overrated." She straightened her tiara. "Eat your heart out, Liz."

Read on for a sneak peek at

THE TRIALS
OF ANGELA

The next delicious romance by

Millie Criswell

Coming in Summer 2002

ONE

Angela DeNero was having a bad day.

Actually she was having a bad life.

As lives went hers ranked right up there with having chocolate-induced cellulite, a refrigerator stocked with nothing but healthy food choices, and jeans that refused to zip up.

There was nothing worse than that.

Except her life.

It sucked.

She suspected she'd feel better in time. She was resilient, after all, and would bounce back.

Just not today.

The dragon she called landlady, Mrs. Foragi, was leaving daily Post-it Note reminders on her door about her over-zealous bulldog, Winston—threats, someone less generous would call them. The law firm she had struggled so valiantly to open was experiencing more than its share of growing pains, like clients who conveniently forgot to pay her. And to top it all off she'd been feeling awful all week with flu-like symptoms. Not to mention that her hair had gone from sleek to curly as soon as she'd stepped out in the rain this morning. Harpo Marx had nothing on her 'do.

Add bad hair day to the list.

So when she entered the police station, Angela's mood was as foul as the weather.

Angela spotted Grandma Flora as soon as she approached the front desk area. The old woman, dressed in unrelenting black like a professional mourner, was seated on a folding chair, a pocketbook the size of Minnesota on her lap, cane resting between her knees, looking more formidable than fragile.

"*Vaffunculo! Bastardo!* How dare you treat an old woman like a criminal! I will call the president of the United States. I voted for him. He owes a me."

"Grandma Flora!" Angela shouted when the woman opened her mouth to say something again, nasty, no doubt.

Grandma turned to look at Angela. "I'va been busted. These pigs are trying to tossa me in the slammer." It seemed obvious that Grandma Flora had been watching *The Sopranos* a little too diligently. "I didn't do anyting wrong. I wanna go home now. *Capisce?*"

Angela heaved a sigh. She understood, all right, but that didn't mean she could make all of Grandma Flora's troubles disappear, though she'd give it her best shot. "I see there's been a misunderstanding, Officer Malcuso. I'm sure we can get it straightened out."

With a look of apology, he shook his head. "No, ma'am. Mrs. Russo was caught red-handed, stealing merchandise from Geppetto's Toy Store. The owner swore out a complaint and is bringing charges against her."

The young officer brushed back his thinning, sandy-colored hair. "Mr. Patel's lawyer intends to speak to the district attorney. If they still want to file charges . . ."

Sitting down next to the old woman, Angela tried to re-assure her, though Joe's grandmother looked more pissed-off than scared. "I think we're in a pickle, Grandma Flora.

We're going to have to wait to see what the store owner's attorney has to say."

A few minutes later, a tall, dark-haired man walked in, whom Grandma Flora seemed to recognize immediately; her eyes lit with love and pride. He was wearing a brown leather bomber jacket over a navy T-shirt, faded jeans, a day's growth of beard.

Angela had to admit he was handsome, in a Russell Crowe kind of way—not pretty handsome, but rugged, virile. The man oozed masculinity.

"Ah, here comes Johnny. Soon he will help you fix tings. A good boy, my grandson Johnny."

Grandson! Angela snapped her mouth shut, raised her eyes from the man's . . . ah, *masculinity,* and hoped she wasn't drooling all over herself.

The man walked over and bussed his grandmother on the cheek. "You've been a naughty girl again, haven't you, Grandma Flora?"

Flora winked at him, and he grinned, obviously used to her antics. "Talk to my lawyer, Johnny. Angela's going to fix tings. Isn't she *bellissima*? And smart, too. She goes to college, like you."

He smiled a hundred-watt smile, and Angela revised her earlier opinion. Flora's Johnny wasn't handsome. He was chocolate, whipped cream, and all things yummy rolled into one fabulous package.

"Very," he replied to his grandmother's question, then said to Angela, "I'm John Franco," holding out his hand. "I'm here on my client's behalf. Mr. Patel owns the store that my grandmother robbed."

Yummy turned *crummy.* Angela's jaw unhinged. "You're *his* attorney? But how can that be? The woman your client's filing charges against is your grandmother."

Looking uncomfortable, John Franco rubbed the back of his neck. "I'm well aware of that, Miss DeNero. But a crime has been committed, and it's my duty as Mr. Patel's lawyer to—"

"She's your grandmother, for godsake! Where's your loyalty? Your compassion? She's an old woman."

Grandma Flora shook her head of gray curls, which were so tightly wound her pink scalp peeked through. "Young people are *stupido*. There isa no respect given to the old anymore."

"Now, Grandma, be reasonable," John said, kneeling down before her and drawing her wrinkled hands into his. "I've talked to my client. Mr. Patel's upset, and he's adamant about bringing you up on charges. I'm hoping to talk to the district attorney, and—"

"And what? Have her put in the electric chair? What kind of man are you?"

His blue eyes turned glacial. "A rational one, Miss DeNero, which is more than I can say for you."

Her cheeks flooded with color. "How dare you! I am not irrational. I'm—" Angela felt nausea rise to her throat and clamped a hand over her mouth. Shaking her head at his questioning gaze, she made a beeline for the woman's restroom, where she promptly tossed up her breakfast.

A few minutes later, somewhat recovered from her ordeal, and a whole lot humiliated, she splashed cold water on her face and returned to find the aggravating man—*traitor!*—with his arm around her client.

"I'm very sorry," she said, grinding to a halt before them. "I think I might be coming down with the flu. I haven't been feeling well these past few days."

Grandma Flora looked concerned. "You need to eat more, Angela. You're too thin."

In an Italian family food was the panacea for everything. If you were sick, you ate to get well. If you felt happy, you ate to celebrate. If you were despondent . . . well, food always made a body feel better, especially if there were sweets involved.

Assuming a professional demeanor, Angela said, "If your client persists in this course of action, Mr. Franco, then I guess we'll see you in court."

He towered over both women, like some mountain of granite, and she had to look up. "I look forward to it, Miss DeNero. But I doubt things will go that far. I'll be in touch." He bent down and kissed the top of his grandmother's head. "I'll see you soon, Grandma. Say hi to Uncle Frank and Aunt Sophia for me."

"*Bah!*" The old lady shook her head. "Sophia Graziano has poison in her heart. I don'ta speak to her unless I have to. She wantsa to have me committed. Says I'ma *pazza nella testa*. Tell me, who coulda be more crazy than my daughter-in-law?"

Eyes wide, Angela shook her head disapprovingly. Grandma Flora seemed a lot saner than a lot of people she knew, including her own father, but she wouldn't go there. That would require entering the realm of the unbelievable— *The Twilight Zone,* without a good script.

The old lady's eyes twinkled, and it was obvious she had enjoyed her escapade, despite being tired. "Are you springing me, like in the movies? Good ting, because I gotta connections back in Italy. You seen *Goodfellas*? You seen *The Godfather*? Luca Brazzi swims with the fishes." She drew a cutting finger across her throat. "That means he'sa dead."

Definitely too much of *The Sopranos*.

"No more shopping for you, Grandma. *Capisci?*" John cautioned from the doorway. But the old lady only smiled enigmatically, which didn't bode well for the remaining merchants of Little Italy.

"See you around, Miss DeNero," he said.

"I hope not," she couldn't keep herself from replying.

THE TROUBLE WITH MARY

by Millie Criswell

THE TROUBLE WITH MARY IS . . . She's unemployed. Her huge Italian family is driving her crazy. Her love life is nonexistent. In fact, she needs a life! So Mary decides to open a restaurant in Baltimore's Little Italy. The place is a big success—until Dan Gallagher, food critic for the local paper, writes a scathing review of her pizza, pasta, and chocolate cannolis. Now Mary would like nothing more than to serve Dan on a steaming platter. Problem is, Mary is the most delectable woman Dan has ever met. And Dan is the most exasperating man Mary has ever encountered. And the trouble with chemistry is, neither one can resist it. . . .

Published by Ballantine Books.
Available in bookstores everywhere.

Coming in Spring 2002
from Ballantine Books

THE TRIALS OF ANGELA

❦

by Millie Criswell

Angela DeNero's life is a mess. She's just broken up with her fiancé, who dumped her for another woman. Her small Baltimore law practice is experiencing more than its share of growing pains. Her smothering, but well-meaning parents have just announced they are moving to Little Italy to be near her. And to make matters worse, she's just discovered she's pregnant.

As if her life wasn't bad enough, Angela has just learned that opposing counsel in the custody proceeding she's handling is John Franco, hometown hunk and cousin to her clients, the Gallaghers. She considers the man a traitor. He considers her a spoiled rich girl from Harvard.

But appearances can be deceiving. Likewise love. . . .

JUST BREATHE

by Dee Davis

For aspiring travel writer Chloe Nichols, escorting a tour group of wealthy old ladies through Europe was supposed to be anything but thrilling. Then she is rescued from an assassin's bullet by a stranger on the train—a perfectly handsome, charming stranger who saves her life with a kiss and asks her to pose as his fiancée. Chloe believes Matthew Broussard is trying to protect her, until the seductive charade becomes part of a lethal international conspiracy in which no one is what they seem—including her captivating hero. . . .

Suzanne Brockmann has taken romantic suspense by storm with her action-packed thrillers. Now she has written the most gripping novel of her career—an unforgettable story of an explosive hostage situation in which two people are caught between the call of duty and the lure of destiny. . . .

OVER THE EDGE

by Suzanne Brockmann

Coming in September 2001
from Ballantine Books

Coming in September 2001
from Ballantine Books

I GOT YOU, BABE

by Jane Graves

On the run for a robbery she didn't commit,
Renee Esterhaus is stuck in the middle of Texas
with a broken car and a sadistic bounty hunter
hot on her trail. Desperate for a way out, Renee
decides to make a promise she never intends to
keep—offer the first man she meets a night of
unforgettable pleasure in return for a ride. A
night to remember, all right, since the handsome guy turns out to be a cop with a pair of
handcuffs and zero tolerance for sweet-talking
criminals. . . .